D0429177

GAME OF THE GODS

GAME OF THE GODS

JAY SCHIFFMAN

TOR

A TOM DOHERTY ASSOCIATES BOOK

NEW YORK

GAME OF THE GODS

Copyright © 2018 by Jay Schiffman

A Tor Book
Published by Tom Doherty Associates
175 Fifth Avenue
New York, NY 10010

www.tor-forge.com

Tor® is a registered trademark of Macmillan Publishing Group, LLC.

The Library of Congress Cataloging-in-Publication Data
is available upon request.

ISBN 978-1-250-30613-5 (trade paperback)
ISBN 978-0-7653-8954-1 (hardcover)
ISBN 978-0-7653-8955-8 (ebook)

Our books may be purchased in bulk for promotional, educational, or business use. Please contact your local bookseller or the Macmillan Corporate and Premium Sales Department at 1-800-221-7945, extension 5442, or by email at MacmillanSpecialMarkets@macmillan.com.

First Edition: July 2018

Printed in the United States of America

0 9 8 7 6 5 4 3 2 1

To my wife, Tamar, my guide and inspiration. You make everything possible. You've shaped me into a man I can generally bear, and sometimes even like. *I only gave you so much to work with*. And to our children, Hannah, Isaac, Josh, Gabby, Ava, and Zach. I never could have imagined how deeply I could love a pack of wild creatures so intent on ignoring me. This book is for you.

ACKNOWLEDGMENTS

My novel begins with the main character reflecting on how little he wants to decide which people should be included within his nation and which should not. I feel the same way about this acknowledgment. I don't want to decide who should be included and who shouldn't. But, it must be done—*or so I've been led to believe.* Why else would every award-winning Hollywood actor go on and on thanking everyone from their hair stylists to their third-grade teachers? Acknowledgments are apparently critical to the success of a well-ordered society.

So here it goes, a bunch of thanks, in time order so that no one can claim preferential treatment:

- My mom and dad, who created me and were always big fans of their creation.
- My sisters, who taught me how crazy my parents were—an essential lesson for writers.
- My college friends, who are constants in my life.
- My wife, Tamar, who is the most generous and loving person I know. I have yet to meet someone more clever or funnier.
- My in-laws, brothers-in-law, and sisters-in-law, who taught me the meaning of family.
- My kids, who shine bright as lighthouses, always helping me to find my way home.
- Debbie Kim and Clarynne Blanchard, who worked alongside me for years, tolerated my insanity, and supported me and this book in every way possible.

- My agent, Bob Diforio, who championed my work, led me to Tor, and shepherded me through the process.
- The publishing team at Tor/Macmillan: Bob Gleason, who gave me invaluable feedback, shaped key storytelling moments, and helped me to see how bad my novel's original title was, and Elayne Becker, who carried my novel through the finish line—no easy task.
- The production team, including Ryan Jenkins, Sean Agan, Eric Gladstone, and Terry McGarry, who trudged through my poor grammatical choices and found errors both glaring and small, and Karl Gold, the production manager who oversaw the project.
- The art team, who designed a cover I love.
- And to my hair stylist and third-grade teacher . . . *because a well-ordered society demands it.*

PART I
THE FEDERACY

1

DARIOX VINYL

The guards open the door to my chambers and usher in a girl, eighteen years old, smelling like urine. Fresh blood is dripping from her nose. Her hair is dyed neon green. I tell the guards to leave. I hand the girl a cloth for her nose and tell her there's a change of clothes in the bathroom. I've gotten used to the fact that teenagers' nerves get the best of them. The Federacy tried to remove the biological impulse to empty our bladders when scared. But nature's a stubborn thing.

What I can't get used to is that so many candidates think they can seduce me. They come out of the bathroom naked—begging with their bodies. Dariox is no different. The second she slithers out with her top off, I force a fatherly smile and guide her back to the bathroom. She sobs on the other side of the door, knowing she has probably just made a terrible mistake. I try to convince myself it will not impact my evaluation.

But it will.

I ask Dariox a question. After years of evaluating candidates for citizenship, I almost always know the answer before I ask. "Why do you have a bloody nose?"

"A rock from the border," she says. "I volunteered with the Civilian Brigade to monitor the Nyton Border Post and a protester threw rock at me."

I don't want to embarrass her and call out the obvious lie. This is her last year to become a citizen and each year her performance gets more and more desperate. Last year she told me she could see the future. She claimed she predicted the riots in the Azarks. For this year's encore, she decided to slam her face into a brick wall and pretend to be a Federacy patriot.

What Dariox and the other citizen candidates surely don't realize is that I have no desire to decide their fate. I have no desire to determine who's in the Federacy and who's outside its protection. I have no desire to handpick the lucky few that will be guaranteed a lifetime of safety. I have no desire to be *that important*.

I am so incredibly important, in fact, that the Federacy's Premier and secretary of war buy my children birthing-day presents. *I am so important* that I travel with ten guards, three of whom are hardwired with detonators. My guards are trained to blow themselves up if it will save my *ever so important* life.

Although Dariox has little chance of becoming a Federacy citizen, I try to give her a fair hearing. It's her last chance and she deserves whatever negligible amount of justice I can dispense. I take Dariox's hand in mine. This is a technique I learned as a young judge. It comforts the candidates and makes it easier for them to be honest. I ask her dozens of specific questions and it doesn't take long before her pile of lies can no longer withstand their own weight. I bite my lower lip, no longer knowing if this is empathy or affect.

"This is your last year, Dariox. I think you attempted the citizenship process as best as you can. But each year I recommend, above all else, that you come back next year demonstrating your character—the character of a Federate. Unfortunately, each year you return my advice with dishonesty." I look out the window and see a small government building on fire in the distance. It looks too small to be the work of the National Freedom Force (NFF). It must be rioters. "No more lies, Dariox. I simply want you to tell me a story about yourself. Don't think about its meaning or how it will impact my decision. All I ask is that it be true."

Dariox looks around the room as if looking for her life's story. The walls are blank but for fourteen plaques—plaques I am legally required to hang—celebrating the fact that for all fourteen years of my service, I have had the highest efficiency rating of any judge. *How so very proud it makes me to see these plaques celebrating how so very important I am.*

HIGH JUDGE MAXOMILLION CONE
HIGHEST JUDGE. HIGHEST EFFICIENCY. HIGHEST HONOR.
THE TRUEST OF FEDERATES.

"You won't find anything at all on these walls, Dariox." I take my finger and point to her heart, then her head. "The story I want is here and here." It's trite, but surprisingly effective.

Dariox has a number of false starts before she launches into a story about how when she was young she wanted nothing more than to be a Federate soldier. Her story, at turns riveting and at turns pathetic, is a direct outgrowth of our educational system's schizophrenia. On the one hand, we teach our young children to have character. The slogan above every education center is:

HONESTY + MORALITY + CONVICTION = CHARACTER
BECOME THE FEDERACY

On the other hand, we teach children the great myths of the Federacy. We teach them the great myths of Our God. We teach them the great myths of the End of the Old Order. We teach them the great myths surrounding the Nation of Yerusalom. Not only are they instructed in the intricacies of these mythologies, they are taught to embellish upon them with great vigor. "Embroider the Nation" is the Federacy's national anthem. Our children and citizens are taught to stretch stories in ways that go against the imposing sign that hangs over every education center's entranceway.

Dariox's story, like so many other candidates', is deeply symptomatic of our education system's split personality. I let her spin her tale for about five minutes before becoming frustrated. "No, Dariox—I want a true story. I'm trying to save your life, for God's sake!" Any other judge would have assigned her to one of the most miserable settlements in the Outer Regions by now.

Dariox snaps. "Fuck you," she yells. She pounds her fist on my writing table. "Go fuck yourself—you hypocrite. I'm just trying to survive." I try not to smile, but I can't help it. For the first time, I believe her.

"Don't smile at me. You make it seem like I'm playing games with you. You're playing games with me. What do you want? *What do you want from me?"* Tears stream down her face. *"What do you want to know . . .* that my little sister and I were raped by soldiers from the NFF. That a Federacy tribunal deemed my mother an 'inconsequential casualty' of a stray Federate bullet. That my father and his bastard sons are all addicted to morzium. Tell me, Judge—what do you want from me?" From the yelling, her nose begins to bleed again. I take out a cloth and wipe it dry.

"Should I tell you how much I hate the fucking Federacy? Should I tell you that if I wasn't so scared of being raped again or captured by mercenaries or strung up by the Rogues that I would never want to be a citizen? Is that what you're looking for?"

I sit back in my chair, satisfied at having won the battle for truth but sad for having heard it. I look out of my window and see three ambulatory transports hovering over the burning government building while suctioning out lives. I put my arm around Dariox and walk her over to the window. "What do you see out there, Dariox?"

Dariox closes her eyes for a moment. She doesn't need to look out the window to know what's going on. She takes a deep breath and opens her eyes. "I see people suffering. There are people in those buildings and they're probably being burned alive." She closes her eyes again and this time keeps them closed. "I see people burning. They're in pain. They're probably terrified." She puts her hand on the window. "I see people dying for no good reason."

"And who's to blame for that?"

Dariox pauses to think. Lies easily roll off her tongue. The truth, however, is a sticky mass. "I don't know—the NFF, the Rogues, the Nation of Yerusalom? I don't know, maybe the Federacy." She removes my arm from her shoulder and thinks some more. "Actually, maybe you—maybe you're the one to blame." Her nose is again bleeding and I go to wipe it, but she pushes my hand away. "You're a good person, right? That's what every single Federacy paper says. *Max Cone, the Highest Judge, is a man of character, a true Federate.* And you were this great military commander before that. You've got all this power and you do absolutely nothing."

She wipes the blood from her nose on her sleeve and looks up at me. *"I think I'll blame you!"*

After I dismiss Dariox, I call in a handful of my clerks to record my decision and file the appropriate documentation. I deny Dariox citizenship. She is smart and passionate—traits I greatly admire. But citizenship is strictly limited and she does not exhibit the character of a Federate. In my professional view, she never will, and maybe that's not a bad thing. I dictate a lengthy outline for my decision, and my clerks fill in the details. Though I cannot assign every rejected candidate to a relatively safe place on the borders of the Federacy, I do for Dariox. She has earned that right, in my opinion.

I leave work just after nightfall. It has been a long week. The Federacy has sustained thousands of casualties at the hands of the NFF and the Rogues, and there are rumors circulating that the Premier is going to ask me to reassume my role as the high commander of the Federate Forces, a request I will have no choice but to refuse. I will never fight for these people again.

My guards open the door to my transport and I am home in fifteen minutes. My two boys greet me at the door and my little girl, Viole, follows close behind. They squeeze me tight, and for a brief moment, I feel something other than numb. Viole wiggles her stuffed bear in my face and pretends to be the bear. "Did you have a good day?" the bear asks. I nod yes—a lie my little girl deserves. My children are my only happiness.

I walk down a long hallway and see my wife staring vacantly out the window watching the owl that lives atop the lone tree in our backspace. I spin around her wheeled chair and kiss the top of her head. As she struggles to squeeze out a smile, drool runs down her cheek. I take out a cloth and wipe it dry.

2

VERITON GLASS

Ten months pass without the Federacy winning a single major battle. The NFF has taken some small settlements in the east, while the Rogues continue their raids in the west. So, I'm not surprised by the early-morning call I receive from Veriton Glass. Like me, he's a former high commander who was later "asked" to become a judge. At one time, I considered Veriton a friend.

All receivers are bugged and monitored by the Federacy, so Veriton's words are guarded. The official policy of the Office of the Premier is that bugging is necessary for the purposes of ensuring that the NFF and the Rogues do not monitor our communications, even private ones. This is partly true. The other part is that there was an insurrection twenty years ago. This insurrection was led by the commander of the military academy Veriton and I attended. All future premiers have been vigilant ever since.

The only place I'm sure is not bugged is my transport. Official transports cannot be bugged. The technological challenge of keeping a supersonic transport off the NFF and Rogue radars, while simultaneously receiving bugged transmissions, is too steep. When Veriton asks me over my home receiver to pick him up on my way to work, I understand he wants to talk about sensitive matters. So, too, does the Premier.

"Things are getting really bad, Max," Veriton says as soon as we start moving. It's a quick trip to work and he has no time for formalities—no time for how're the kids, how's the wife. As we speed through the Valley of Pines toward the Federacy Omniplex, Veriton stirs nervously in his seat and talks quickly. "Did you hear the NFF and Rogues are in serious talks to reunite? I hear that Chancellor Vrig had Commander Phode over to his summer estate and things went well . . . *very well*. Vrig wants to bring the Rogues back into the NFF, and however pure Phode is, I believe Vrig has named his price."

Veriton looks over at my guards, who are seated in the front compartment of my transport. He wants to make sure they cannot hear us. He leans close to me and lowers his voice. "Our brilliant Premier thinks he can keep the Rogues and NFF apart by conducting some kind of amateurish propaganda campaign. He thinks he can fan the flames of dissent by artificially inflating the price of hydrogen-based military commodities. Of all things, *this* is what he thinks will stop them from reuniting. He doesn't get it. He doesn't understand the first thing about military strategy or politics. His naïveté is pathological." Veriton genuinely dislikes the Premier—probably because Veriton, quite wrongly, believes he could have been Premier.

"Does the Premier really think the Nation of Yerusalom is going to help us fight the NFF," Veriton says. "He can't possibly trust the Holy Father. *He can't be that stupid.*" Veriton can tell I'm getting uncomfortable, so he decides to throw the Premier a backhanded compliment. "Look, he has effectively consolidated power within the Federacy and limited the influence of the Abstainers over the last decade. My hat's off to him. But he has no focus—no strategic hierarchy. The NFF is gaining territory every day. We are supposed to be the most powerful nation in the world. We have the greatest military. We have the greatest intelligence apparatus. How can *we* be losing the war? It makes no sense. It's almost as if he's purposely letting them win." Veriton rubs his forehead. "While we fight the NFF and Rogues, our *good friends* in the Nation of Yerusalom are growing stronger. The Holy Father has been meeting with cartel leaders in Kolexico and there are rumors that one of his senior lieutenants is about to marry a powerful ally. That sneaky son of a bitch is up to something." I shake my head in disgust. I have my doubts about the Holy Father, but Veriton shouldn't be talking about him this way.

"The Premier is blind to what's happening, Max. Our military leaders are losing faith. And I don't need to tell you, when commanders lose faith, soldiers lose faith, and that's how wars get lost." He looks up at my guards again. "You know the Premier better than I do. What the hell is going on with him?"

"Don't ask me questions like this, Veriton. You know I don't get involved in politics anymore. I leave the politics to people like you. I'm just a judge."

"You've become a cheerless bureaucrat, Max."

"You're right about the cheerless part."

As we weave our way through the Calcium Mountains, Veriton continues asking me about the Premier's motivations. He thinks I know more than I do. He is persistent and focused, just like when he was the Federacy's chief law advocate. He made a much better advocate than judge. But I'm a terrible witness. Unlike Veriton, I'm quite adept at saying nothing. This drives him crazy.

"Throw me a bone, Max. For God's sake, we went to the academy together. We fought together. We were inaugurated together. You're like a brother to me." I remain silent. He knows I no longer see him as a friend, and I never thought of him as a brother. I don't trust Veriton. It's nothing he specifically did. I just can't trust *his kind* anymore. Not after what they did.

Veriton quickly loses his temper and strikes at me as only he can—like an angry child. "You're too serious, Max," he says. "Way too serious." He knows exactly where he wants to take his insults—where he wants to lead his witness. "You need some fun in your life, right? Some adventure? Some debauchery, don't you think? How about we get you a whore? I know this gorgeous girl with really big breasts, a nice round behind, and beautiful soft brown skin. This girl's a real pro. You need a good time, Max. When's the last time that wife of yours was able to . . ." Veriton's voice trails off. He wisely doesn't finish his sentence. I can take a joke, but not one at the expense of my wife. She has suffered enough. Veriton knows that she and I can no longer have sex. The Federacy made sure of this.

I unlock my restraints and slowly stand in front of him. I firmly place one hand on Veriton's shoulder, while motioning to my guards to stand down with the other. My thumb is near his jugular. He immediately understands my intent. I was a junior officer in his brigade before I took away his command. He has seen me exercise my will before.

Veriton waves his hand as if holding a white flag. "That was out of line,

Max. A bad joke at the expense of one of the Federacy's great women." I take a deep breath—one that could remove all the oxygen from my transport. There are few things I work harder at than controlling my temper. And there are few things that make me angrier than a slight to my wife. As I said, she has suffered enough.

"There was a day, Max, when you would have bashed my skull in for such an insult. Now, you can just snap your fingers and your guards will drag me to the gulags. It's a better form of power, don't you think?"

"Actually, I would prefer to bash your head in."

Veriton gives me an uneasy smile and an even more uneasy laugh. He tries to direct the conversation back to safer ground. "Seriously, don't you prefer political power over the brute strength of commanding a brigade?"

"Not really. I prefer the simplicity of my days as a soldier. It was a more honorable form of killing." I apply slight pressure on Veriton's shoulder, lowering him deeper into his seat. I want to tower over him. "Every day I sit behind my shatterproof glass—sweet artificial air pumped into my chambers—and I deny teenagers citizenship. I send them out to the furthest reaches of civilization. No food. No protection. No chance they'll survive. I send them out to die. I kill kids every day. I liked it better when I was a teenage soldier and I took their lives with my own hands. It was more honest."

"I remember a time when you were at least a tiny bit fun, Max."

"Those days are long gone."

Veriton does not say another word during the trip. We both sit silently, looking out the window, occasionally taking note of the embers of the NFF's war with the Federacy. Veriton understands how to manipulate me, but he also understands his limits. He knows that there's no reason to talk any further.

As my transport closes in on the Federacy Omniplex, Veriton reaches into his coat and hands me a circular device about the size of my hand. It is strangely heavy. "It's called a Palmitor," Vertion says. "It will explain to you how it works and it will give you the information you need. Please pay attention to what's on this device, Max. I hope it will make you come around to my way of thinking. Either you lead the Federate Forces again, or we're doomed. That's the one thing the Premier has right." As Veriton walks out, he says, "I should have just given you this first. I'm sorry. I'm really sorry, Max. No matter what you think of me, I am your friend—maybe your only friend."

As Veriton leaves, I stand up and instruct the transport driver and my guards to head to my chambers. I hold the device in my hand for a few minutes. I'm reluctant to do anything with it. When someone like Veriton hands you a powerful instrument like this, it can only be bad. Eventually the device just starts speaking. It says that it will assess the likelihood of certain future events happening. According to the voice coming from the device, it assesses electric currents in one's brain, calculates different types of biometric feedback, algorithmically sorts through external information, and stochastically builds different future scenarios, one of which is presented as most likely. I'm skeptical, to say the least. But for reasons I cannot fully understand, I'm nervous to use this device.

I sit back down and the device instructs me to place its platinum side in the palm of my right hand. The device starts to beep and tiny metallic balls—maybe thousands of them—begin to roam my palm. The machine warms and I feel electric pulses shoot from my fingertips through my right arm and then to my spine and head. It's a highly unsettling feeling, especially the electric currents running through my brain. What bothers me most about the device is how well it's designed. It seems too well designed to be a complete fraud. And Veriton, one of the more cynical people I know, gave it to me. He obviously believes in its power.

My hand tightens around the device and it begins to beep more quickly. I don't like the way it feels. I don't like the beeps. I don't like the vibrations. I don't like the movement. There seems to be something deceitful about this mechanical dance. But it is *so heavy* in my hand. Part of me thinks that because it is so heavy—so full of weight—that it must speak some sort of truth. I grip the device as if I want to squeeze the life out it. As the device's beeps reach a frenetic pace and the skin on my forehead starts to tingle, the machine becomes exceedingly hot. Then, abruptly, a loud buzz comes over the device, followed by an orchestral ding. The metallic balls recede. The device slows. It cools down. It's done. The motor's hum becomes quiet and a different voice, a female one, comes on. "Your results are ready for viewing." A small monitor rises from the top of the device. It turns and faces me. It looks at me as if sitting in judgment. I watch the monitor tell me its vision.

I have seen war from the battlefield and the war of citizenship. I have sent tens of thousands of young people to certain deaths. But what I bear witness to on this screen is unfathomably crueler. The destruction I see knows no bounds. It is a kind of destruction that defies all decency. I see the end of reasonableness. I see the end of truth.

And it was just as Dariox said to me before I denied her citizenship. I am to blame.

3

PIQUE ROLLINS

Citizen candidates usually come to their First Interviews wearing their best ecclesiastical clothes, and holding a picture of the Holy Father. The relationship between the Federacy and Our God, the One True God, is a close one, and the First Interview is something like the Old Christians' Confirmation. The First Interview begins with an elaborate ceremony in which a judge initiates a candidate into the class of citizen candidates. The ceremony is followed by a formal interview in which the judge begins a five-year process of determining whether the candidate is worthy of citizenship. Each year, from the ages of thirteen to eighteen, the candidate appears before a judge for an extensive interview. After five years of evaluating the merits of the candidate, the judge makes a recommendation as to whether to grant or deny citizenship. As the Highest Judge, I must approve all recommendations of lower judges and I alone make the ultimate decision about citizenship, subject to the Office of the Premier's veto.

The initiation ceremony is held outside the judge's chambers in an open theater. The candidate's family and mentors, Federacy priests, representatives from the Holy Father, military guards, and a choir are all in attendance. I dread everything about these ceremonies—mostly because more than ninety-nine percent of candidates will be rejected and so it's a waste of time. But I have been assigned a young teenager from outside the Federacy, which is rare, and I have been asked by the Office of the Premier to personally handle her candidacy, which is even more rare.

Pique Rollins, a thirteen-year-old girl from the Anterior Region, enters my chambers wearing everyday clothes. She holds no picture of the Holy Father. She has no family in attendance. During the initiation ceremony, she sits silently, neither smiling nor frowning. While most candidates eagerly sing along with the choir's "Embroider the Nation," Pique quietly taps just one foot. Pique says her vows to Our God and the Federacy, but before each vow she says, "As you've requested." I'm not sure if the citizenship rules permit such a qualification, but I allow it.

After everyone in attendance watches a video of the Premier congratulating the candidate on the beginning of the citizenship process, the initiation ceremony comes to a close. I motion for the candidate to follow me into my chambers. I begin most First Interviews the same way. I say nothing. I wait for the candidate to speak first. I usually will remain silent for up to ten minutes. Most candidates will say something before the ten minutes pass. Of those candidates, more than half will say something that immediately demonstrates they are unworthy of citizenship. The other half eventually demonstrate their unworthiness in the next few minutes of the interview. I then proceed to waste the next five years trying to prove to myself that my initial instincts were wrong.

Pique is that rare candidate who says nothing. She politely makes eye contact with me, and after a few minutes takes out a pad and begins sketching. There is no specific rule forbidding this, but it seems wrong to me, perhaps even rude. After a minute or two of silence, I point to the pad and shake my head in disapproval. But I don't say anything. She ignores me and continues to sketch. We both sit in silence for about ten minutes before I give up and ask her what she's drawing.

"Your chambers," Pique says.

"Why?"

"It was the most useful thing I could think of doing. I was getting kind of bored just sitting here."

I ask her if I can see her work, and she hands it to me. I look at her sketch. It's a meticulous drawing of the room we're sitting in by someone who appears to be schooled in the high science of interior engineering, which of course she cannot be, because she is too young and comes from the Anterior Region. "Why are you sketching my chambers?"

"I don't know," she says. "Maybe one day I'll be a judge and I'll need to know how to decorate this place."

I want to laugh, but I don't. It's too early in the process to have that kind of familiarity. "Well . . . you will need to become a citizen first."

"Oh, I'm pretty confident you'll want to make me a citizen."

"And *why* are you so confident?"

"Because I'm a talented fighter and I don't lie." Pique stands up. She is no more than 150 centimeters tall. She looks nothing like a fighter and her boast about being a talented one seems like a lie. She sits back down on her chair with her legs crossed. She looks tiny. She repeats herself: "All you need to know about me is that I'm a talented fighter and I don't lie. *That's what you Federates are looking for, right?*"

Pique and I are off to a strange start. "So," I say, before taking in a long breath. "You're a talented fighter and you don't lie. Presumably you have some weaknesses?"

"Clearly." Her response is quick. She stands up again. "I'm small. I'm very, very small. And *your doctors* say I'm done growing." She says "your doctors" in an unusually incriminatory manner. "But I'm fast. Fast in every way. My uncle Trace says: Fast feet. Fast hands. Fast mind." She then winks at me. *A thirteen-year-old girl from the Anterior Region winks at me, a high judge.* I know how pompous I sound, but it's highly unusual. After her wink, she says, "But Uncle Trace is a morzium fiend. So what does he know?"

It surprises me that Pique mentions her uncle so early in the citizenship process. In the preinterviews, her mentors told me that they coached her not to do this, out of respect for the Premier and the Federacy. Trace is an Abstainer. At one time he was a leader of the Abstainer movement. The Abstainers have no military, but the Premier still sees them as a significant threat to the Federacy. He's wrong.

I don't respond or react to Pique's mention of Trace. I want to get to know Pique and I know that any further talk of Trace will cloud my judgment both in favor of Pique and against her. My view of Trace and the Abstainer movement is irrelevant to her citizenship process. A thirteen-year-old girl stands before me. One I do not understand.

"So do you have any other weaknesses?"

"Sure. I already told you them. I'm a talented fighter and I don't lie."

"You said those were your strengths."

Pique smiles. She then rests her chin on her closed fist and schools me with her eyes. She doesn't say anything, but I know what that look means. *Come on now, Judge, my strengths are my weaknesses. This is true with anyone. You should know that.* Pique is now playing on one of my greatest weaknesses—I am truly charmed by the truly charming. Pique radiates this quality. I wish I could bottle it and spray it all over the Federacy Omniplex.

We talk for another three hours, about her studies, her thoughts on the NFF and the Rogues, her interest in science, her extended family, her lack of any true friends, her disapproval of the Abstainer movement, her love of drawing, her volunteer work with injured animals, and a multitude of other topics. She is gifted in so many ways and mature beyond her years. I have never had a more forthright candidate. I would wager my entire fortune that she does not lie once. If I were an impulsive type, I would grant her citizenship on the spot.

As we are talking about her maternal grandmother, Aquarius Rollins, a trailblazer in the Abstainer movement, Pique looks down at her chronometer and abruptly wraps up what she is saying. "May I use the bathroom," she says. She smiles at me again. This time, her smile seems less innocent—less like a thirteen-year-old's smile. It sickens me to say, but it's almost seductive. She is only thirteen years of age, but she is fully mature, pumped with synthetic growth hormones that increase her biological age. She is legally approved for sexual intercourse according to *The Federacy's Cohabitation and Copulation Regulations.* I worry she will return from the bathroom as Dariox did. As so many candidates do.

After a few minutes of water running and the toilet flushing, Pique returns from the bathroom. Her hair is slicked back with water and pulled into a tight ponytail. The ponytail is tucked back into her shirt so that she looks like a boy.

"You thought the worst of me, *Your Holiness.*"

"It's 'Your Honor' or 'Judge' or just 'Max'—*not* 'Your Holiness.' And yes, I thought the worst."

"I told you. I don't lie. Seducing someone to get what you want is a kind of a lie, right? And you know by now that I'm being honest."

"Yes, you've said you do not lie and I probably believe you."

"You know it's true."

"Maybe, but you've also said you're a talented fighter and I find that hard to believe."

"Yeah, so that's the trick. There's no easy way to prove that."

"Well, I believe—"

As soon as "believe" leaves my lips, Pique slides through my legs. She's a flash of light. Before I can turn around, she rips the loops that hold my robing suit's belt in place. As I lower my arms to stop her, she instantly breaks the last belt loop, lifts the belt up around my arms, and quickly tightens it so I can't move my arms. It's so tight that I become short of breath and light-headed. She then kicks out my legs by striking the back of my knees. I fall onto my stomach and she uses a cable she ripped from the latrine to tie my feet together.

It takes Pique all of five seconds to have me completely secured. It takes another sixty seconds before five of my best guards can secure Pique. She is lightning—fast, powerful, destructive. She is almost not human. She knocks out four of my guards cold. It is not until the fifth guard pulls his weapon that she stops, and I'm pretty sure based on what I just witnessed that she could have disarmed him too if she so chose. For a second, I think the tales of the halfling breeds from the Anterior Region are true. But those myths have been widely debunked.

As they carry her away to the Omniplex Detention Center, she smiles at me and says, "You thought I was going to come out of that bathroom naked." She shakes her head disapprovingly. "You're supposed to be a judge. A judge of character." She then mocks me by repeating what my fourteen plaques say in her squeakiest voice. *"High Judge Maxomillion Cone. Highest Judge. Highest Efficiency. Highest Honor. The Truest of Federates."* There is a certain empathy in her cajoling, like a younger sister teasing an older brother whom she admires. At least that's what I hope.

As the guards carry her down the hallway, the last thing I hear her yell is "I told you, *Your Holiness*. I'm a talented fighter and I don't lie."

4

EMMIS CONE

As I take my transport home, I cannot stop thinking about Pique. I know that she is more than just a charismatic girl from the Anterior Region. She is the granddaughter of Aquarius Rollins and the niece of Trace Rollins. The Premier asked me to personally conduct her First Interview. She has strength and speed that are beyond human. I know she came to me for some reason other than just trying to get citizenship. The Premier's office must know this, too.

For now, Pique is a prisoner of the Federacy charged with assault of a high Federacy official. I wish I could just order her release, but if I want to help her, I can't. Appearances will matter. I must let her remain in the detention center and pretend I'm disinterested, even though I'm anything but. I just met Pique, yet I felt an instant connection. She is special, and because of my complicated relationship with the Premier, I must hide that fact.

I exit my transport and walk into our house. I am greeted by Viole first. She is quickly followed by her older brothers, Kase and Jax. Viole jumps up and tries to kiss me on the cheek, but the kiss lands on my nose. Jax rushes up to me and excitedly shouts, "I won at Ladders today in school. And I got a one hundred in—"

Kase cuts him off. "Dad, Dad, are we going to the films tonight? Please. You promised." I have far too much work to go to the films, but I say yes anyway. "We're all going to the films and then out for cold cream." They all smile and tell me I'm the best dad in the world. I like that. That's the only thing I genuinely want to be the best at, and that includes being a husband.

I walk to the colidor to get Viole a canister of fortified juice. The colidor's monitor flashes through the children's projects from their primary-education centers. I freeze on one of Jax's poems. He is my middle child, and like many a middle child, the most understanding. I read his poem about Emmis.

MY MOTHER'S CHAIR
My mother's name is Emmis Cone.
She's the only mother I've ever known.
She lives her days stuck in a chair.
The only thing she does is stare.
I miss the days of kisses and hugs.
But it seems her brain's been eaten by bugs.

SCRIPTED BY STUDENT 3-C: JAX CONE

After the film and cold cream, I get my kids ready for bed. I read them the story of Jeremiel from the Book of Our God. They ask me questions about whether Jeremiel really talked to Our God or really separated the salt from the Sea of Sorne. I tell them a partial truth—I don't know. Viole falls asleep in my arms and I carry her off to her room. When I return, Jax and Kase are snoring in their bunks.

I let the nurse leave for the night and ready a bathing pool for Emmis. I wheel her to the bathroom and begin removing her clothes. As I take off her underwear, I feel as though she smiles at me. She still looks beautiful. I remove her shirt. Her breasts are still firm, though smaller than when she was well. Her legs and arms have not fared as well. They are twigs. Her muscles shriveled. And her back is arched like a 125-year-old woman's. Her face, though, is as beautiful as it was the day the Holy Father bonded us.

I bathe her. It's a perverse feeling—excited by touching her, but not wanting to be excited for fear of taking advantage of a person who lacks the ability to consent. She is my wife and yet she is off-limits to me.

I tell her about my day as I rub foaming solution on her back. I feel her heart pick up its beat as I mention Pique. When I tell her how Pique slid through my legs and tied me up, Emmis's eyelids begin to flutter rapidly. It is these little gestures that make me believe that Emmis will return to me one day and I will again be whole. It is these little gestures that remind me that one day I will kill the people who took Emmis away from me. It is these brilliant little flutters that give me the patience to lie in wait—to lie in wait for the right moment, when I will rip out the hearts of the men who did this to her.

It is undeniably true that Emmis was "a traitor" to the Federacy. Her scientific work had more to offer than the Federacy's closed walls and closed minds. She could never specifically tell me about the details of her work, because it was too dangerous for both of us. I knew that her specialty was the study of the physics of divinity, but that's all she would tell me. I do know that her work for the Federacy's Divinity Labs was transformative and that it transcended the very idea of the Federacy. I know she shared her classified findings with those she shouldn't have. I know that the established class couldn't have this. I understood their fears and their need to send a stern message. But to take her away from her children was unconscionable. So I lie in wait for the right moment, nourished by these little signs of hope.

When the day comes, I will let the Premier know that I made a conscious decision to spare his life. I will let him know that he came dangerously close to being killed by me. I will let him know that he is being spared because his crime was the crime of cowardice. He did what *he could* to stop the procedure. His weakness is not worthy of death.

But I will destroy everyone else. The head of the Federacy Tactical Intelligence Service (FTIS). The Council of Three. The Lord Regneon. The Committee on Tyranny. The Rector of Treason. I will rip through their chests and pull out their hearts. Just as they have pulled out mine.

In all likelihood, Emmis will remain in her wheeled chair for another eternity. But when I tell her that I finally ripped out the hearts of the men who ordered the procedure, her heart will pick up its beat and her eyes will flutter.

5

SPIRO DE YERUSALOM

I'm surprised by the Office of the Premier's decision to keep Pique in the detention center for twelve days before granting her an initial hearing on the assault charge. The office assigns Veriton to preside over the hearing. As the highest judge in the Federacy, I have the authority to undo this decision, but it's best if I do nothing. The only request I make, and it's a formality, is to attend Pique's hearing before Veriton. The office stalls in approving my request, but eventually realizes it cannot deny it without me becoming suspicious of their motives.

After almost two weeks of detention, Pique is brought into Veriton's courtroom in electracles. I can't help but think she could break out of them at any time if she wanted to. I sit in the back of the courtroom, and Veriton gives me a peculiar smile. I'm not sure what that smile means—if it's about what I saw on the Palmitor or if he knows something special about Pique's case. Either way, I suspect I will soon be receiving a call from him requesting a ride to work. I smile back at Veriton, and just as I do, Pique winks at me. I don't want to, but I automatically wink back.

The clerk of Veriton's court appears in the center of his chambers. The clerk is standing on a raised circular platform, and a spotlight is shining down from the ceiling. "Please all come to order—for Judge Veriton Glass shall now begin the violation inquiry proceeding in the matter of *The Federacy versus Citizen Candidate Pique Rollins*. His Highest Judge Maxomillion Cone and

Sir Croix Ripevine of the Committee on Tyranny are in attendance. Pique Rollins, please rise and take the oath of the accused."

Pique stands. She looks even smaller than I remember. The lights, the staging, the microphones, and the positioning of all those in attendance are carefully orchestrated elements of interior engineering. The accused is intended to look small and the judge large. Interior engineering is a high science taught in all the best tertiary-education centers. Though Pique is too young to be trained in this science, I remember her sketch of my chambers from our initial meeting. She had a strong intuitive understanding of the architectural and acoustic hierarchies of interior engineering. As she stands on her small, poorly lit platform, she must understand how tiny she looks to all in attendance.

The clerk's spotlight brightens as he addresses Pique. "Citizen Candidate Rollins. Please place your hand on the Book of Our God. Please solemnly listen to the oath of the accused and then answer in the affirmative." Pique places her hand on the Book of Our God, but she touches the cover as if it's a sharp blade. The clerk reads the oath: "As a citizen candidate under the dominion of the Federacy, and as a fully realized human being living and thriving under the Federacy's protection in this year 210 After the End of the Old Order, you pledge to be forthright and exhibit the character of a Federate in responding to the inquiry of Judge Veriton Glass."

"As you've requested, I do." Veriton doesn't contest the qualifying "as you've requested," but there are some in the audience who are aghast, particularly that bastard Croix Ripevine.

Pique's platform automatically rotates away from the clerk and toward Veriton. The clerk reads the charges against Pique and asks her whether she wants an advocate to represent her. "I don't need an advocate. I've got a friend in the audience. He'll defend me." She winks at me and I don't feel the least bit uncomfortable, though of course I should.

"Very well," the clerk says. "How do you plead to the charge of assault against a high officer of the Federacy?"

"That would be guilty." Pique pauses for effect and seductively says, "Very guilty."

Veriton can't contain his smile. The only person in the chambers not smiling is Ripevine. A soft glow backlights Veriton's imposing judicial throne.

"Young lady, at this point in the proceeding, most people select an advocate and most people choose to be not guilty irrespective of the facts."

"Wouldn't that be lying, *Your Holiness*?"

"I would really prefer it if you called me 'Judge,'" Veriton says. This time his smile uncontrollably overtakes his entire face. "And no, it would not be lying. It's a procedural maneuver which simply says you are not ready to admit guilt. It's perfectly in line with the character of a Federate."

"I'm not a Federate, sir. I'm just a little girl from the Anterior Region who hogtied one of your fancy judges. I am *very, very* guilty." It's hard to tell who is smiling more, Veriton or me.

"Again, I remind you, Ms. Rollins, that it is customary for Federates or even citizen candidates to—" Before Veriton can finish, a massive explosion rocks the chambers. The lights go dark. A pulsing electric current washes over the room, short-circuiting most of the chambers' technologies. Smoke fills the room, and as the emergency lighting flips on, I see a large cloud of smoke mushrooming up to the vaulted ceiling. This billowing dark cloud is pierced by a single blue spotlight that appears in the center of the chambers. I expect to hear people screaming, but there is complete silence. I'm shocked. Everyone's frozen.

Out from the blue circle of light, a man wearing a long robe appears. It is inexplicable how he appears from thin air. He is tall and thin and his robe is red velvet, richly adorned and perfectly tailored to the body of the man that inhabits it.

"Hello, Federates," the man says. His voice is a strange mix of earnest cordiality and mocking contempt. "Warmest wishes from the Holy Father himself." The man tightens the belt around his robe and looks up to the frozen audience. "I mean none of you any harm." He shakes his head. "Forgive me. I misspoke. I meant to say that I mean *very few* of you any harm. But please know that the Holy Father does not wish violence upon his friends and he considers the vast majority of you as friends. The Nation of Yerusalom and the Federacy are good friends. So you are entirely safe." Again, he shakes his head. "I should have first introduced myself—please forgive my rudeness. Some of you may already know me, but for those who don't, my name is Spiro, Spiro de Yerusalom. I am the Holy Father's senior emissary." I don't know how many people know who Spiro is, but I certainly do. And that he's here isn't a good thing.

I feel as though my body is ten times its weight, but I can still move. I pull myself up from my seat and try to run toward Spiro, but the weight is too much initially. The more I move though, the quicker the gravitational force diminishes. Eventually, I am able to run full-speed at Spiro. I am weapon-less, but I will bash his skull against the podium. I manage to get down a half a flight of stairs before Spiro makes eye contact with me and swiftly raises his hand. I'm instantly hit by an electric current, which races through my body and goes straight to my heart. The shock to my lungs burns at first, but when the pain subsides, I realize that my heart is beating very slowly and nothing else is moving. My chest, arms, and legs are glued down by a gravitational force I can't comprehend. I have never experienced anything like this. Only my head can move, and not well. I lift it up, and in that moment, I realize Pique is gone.

"No need to get violent, Judge Cone. Like I said, we're friends. The Holy Father and I are enormous admirers of you and your work. As a small token of my admiration look what I have done for you." Spiro points over at where Sir Croix Ripevine was sitting and then dramatically raises his hands above his head. He points up to a titanium crossbeam where Ripevine is dangling from a robotic noose.

"Vengeance is sweet, is it not? That miserable man—one of the perpetrators of that most heinous crime against your wife—is now dead. Consider that a gesture of goodwill from the Holy Father and me."

I try to speak, but my head is now rendered immobile and my mouth and vocal cords feel as though they have been untethered from my brain. With the exception of Pique, who is gone, and Ripevine, who is dead, everyone else is held motionless by some electrical or gravitational field that I have never in all my years of warfare seen. Spiro sees that I'm trying to talk and he quickly flicks his index finger in the air. My mouth and vocal cords, but nothing else, are restored to normal.

"What have you done with Pique?"

"She's safe. You have nothing to fear." Spiro approaches me. "We've been studying you for quite some time, Judge Cone. Like Pique, you are one of the most talented individuals we have ever come across. You have the Divine Spirit inside of you. You are a judge among judges—a master discerner of great character. You knew Pique was extraordinary. You probably knew right away. Am I right or am I right?"

"Apparently you're right," I say.

"A sense of humor, too. I love that."

"Are you going to tell me where she is?"

Spiro comes uncomfortably close to me. His lips are far too close to mine and his breath smells medicinal. My head has regained some ability to move, so I turn it to the side to avoid his uncomfortable proximity. As I do, I notice out of the corner of my eye that Veriton is also gone. Spiro pulls my face back toward his. His smile is wide and disturbing. He puts his hands on my shoulders and whispers into my ear. "In approximately four hours, Pique will be in the Nation of Yerusalom having Damascian tea with the Holy Father. Now I want you to imagine that you are sitting right there, next to Pique. You watch her every move. As she sips her tea, the Holy Father tells her to try adding some honey goat's milk. She adds the sweet milk and winks at you. You have an uncontrollable desire to wink back. Indeed you do wink back. You then turn to your right—or maybe it's your left—and you notice something strange. You notice that Veriton Glass, that colossal jackass, is sitting beside you motionless. You ask me why he's not moving. I tell you that he's not moving because he's dead. You ask me how he died and I tell you I killed him. Then, you ask me why I killed him. I pause for a moment—perhaps just to add some dramatic effect to the situation—and then I give you the answer. I killed him because he gave you that *fucking Palmitor*."

6

THE HOLY FATHER

"Fucking Palmitor" are the first words I remember upon waking up in a velvet chair with Pique on one side and Veriton's dead body on the other. "It is so good to see you again, Judge," the Holy Father says. My vision is a bit blurred, but his voice is unmistakable. "It must be ten . . . fifteen years since I bonded you and Emmis. It's been too long." As my vision improves, I notice the Holy Father making his way toward me. "My deepest apologies, Judge." The Holy Father pours me a cup of tea and then motions to two lifelike beings, not entirely human, but also not entirely robotic, to carry Veriton's body away. "I must indulge some of Spiro's theatrics. He is profoundly talented. If I took away his creativity—if I dampened his untamed spirit— he might lose some of his greatest endowments. As you well know, Judge, talent comes in all shapes, sizes, and characters. And it must be nourished at all costs. You find and nourish great *Federates*. I find and nourish great *Spirits*."

My head and body feel like they have been stuck in a gravity vise for a week. I can barely move my legs, and my organs feel like they're on fire. Without me uttering a word about the pain, the Holy Father says, "It will wear off. Drink your tea, *my son*." I don't like that he calls me his son. The fact that he calls every man who is not openly his enemy "my son" is a pretension I could surely live without.

The Holy Father, according to most accounts, is 195 years old, which makes him about a century and a half older than me. He was born just after the

End of the Old Order and he is the grandson of the heroic Cardinal of Petyrs-burg, whom most history books hail—rightly or wrongly—as the Father of the New Order. The Holy Father seems to be ageless. His face is covered with a skin-colored adhesive material that, I assume, protects him from the sun's ultraviolet rays. His eyes and mouth, which peek out through this ad-hesive mask, show no signs of aging. They must not be his original parts.

"Rest up, my son." He pats the top of my head and then places his hand on Pique's shoulder. Pique is sketching the inside of the room we're in. I'm extremely groggy. But based on the volume of books and the ornate gold ceil-ing, I assume we are in the Golden Library of the Holy Temple. The Holy Temple is attached to the Holy Father's residence, and its library is the larg-est repository of books in the world. Few people have ever entered its sup-posedly hallowed halls. There are legends that suggest that the ceiling of the Golden Library can be unlocked and a portal to the Heavenly Kingdom will appear. When asked by the Federacy's state media about the truth of this legend, the Holy Father refused to deny it.

"Why am I here?" I ask the Holy Father. I want to let him know I'm angry that I've been abducted, but I can barely muster the energy.

"I will answer all of your questions in short order. But for now, if you don't mind, I would like for you to drink your tea." The Holy Father is not engag-ing me in a conversation. He clearly does not view me as his equal. He's telling me what to do. That is what the Holy Father does. He speaks and people listen. He orders the lifelike beings, which he calls DAKs, to bring me more tea and inject me with stolion, which should slowly alleviate my cloudiness. I can't be sure, but based on my knowledge of Yerusi military jargon, I believe that "DAK" stands for the functions of this humanoid—dedicated autonomous knowing.

"I want you to sip your tea slowly," the Holy Father says. The Holy Father is gracious, but that doesn't mean he has a high threshold for dissent. "I want you to concentrate on the fact that each sip is an opportunity to be renewed. Let the warmth of the tea fill your body. Let it flow through you and restore your strength, just as the Divine Spirit renews us each and every day."

I look up at one of the Golden Library's many balconies. I notice that Spiro is looking down at us like a hawk watching its prey. "Isn't this glorious," he says. Spiro is perched above me watching my every move. "It's the second coming of the Sacred Trinity." Spiro rarely laughs outwardly, but every word he says is steeped in his own amusement. "Our New Trinity—the Holy Father, the Judge, and the Holy Son Pique, gender notwithstanding."

Before I have an opportunity to say anything about how much I would like to bash Spiro's head in, Pique turns to him. "And who are you in this little story, the Fallen Angel?" She then lifts her right hand in the air as if reaching for an imaginary rope—one that is attached to Spiro's neck. She yanks it and Spiro somersaults off the balcony and lands in front of her. Neither of them says a thing to the other and I don't know if she actually made it happen or he pretended. Pique simply turns to me and whispers in my ear, "Just know, I'm on your side. No matter what happens, never forget that." She smiles and adds the dig *"Your Holiness."* I don't have the strength, or even the inclination, to stop her from making fun of me. If Emmis could talk, she would probably say I sort of like being teased by Pique.

"Please drink up, my son," the Holy Father says. He looks at Spiro like a disappointed parent. He turns back to me and says, "It will help you overcome the effects of Spiro's overzealousness. He needs to learn to control his gifts." I see Spiro fight back a smile, which the Holy Father responds to with an angry squint of his—or someone else's—Neptune-blue eyes. I sip my tea, but it doesn't help my pounding headache or the fact that I can't think straight. I have never tried morzium, but I assume this is what it must feel like when the high ends.

"I would like us to gather in the library's Summit Room. The DAKs will bring your tea and we can begin the process of enlightening you, Judge. Soon you will know all there is to know about our greater purpose. But you must be patient. Our journey is long and our path will take many turns."

As I rise to my feet, my knees buckle. Before I can fall, Pique's arms are around me and I am using her for support. I am many heads taller and weigh more than twice as much, but Pique easily supports me. It feels as if she could lift me over her head with one hand. As she carries me, I feel a connection to her. My thoughts are cloudy, and I don't know if it's something instinctual like the fact that she reminds me of my daughter Viole, but I feel a certain kind of familiarity, a certain kind of trust. It's not rational, but the feeling is inescapable. She guides me through a mahogany archway into a meeting room with a large table and twelve hoverchairs. The walls are covered with seemingly endless shelves of books that stretch up to the vaulted ceiling. There are copper-coated ladders everywhere and the books closest to the ceiling seem as though they are hundreds, if not thousands, of years old.

The two DAKs arrive with our tea, and the Holy Father quickly motions for them to leave. Over the next twenty minutes, the Holy Father gingerly climbs ladders and pulls books from the bookshelves. He scrutinizes different books and reads passages to himself, but says little. Occasionally he smiles while reading a passage and says, "Yes of course." When he looks at Pique, she ignores him. She refuses to make eye contact, and although it seems they know each other, she clearly feels uncomfortable around him. Whenever Spiro tries to talk, the Holy Father tells him to "enjoy the silence" and Spiro closes his eyes and folds his hands as if praying. My head is still heavy and I'm content to sit in my deep haze sipping tea. For a brief moment, I think that maybe I shouldn't be drinking this tea—maybe something's wrong with it. But that thought, like all others, quickly passes.

Eventually the Holy Father slides a pile of books across the table to me. "The real answers you want are in here. They will answer your questions in ways that will be more fulfilling than if I spoon-feed the answers to you. But first—because I remember what it's like to be young and impatient—I will give you the superficial answers you so desperately crave. The first thing you need to know is what transpired in the Federacy." The Holy Father looks at Spiro. He's disappointed. "My orders were not honored and Spiro escalated matters far beyond what I intended. My goals were simple—exterminate Judge Glass, recover the Palmitor, and bring you and Pique to the safety of Yerusalom."

The Holy Father's fingers are long and thin and covered in the same skin-colored adhesive that masks his face. He holds up his index finger and says, "Most importantly, I need you to know that I have rescued your loved ones and placed them under my protection." I rise to my feet and try to find my balance. "I have Emmis and your three children nearby in a secure location—far away from those who would do them harm. The Federacy would have assumed that you are cooperating with me and they would have taken them to use as pawns. They have harmed Emmis in the past and they most certainly would do it again."

I place my hands on the table and try to bring myself back into reality. "If any harm—"

"There will be no harm, Judge. But please let me finish." The Holy Father looks at Pique and she immediately turns her head away. "Spiro decided in his abundant wisdom to kill all those in attendance at Pique's hearing, including what we later learned to be some very close relatives of your Premier. Ever resourceful, Spiro made the whole thing look like it was the work of the NFF. The NFF knows it has been framed for the mass murder of innocents, and so, unfortunately, there is a chance they will blame you. So, with all this confusion in the air, I immediately ordered one of my commando teams to secure your family and bring them to Yerusalom."

The tea, the long breaths, and the injections of stolion the DAKs gave me cannot fully wake me out of my stupor. But hearing that someone took my family—for whatever purpose—brings me back to life. I walk toward the Holy Father, my eyes never leaving his. The Holy Father absorbs my glare. He does not look scared, but he quickly flashes a look to Spiro, who in turn discharges an electric current that glues me to a nearby seat. I am frozen from the waist down. "Please, Judge," the Holy Father says. "Give me a chance to explain everything to you. I know that as a judge you treasure truth above all else and I shall provide you with the truth."

As Spiro moves closer to me, I lunge for a book, and before Spiro can do a thing, I smack him across the head with it. The electric current weakens as he loses consciousness. Before he can stand, I elbow him in the head and break open a huge gash above his brow. He immediately collapses and I am free. I quickly take off my belt and bind Spiro's hands. I find a nearby closet and throw him in it. When I return, I see Pique whispering something to the Holy Father.

"Take me to my family immediately."

"I promise they're okay, Judge," Pique says. "I would never let anyone harm you or your family. Emmis and the children are—"

"That's enough, Pique," the Holy Father says. "What you did—seeking the judge out—was rash and irresponsible. You set us all back. The judge needs time to adjust. Trust comes slowly to most—especially those who have perfected the art of judgment."

"That's fine," Pique says to the Holy Father. "But make sure you treat the judge with respect. He's not your servant. He's your equal."

The closet door flies open and Spiro wobbles out. He undoes the belt around his hands, and waves them in the air, signaling that the fight is over. He staggers over to the Holy Father and falls into a hoverchair. As he wipes away the blood on his brow, he says, "I couldn't help but overhear what Pique was saying about treating the judge as an equal. As you know, Father, according to the most recent Palmitor results, the judge may be more than just your equal." Spiro smiles.

"Let's not get ahead of ourselves," the Holy Father says. The Holy Father is not one to show a great deal of emotion, but he does not take kindly to being challenged. He sucks in a deep breath, trying to rid himself of his anger. He then folds his hands together. "Judge, give me a few moments to explain myself and then I will personally take you to your family. You have my word. There will be no deception and Spiro will be on his best behavior."

"He better be," Pique says. "If not, he'll deal with me." Pique turns to me and whispers in my ear. "I think you should hear the Holy Father out—lies and all."

"I will give you five minutes," I say. "But it's for Pique, not you." I set my chronometer and show it to the Holy Father. "When it goes off, you take me to my family."

The Holy Father wastes no time. He motions for the DAK standing just outside the door. The DAK quickly enters the room and hands the Holy Father the Palmitor that Veriton gave me. "We recovered this from your home. We think we know what you may have seen. But I would greatly appreciate you telling me. What did you bear witness to, my son?"

"*You're* asking *me* questions," I say. "I'm waiting for you to give me answers. The clock is running."

"It would be helpful if you would indulge me just a bit longer. The Palmitor, as you might suspect, is an imperfect device. It has embedded content schemas, but it also relies heavily on the biometric feedback and synaptic references of its holder. It delivers very different information depending on who is holding it, when they are holding it, and what emotions they are experiencing at that time. The Palmitor is a mirror of sorts—a powerful one at that—but between the content algorithms and the peculiarities of the biometric architecture, it can greatly distort the truth. It can become a stochastic kaleidoscope, a warped amalgamator of fact and fiction."

The Holy Father gently places the Palmitor on the table. "I hope and pray you are like your fellow countrymen in sharing the Nation of Yerusalom's belief in the Sanctity of the Divine. We are a nation of belief—belief in the capacity of humans. We have faith that humankind advances by practicing the tenets of Our God, the One True God. The Palmitor was built to enhance our faith in this sanctity. It was built so that we can grow closer to, and be more connected with, divine providence—or in laymen's terms, the future. When laboratory conditions are perfect, the distance between the Palmitor and the divine is minimized. But when conditions are unregulated, the results can be disastrous. And this is precisely why Judge Glass was so reckless in giving you this Palmitor."

"What *do you* think I saw?"

"I would prefer if you answered me first. But I know my time is winding down and a promise is a promise." The Holy Father almost laughs. "You are a stubborn man, Judge Cone. You want me to speak first—I will speak first. The truth is I don't know exactly what you saw. But I know something about what you might have seen, because my scientists were the ones who created the Palmitor and programmed the original content. But Veriton, who I thought was working to further mutual interests of ours, stole my creation. He had my Palmitor hacked and modified so that he could convince you to take over the command of the Federacy troops. He truly believed the unthinkable—that the NFF and Rogues would eventually defeat the world's most powerful military. The Premier was on the fence about reinstating your command and there was a lot of resistance from the political elite—you know, those same *noble men* responsible for Emmis's procedure. Veriton needed you to actively seek out the reinstatement, and he knew how hard that would be. So he stole my Palmitor."

The Holy Father picks up the Palmitor and runs his hands across it. "You could have seen any number of things. If I were a betting man, which of course I'm not, I would say you saw yourself as a failed leader, one who refused to lead or maybe acted recklessly. I can't be sure. Maybe you were leading the Federacy, or even some breakaway group. Perhaps you made an irresponsible decision to use some *vehicle of immense devastation*, like your nation's Phoenix VOID system. Perhaps you unintentionally caused some kind of cataclysmic collateral damage or maybe you even blew up the entire planet. Perhaps you saw your entire family vaporized by these VOIDs." The Holy Father smiles and I don't like it. "Is that about right, my son?"

Before I have a chance to answer, the Holy Father adds, "Oh yes, and you believe that you are entirely to blame for these choices. You and you alone control the fate of our planet and you make a terrible decision that leads to our massive annihilation."

"The Palmitor is witchcraft," Pique says. "Tell him the truth."

"Please, Pique," the Holy Father says. "You do not know of what you speak. The Palmitor is far from witchcraft and I insist that you exercise some restraint." The Holy Father places his finger over his lips. He doesn't want Pique to say another word. "What Pique is trying to suggest is that Judge Glass only wanted to show you a partial truth, one that advanced his views. I, however, want to show you the whole truth. If you are patient and let me lead you down the path, I will take you to the truth. The Nation of Yerusalom needs people like you and Pique, and if ever she would return to us, your dear wife Emmis. We need exceptionalism. We need people who understand the boundlessness of human capacity. We need great judges and great thinkers. As you know, Emmis's work focused on the intersection between knowledge and the divine. This is precisely what the Palmitor does. Remember what the Book of Our God says, my son. 'God created the human in the hope that he could do what is divine.'"

My chronometer goes off. "Let's go. I don't care about the Palmitor or the Book of Our God or anything else. I want to see my family."

"Very well, my son. There are more answers in a hug from a youngling than there are from the mouth of an old man. Let us go see your family. I shall take you myself."

Pique stays close to me as we walk down a winding corridor, trailing the Holy Father's cape. There are no Yerusi guards anywhere. There are only a handful of DAKs, each of which bows to us as we pass them in the corridor. We walk for about ten minutes in dimly lit hallways with strange Gracian music playing softly in the background. Somewhere along the way the lights grow even dimmer. I can no longer see the Holy Father ahead of me. I walk faster, hoping to catch up, but he's not there. It's as if he's disappeared into thin air.

I am left alone with Pique, standing in front of a sliding door marked VISI- TOR QUARTERS. I go to press the button to open the door, and Pique stops me. She takes my hand and holds it tight. "I'm on your side, Judge. Please, no matter what happens, never forget that."

I press the button and the door opens slowly. Pique knows there is some- thing on the other side of the door that's not right. She tightens her grip, and my heart starts to beat faster. A flickering light comes on and I'm immedi- ately hit by a rancid smell. I step forward into the room. The floor is sticky. I take two steps in and see something no man should ever have to see. They're on the floor facedown. I can't breathe. I don't want to breathe. They're not moving. I kneel down to touch Viole. She's cold and stiff. She's dead. They're all dead. My whole family—they're all dead.

PART II
THE ABSTAINERS

7

NAYLA ROLLINS

I wake up on a dusty path. The sun is burning hot. Drums are playing in the distance, beating out rhythms similar to the banging in my head. I touch the heavy beard on my face. I must have been unconscious for days . . . more like weeks. I look down at my hands and there is no blood on them. I clearly remember holding Viole. I remember stroking Jax's bloodied head. I remember holding Kase's sticky hand. I remember wiping away the blood from Emmis's face. I should be covered in blood. How can this be?

I must focus.

I rise to my feet and instinctively follow the beat of the drums. I try to get the images of my murdered family out of my head. But I can't. I want them back. I need them back. I can't have them back. I keep telling myself, *I can't have them back*. I walk to the rhythms of the drums repeating my awful chant: *I want them back. I need them back. I can't have them back.* This march goes on and on and on. The only thing that occasionally breaks it is the thought of Pique. *Is she okay?* I know she had nothing to do with this. I know.

I follow the sound of the drums. As they get louder, the repetitive beats begin to fill my head, temporarily pushing aside the most painful images of my family. I'm exhausted. My steps start to slow and my march can no longer follow the drums. My feet now take their cue from the beating sun. Our star is merciless. I am high in the hills. Sun-parched hills with thin air.

It is mind-numbingly hot—far too hot to be the Federacy or the Nation of Yerusalom. I must be close to the equator.

I look up toward the sun, and as soon as I take my eyes off the trail in front of me, I trip over a rock. I am weak and dehydrated. I fall forward and roll a few meters into the brush. I get up and see a small trail of debris behind me—nutrition unit, books, and a micropak. I realize I must have been wearing this pack the whole time. I gather the pack and its contents. I notice that the books are some of the same ones the Holy Father intended to give me. There is a water bottle, omega supplements in the nutrition unit, and an envelope with the Holy Father's seal. I open the envelope.

On this 42nd Day of May, 210 A.E.O.O. Praise All that is Divine.

Dearest Judge:

My most heartfelt condolences on the devastating loss of your family. This life is cruel and your loved ones were victims of its deepest cruelties. May they rest in peace in the light of the Divine Spirit.

I have no words to ease your pain, but I have taken the strongest actions in the name of your family and the name of the Nation of Yerusalom. On my command, we immediately executed fourteen of the perpetrators of the crime. They were mercenaries, the MO-4 Corps, hired by the Federacy.

So that we are entirely clear, *I am the one to blame* for not sufficiently protecting your family. I ask and pray for your forgiveness. I should have protected them. I failed you and will live the rest of my days knowing this.

They killed your poor Emmis, Jax, Kase, and that little darling of yours, Viole. I am to blame and I will show not one ounce of mercy towards the perpetrators of this heinous crime. I will slaughter without regret every single mercenary, every single Federate soldier, and every single member of the Federate Aristocracy who was involved in this crime. This depraved attack was a direct order from your Premier. I will bring him to you—roped and gagged—for you to do as you wish. That will be a small measure of my penance.

We sent you away from us to protect you. Currently, there is a consortium of over twenty hired mercenary groups looking for you. The Federacy wants you dead and the price they have paid is steep. The Premier fears your retribution and so he needs you dead. Therefore, we have airlifted you to safer ground. Neither I nor my staff knows where you currently are. A special Palmitor determined where you would be safest and one of my elite DAKs secretly arranged the rest. If we knew your location, we would become a liability to you. We took enormous precautions to ensure that your whereabouts are unknown to the world, save for one contact. You and the contact will be united shortly.

We know you will be skeptical of this letter and our intentions. We know that there is no way for you to currently trust us. We know that you will need time to reflect and time to heal from your loss. But, I need to make you aware of one critical fact. The MO-4 has captured Pique.

Our initial intelligence reports suggest that she was taken back to a secret detention facility in the Federacy and that they're convening a Capital Crimes Tribunal. For public appearances, they are accusing her of the death of you and Judge Glass.

No one knows the Federacy like you. You need to save Pique. You need to bring her home to me. You, Pique, and I need to be in Yerusalom. War is coming, and it will not just be a war for men. It will be a war for the gods.

May Our God, the One True God, open his heart to you. May he heal your wounds. May he cast aside your enemies. May he bring you and Pique safely back to me.

With an Open Heart and Boundless Love,
The Holy Father

I place the letter back in the envelope and open the bottle of water. I take a sip, but I'm too nauseous to eat any of the supplements. I know that the

Holy Father's letter is filled with lies. But I also know some of it must be true. The best manipulators provide just enough truth to disguise their lies.

I'm pretty sure the Holy Father is lying about not wanting to know my whereabouts. He couldn't give up that kind of control. It's not in his nature. I search my micropak, clothes, and body for positioning devices. He has to be tracking me. But I find nothing. I go back and forth in my head over whether I should even keep the micropak. I decide that the books may provide some insight into the Holy Father's motivations and I need something to carry them in. I put the micropak on and head back toward the trail.

The trail climbs for another few hundred meters and then descends into a valley. The trail is mostly clear, with the exception of some low-growing desert weeds and cactus. I eventually reach a hilltop on the trail. I look down and see where the drums are coming from. There's a group of people in the distance. Most of them are gathered around a triangular stage with a white canopy. I pick up a few large rocks and stuff my pockets with them. They're the only weapons I can find. I head down the hill trying not to attract attention.

I find a patch of thick shrubs close to where the people are gathered and hide behind them. I don't think anyone sees me. There are two women in their twenties standing on the stage. They are wearing sheer white gowns without any sleeves. The sun beats down on their bodies, and their bronzed skin glistens with sweat. The young women are stomping their feet in unison and kicking up white flower petals that are spread across the stage. They are holding hands and swaying to the drumbeats. An attractive young priestess with long curls of blond hair places her hands on both of their heads and says, "Sealed are you. Bonded are you. Blessed are you. True are you." The women spin around in a circle. Their foreheads have a sacred mud eye on them like those worn by the ancient Iyandians. Sweat is pouring from every part of them and their dresses are sticking to their bodies. The dresses no longer hide what's beneath them.

Eventually, the two young women collapse to the ground, one on top of the other, and they kiss. It is the kind of kissing that we in the Federacy would do only behind closed doors. When they are done, they stand and everyone applauds. The priestess takes both of their hands. "You are bonded in marriage." The priestess hands them a glass of mulberry wine. They drink from it and say, "Bonded are we. Blessed are we. True are we."

The priestess comes off the stage and walks straight toward me. She knows exactly where she's going. She is someone who is very much at ease with herself. I am tightly grasping a rock in my right hand, but something tells me to drop it. Maybe it's just because she's beautiful. "We've been expecting you, Max. I'm Nayla. It's wonderful to finally meet you in person."

She reaches her hand out and I take it. Her hand is warm. She pulls me toward her and throws her arms around me. Her sweaty body glues to mine. I feel something I haven't felt since I saw my family lying on the floor in a pool of blood. I feel a slight desire to live.

But it passes quickly.

8

AQUARIUS ROLLINS

"Come on in, Max," a gray-haired woman says. Nayla opens a see-thru screen door to a strange home that is covered in a wood-like material I have never seen. I touch the material as I walk in. Nayla notices my confusion. "They used to call them shingles," she says.

"I'm Aquarius Rollins," the gray-haired woman says to me. She leads with a handshake, but her real purpose is a hug. "I'm Nayla's mom, and maybe more importantly to you, I'm Pique's grandma." The strangeness of landing at the door of Pique's grandmother is not lost on me. But strangeness is a *relative feeling*, so I'm not overly concerned.

"It's nice to meet you," I say politely. "I've heard a lot about you." I try to unlock myself from her embrace, but she's not ready to let go. She eventually allows me to step back, but she keeps hold of both of my hands. "I've heard a lot about you, too." She grabs my face and holds it between her hands. She stares into my eyes as if she's known me forever. She asks me to follow her to the kitchen. I have never seen a kitchen like this. Gas comes up through burners. The colidor, if that's what it is, has a glossy plastic veneer. The eating table is made of wood and it's stained a dirt-brown color. "You hungry, Max? I was born to feed. Let me make you something."

"I'm sorry, but I can't eat."

"Nonsense. You're going to eat." She shakes her head. "We're here to grieve with you. It's no accident you're here. You were sent to us. So you sit yourself down and we're going to eat together. And we're going to talk about love. We're going to talk about loss. We're going to break down. And we're going to cry together. We're going to cry a lot. And eventually, we're going to pick ourselves up and move on. 'Cause that's what our crazy race of people does. We grieve. We heal. We pick ourselves up."

"How do you know what happened to my—"

"Pique of course. She told us to expect you."

"Is she okay?"

"She's fine. No one can harm that little girl. You should know that by now."

"Where is she? Does the Federacy have her? How are you talking to her?"

"Slow down, Max. There's plenty of time before you have to put your soldier uniform back on. We'll get to all of it. Just have a little faith and little patience. I'm here to help you move on. We all need to move on."

"I'm sorry, Ms. Rollins, but—"

"It's Aquarius."

"I appreciate your kindness, Aquarius, but I'm not in the habit of trusting people I just meet—especially not after what happened to my family."

"Now's the time to trust, Max. We're Pique's family. *We're your family.*"

"I'm a little confused. Forgive me, but I don't even understand how I got here."

"I promise—we'll get to all that in a few minutes. But you're dehydrated and you haven't eaten in days. So for now, I need to get some food and liquids into you. And while I'm doing that, why don't you ask yourself this one question: *Do you feel good here?* You like sitting in my kitchen with me and Nayla? You like the smell of those cinnamon cakes coming from the oven? Why don't you just turn that big fancy brain of yours off and ask yourself a simple question. *Does your heart tell you that you're in the right place or the wrong place?*"

I don't answer. I know it doesn't feel wrong, but I'm incapable of feeling that anything is right.

"You're safe here, Max. Nayla and I are going to take good care of you."

A door swings open and a huge man with out-of-control hair and a large stomach storms into the room. "Sure, you make your famous cinnamon cakes for the big-shot judge from the Federacy," he says, laughing.

"Trace, you watch yourself," Aquarius says. I notice that she wipes away a tear with her handkerchief.

"I'm just trying to keep things light, Mama." He walks toward me, arms wide open. "Get over here, Max, and give me a big hug." I do not hug as a general rule. I indulged Nayla's and Aquarius's hugs to be courteous. But being squeezed by this enormous man is really not my idea of a good thing. As much as I try to resist, he has his hug.

"I'm going to take care of you, too, Max."

"Why don't you worry about taking care of yourself," Nayla says. "We're going to mourn with Max and you better be on your best behavior. Max has been through a lot."

"I'm sorry, Max," Trace says. He swallows hard and mumbles something under his breath. I can't be sure but I think he says something about the Holy Father.

Aquarius offers me a juice, a cinnamon cake, and a napkin. I feel compelled to take the cake even though there is no possible way I can eat it. It smells like something baked by the gods, but my stomach isn't interested. I sip the juice and pick at the crumbled topping, trying to be polite. Aquarius stands up slowly and moves her chair closer to me. Everything she does is in slow motion. She watches me as I move the cake around my plate, but doesn't say a word. Trace and Nayla sit at the table and Aquarius serves them cake, too. No one says much, although it's clear Trace wants to talk.

As I mindlessly poke at the cake, an image of Viole sitting in her own blood barrels its way into my head. "Are they really dead?" I think I'm saying this in my head, but I say it out loud. I want to cry, maybe even scream. But I'm still a soldier. I'm a high judge. I'm a man who values dignity. Men like us don't cry. We don't scream. And we certainly do not act hysterical in front of strangers.

"I wasn't there, Max," Nayla says, choking up. She places her hand on mine and says, "Pique doesn't remember much. She remembers being pulled away by a team of heavily armed soldiers and you yelling that they killed your family. Then she was injected with something and went unconscious."

"Pique told you this?"

Nayla wobbles her head from side to side as if to say *sort of.*

"Well, did she?" I say this like a commander and I can tell that Nayla doesn't like it.

"Yes, Pique and I talked about this." Nayla doesn't want to say another word about it. But Trace does. Just as he opens his mouth to talk, Nayla covers it. Trace pushes her hand away and starts talking at the speed of light, trying to get the words in before she stops him. "They communicate by manipulating electrical fields in the ionosphere. They're basically satellites that transform electric currents into information." Nayla tries to stop Trace, but he won't listen. "All the Rollins girls do it. My mom does it. Nayla. Pique. Emmis. You must know, Max—Emmis is the one who came up with the idea. Apparently us guys can't do it—something to do with the electricity and the pH of the eggs or the estrogen or the chromosomes or something."

"I'm sorry—did you say *Emmis*?"

Nayla quickly grabs one of my hands, and Aquarius takes the other. They nod back and forth at each other, trying to decide who will speak first. Aquarius takes over, but she struggles to get the first words out. "This isn't easy to explain." Aquarius searches for the right words. "Emmis was a great person and a devoted wife. But she kept some things from you. She had to." Aquarius coughs into her handkerchief. I see a small amount of blood. "She loved you very much. You know that. But she could never be fully honest with you about us. We're Abstainers, Max. We abstain from all sorts of things, including the Federacy's rules. You are the very embodiment of the Federacy— decorated soldier, commander of the Federate Forces, high judge. So Emmis had no choice but to live separate lives between our two worlds. She couldn't tell you about us and we were never allowed to meet you or your beautiful children. I hated it, but she gave us no choice."

Aquarius tries to go on, but the words are too painful. She starts to cry, which causes her to cough. "It's okay, Mama," Nayla says. "We're going to be okay." Nayla stands and rests her cheek on the top of Aquarius's head. She rubs her mother's back. After a few seconds, she lifts her head up and smiles at me. "I'm Emmis's sister, Max. We're her family. We're your family."

I look around the table. Their resemblance instantly hits me. I see Emmis in all of them. I see Pique in all of them. I see Emmis in Pique and Pique in Emmis. I see my children in them and have to fight back the tears. I'm sad and I'm hurt by Emmis's deceit. I feel lost. I purposefully drop my napkin on the floor. I reach down below the table to get it. I stay there for a brief moment, just long enough to gather myself so I don't cry.

9

PIQUE

Aquarius eventually takes me to Pique's room so that I can try and get some sleep. I'm exhausted, but I doubt sleep is in my near future. This strangely colored room—green walls and rust-colored carpeting that seems to grow like thick grass—was also Emmis's childhood room before she left for the Federacy. Aquarius points out a picture of Emmis and tells me she was twelve in the picture. Aquarius then picks up a picture of Pique and holds it up next to Emmis's. "They look like twins, don't they," Aquarius says. She then plants a kiss on my forehead and says Nayla will be up in a little while with fresh linens.

Nayla comes into my room holding bedclothes and candles. She places the scented candles throughout the room and lights them. Without saying a word, she removes my boots. She then takes my hand and leads me to a type of bathing station I have never seen. There is hot water spraying from a metal-plated disk, and it is falling into a small drain. I can't place the material of the glossy structure containing the water, but I believe the tiles surrounding it are made of something they used to call "ceramic."

Nayla smiles at me as she removes my socks. She then tries to take my pants off and I stop her. "It's okay," she says. "I'm here to take care of you. That's all." I allow her to remove my pants and then the rest of my clothes, but I turn my back to her. She turns me around. "Would you feel more comfortable with a towel," she says, staring just below my waist. I'm embarrassed by what's happening there, but she's clearly not. "There are no wrong feelings here, Max. You can be excited by me. I'm a woman capable of pleasure and you're a man with desires. That's not wrong. I want you to know you're safe here, no matter what you're feeling." She places the towel around me, but I still feel uncomfortable. I'm not a prude, but I'm not used to this kind of Abstainer openness.

Nayla begins by trimming my beard with clippers. She then lathers my face with a shaving brush and takes off my beard with a motorized razor. She then suggests that I remove my towel so that she can shower me. "I can do it myself," I say.

"Max, nothing is happening here. I'm not trying to have sex with you. I want to clean you. I want to care for you because you need love. That's all." She removes my towel. I face away from her and she washes my back and legs. It's too much for me. I take the soap, pull some kind of archaic rubber curtain closed, and tell her I will do my front. She laughs as I pull the curtain closed.

I dry off and cover myself with the towel. She waits by the bed with a robe. "It's not a judge's robe, but it's the best I could do."

"It's fine. Thank you, Nayla."

"I could stay with you for a little while and keep you company while you fall asleep."

"That's very nice of you, but I need rest. I'm going to find Pique tomorrow. I want to get an early start."

"You're right. *We will* need to get an early start."

"I'm sorry, but I don't think *we* will be doing anything together." I say this as politely as I can, but I'm sure it comes off as if she is one of my soldiers and I'm giving her a direct order. "I'm going to be killing people along the way. I don't need a priestess at my side."

"Who do you think taught Pique to fight?"

"I don't know. *Her father?*" As soon I say this, I realize it is wrong on so many levels.

"I don't think so," Nayla says. Her entire body clenches up. This is the first time I see even the slightest hint of animosity in Nayla, and frankly, it's not so slight. "Pique doesn't have a father."

I try to apologize, but Nayla cuts me off. "Max, I'm going after Pique.

I will go with you or without you. I've just been waiting for you, because Pique asked me to."

"I will be killing people—sometimes just because they're in my way. I'm not an expert on the Abstainer movement, but I'm pretty sure it frowns upon killing for a cause?"

"Yes, it does. But I'm going anyway."

"Will you be killing people with me? Or will you be lighting candles and bathing naked strangers?"

"I didn't realize you were so funny," she says. "I'm an Abstainer. We don't believe in killing in the name of some ideology, and that includes the notion of retribution. Vengeance is a poisonous thing. You're a big-time judge, Max. You should know that." I hear Pique in her mother's voice.

"Is that a *yes* or a *no*," I say coldly. "Will you be killing with me?"

"I will kill if my life is immediately threatened."

"What if I'm threatened or if Pique is threatened?"

"If anyone threatens my daughter, I will slice them in two." Nayla kisses me on the cheek. "*You*—I will have to think about."

10

JAX, VIOLE, AND KASE

There's no way I can sleep. I can't get the images of Emmis or the kids out of my head. I begin walking quickly from one end of the room to the other—anything to take my mind off of them. I pick up a picture of Emmis on the dresser. *You and the kids are okay, right? You're all sitting in our backspace right now. You're in your chair, right? You're safe in your chair. You were never in Yerusalom. Please tell me you were never in that godforsaken place. None of you were there. Why would anyone hurt you? Why would any man strike a helpless woman in a wheeled chair? Why would any man stab an innocent little girl or use the butt of a gun against my boys? It couldn't have happened. You're alive. I was drugged. It was that tea or what the DAKs shot into me. I imagined the whole thing, right? It was the drugs. You're all alive. Please tell me you're alive.*

There's no use in even trying to sleep. Every time I close my eyes I see the bloodied faces of my children. And on the few occasions when those thoughts pass, the only thing I can think about is how Emmis lied to me throughout our entire marriage. I decide to go downstairs. I turn on the lights and see Aquarius sitting in the dark at the kitchen table. She looks up. "Can't sleep?"

I nod.

"I wish I could find the right words for you, Max—the right words to let you know how sad I am for you." She is about to cry but catches herself. She's a strong woman. By all accounts, she was a strong leader. "If there was a

God—you know *that God* the Federacy and Nation of Yerusalom are always talking about—I would punch him right in the nose." She pushes herself up from her chair and moves toward the thing that looks like a colidor. It's a trek for her. Halfway through her journey, she pulls out her handkerchief and coughs into it. "I could say something trite right now if you want, but you just don't seem the type."

"No, I'm not. I'm a coldhearted-truth kind of person. I don't like it when people lie, even when it's to protect someone they supposedly love." There's an edge to my voice and it's not lost on Aquarius.

"The truth is a means to an end, Max. But it's not always the best end."

"I think of it as an end in itself—especially in marriage." There is less edge in my voice, but my intentions are clearer.

"I understand how you feel." Aquarius takes out an apple pie. She cuts a huge piece of it, slowly makes her way back to the table, and drops the piece down in front of me. She then pours me some tea. "I've read a lot about you, Max. You're about as honest as they come and you expect the same from others. I'm sure you demanded honesty from the troops you commanded and the government officials who worked for you. And most of all, you demanded honesty from your family. You expected complete truthfulness from Emmis. I get that, Max."

"I understood that her work was classified," I say. "I understood that she couldn't tell me certain things. I'm fine with that. But she lied to me about who she was. She lied about where she came from. She lied about who her family was. She made up all sorts of stories about these fake parents of hers who died in the Fifth War." I slide the piece of pie away. "Lies are like mice. You see one on the kitchen floor, and you know there must be hundreds more hiding in the walls."

Aquarius smiles at me as she pushes the plate back in front of me. "Just eat your pie, Max. That's an order!" It's hard not to smile back at her. She's dying, but yet she's so full of life. She points at the plate of pie. "How about you eat, while I try to defend my daughter?"

She puts away the rest of the pie and tidies up as she talks. "Emmis was not some simple girl from the Anterior Region. She wasn't even an Abstainer. She never believed in anything we stood for. One thing you have to realize is that when she refused to become an Abstainer, and decided she needed to leave us, it broke my heart. She chose the Federacy over her own family."

Aquarius wipes some crumbs off the table. "Smart as you are, Max, Emmis understood things you could never fathom. When she was just a young girl—eleven, I think—she deciphered this centuries-old mathematical problem I'd never heard of. It's called the Book of Our God's Paradox of Boundless Polygons. You ever hear of that?" She doesn't wait for me to answer, but I would have said no. "I was told that she was one of only seven people in history to have done this. And she is only one of two people to do it under the age of thirty. She wasn't like you or me. You have to understand that. So if she felt like she had to lie to you about her work or her family—then she had to lie. You have to trust her on that. My girl loved you and her kids more than anything. Please, for the sake of anything good left in this world, please know that my little girl loved you."

Aquarius sits down at the table. She can't talk about it any more. I don't feel any better listening to Aquarius's explanation. If anything, I feel worse. But there is no reason for her to know that. She just lost someone she loves, too. So I lie. Apparently, according to Emmis and Aquarius, this kind of thing is sometimes okay. I reach across the table, take her hand, and lie. "I understand now why Emmis did what she did."

11

RAY TYNE

I head back to my room, but I've given up on the idea of sleeping. I grab one of the books from the micropak I was given. The Holy Father originally picked out twelve books for me to read, but there were only five in the micropak. He apparently did not want me carrying all those books in the desert heat. I pull out the books and stack them so I can see all their titles.

> *Jo-Jo a Go-Go*
> *Saool Forque: The Bloke Who Broke the World*
> *Abraham Lincoln: A Biography*
> *Electric Gods and Other Love Stories*
> *Who Wrote the Book of Our God?*

I pull out *Saool Forque: The Bloke Who Broke the World,* mostly because I have no idea what the term "Bloke" means and I don't think you can tell much from a title anyway. *Who Wrote the Book of Our God?* looks more important than a book about a "Bloke," but looks are deceiving.

I quickly turn to the center of the book, which contains the author's biography, middle notes, pictures, and legal information. The book was published before the End of the Old Order. As was customary at the time, the book reads from the center out. It was written in Arabic—the predecessor to modern-day Erabiat—and reads from right to left going from the center of the book to the front of the book. The same text—*or at least what was supposed to be the same text*—was written from left to right in English, a close cousin to our modern language, Anglicote. The English part of the book reads from the center of the book to the back. As strange as it sounds, in those days, billions of humans were what they called "bilingual"—meaning they spoke Arabic and English. Of course, synthetic developments in Erabiat and Anglicote, and the rise of the Digital Creo-Linguistic movement, changed the need for bilingualism.

In those days, language was one of the Big Three—the three reasons for disruptions in political stability, including the most extreme of political disruptions, war. Hydrogen can be blamed for the other two reasons—hydrogen mixing with oxygen (water) and hydrogen mixing with carbon (petrofuels). But language was the most interesting disruption, and in the end the most important because it caused the greatest wars of all. It was disagreements over the interpretation of words—in religious documents, treaties, constitutions, judicial edicts, transnational corporate documents and the like—that ultimately were responsible for the End of the Old Order.

I flip to the author's biography. Maybe it will shed some light on why the Holy Father wants me to read this book. Maybe it will shed some light on why the Holy Father wanted me in Yerusalom in the first place.

ABOUT THE AUTHOR

Ray Tyne is a former assistant speechwriter for the Great Anglican Nation's Minister of Good Humor. Tyne was born in Liverpool in the U.K. Province. His parents were hand-to-hardware workers with few sanctioned privileges. A young Ray Tyne worked his way through the best Anglican schools, graduating top honors from Oxford University with a doctoral degree in fine humor.

In A.D. 2449, Tyne was wrongly convicted of recklessly providing support to an enemy territory through dissemination of state-prohibited propaganda. He was incarcerated in the same penal facility as a great man by the name of Saool Forque. Tyne and Forque became close friends and confidants. Tyne's mission in life is to promote the teachings of Saool Forque.

Saool Forque: The Bloke Who Broke the World is Mr. Tyne's only book. It received the Ledbetter Award for the Most Unexpected Piece of Nonfiction in The Great Anglican Nation and was made into a TV movie starring Sir Franklin Haux on the GAD Network.

Mr. Tyne now lives in New York Proper with his wife, Ayn, and their two dogs, Barack and George. Nothing makes him more proud than to say he is the father of Cecilia Forque. It is to her that he dedicates this book.

I thumb through some pictures of Saool Forque and Ray Tyne. Most of them are pictures from the penal facility. They are in white-and-black jumpsuits that make them look like silly zebras. There is a picture of Tyne bending down on one knee and kissing the hand of a clearly uncomfortable Forque. That picture is my favorite. Forque's discomfort is earnest. If there is one thing I learned as a judge, it's that you can't fake humility.

I turn to the first page. The chapter is entitled, "What's a Bloke Like Him Doing in a Place Like This?"

I had no idea what Saool Forque looked like. My government had burned an impression of him in my head, but it was of a shape-shifting military beast that could slice through a thousand soldiers with one swipe of his laser. When I first met Saool in the mess hall, I was pleased to find that the official reports were mostly propaganda. Saool was indeed huge in physique, standing more than 2 meters tall and weighing approximately 150 kilograms; but he was no beast. His eyes were gentle. Soft. Sweet. Simple. Eyes that saw the world anew each day.

I got to know Saool over our lunches in the mess hall. He graciously would ask me to join him. A pale-skinned Protestant bureaucrat from The Great Anglican Nation dining with a brown-skinned General in the Kingdom of the Blessed Erabian States. It was not just that we were from enemy nations or that our religion, language, and skin color were different. It was that I was a low-level political hack in my country and he was a celebrated military demigod in his. I was unknown in his lands and he was Public Enemy #1 in mine. I was the court jester and he the king.

We bonded over the most miserably unpalatable meatloaf one can imagine. We would both eat slowly (for different reasons) and smile (for very different reasons). I found humor in the lack of humanity and he found humanity in the lack of worldly needs. We greatly enjoyed laughing together. Deep, pit of your stomach laughter. He loved my jokes. Or I should say he loved the camaraderie of sharing a joke and transcending the space between talker and receiver. He even laughed wildly at my off-color jokes— for which he certainly took no selfish pleasure. I would tell him a joke about two Muzlim holy men who meet a prostitute in a drinking hole, and he would smile widely the entire length of the joke and then laugh boisterously at the punch line. But clearly the insults to religious authority were not what made him smile and laugh. For Saool, a conversation was a musical improvisation of individual voices finding a common space to share and transcend.

Our lunches were more comical than divine, but that was only because Saool was never dogmatic about what he preached. The dogma came more from my tired and angry warm-up routine.

Saool and I fell into a rhythm of sorts. Food would be served by two fat Aziatic women in the mess hall: one who smelled like raw onions and spoiled greens and another who I wished only smelled that vile. About a hundred or so inmates would quickly eat their slop and then gather around Saool's table. I thought about charging for the limited seats at our table, and I was even stupid enough to tell Saool my idea. But Saool simply laughed and I understood that to mean no. He never told me I couldn't charge. But being around Saool, you had no choice but to make the right decisions. His laughter was like a moral lubricant that forced the mechanisms in one's mind to function rightly.

After I would warm up the crowd with a routine about the sexual proclivities of the Great Anglican Priests or the insipidness of the Muzlim counter-revolution, he would speak. He would stand up very slowly. He would never rush in to talk, and though he smiled, he never had any great love of speaking. If he could share his wisdom some other way, he surely would.

He would have 100, sometimes even 200 or 300, inmates surrounding our table, mouths agape as he revealed to us the nature of divinity as seen through our earthly limits. He would explain how every ray of light that we share is a metaphysical—as well as biological, chemical, and quantum—bond. He would explain God as a relationship or a bond between two individuals. He called it the *Infinite T.*

Our discussions together at the mess hall were an event—the event. It was like the most popular college seminar at Oxford. But Saool's event was a mind-bending trip, a seminar through the eyes of a person looped into a frequency of cosmic truths. At the end of every day's discussion, which from my perspective was sometimes an angry debate between me and him, he would pick me up or pick up any other Anglicans that debated him, and he would hug and kiss us. He would profess his love for us and call us comrades, an almost sacrilegious compliment from a General in the Kingdom of the Blessed Erabian States.

It will be hard for people to believe that Saool Forque went from being one of the world's most efficient killers to becoming one of the world's greatest voices for peace. But it is true and it demonstrates a fundamental premise of Saool's Infinite T. The space between God and two or more individual souls is infinite in both its distance and proximity. We can always get further and closer along the T and bend it in ways that reshape our morality, as well as our future.

Saool Forque murdered tens of thousands of Anglicans on the battlefield. But he is also the same Saool Forque who later identified the connection between pure, unadulterated love of fellow humans and the mutations of human biology, metaphysics, and divinity. Saool the Terrible, Saool the Great, and all other time-based personas of Saool are part and parcel of the same Saool Forque. And to be Saool Forque is to see the world through the eyes of a child.

To understand Saool, you must know what happened to him at the end of his days as a General. He had a glorious vision one day on the battlefield, and his eyes, those of an adult at the time, were completely obliterated. The vision simply just appeared before him—a great vision like the great visions of prophets past. Saool was standing on the battlefield and he saw the Infinite T in an array of dead soldiers. Anglicans and Erabians were holding hands in death on a battlefield. They were arrayed in the shape of an infinitely elastic T, undulating between waves of infinite space and collapsing towards nothingness. Saool's battle-weary eyes perceiving light in ways unimaginable. The Infinite T revealing itself—rain mixing with light, light mixing with blood, blood mixing with the divine.

After the revelation on this love- and blood-soaked day, Saool asked his unit to return to camp without him. Saool fired up his transport and headed west for a brief, but important stop, and then north to London. And on September 33, 2448, he turned himself over to the Anglican authorities. The world was shocked. The "Butcher of Brisbane," the "Jersey Jihadist," the "Mastermind of the Dublin Massacre," just showed up at a local constabulary station in London and turned himself in.

After a closed military tribunal, he was sentenced to life in prison. The Anglican Congress tried to pass a special law allowing for the death penalty for those convicted of killing more than 10,000 people. But the special measure failed by a handful of votes. Thank God for petty Anglican politics.

I wake up to the sound of someone knocking on my door. I must have fallen asleep while reading the book about Saool Forque. It is lying open on my stomach. The last thing I remember reading is that right before heading north to turn himself in, Saool Forque blew up part of a wall in Yerusalom dividing the Jewish Protectorate of the Great Anglican Nation and the Palestinian Principality of the Kingdom of Blessed Erabian States. He arranged the debris from the wall in the shape of a T.

12

TRACE ROLLINS

Before I have a chance to say "Come in," Trace rushes into my room. This large sad man plops down on my bed. The sun is up, which makes it somewhat less awkward, but I still don't like it. He sits uncomfortably close to me and starts talking. The words pour out of his mouth. "I loved her. I loved Emmis so much. When Mama told me she was gone, I flew out of the house and injected myself with a barrel of morzium." I am barely awake and Trace, who twenty-four hours ago was a stranger to me, is baring his soul. He wipes his nose dry on his sleeve. "I took myself as high as a satellite, orbiting in a cloud of messed-up-crazy, brother. The morzium shot through my veins like a rocket. I felt like every part of my body was going to explode. I started seeing things. Crazy things. Fire was shooting out of holes in the ground. Demons were dressed in velvet robes. Then some outrageous wormhole appeared and I was transported to Yerusalom. I saw Pique bound in chains. I saw hundreds of Yerusi guards with smoke coming out of their noses and daggers growing out of their fingers. Then the Holy Father appeared to me as the Devil himself. He snapped his fingers and the Yerusi guards ran at Emmis with knives. They cut my sister to pieces. They cut your poor little babies to pieces. Next thing I know, I'm on top of a hill—a real hill—a mile or so from my house, and my shirt is drenched in sweat and my fists are covered in blood. I must have fought a nearby tree thinking it was those guards. That tree was real messed up."

Trace stops talking, and tears pour down his face. I have no choice but to awkwardly put my arm around his shoulder. "I'm really glad you're here, Max. I've never had a brother. But I kind of feel like maybe you and I could kind of be—"

Nayla and Aquarius enter the room, and Trace quickly stops talking. He's embarrassed, and I'm thankful for the intrusion. Like Trace, Nayla and Aquarius just seem to walk into rooms without being invited. It's not rudeness. It's openness. Federates are all about boundaries. Abstainers are about breaking them down.

"It's time for our morning meditations, Trace," Nayla says. "Will you join us, Max?"

"I don't know about Max," Trace says, "but sure as hell I'm not joining you." Nayla doesn't take the bait. She ignores Trace and waits for me to answer. I stumble a little and then say, "Thanks for the offer, but I think I'll just get my things together and get ready to go."

"If it's not too much trouble, Max, I would like for you to stay while we do it. You can just watch."

Trace and I sit on the bed like petulant children while Nayla and Aquarius kneel to the floor. They sit on the rust-colored carpet with their palms facing the sky. "Thank you for hearing our words. Thank you for being present. I am Nayla. This is my mother, Aquarius. These are my brothers, Trace and Max. We are in the room of my sister Emmis and my daughter Pique. We are a family filled with love. We are present. We hope that we bring virtue to the day and goodwill to all we meet." She rises to her feet and helps her mother stand. Aquarius and Nayla chant:

> *Our suffering is like water.*
> It ebbs. It flows. It roams. It returns.
> *Our suffering is like water.*
> It follows. It compels. It evaporates. It returns.
> *Our suffering is like water.*
> It moves. It changes. It leaves. It returns.
> *Our suffering is like water.*

Nayla pauses for a moment and asks me if I would like to chant with her. I feel beyond uncomfortable at this point. I would rather run naked through the Omniplex. But I feel I should do it out of respect for Aquarius. Trace makes it easier for me. "We're not doing any of this nonsense," he says for both of us. Aquarius gives Trace a dirty look, and she and Nayla continue chanting:

> Truth survives without a name.
> Suffering survives without a name.
> *We survive without a name.*
> We are a wave without a sea.
> We are a river without a bank.
> We are a storm without a sky.
> *We survive without a name.*
> We are a . . .

Out of nowhere, the hair on my arms suddenly stands up. It is a perfectly clear day, but I hear the faint sound of thunder in the distance. The smile on Nayla's face quickly vanishes. Her eyes mechanically snap shut as she grimaces in pain. "It's okay, honey," Aquarius says to her. "It will be over soon." Sweat forms just above Nayla's upper lip and her jaw clenches tight. Her blond curls become a scattered mess, pointing in all directions from the static charge. Her face warps as if it's made of rubber. She squirms as the electricity runs through her body. She covers her face with her hands. Trace gets up from the bed and goes to hold Nayla's hand, but before he can, Aquarius bats him away. "You know it's not safe to touch her, Trace." Nayla starts to shiver as if she's come in from the cold. She opens her eyes and shouts out, "Pique wants us to meet with the Rogues, Max. They will help us."

"*What the* . . . that's crazy," Trace shouts, just before I can.

"I won't be meeting with the Rogues," I say calmly. I'm skeptical that Nayla spoke with Pique, but after experiencing firsthand what Pique can do—not to mention what Spiro did to me—I can't dismiss it.

Nayla catches her breath, and the moment she does, she says, "Let me guess, Max. You're not going to meet with the Rogues because you're a Federacy judge and the Rogues are sworn to overthrow your precious regime. You realize how crazy that sounds in light of recent events. The Rogues are no more your enemies than the Federacy. It wasn't the Rogues that performed that procedure on Emmis and it wasn't the Rogues that killed your family."

"Well, I agree it wasn't the Rogues, but I don't think it was the Federacy either," Trace says. I know Trace thinks it was the Holy Father. I'm not sure what the Holy Father's role is in all of this, but he clearly knows more than he's telling me.

"You should at least reach out to the Rogues," Nayla says.

"For years, they wanted me dead," I say. "I can't think of a good reason why they would help us." I stand up and walk toward Nayla. "Even if they did want to help us, I don't want it. I was the high commander of the Federate Forces. You think I need the Rogues to help me? You think they're going to teach me something I don't already know?" I realize I'm being defensive, but I don't want to be questioned, especially not by some Abstainer priestess I just met.

"The Rogues and NFF are winning the war," Nayla says. "That's what everyone—well, everyone outside the Federacy—is saying. The Rogues obviously know some things about the Federacy—*like how to defeat them.* Maybe they could help."

"I don't need a bunch of wild-eyed revolutionaries to help me bring back Pique. And I definitely don't need some amateurish Abstainer telling me what to do."

Aquarius sits down on Emmis's bed. She pats the spot next to her and motions for me to come and sit. I know what's coming next. I sit next to her and she puts her arm around me. "You probably don't like my arm around you. You probably don't feel all that comfortable with me saying that you're my son. Emmis was that way, too. She didn't go for all that mushy stuff. But I'm a lot older than you and I'm going to give you some advice." Aquarius leans in. "A man can only be a good man if he's got faith in the women around him. If those women are good women, you've got no choice but to trust them." She slowly lifts herself up off the bed and takes a step toward the door. "Emmis, Nayla, Pique—those are some of the best damn women you will ever know." She coughs, and whatever's growing inside of her stakes a bigger claim.

"You're going to have to start trusting my girls. You need more faith in them. I know you're suffering. I know you're grieving. I know you're hurt that Emmis wasn't completely honest with you. But you have to get this straight in that brilliant little head of yours, Max. She had to lie to you. It was one lie she told and it was the right thing to do. That's all. The rest of it was the truth." Aquarius coughs again. "I don't lie. Nayla doesn't lie. And Pique doesn't lie."

"I lie all the time," Trace says, smiling. "I've got no problem with it. Apparently truth telling only runs on the female side. Telepathy and truth. Us guys, we're just a bunch of handsome liars."

Aquarius slowly makes her way to the bookshelf by the door. She picks up the book about Saool Forque. *The Bloke Who Broke the World,*" she says, smiling. "Good story. Don't know if any of it's true, but some of us early Abstainers gave it a read. We don't buy into a lot of these myths, but we certainly value good science and good ideas about how humans should behave toward each other. And this book's got a little bit of each. Let me guess, the Holy Father asked you to read it. Told you it's got all the answers, right?"

I nod.

"Well, like most things in life, he's sort of right and sort of wrong. You want the answers—look to the people in your life who care about you." A cough stubbornly sticks in her throat. "You want to know what the most important thing in life is?"

I shrug.

"Surround yourself with people who care about you. That's a pretty good answer to just about anything that troubles you." She walks out the door, and Nayla and Trace follow.

Aquarius is halfway down the stairs when she yells back to me. "If my girls think you should pay a visit to the Rogues, then you should pay a visit to the Rogues."

13

EMILE PHODE

The commander of the Rogues is Emile Phode, a shrewd and capable leader a few years older than me. When Phode was a young colonel in the NFF, he became deeply troubled by the NFF's senseless brutality and decided he had no choice but to revolt against the NFF and one of its senior military leaders, Anther Vrig.

The NFF has volumes of military manuals on the permitted uses of state-sanctioned terror, and Vrig, who wears the title Chancellor as if it somehow immunizes him from war-crime charges, has terrorized every civilian population he has conquered. Vrig employs terror as a means of control. According to Federacy military psychologists charged with studying Vrig, his decision to use terror is a product of a ruthless political calculation, not his moral depravity. In my view, this is a distinction without a difference. I think many of these experts have become far too enamored with their subject. One prominent expert I met went so far as to say that if Vrig thought he could subdue the population by showering the people with gifts, instead of dousing them with terror, he would. Not the most dispassionate scientific analysis I can think of.

Based on what I know, Phode is a political reaction to Vrig. Phode is a man of honor who rejected the NFF's brutality, and maybe more importantly, rejected its hypocrisy. Decades ago, the NFF broke away from the Federacy because corruption and cronyism had spread through the body politic like cancer. But over time the NFF became just as diseased and Phode wanted no part of it. Just as the NFF rebelled against the Federacy, the Rogues rebelled against the NFF. It is a political truism that a society with roots in rebellion will eventually be the victim of its own rebellion. Best of luck to the Rogues—they will probably reap what they sow.

After much deliberation on Phode's possible motivations and the potential risks to our safety, I decide to meet the Rogues. Although I cannot trust a nation that has long been my sworn enemy, I cannot discount what Aquarius and Nayla have said. If the Federacy was behind my family's murder, and if it has Pique, then it is now my enemy. This makes the Rogues my enemy's enemy and therefore a potential friend. I don't have a lot of good military options to help me bring back Pique, and the Rogues may be my best hope.

Through secure military back channels, I reach out to an acquaintance of an acquaintance and eventually connect with a Rogue contact who has Phode's ear. The senior communications officer I speak with tells me that Phode was expecting my call. My conversation with the officer is short and she makes it clear that she is permitted to discuss only two things: the specifics of how we will rendezvous with them and assurances that no harm will come to us. Nothing else can be discussed, but I'm as satisfied with her answers as I will ever be.

Following break-meal, Trace goes out to a strange little house in the backyard that he calls a "shed." He brings back some ancient firearms—two shoulder rifles and an assortment of handheld guns. He drops them on the kitchen table and Aquarius is mortified. "Where did you get these?" Before Trace can answer, Nayla is gathering them up to take them back outside.

"Hold on," Trace says. "We're not going into Rogue territory without arms."

I laugh. And so does Nayla.

"You have those special hands of yours, Nayla," Trace says. I don't know exactly what Trace is talking about but I assume she has powers similar to those I saw Spiro and Pique use. "I get why you don't need a gun. But Max and I need something to fight with."

"You'll fight with your mind," Nayla says. "The Rogues aren't barbarians. There's a reason that Pique wants us to meet them and I trust her judgment. Showing up with guns won't help our cause."

"Especially not these guns," I say. "They should be in a military museum."

As Nayla tries to return the guns to the little house, Trace yanks them from her and angrily tells her he'll do it himself. I notice through the window that Trace has no intention of returning the guns. Instead, he puts them into the back container of his rusty old land transport, which is presumably going to be our means of transportation.

When Trace gets back, I sit him and Nayla down at the kitchen table. "Before we leave I want to get one thing clear." I pause. As I have always done with my troops, I set the tone for who is in command. I look down on the ground for an unreasonably long time. Then, I slowly raise my head, making sure to never lose eye contact. I look over their heads as if talking to someone or something beyond them. It's all an act, but sometimes leadership requires a bit of drama. "I'm in charge. Whatever I say goes."

Nayla nods in agreement. Trace gives me the Federacy salute. He's mocking my authority, which isn't a good sign for what lies ahead. But I do think he understands. I move closer to him. "Let's start by you taking those ridiculous firearms out of the transport. The first thing the Rogues will do is check the back container of the transport. Let's try to be smart, Trace."

I then turn to Nayla. "What exactly can you do with your hands?"

Nayla doesn't want to discuss it. She lowers her head.

"Just tell him," Trace says.

"Emmis would be able to explain it a lot better than I ever could," Nayla says in a soft voice. "All I know is that if I concentrate very hard and focus on a certain part of my brain, I can move electricity. It's not always reliable, but sometimes it works all too well."

"Pique, too?"

Nayla wants to talk about this even less. It's clear she doesn't want Pique to have this power. Her voice is almost a whisper, and it's filled with regret. "Pique is far more powerful than I am. She's capable of things that are beyond . . ." Nayla stops.

"Well, I'm going to have to ask you a favor," I say. "Please don't use your powers unless I ask."

"It's no favor. I hope you never ask me."

Aquarius walks into the kitchen just as I'm telling everyone it's time to go. She is very weak and her skin even paler than the day before. She walks by, taking small steps and holding on to the appliances. One step to the thing they call a "stove." Another step to the thing that looks like a colidor. And another step to the table. She wiggles her fingers for me to come close to her. She kisses me on the cheek. "Take care of yourself, Max. And take care of them, too."

Nayla and Trace move toward their mom. They don't say a word. The three of them hug as tightly as they can. There is no air between them—no room for doubt about the strength of their commitment to each other. Trace and Nayla kiss Aquarius and quickly walk away—trying futilely to hold back their tears. They know what I know. This is the last time they will see their mother.

14

COLONEL FRAYNE

We board Trace's rickety land transport and head down a dirt path with food, water, and a cartogramic register. We are going to travel on back roads for a few days in a north-by-northeast direction in an attempt to avoid Federacy spies or hired mercenaries. When we reach our initial destination, the cartogramic register will send out a signal on a Rogue-protected frequency, which the Rogues will lock in to. We will then be guided in under the cover of a high-security tracking beam. The Rogues don't want the Federacy, and maybe even the NFF, to know what's going on.

Trace drives most of the way, and other than the fact that I've become an insomniac, the first few days are uneventful. On day five, we cross the Trio Riviera, which is about ten hours from our initial destination. Nayla knows how little I've been sleeping and she says I need to try and get some rest. She's right. My mind is muddy, and if I want to be effective when I meet Phode, I need more clarity.

I eventually fall into a heavy sleep, dreaming of Emmis and the kids. It's nice. They're all swimming and playing on the beach and I'm just watching them from a beach chair. When I wake up, my head is lying on Nayla's lap. She is stroking my hair and singing a sweet and melodic version of "Embroider the Nation." I slowly raise my head from her lap. I wonder how it is that an Abstainer can happily sing along to the Federacy's national anthem. "Really," I say to her. "'Embroider the Nation'?" She laughs and says, "It's a beautiful song. The words are deplorable, but the melody is nice. I thought it would help you sleep. You need your rest."

I let her continue stroking my hair even though it feels inappropriate. I doze in and out of sleep, and when I finally awake, I feel a little bit like me again. Nayla seems to have a knack for restoring me. But it's confusing. She looks so much like Emmis. She feels so much like Emmis. The way she touches me has to be wrong. I sit up and feel less confused once I move away from her.

Another hour or so passes before the cartogramic register starts beeping. I look out my window and notice the road narrowing. The road rises into the hills and then drops steeply to the west. To the east, there is a more gradual slope to a riverbank. The beeps start softly at first, then gradually become louder as we approach the point at which we will rendezvous with their tracking beam.

As we close in on the site, I try to focus more closely on the road ahead. The beeps begin to fire faster. We're probably no more than a kilometer away. My eyes are straining to see the road, but I think I see something ahead. I can't make it out because we're going too fast. "Slow down, Trace." I quickly realize it's a gigantic sinkhole in the road. Trace isn't slowing down fast enough. We continue to speed toward the sinkhole and what I think is a newly paved detour to its right. "Stop," I shout. "Hit the brakes! Hit the brakes! It's a trap!"

Trace slams on the brakes, but the decline is too steep and the transport's forward thrust too much. Trace tries to deploy the old transport's reverse thrust, but it's too late. It's the sinkhole—a certain death—or the detour, probably a terrestrial explosive and a likely death.

"Detour," I shout. "Hard right!"

Trace quickly turns the controls to the right. We hit only a portion of the newly paved road. The front left tire snags a terrestrial explosive and there's a huge explosion. We tumble front over end, then side over side. We spiral out of control toward the river. The transport spins in every direction and then luckily hits a patch of trees by the bank of the river. The trees save our lives.

Smoke fills the transport, but no fire. There's broken glass and mangled metal everywhere. "Is everyone okay?"

"We're fine," Nayla says. She reaches into the front of the transport to grab Trace's shoulder. I look out of the transport's shattered windows and realize we're not fine. We're surrounded by heavily armed forces. About twenty-five MO-4 mercenary troops quickly form a circle around the transport. The lasers from their weapons pierce through the windows and fix themselves on our heads.

"Take them down to the river," shouts one of them. Three guards reach into the transport and pull me out. I am then dragged by my legs down to the river. Nayla and Trace are dragged behind me. I'm immediately approached by a tall man with thick gray hair. "On your knees, Judge. I'm Colonel Frayne. I have been granted authority by the Office of the Premier of the Federacy, through a special order from the Committee on Tyranny and the Rector of Treason, to bring you, High Judge Maxomillion Cone, in on the charges of conspiracy to overthrow the Federacy and the murder of Judge Veriton Glass. I can bring you in dead or alive according to the order. The Premier has indicated a preference to bring you in alive, but I don't necessarily share that preference. So, one wrong move and I will put a slug in the back of your head."

Nayla closes her eyes and begins rubbing her hands together. There is a slight smell of burning, and the hair on the back of my neck starts to stand. I feel the electricity quickly building. Nayla is readying for a fight. "No," I tell her, motioning for her to put her hands down. I know I can get out of this without relying on her risky magic. I know that if the MO-4 found us, the Rogues will soon find the MO-4. The Rogues are light-years ahead of a mercenary group like the MO-4. They will know something went wrong. It's just a matter of time before they realize the discrepancy between our cartogramic register and their tracking beam. If I can stall long enough, they will find us. I know what to do. I know I need to buy time.

"I need to live," I say. I make my body shake and talk quickly, with several well-timed cracks in my voice. "Please, I just lost my family." Acting is something I am surprisingly good at. It started when I was a young child and I had to make my father believe I didn't hate him. "It would be dishonorable under the Federacy Rules of Morality in Warfare to knowingly kill the sole remaining member of a recently killed family." Trace and Nayla are initially confused by my show of weakness, but they quickly catch on.

"You're *the* Judge Maxomillion Cone," Colonel Frayne says. "You're the storied commander responsible for defeating the NFF in the Battle of Indoko? You're the mythic fighter that everyone is always talking about? You're quivering like a girl." Most of the MO-4 troops laugh. *Perfect.*

"I'm human, sir."

"You're a pussy, if you ask me."

All of the MO-4 troops are now laughing loudly.

"If you'll indulge me, Colonel, I can tell you the story of how I really won the war. How I really won the Battle of Indoko."

I notice that the MO-4 troops are now all staring at me with great intensity. The Battle of Indoko is taught in all the great military academies—Federacy, NFF, Nation of Yerusalom, Rogues, Artiqua, Iberion, Kolexico. Most mercenaries are former soldiers from established militaries, so they were all taught about this battle. I led a thousand Federacy troops to victory against a force that was at least fifty times the size. I defeated the NFF troops by an improvised military technique that grew into a theory of asymmetric warfare called DROPS: dynamic redistribution of permeated strategies. Now, academies teach an entire curriculum on this technique.

Colonel Frayne motions with his hand for me to continue. I launch into a story about how it was never just a thousand Federacy troops. I explain that we had undercover paramilitary mercenary groups just like the MO-4. I begin mentioning names of great mercenary leaders the troops have heard of—leaders who were legends. I explain how instrumental they were in the battle. I weave a passionate tale of the role of mercenaries in famous Federacy battles and in particular their role in winning the Battle of Indoko. I explain how the great mercenary general Qio Zarks was really responsible for the idea of DROPS. I explain how a smart young mercenary by the name of *Victor*—you would think they would see through my ridiculous choice of a name—was the real hero. I explain that Victor killed the last fifty NFF soldiers by having them position themselves in the direct line of the exhaust of an airtanker. This really gets the MO-4 troops going.

All the while, I am listening for the Rogue helicrafts that will surely be coming. As I tell the MO-4 about how General Zarks saluted the young soldier Victor, I'm getting them drunk on their own fantasies. I'm feeding their primitive egos. I'm assuring them that I am weak and they are strong. I'm pumping them up with confidence. I want them focused on anything but the fact that they have a killer on his knees who is currently plotting their death.

A few minutes into my story, I hear the faint sounds of the helicrafts' blades. I begin speaking louder, trying to muffle the sounds. I tell them how brave General Zarks and the young soldier Victor were and how wrong it was of me to take credit. I raise my voice. "I am so embarrassed by the honors given to me. High Commander of the Federate Forces. It was a lie. A huge lie. History should be rewritten to laud the work of the great mercenaries—

"Nayla, now," I shout. She knows exactly what I mean. From across the river, four heavily armed helicraft rise up from a ridge. Nayla shoots out an electric current that is weak but immediately stuns the MO-4 closest to us, including Colonel Frayne.

"Roll to the river," I shout. "Stay down." I want them to stay low to the ground and be the smallest targets possible. We hit the ground and start rolling. Projectiles shoot out from the helicraft. We get to the river, and hide by the bank as the helicraft rapidly fire projectile after projectile. The helicraft's guns rip the MO-4 to shreds. In less than thirty seconds, most of the MO-4 are dead or badly injured. I run back up the bank and grab a dead mercenary's weapon. I quickly shoot and kill three MO-4. It looks like there are only two left standing. One is a low-level soldier, and the other is Colonel Frayne, who is hiding behind a boulder. I run toward Frayne. I fire a shot into his legs and take out his kneecap. He screams in pain. He lifts his hands in the air and surrenders. Through the pain, he shouts to the one remaining soldier, "Drop your weapon. It's over."

The helicrafts stop firing and land. We are locked in to their monitors, and they know I have the two mercenaries secured. I move quickly toward Frayne with my gun on him. "Keep your hands on your head, Colonel," I shout. I remove his weapons.

"Are you going to read me the Federacy's Rights of Prisoners of Warfare?" Colonel Frayne says. "They're supposed to be universal regardless of membership, tribe, or statehood."

"Are you joking? I'm not a member of the Federacy anymore."

"What are you going to do to me?" Frayne is nervous.

"That depends on what you tell me. If you answer my questions correctly I can assure you I will not kill you or torture you in any way."

"I will tell you whatever you want to know."

"Good." I watch Frayne's eyes and mouth closely as I ask my first question. They are the places on one's face that tell the most. "Did the MO-4 kill my family?"

"No, Judge. Absolutely not. We would never take a job like that."

"Then who killed my family?"

"I have no idea. But as Our God is my witness—and on the lives of my own children—the MO-4 had nothing to do with the killing of your family. I would never take such an assignment. If you have ever heard anything about my reputation, you would know I am a cold killer, but I only kill other soldiers. We would never kill innocents."

I'm convinced Frayne is telling the truth.

"Do you know anything about who killed my family?"

"I'm very sorry, Judge, but I don't. The mercenary world is a small one and there's always chatter about big assignments. I haven't heard a thing about anyone being hired for that job. If I were a betting man, I would say it wasn't mercenaries. Killing kids isn't our thing."

"You heard nothing? Nothing at all?"

"There aren't a lot of secrets in my world. I probably would have heard something. The truth is that most of the major groups are tied up in the Artiqua excursions and the NFF's skirmishes with the Federacy in the Penumbra."

I'm satisfied with Frayne's answer. I believe him. Mercenaries tend to execute and leave. My family was butchered.

"Next question, Colonel. Did the Federacy send you to capture me?"

Frayne answers yes quickly. Too quickly. His mouth curls and contorts in a strange way.

"I'll ask you again. Was it the Federacy or someone else?"

Frayne is not a stupid man. He slows down his response this time and keeps his face straight. "It was the Federacy, sir. They want you—"

"He's lying," the other soldier shouts. "It wasn't the Federacy."

"Quiet, Corporal," Frayne shouts. "That's a direct order."

"Let him speak," I say.

"Forgive me, Judge Cone. There are rules relating to questioning when there is a superior officer in the presence of low-level soldier and I insist—"

"You will insist on nothing," I say. I rip off a part of the uniform of a dead soldier lying nearby and gag Frayne. As I do, I see three Rogue soldiers rapidly approaching on foot. Their weapons are drawn and they are moving quickly toward me. I do not think I'm in danger, but I feel electricity in the air and know that Nayla is preparing for a possible fight. I turn to her and signal for her to stand down. The Rogues are now a hundred meters from me and they are shouting for me to step aside.

"Continue, Corporal. Who sent you?"

"It wasn't the Federacy. I know because I saw the colonel meet with a man who gave him forged Federacy orders. The man had on a uniform and I'm pretty sure—"

Two shots are fired—one to the head of the corporal and the other to the head of Frayne. Both fall over dead in an instant.

"Are you out of your minds," I shout. I turn around and see that the three Rogue soldiers have returned their weapons to their holders. "I was about to get important intelligence out of them!"

A young female gunner approaches me. She removes her helmet, and her dyed neon-green hair pours out. "What were you thinking," I shout. "I had them under control!"

"We had direct orders from Commander Phode to take no prisoners," the gunner says.

The gunner abruptly stops talking. She takes a long look at me and laughs. Her smile grows wide. "If I knew this mission was to save you, I would have thought twice about it."

"*Dariox?* Is that you?"

"I may not be Federacy material, but I'm good enough to save your sorry ass!"

PART III
THE ROGUES

15

MAVY SWAY

We are transported in one of the attack helicraft to a small man-made island in the Pacifiqua Sea. We take no prisoners back with us, because *there are none.* Phode ordered everyone killed. Even the injured mercenaries were summarily executed by the Rogues. I tried to stop the Rogues from doing it, but it was either fight them to save a few dying mercenaries who not long ago wanted me dead or accept this as the price of getting the Rogues' assistance. I chose the latter.

We land on top of a steel and glass building that resembles a modern-day version of the famous San Bernardino Basilica in Yerusalom. When the door to the helicraft opens, I am immediately greeted by Emile Phode, which is a thoughtful gesture on his part. He reaches for my hand as I climb out of the craft. "Judge Cone, welcome to Rogue headquarters." He holds my hand for longer than normal and says, "I know we come from different sides of the war, but you have my assurance that you are safe here." Phode's voice is deep and deliberate. He is short in stature, but exudes strength and confidence. He immediately wants me to understand the terms of our stay and his cooperation. "You have my word that you and your two compatriots will be protected at all times while in Rogue-controlled territory. When you are not in our territory, you may or may not have my assurances of this protection. It will depend on your actions and you meeting certain well-defined and reasonable requirements. For the time being, though, we can say that you and I are allies. Temporary allies."

Phode has a reputation for honesty, so I take him at his word. More importantly, it's my experience that when a man in power tells you he will help you, but only over a short period of time and with a number of qualifications, his statements tend to be credible—far more credible than those of a man who promises any and all assistance.

Nayla, Trace, and I follow Phode, Dariox, and a handful of armed guards down a stairway toward a low-lying rock and metal bridge that goes far into the Pacifiqua. The mainland is in the distance to our backs. We walk out into waters that are heavily patrolled by Rogue helicraft and waterships. Rogue headquarters is far more fortified than Federacy intelligence led me to believe and far more fortified than the Omniplex.

The Rogues rebelled against the NFF about fifteen years ago. But there was never a war. The rebellion was brief and contained. The leaders of the revolt simply chopped the head off the snake. Twenty or so top military brass and government officials were killed, but not the Chancellor at the time, and not Vrig, who was a senior general. It was a surgical strike to send a message that there was a new regime in place and a new way of ordering relations. Within days of the strike, the two sides agreed to end the violence. This was followed by a long and chilly peace.

The Rogues' rebellion cleared the way for Vrig to take control of the NFF's military apparaturus and eventually the chancellorship. Some Federacy intelligence agencies believe that Phode coordinated the coup with Vrig. But I doubt a man like Phode would ally himself with a man like Vrig. I know that Phode wanted to spare as many of his fellow soldiers as possible, and Vrig would have been the one able to make that happen. So there may have been some low-level coordination for that purpose alone.

I think of the NFF and the Rogues as being like an extended family—a family with deep distrust and estrangement, but still a family. They have numerous fundamental differences—religion being one of the biggest. Vrig despises religion in all forms. He especially despises the brand of religion practiced by the Holy Father and the Nation of Yerusalom. Vrig has done his best to eradicate religion from all aspects of NFF life. Phode, on the other hand, is a believer.

The one area where there is little disagreement is military operations. The NFF and the Rogues have a common cause—the destruction of the Federacy. Over time, the NFF and the Rogues settled on a de facto division of military operations based on their headquarters, territory controlled, and military capabilities. The Rogues control the Pacifiqua shoreline and anywhere from 500 to 1000 kilometers inland depending on the latitude and the year. They currently control most of what used to be Calyphornia, as well as some of the former northern principalities. In the Federacy we call the land the Rogues captured the Boomerang because of its shape. The NFF, whose population outnumbers the Rogues' by roughly five thousand to one, controls military operations from the shores of the Atlantique to the Myssisipe Waterway.

Like any broken family, the Rogues and the NFF could barely communicate without it quickly breaking down into a fiery war of words. For years, the Federacy tried to fan those flames, but it always backfired. Nothing can bring a broken family closer than an outsider.

As we walk out into the sea along along the bridge, seagulls circle above us. This is the cleanest non-artificial air I have ever breathed. I put my hand on Phode's shoulder and gently turn him around. He is a commander of troops as I was. He understands my blunt act, but knows it's not menacing. "I only care about two things in this world, Commander. Avenging the death of my family and finding Pique."

"Why tell me this, Judge?"

"Because I believe you can be honest with me if you know how simple my wants are."

"My deepest sympathies on your family. I was appalled to learn that innocents were killed in this petty war we are all fighting. *And for what?* So that we can control all the hydrogen. So that I or the Federacy's Premier or that monumental fool Vrig can rule over a few hundred million people. It's absurd. We live in a world where avarice rules and absurdity follows."

Phode rubs his beard. "I would want to know who killed my family, too, and I would want to torture them slowly. But I can't help you in that regard. I simply don't know who did it." Phode reaches over the bridge's ledge, picks up a rock, and throws it into the ocean. "I can tell you one thing I do know and this should alleviate some of your suspicions. I can tell you who is *not* responsible for this heinous act."

Phode pauses again. He is a very careful man. He rubs his beard once more, which I believe is his tell—one indicating honesty. Lately, I have been doubting my ability to judge character through these simple bioresponsive gestures. But I feel strongly that the next words out of Phode's mouth will be honest ones.

"It was not the Holy Father," Phode says. "I know you have suspicions that he was involved. Based on what I know, I, too, would be suspicious. But I'm certain he was not involved. I know this man. He is a political animal and not one who can easily be trusted. That, there is no question. But he would not kill innocents. The Holy Father would never, under any circumstance, kill an innocent woman or child. Such a killing is an abomination. I feel that way. You feel that way. And I am a hundred percent sure the Holy Father feels that way."

"Yes, but would one of his people, someone like Spiro de Yerusalom, do it? That man seems capable of any and all sorts of abominations."

"I am very familiar with the *work* of Spiro de Yerusalom and it is highly unlikely that he would do anything without the Holy Father's approval. Spiro owes his life to the Holy Father."

We walk another few hundred meters out on the bridge to a stone and glass building that stands confidently on a small man-made island. The windows from the building take in the ocean and sun. Intense surges of blue and green light pour through the glass. We walk through sliding doors into a long hallway, and after a few turns, are guided into a circular room with floor-to-ceiling glass. The room is surrounded by whitecaps on all sides and is connected to a small bridge that leads to a floating helipad in the ocean. Nayla enters first, followed by Trace, then me. Sitting at the end of a large glass table is one of the most beautiful women I have ever seen. I am instantly taken in by her silky brown skin and penetrating green eyes. She plays with her tightly curled hair, individually wrapping each curl around her fingers. The light from the sky and sea turns her white dress a shade of turquoise. Trace's eyes are fixed on her. She stands as I enter the room. Her tall and slender body is etched with flawless turns. "An honor, my brother," she says as she kneels before me. She kisses my hand. Her lips are warm and her breath is soft. Phode introduces her: "Judge Cone, this is Mavy Sway, my chief counselor."

"Come on now, baby," she says laughing. "Don't forget fiancée. No reason to hide that."

"In all things, my greatest asset," Phode says. He walks behind her and reaches up to put his hands on her shoulders. She bends down so that he can kiss her. Phode says, "Love is a strange thing, Judge. I was initially forced by an ecclesiastical order to "propose" to Mavy. But now, nothing could keep me from this woman. She is my light, my strength, my sight, my sustenance."

"What Emile means is that my father thought that a marriage between us made heavenly sense. My father is always right in matters of the heart."

"Your father is the worst kind of political creature, my dear," Phode says. He laughs. "But he knows love." Phode pokes Mavy in her side. "Your father has certainly loved enough women of his own. How many mistresses does he have?"

"I've lost count," Mavy says. She's not happy with Phode. He feels bad and tries to kiss her, but she stands up tall and makes him stand on his toes. She then smacks him hard on his backside. "You shouldn't speak ill of my father."

"You're right." It is clear that Phode is very much in love with Mavy. "The day your father came to me *to request* that I marry you was a blessing. I didn't know it at the time. But perhaps he was one step ahead of me. He's an extraordinary man. I mean that most sincerely." Phode looks at me. "I'm sure you agree, Judge."

"I guess," I say. I'm not sure how Phode expects me to answer. I look at Nayla to see if she knows what Phode is talking about. Mavy notices my confusion and says, "You don't know who my father is, do you?"

"No," I say. "I'm sorry, but I don't."

"My father is your father. He's everyone's father."

"I'm sorry, I'm not following you."

"My father is *the* Father. The Holy Father."

"That can't be," I say. My response is a bit on the childish side, like that of a child the first time he is told there is no such thing as the tooth fairy. "There is the Sacred Oath of Celibacy—no relations after fifty. The Ceremony of the Half Century. The March of the Many to the San Bernardino Basilica. Not to mention that every Father since the End of the Old Order has been castrated on his fiftieth birthday."

"Oh, he's not castrated," Phode says. Mavy gives him an ugly look.

"It's what the people need," Mavy says. She doesn't mean to be condescending, but condescension is not an intent-based offense. "Father loves family. He loves all of his children. Father made a decision to bring life into the world—life of His Blood. Father believes that when the End of Days comes, family is what will matter most. The love of a child will bring peace on earth. This is Father's holy purpose."

"Get the fuck out of here," Trace yells. He has been instructed by me not to talk at all while in the presence of any Rogue. But to say Trace is a bad listener would be an understatement of epic proportion. His impulse control is limited—he needs to be heard. "The Holy Father wants to get in between a woman's legs, just like any other man. He wants to take his prick and stick it in some woman's hole. He's no different." Trace is very proud of his outburst. He feels as if he's on a roll. "No disrespect to your dear old dad, but he's a man, thinking with what's between his legs and wanting what's in between hers."

Phode grins. He is clearly amused.

Mavy is not.

"Father is not your average man," Mavy says calmly. She begins to pace, dramatically clearing a space for herself. "It's Trace, right? You're Trace Rollins. You used to be a leader in the Abstainer movement?"

"Yes," Trace says, a little less confident than before.

"Then something happened to you, right? Some kind of transformation? You went from being a firebrand of sorts to becoming a morzium fiend. What happened to you, Trace?"

"I had an epiphany. I realized that my bullshit was the same bullshit as everyone else's bullshit. I realized that thinking that no *ism* mattered was as much bullshit as thinking any specific *ism* mattered." Trace's smile grows wide. "So I got high."

"Well, you're right in saying that *your bullshit* is bullshit. And perhaps morzium is the fix for that. But Father's beliefs are genuine. They are steeped in the authenticity of divinity. Father's faith comes directly from his connection to Our God."

"You're just saying a lot of nonsense. But if it gets you through the day, lady, good for you."

"What you are too myopic to see is that Father is concerned with the divinity of humankind. The inspired efforts of his flock drive his actions. Father's every waking breath is about love, peace, and the sanctity of the human spirit. He brought life into this world because he prayed to Our God and Our God commanded him to do so." Mavy marches up to Trace. She is almost as tall as he is. She reaches down with her right hand and forcefully grabs his crotch. "This needy child in between your legs may command you." She squeezes tight and turns it. Like a puppy whose tail has been stepped on, Trace lets out a yelp. "But Father is commanded by only one thing, Our God. Father follows the commands of the Great Inventor of the Universe, the God of All Creatures, the Heavenly Being who sacrificed himself upon Lyncone's Altar to atone for our sins. Father is commanded by Our God and by Our God alone."

Mavy lets go of Trace's crotch. She turns her back to him and walks away. "It is not for people like you to sit in judgment of men like him. While he opens up the heavens to the masses, you hide in your morzium. He is the trustee of humanity and you're an Abstainer who wishes to sit this one out. It's laughable. You want to abstain from the pain and suffering that is humanity. You want suffering to be like a catchy slogan from an acne advertisement: Here today, gone tomorrow! Suffering is not a pimple. Suffering is the friction between humanity and divinity. To become divine is to suffer. Abstainers are the lowest form—"

"Enough already," Nayla says. "We appreciate you helping us. We truly do. But do we need to suffer through your insults and lectures? Is this the kind of suffering you're talking about? Because if it is, rest assured, we're suffering."

Before Mavy has a chance to answer, Phode steps in front of Mavy. "Forgive us, Nayla. You, your brother, and Judge Cone are our guests. Mavy is very protective of her father. We all want to protect our loved ones. It is in our biology and our humanity."

"I have a daughter who I need to protect," Nayla says. "I'm not sure whether it's biology or humanity. But what I am sure of is that no one will stand in my way. If the Holy Father is on my side, then he's okay in my book. If he's against me, he's not."

Mavy faces Nayla. "I will not tolerate you casting judgment, one way or the other, on the Holy Father. You are in my dominion and you will refrain from even mentioning his name in my presence."

Nayla storms over to Mavy. She looks deep into her eyes and reaches down and grabs what lies between Mavy's legs. She sends a powerful electric current up through Mavy. The childlike scream that comes from Mavy shakes the glass walls. Nayla looks possessed. "If you're on my side, we're good. If you're not, we're not. It's that simple."

16

KENE YORNE

Over the next few days, Phode and I get to know each other. We meet regularly and discuss tactical plans to extract Pique from the Federacy. I'm impressed with Phode's knowledge of military strategy and I'm fortunate to have the opportunity to collaborate with a mind as sharp as his. Phode is generous with information, a sign of an astute military leader. He shares every last bit of intelligence, classified or not, regarding Pique's detention. Rogue intelligence reports are highly detailed. In fact, they are far better than the intelligence I used to receive when I was a Federacy commander. I'm starting to understand why the Federacy, a much larger and more powerful entity than the NFF and the Rogues combined, is losing the war.

According to the assessments, FTIS, an elite military unit, is holding Pique in a secret detention center in a remote part of the Federacy, a region often referred to by its colloquial name, the Caps. There are approximately 250 specially trained guards holding her and a few dozen other high-security prisoners. They intend to convict her of high treason and conspiracy to overthrow the Federacy.

Phode doesn't say much about the Federacy's motivations. But based on the intelligence, my best guess is that the Federacy is using her to get to me or the Holy Father. The Federacy wants to negotiate a new military pact with the Nation of Yerusalom. The Premier understands that he is losing the war against the NFF and the Rogues, and he needs the Nation of Yerusalom to enter the war. What the Federacy obviously doesn't understand is that the Nation of Yerusalom and the Rogues are already working together against the Federacy. And although Phode doesn't say it, I'm reasonably certain the Nation of Yerusalom and the Rogues are aligned against the NFF as well.

Phode is forthcoming about anything related to Pique and her detention, but extremely tight-lipped about all other things. He will say nothing about the hydrogen price wars or recent high-level defections from the Federacy to the NFF. He will not speak at all about the ongoing negotiations between the Rogues and the NFF or why he is so committed to the Holy Father, beyond his impending marriage to Mavy. He clearly doesn't trust the Holy Father. My sense—for whatever that's worth these days—is that he owes the Holy Father or the Holy Father has something on him. It can't just be his love of Mavy and I don't even think it's political expediency. That just doesn't seem like Phode. Although Phode is clearly in love with Mavy, he is shrewd enough to know that her motives may not be entirely pure and the Holy Father is not a trustworthy ally.

From our first day together, Phode insisted that our extraction team be small and that under no circumstances should Trace or Nayla be a part of it. On these two points, I'm in complete agreement. In fact, there is very little disagreement between us as to any decision or tactic. As a commander, Phode is everything Veriton—rest his wretched soul—was not. Phode is a man I could have served under, and based on his humility, I believe he willingly could have served under me. Veriton was capable of serving only Veriton. Phode and I have something significant in common. Because we couldn't trust or respect people we served under, we took away their commands.

It takes a lot of convincing, but Trace and Nayla eventually acquiesce when I explain to them that they're not coming on the mission. I convince them I need trained military personnel and that it's more important that I have friends on the inside of Rogue operations than friends in the field. The operation will be run through the Rogue command center by Mavy's right-hand man, Kene Yorne. I want Nayla near him at all times. Yorne defected from the NFF about two years ago and I don't trust him—or Mavy for that matter. If this mission fails and I get killed, I want to know that Nayla and Trace are safe and have a fighting chance to survive.

The extraction team consists of Mavy, Dariox, Kene Yorne's twin sister,

Asio, and a young soldier from Kolexico named Shifa Teal. Mavy and I will extract Pique. Shifa will be the pilot. Asio will be our electrical-fields, communications, and digital-ammunitions expert. And Dariox will be what the Rogues affectionately call the Killer.

Phode gave me his best. An all-female team. Classic Rogue.

Our plan consists of flying a dangerous serpentine route that winds through the Caps. While jamming the Federacy's radars and dodging anticraft weaponry, we are going to land the helicraft right in the middle of the detention center. From the moment we land, we estimate we will have three minutes to extract Pique before being overwhelmed by FTIS forces. The instant our landing gear hits the ground, we will emit a powerful cloud of electrical disjoints. This should temporarily disrupt all communication and disorient human resources. Then, while the others create massive distractions on the east and south sides of the camp, Mavy and I will begin burrowing under the northernmost wall of the main holding center. Using a highly sophisticated cartogramic drill developed by a team of Yerusi scientists, we will burrow underground and come up near Pique's cell. We will need to move quickly and get a mask over Pique, so that when we detonate the meylon canisters, she will remain conscious. We will have about one minute from the time the meylon knocks out the nearby guards to get back through the burrowed tunnel and escape. The plan is extremely dangerous and full of risks. But it's the best we have.

17

SHIFA TEAL

It is standard Rogue procedure that a week prior to a mission the forces embark on a twenty-four-hour team-building exercise called Trial and Bonding. No one will explain to me exactly what happens on these Trial and Bonding experiences, but there are some less-than-subtle clues that concern me.

Shifa Teal, a young and carefree girl who exudes the fullness of life, introduces herself to me and says, "Don't you worry. We're going to take real good care of you, Max." She slowly licks her lips and seductively says, "I can call you Max, right?" Just as I am saying yes, she places her hand on my cheek and gently lets it slide down the back of my neck. Phode also has me worried. As I am readying my micropak for the trip. He is more serious than usual. "Whatever happens during this—whatever Mavy decides—I'm okay with it. You and I will be okay. We are a young culture of warriors, so we need our traditions, however fledgling they may be."

We are instructed to gather in the circular glass meeting room that sits in the Pacifiqua. We are told about the route to the Trial and Bonding retreat and the flight time, but little else. When the briefings are over, I grab my micropak and head toward a glass door that leads out to the bridge that connects the meeting room to the floating helipad. I am a few meters from the door when I turn to say good-bye to Nayla. She quickly runs up to me and hugs me tightly.

"It's only twenty-four hours, Nayla. I'll see you soon."

"I know. I'm just worried about you."

"I'll be fine."

She pulls me close and whispers in my ear. "I just don't trust Mavy. She's a manipulative liar, just like her father. You can't forget that."

Although Mavy is on the other side of the room, she somehow hears Nayla. She takes her time walking across the room, but everyone knows she's coming. She stops just inches from Nayla's face. Their noses practically touch.

"Max, should remember *what*," Mavy says. Her tone is that of an aristocrat commanding someone beneath her to answer her question. She is quite comfortable letting others know that she is the purest breed in the room. That she is the bastard daughter of the Holy Father does not change the fact that both of her parents, the Holy Father, and her mother, a Baroness from Iberion, are of bloodlines considered *most pure*. She looks down on Nayla. She looks down on her common stock, as well as her "silly little Abstainer ideals."

Nayla doesn't respond to Mavy. She doesn't want another confrontation. Mavy is about to go on a mission to rescue Pique and Nayla doesn't want to jeopardize it with another fight. She has to swallow her pride for Pique's sake. So she simply takes three steps back and lowers her eyes. Mavy quickly eliminates the space.

"Please Nayla—share with me your deep insights."

"I have nothing to say."

"Very well, I will say it for you. You told your brother-in-law, whom you love so dearly, that I'm a liar. A manipulator. You believe that I'm a person without character. Perhaps you mean 'Federacy character' or 'Abstainer character' or some other definition of that funny little word you people like to throw around. Well, my dear, perhaps I don't have this *character* you speak of. But I am no liar. I am no manipulator. You think I'm some voracious political beast who craves power at all costs. You think I am ego—pure unadulterated ego. Nothing could be further from the truth. I am the daughter of the Holy Father himself. I am an emissary of Our God. I am his humble servant. I am his loyal vassal. I follow his orders. And his orders, so that we're clear, command me to protect you, the judge, and Pique. Through the Holy Father, Our God has spoken to me. I am to save your little girl."

"I pray this is true," Nayla says. Her eyes slowly rise and meet Mavy's.

"I will bring home your little girl. You have my word."

Mavy's smile quickly turns from triumphant to chilling. She has put Nayla in her proper place, but that's not enough. Mavy moves in for the kill. She places her mouth close to Nayla's ear. "You also have my word that I will keep Pique's dirty little secret. I will keep your dirty little secret."

Nayla's face turns pale.

"Look around you, my dear," Mavy says. She dramatically swirls her hands through the air, pointing at the walls. "Glass everywhere. You shouldn't throw stones."

18

ASIO YORNE

We board a superhelicraft unlike any I have ever seen. As we take off heading west into the Pacifiqua, I feel a magnetic attraction, a ricochet-like force into the sky. I have never flown at this kind of speed. I can't imagine the Rogues built this without the help of Yerusalom.

Dariox is seated on a platform above the main fuselage. It is encased in clear projectile-proof glass. I am seated in the back of the craft next to Mavy, and Asio is to our right. Shifa sits in her own glass bubble below the helicraft, and all I can see is the top of her frizzy hair sticking up through a cutout in the floor of the craft. Mavy informs us that this is the craft we will use during the extraction.

We fly only a few meters above the water at lightning-fast speed, and at times, the craft sucks up the water and shoots it back down for added propulsion. I have never seen such a thing. We are traveling at least five times as fast as my own transport's top speed, and I have a strong feeling we can fly much faster. I had heard rumors that the Rogues' aircraft had surpassed the Federacy's, but they were just rumors.

After a thirty-minute flight at supersonic speeds, we land on a beautiful volcanic island with large peaks and waterfalls. We step out of the craft onto a white sand beach with palm trees. "Why are we training in a tropical location?" I ask. "Our mission takes us through the mountains. Subzero temperatures. Twenty-meter snowdrifts. Jagged cliffs. *This* is a vacation spot."

"It's time to bond," Dariox says. "This isn't about training for our mission."

Mavy strides over—long graceful steps that easily glide across the earth. "I don't like having to explain this over and over, Dariox. Trial and Bonding *is* training. It's an integral part of our journey toward oneness." Mavy shakes her head in disappointment. She looks at me, while talking to the others. "Dariox is very new to us, but she's extremely talented. I'm sure you will see that."

"I know," I say.

"Yeah right," Dariox says. "You threw me away like a piece of garbage because I didn't fit some stupid Federacy checklist." She's not wrong.

"You two are going to need to kiss and make up," Mavy says. "But the intimacy part of the Bonding won't happen until later." My heart races. I'm not going to be intimate with Dariox, or anyone else for that matter.

"Max, the Trial is a tradition of great significance and meaning to the Rogues," Mavy says. "It is a ritual of virtue, camaraderie, cohesion, and clarity. So I ask for your formal consent to partake in the tradition."

I nod with as little enthusiasm as I can. I want to get Pique back, and if participating in this weird experience will help, I'll do it. But I'm feeling pretty uncomfortable right now.

And then things get *really* uncomfortable.

In an instant, Mavy unrobes herself. *Oh my God. She's perfect-looking.* Then, she does the same to Dariox, Asio, and Shifa. They are all naked, bathed in the tropical sun. Sweat quickly forms over their young bodies. *This isn't really happening.* "You're next, Max," Mavy says.

"I would rather not have—" Dariox places her hand over my mouth, while Asio and Shifa begin taking my clothes off. I put up a little bit of fight. Mavy sees this and says, "Out of respect to us and the process, please allow us to remove your clothes. This is more than just being unclothed. It is about being naked. It is about being exposed before each other. We need to uncover our weaknesses—our vulnerabilities. Clothes are but one superficial way in which we hide our inhibitions."

Mavy finishes removing my clothes and then directs us all to the beach. When we get there, she turns her back to us and looks out onto the ocean. She screams, "We are one! We are one! We are one!" She turns back to us and claps her hands three times quickly, and the others drop to their knees in a straight line in front of me. They have done this before. Mavy places four gray squares of paper in my hand and kneels before me. The four kneeling women stick their tongues out. I am to perform some warped version of the Old Christians' communion. I place the paper on their tongues. As I do, each one rises and kisses me with her mouth open. With their tongues, they guide the paper back into my mouth. I immediately start to feel intoxicated. The high reminds me of the medical analgesic delphium, but with a slight hallucinogenic nuance.

The women join hands and chant:

> *We are One! We are One! We are One!*
> *Work as One! Win as One! Seek as One!*
> *Take as One! Move as One! Reap as One!*
> *We are One! We are One! We are One!*

They form a circle around me and attempt to bind my hands. I pull away and Mavy smiles at me. Her eyes try to tell me that it's safe to play along. It's only after Dariox nods that it's okay that I allow them to bind me. I can trust Dariox. Even if I couldn't, after all those years of evaluating her, I'm an expert at knowing when she's lying.

They blindfold me and tie my arms and legs together. They sing "The Rogues' National Hymnal" and carry me on their shoulders like a log. They walk for about twenty minutes before we arrive at what sounds like rapids—very loud rapids. I don't like this. "What's going on?" I ask. Too late—they drop me in the water. My head immediately starts pounding from the cold. The water is surprisingly frigid and the salt strong. It stings. I can't breathe. An image rushes into my head. I need to fight it back. It's my kids—their murdered bodies floating in this river. I can't go there.

The current quickly takes me toward a thunderous fall of water. I slam into a sharp rock that juts out of the river and the current quickly submerges me beneath the surface. There is a colossal downward pressure of water that I can't fight. I'm blindfolded and I have no idea which way is out. But I feel a very clear pull. The rapids are dragging me toward a waterfall. A sharp object slams into my leg and tears open a gash. The salt in the water stings the fresh wound. I can feel the warm blood mixing with the cold rapids. The water begins to churn more violently. I'm getting sucked toward the drop. I flail my legs, trying to swim to one side, but the waterfall has me. I'm going over and there's nothing I can do about it. I'm helpless.

The sound of the water stirring fills my ears and I become more and more disoriented. It's impossible to catch my breath. I'm taking in a lot of water. My throat feels raw and my stomach feels like it's ready to burst. With each gasp for air, I swallow more water, but there is nowhere left for it to go.

The rapids have me in a stranglehold. I am spinning in every direction, but there is an unassailable pull, as if I'm tied to a destiny at the bottom of the falls.

I begin to lose consciousness. Then, I hear a sharp sound above me and something pierces through the water. It sounds like a boulder fell in and is heading toward me. My blindfold has been ripped to shreds by the rock and river, but I still can't see. My vision is completely blurred. I can see only vague shadows. But whatever pierced the water is coming toward me. With my bound hands, I reach for it.

And thankfully, it reaches back.

It's a woman's hand that stretches out and locks with mine. I am quickly pulled out of the water and snapped straight into the air, high above the river. The hand that saved me reaches down and removes whatever remains of my blindfold. It's Asio.

She's attached to a retractable cable that connects to a zip line that spans the waterfall's drop. Holding me with her bare hands, she is the only thing that stands between me and a 150-meter plunge to a certain death. We are suspended over the falls for a good few minutes. "I'm not letting go," she says. "I have you."

The feeling of dangling over a fall, completely naked, with only Asio between me and my death, is exhilarating. I wish it would last forever. The time passes too quickly. I don't want her to, but she releases the lock on the zip line and we fly across the river to the bank. We are alone on one side of the river while everyone else is on the other. Asio hugs me for a long time. She will not let go of the hug. It is an awkward feeling hugging her naked, but the delphium-like drug is powerful. It overcomes some of my self-consciousness. She puts her lips close to my ear and speaks softly. "I'm excited about what's going to happen later." She looks down below my waist. "Looks like you are, too."

Asio then asks me if she can tie me up and blindfold me. I'm not quite sure if it's the drug, the excitement of dangling over the cliff, her hugging me, or that I've completely bought into the Rogues' tradition of Trial and Bonding. But I quickly say yes. I have not felt this good in a long time.

I hear the others swim through the rapids to our side of the river. I am again tied up and carried on their shoulders. They march singing a song with no words. Time is becoming less relevant to me and I cannot say how long they march for. But they are breathing heavily. They come to a stop and gently place me on the ground sitting up.

I quickly hear two sounds that stand out. The first is clear to me, while the other is not. The first is the sound of digging. They have old-fashioned manual diggers and they are digging a trough or hole of some sort. The second sound is a muffled hiss, like the release of carbon from a canister. But it's more erratic, angrier.

I am lifted up and placed in the hole they dug. It is deep and narrow, and appears to be perfectly constructed for me to stand in. I am not nervous—not yet.

But then I begin to hear the rumbling of the diggers again, and the small space between me and the sides of the hole begins to disappear. They slowly fill the hole with stones. First they cover my feet, then my legs, and then my chest. They pause for a minute, which gives me time to get nervous. My chest instinctively pushes against the stones as if it's trying to break free. My brain is not yet as scared as my chest. Finally, they fill the hole with small stones and dirt—all the way up to my chin. There's no way I can get myself out. Then they remove my blindfold. I initially think this is a kind gesture, but that soon changes. Each of them comes over to me, lies on her stomach, and kisses me on the lips. Dariox kisses me last and gently brushes the hair away from my eyes. "I've got you," she whispers.

Mavy tells everyone to join hands as they form a circle around me. As they walk around holding hands, Mavy says, "You're a brave man, Max Cone. You're a wise man. You're an honorable man." The circle slows down and Mavy says, "I want you to know that if you die in this Trial, I will give you a burial fitting of Our God."

Dariox rolls her eyes.

The circle disbands and Mavy tells Dariox to get started. Dariox runs toward the palm trees in the distance and disappears behind them. I hear

some shuffling and she returns with a crate. The hissing gets louder. She removes the top of the crate, runs back behind the trees, and disappears. Mavy,
Shifa, and Asio follow. I am now alone with the hissing crate. I know what's
next. My brain catches up to my chest.

Snakes. Ten. Twenty. Thirty. Maybe as many as a hundred of them slither
up to the top of the crate and fall out. They seem like they're in a tremendous hurry to go somewhere. I don't know much about snakes—only enough
to know I'm scared of them. I assume, by their fangs, that they're poisonous.
Even though I know it's futile, I try to wiggle my body out of the hole. The
more I wiggle, the quicker the snakes come. They must sense the vibrations—
that or my fear. I stop moving, but it doesn't matter. They're on to me.

Like a tide coming in, the snakes begin to come closer and closer. A few
of the large snakes jump out ahead. They are brown and their mouths are
black. They move at a quicker pace than the rest. "Mambas," I hear Mavy
shout. "Go!"

The snakes are only ten meters away when I see Dariox jumping over the
slower snakes in the rear, making her way toward me. She is running full-
force, armed only with an Old World laser machete. One snake reaches me
first. I can see its cold eyes and determined tongue. Dariox is running at full
speed, raising her machete above her head. The mamba coils. It readies
itself to strike. It flings itself at me. Dariox dives in front of me and absorbs
the mamba's bite on her leg. She screams at the top of her lungs as she drops
the machete down on the mamba, splitting it in two. She then hobbles to her
feet in front of me, protecting me from the next wave of approaching snakes.
With great precision, she slices the next snake. And the next. And the next.
She spins, and turns, and leaps like a great dancer, acrobatically slicing snakes
in two. Her dance with the snakes is both beautiful and grotesque. Snake
parts are everywhere and their halves writhe in a gruesome dance with death.

When the last of the snakes is killed, Dariox runs to the crate the snakes
came out of and opens a package affixed to the side of the crate. It's an injec-
tor and she immediately stabs herself with an antineurotoxin shot. She falls
to the ground and passes out. Mavy picks her up and treats her wound while
Asio and Shifa dig me out of the hole.

The last two Trials are less intense, not because I'm less likely to die, but
because I know, for sure, they won't let it happen. When Shifa and I fly up at

ten thousand meters in the helicraft and she jumps out, I'm not nervous. Even though I'm bound to one of the helicraft's seats—and I'm alone at a thousand meters speeding to the ground in a nosedive—I'm calm. I know someone's coming.

Of course I'm right. At the last minute, Mavy flies through a suction port-hole on the side of the craft, sits down at the controls, and lands us, right near our camp. *Apparently Mavy flies helicraft, too.*

And when I get placed in a maze of fire—impenetrable concentric circles of fire and explosives that do not allow me to move more than a few meters in any direction—I know I will be safe. I know help is coming. So when Shifa jetpacks in just before the blaze swallows me, all I say is, "What took you so long?"

The Trial comes to a close and I feel like a huge weight has been lifted off my shoulders. I feel alive. I know it won't last, and I know the drug is part of it, but it feels good.

As the sun starts to set, Mavy announces that the Bonding will begin in a few minutes. She again heads to the beach and directs us all to follow. Every-one kneels before me again, and Mavy hands me four circular blue pieces of paper. We perform the same ritual. One by one, I place the paper in their mouths. They swirl it around and kiss me, sliding the paper back into my mouth. We are intoxicated in an instant. It's a different kind of high than the first, but just as strong.

Night is coming, so Asio and Dariox build a fire. Mavy excuses herself, and when she returns, she is holding a small box. She looks inside the box and says, "This will determine how we Bond. How we connect. How we touch."

She takes out a shiny metal object and raises it above her head. It's a Palmitor.

19

DARIOX

Mavy opens a side compartment on the Palmitor and places a small circular operating license into it. "It's a highly specialized experience," Mavy says. "There is no other license like this in the world." She seems very proud of this. "We're not going deep into your consciousness, Max. We're just going to quickly browse your desires to ensure that we maximize your pleasure."

"Who dreams up programs like this?" I ask. I try to act nonchalant, but the fact that this machine is going to browse my desires—my *sexual* desires— scares the hell out of me. The fear doesn't last long, though. The drugs quickly take control and squash my fears as if they're tiny, inconsequential ants. *These drugs are bullies.* They run through my body destroying any and all inhibitions. By the time they're done, I feel very little of anything. I'm utterly numb. All senses are deadened.

I soon find myself repeating the same thing I just said. "Who dreams up programs like this?" Then I realize I'm not sure if I said it again or I'm just remembering the first time I said it. This cycle goes on for a while—*or maybe it's a very short time.* "Who dreams up programs like this?"

Mavy raises the Palmitor above her head. "Let's all praise the sister behind the Palmitor!" She takes the Palmitor to the other women, and each of them takes her time holding it and examining it as if it's a meteor that's just fallen from the sky. "That's right—praise the sister who brought this gift from God to us." She hands the Palmitor to me and smiles wide. "Obviously, you're the one person here who knows the most about it." She asks me to kiss it, and I of course refuse. There aren't enough drugs in the world to make me kiss a machine. She then says, "You want to talk a little bit about this wonderful device and the sister responsible for it?"

"Why would I know anything about it?"

"How high are you, Max?" Mavy sees the look of confusion on my face, and when I tell her I have no idea who created it, she realizes I'm being honest.

"You really don't know." She shakes her head. "That is so sad." Mavy seems upset, but I can't tell if she's being genuine. She moves close to me. I feel her warmth. "I don't understand why she didn't tell you. But that's not for me to judge." She puts her hand over my hand, the one holding the device. "I'm sorry. I thought you knew." She then raises it and places it softly on my cheek. "Your wife created the Palmitor."

I'm in a highly drugged state. My thoughts are about as clear as morning fog. But I'm almost a hundred percent sure Mavy just said that Emmis invented the Palmitor. Emmis kept secrets, but I can't believe she kept *this* secret. I'm not sure what to think, and honestly, it's so hard to think at all right now that I just want to return to my state of unconsciousness. Before I do, I decide I need to come up with some explanation for why I didn't know that Emmis invented the Palmitor. I don't want Mavy thinking that Emmis lied to me. I don't want Mavy thinking that there were flaws in my marriage, which is crazy, because of course there were. There were many flaws—many lies.

"My wife's work was highly classified. I was the highest judge in the Federacy. For the sake of the nation, we had to keep our work private from each other. So I'm not surprised she didn't tell me. She was simply being a true Federate."

Mavy laughs. It's not mean, but it's certainly patronizing. "Of course you also know then that Emmis, that *true Federate,* was working for my father. The Nation of Yerusalom commissioned the Palmitor, as well as the rest of Emmis's real work. What she did for the Federacy was simply a cover. She worked for us. Once the Federacy found out, she could have told you. I assumed she had. The Federacy knew she worked for us for years, well before they decided to perform that unholy procedure on her. We never told her to keep secrets from you. I'm sorry to say it, but she hid it from you for one simple reason—*she didn't want you to know.*"

I try to capture that thought in my brain, but it runs away from me. It runs really fast. The drugs won't allow me to focus on anything for more than a second. I'm just trying to remember what I was even trying to remember. It's a vicious circle. One I cannot fight. My mind is a black hole from which no rational thought can escape.

I give up trying to remember. I have no choice.

Night has fallen and Mavy lets us know that the Bonding will begin. She kisses me on both cheeks. I know she said something that bothered me at some point, but I'm not sure what it is. "Are you ready, Max?" She doesn't wait for me to answer. She activates the Palmitor. "Please firmly hold the Palmitor, Max." The Palmitor begins to hum. "I want you to think about each of us. I want you to imagine what it would be like to be with us."

I have trouble focusing, but a few thoughts try to take hold. I think about Dariox in my chambers during her final citizenship hearing. I think about how she slithered out of the bathroom trying to seduce me and how I guided her back to the bathroom. I think about the exhilaration of dangling over the falls with Asio holding me. I think about Shifa jetpacking in to save me from a wall of fire. I then think about Mavy. I think about what it would be like to be with her. She's the only one I would want.

I try my hardest not to think about Emile or Nayla. They would be hurt if I was with Mavy. I try to push them out of my head, but I can't stop thinking about them. I can't stop hearing their voices in my head. Voices of reason. They tell me what I already know. I shouldn't be with Mavy. I can't be with Mavy.

I tighten my grip around the Palmitor. It feels very different from the one Veriton gave me, but again I feel like I want to strangle the life out of it. Again, I feel like I don't want to hear what it has to say. This Palmitor is lighter and moves more quickly. It emits a few high-pitched beeps and begins to warm and expand slightly. Small circular balls on the bottom of the Palmitor move across my hand, methodically uncovering every physiological and electrical clue they can. After a minute, the Palmitor lets out a soothing harp-like sound and it's done.

Dariox takes the Palmitor from me and hits a button. Then, a monitor pops up for everyone to watch. Before she presses play, and before I can say no, she places yet another drug-laced piece of paper in my mouth. Mavy tells me that this drug is specifically designed for pleasure. I take it, and my brain feels as though it is spinning above my body.

Dariox hits play, but I can't focus on what's on the monitor. My head is a hazy mess. The only thing I hear is Dariox laughing sweetly, and before I know it, she has taken my hand and we are walking toward a spot near some rocks and the incoming tide. Dariox puts me on my back and climbs on top of me. She sits on top of me for a long time. She doesn't move. She looks into my eyes and smiles. She moves her hand through my hair and says, "Everything is going to be okay. Remember, I got you." She then wraps her legs around me and squeezes her thighs against my hips. She wiggles her backside and I am soon inside her. She places her hands on my chest and pushes against me to move up and down. She is in complete control of her body and mine.

The air is warm and moist. She kisses me. I taste the salt. Sweat covers our bodies. She takes her hands off my chest and grabs my arms. She pins my arms to the ground and drops her body on top of mine. She moves more quickly and our bodies stick together with sweat. I'm lost in her. There's not a thought in my brain.

The last thing I remember is Dariox kissing me when it was over. But when I wake the next morning, it's Mavy who's lying nearest to me. She and I are naked. My hand is outstretched and near her breast. I don't remember being with her. I only remember Dariox. But by the look Mavy gives me when she wakes, and the fact that we are lying near each other naked, we must have been.

Mavy gets up slowly. "The Trial and Bonding is over," she shouts. "Praise God in all his glory!" We all get dressed and Mavy gives each of us one last piece of drug-laced paper. We take it, and she says, "We take this last gift from Our God—*so that we may try to forget.* We thank you God for this beautiful experience. But you know how weak we are. You know our penchant for jealousy. You know our limits. So we take this gift and we thank you. We thank you, God, for letting us be human."

20

CECILIA FORQUE

I don't feel quite right on the flight back to Rogue headquarters. The drugs have taken a toll. So has the Bonding. Although I remember very little from it, certain parts of my body seem to recall the events in great detail. Some part of me likes the idea of this and some part of me is repulsed by it. There is a fine line between losing one's self and finding one's self. With sex, this is especially so.

When we land at headquarters, Nayla and Trace are waiting for me. Nayla runs up to me and hugs me. I want her hug about as much as I want dysentery. Maybe it's because I think I just had sex with other people and I feel guilty toward Emmis or even Nayla. Or maybe it's something else—like the idea that I can't fully trust Nayla's motives. Either way, I don't allow her to hug me for very long. This upsets her. It upsets her too much, in my opinion. "Are you okay?" she asks after I gently pull away. She then looks at me strangely. "I missed you."

"It was only a day." I pat Trace on the back, and force a smile toward Nayla. I don't want to seem unkind. "I'm tired and I need some rest."

As I head back to my quarters, Phode slides in front of me. He places both of his hands on my shoulders. "Can we talk, Max?"

"Can we do this tomorrow, after I've showered and rested a bit?" Phode looks disappointed, but he nods okay.

I return to my quarters, shower, and lie down on my bed. I don't want to think about anything. I want to read a little and go to sleep. I open up *Saool Forque: The Bloke Who Broke the World.* I am near the end and I still have no idea why the Holy Father wanted me to read it. Without question, Forque transformed himself into a good man who tried to do his part in bringing about change within himself and beyond. He was ahead of his time with his Infinite T theory. That the space between the divine and two or more individual souls is infinite in both its distance and proximity is an innovative hypothesis, especially given the lack of schooling or science at Forque's disposal. His theory that an individual can move farther and closer along the T and bend the T itself in ways that reshape time and space—in other words, the future—is an interesting one. But I can't believe this is what the Holy Father wanted me to take away from this book. Though I've never associated any of Forque's theories with Forque himself, they are well-known theories that have been widely discredited.

I read the last chapter of the book, an overly sentimental homage to Forque that glosses over his early life as a ruthless commander in the Erabian military. This lionization of Forque is a bit much, so I quickly move through it. But the last few pages of the book capture my attention.

Two Muzlim men draped in white gowns killed Saool in the most cowardly and undignified of manners. Though a heavenly man, Saool had bodily functions like all of us. He was sitting on a receptacle performing a bodily requirement, when these creatures slithered up to him and slayed him. With shards of glass in hand, they snuck up behind him as he wiped his arse, and slit open his jugular.

I was the first to arrive. I saw these cowards. Their white gowns speckled with holy blood. They were smiling, standing over Saool as the blood spilled out onto the loo floor. I yelled at the top of my lungs, "They killed Saool! They killed Saool!" I am not a man of violence or a man of size, but I charged these killers. They quickly dispensed of me. One punch to the face and I was sent flying. But within seconds, Saool's flock appeared and quickly avenged his murder. The two Muzlim men were kicked and pummeled by a mix of twenty or thirty Anglican and Muzlim men. They were hit so hard and so repeatedly that their heads flew off.

Saool would have been devastated at the sight of his students pummeling his killers.

Saool's Last Will and Testament was peculiar, even by Saool's standards. He wrote it a year before his death. It merely requested that the Executor, which was me, do four things. First, I needed to ensure that all his money, which was quite sizable, was donated to the Yerusalom Foundation for the Linguistic Partnership of Erabians and Anglicans. Saool had the foresight to know that the major wars of the next decade would be fought over language and would be devastating. (An unfortunate aside: It turned out that the money was pissed away by a future director of the foundation. He liked to diddle little boys and needed to pay them handsomely to keep them quiet. So he stole all of the foundation's funds.)

Second, Saool's will requested that I read a passage from the Queen Ziobeth Anglican Bible. Saool asked that I read this passage *and only this passage* at his funeral. Under no circumstance was there to be a eulogy or any mention of him at his funeral. There would simply be a reading of the passage. So I read it in front of the entire prison population. It was the single least moving eulogy ever given:

Adam lived 130 years. He had a son in his own likeness and called him Seth. He had sons and daughters.

Seth lived a 105 years and had Enos. He had sons and daughters. Enos lived 90 years and had Cainan. He had sons and daughters. Cainan lived 70 years, and had Mahalaleel. He had sons and daughters.

Mahalaleel lived 65 years and had Jared. He had sons and daughters. Jared lived 162 years and he had Enoch. He had sons and daughters. Enoch lived 65 years, and had Methuselah. He had sons and daughters. Methuselah lived 187 years and had Lamech. He had sons and daughters.

Lamech lived 182 years and had a son. And he called his son Noah, saying, "This same shall comfort us concerning

our work and toil of our hands, because of the ground which
God has cursed."

Noah had Shem, Ham, and Japheth. And God rejoiced.

When I read this passage to the prison population there were
blank stares everywhere. The only faces that seemed to pay attention were two heads fixed upon spikes. The prison guards made
sure Saool's killers were paying close attention to me. Their eyes
were wide open as I read, as if they—and perhaps they alone—
understood Saool's purpose.

The third requirement of Saool's will brought me the greatest
gift of all. Saool, who was never married or parented a child,
wanted me to locate his stored semen. His will identified the
location of the facility in the Blessed Borough of Saoodi Lower
Erabia and it instructed me to take possession of his semen. The
will further instructed me to find a woman with a big mind and
an even bigger heart and inseminate her. The one woman I knew
that would fit this bill perfectly was my wife.

Last, he wanted me to make sure that he had an unbroken line
of descendants, who would always carry his name. I have done my
best to explain this to Cecilia and to ensure she will do the same
with her offspring and so on and so on.

I love you, Saool Forque. I love my wife, Ayn.

I love our daughter, Cecilia Forque, with each and every mil-
limeter of my heart.

Thank you, Saool. You have given me the most wonderful gifts.

THE END

21

MAVY AND EMILE

The next morning I wake from a deep sleep to knocking on my door. I open it to find Phode standing there. He's sweating and his eyes are red. "Good morning, Max. I hope you slept well."

"Yes." I give him a quizzical look. There is no reason for him to be at my door first thing in the morning. "This is the royal treatment," I say. "The commander of the Rogues coming to personally provide me with a wake-up call."

"You know I have no sense of humor, Max. Please do me the courtesy of meeting me at my office by nine."

"Of course." There is something off about Phode. I wash up, gather some intelligence documents, and head for his office. About halfway there I'm stopped by Nayla. It feels as though she's been waiting for me around the corner. I can't catch a break this morning.

"How did you sleep, Max?"

"Why is everyone so concerned with how I slept," I snap.

"It's a harmless question."

"I slept fine." My tone is not improving.

"So how was it?"

"My sleep?"

"Not your sleep. The Trial. The Bonding." She pulls a loose thread from her shirt and nervously wraps it around her finger. "Rumor has it that everyone has sex with each other. *Did you enjoy having sex with everyone?*"

"I don't remember very much, Nayla. And I don't think I like the way you're questioning me."

"Did you have sex with Mavy? Honestly, that's all I really want to know. Did you sleep with her?" She's agitated. Her eyes begin to water. "Please tell me you didn't."

"I honestly don't remember. I think I took something. I think we all took something to forget."

"So *you did* have sex with her."

"I don't know." I'm almost yelling at this point. "I told you I don't know whether I slept with her and it's none of your business if I did or I didn't."

"Don't yell at me, Max. I care about you. I really care about you." She takes a deep breath and begins to cry. "I think, I mean maybe, I think I'm beginning to fa—"

"Don't finish that thought. You're Emmis's sister. I'm her husband. You're the aunt to my children. I'm the uncle to Pique." I walk closer to her and try, unsuccessfully, to hide my frustration. "Your jealousies make absolutely no sense. You're an Abstainer. A priestess. You can't possibly care who I have sex with. I thought Abstainers left all of the 'Old Morals' behind. *What the hell is going on with you?*"

Nayla storms away from me. She quickly walks down the hallway. Just before she turns the corner, she yells back at me, "I don't care who you sleep with, you selfish bastard! It just can't be her!" She then takes off running away from me.

I walk down the hallway feeling guilty and reluctantly make my way to Phode's office. I'm not in a good mood. Neither is he. I push open two large doors, which automatically close behind me. I see Phode. He is in the back of his enormous office pacing between two floor-to-ceiling windows that overlook the ocean. His shoulders are slumped and his hands folded behind his back.

It is strange that a man like Phode doesn't have a writing table to sit at. Instead he has a large circular lounge with ten cushioned back supports. The lounge sits on a tiled floor and surrounds a pool of water. There are five retractable monitors placed equidistant around the lounge. Besides a small towel container near the lounge, the only other thing in the office is a huge display case with what looks like war mementos, plaques, and immense ceremonial glass orbs that represent Rogue "oneness."

Phode walks over to the lounge. He points his hand upward, and the monitors retreat into the ceiling. He then takes off his shoes and socks, sits down on a cushion, and places his feet in the pool. He motions for me to sit across from him, and asks me to remove my shoes and socks and place my feet in the pool too. I am in no mood for this touchy-feely nonsense, but I take my shoes and socks off and put my feet in anyway. Phode rubs his beard as we sit silently. He stares at the pool. I like Phode a great deal, but sitting in silence, dipping our feet together in a pool, is too much.

He slowly begins to move his feet, creating little circular ripples in the pool, which spread toward me. His eyes focus on the little waves he created. About five minutes pass, and finally, he looks up at me to speak. "I know you slept with Mavy."

I don't want this, I think to myself. *I'm exhausted and I just don't want to talk about it. But I guess I have to.* "I don't know whether I did or didn't."

"I know that, too." He continues to swirl his feet in the pool. "Please just hear me out before saying anything." Phode swallows hard. "I had the entire Trial and Bonding recorded. It is part of our tradition and young societies need tradition. I needed to see it." His feet move more quickly, and the ripples become more wavelike. "It made me jealous. Wildly jealous. But I hold no ill feelings toward you." Phode tugs hard at his beard and looks down. "It's awful for me, Max. I love Mavy and I know that she cares about me, but not in the same way I care about her. Given her leadership position, she could have easily altered the Bonding experience in order to remain true to me. It would have been a loving gesture on her part. She knows of my jealousy, as well as my insecurity. She knows I am reactionary in this regard and that I still value the Old Morals."

"I honestly don't remember a thing."

"As I said, I know you don't." Phode then reads my mind. He is a man acutely aware of what others are thinking. "Please know, Max, I was not watching you have sex with the others. I'm not a deviant. I mostly listened and only enough to know what transpired. I watched only enough to understand motivations. I would, however, like to share something with you. But it may embarrass you." I am beyond embarrassment at this point. I shrug my shoulders, and Phode takes this as my consent.

"You were very tender and caring when you were with Dariox."

"Why would that embarrass me?"

"You are the highest judge in the Federacy. A lethal military commander from every text I have read about you. *Honorable,* yes. But *tender* and *caring*? That does not seem part of the profile." Phode pulls his feet from the water and gets a towel from the container. If Phode were the premier of the Federacy, and not someone who still thinks of himself as a soldier, some attendant would run over now and wipe his feet.

"After you finished having sex with Dariox, you insisted that you both get dressed. You sat in front of her and took both of her hands in yours and you said that you were sorry for the way you treated her. You said that you now realize she was deserving of citizenship. She broke down crying and you held her in your arms. You then told her something very interesting. You told her about your feelings toward me. You said that I was a man of honor and that she was better served by being a Rogue than a citizen of the Federacy."

Phode dries his feet and puts his shoes on very slowly. He's in no rush. This entire conversation is hard for him. "I thank you for that, Max. There could be no higher compliment than to be told you're an honorable man from another honorable man."

Phode grabs another towel, walks over to me, and sits down. Our shoulders are touching as if we're old friends. I guess we are friends. We both look out through the massive windows in the back of his office. We watch the waves crash over a jetty. He hands me a towel for my feet and I dry them. "I am weaker than I would like to be. Mavy clouds my judgment. It was interesting for me to see your Palmitor results during the Bonding. You were precisely like me when it came for your desire to be with Mavy. You lusted for her, as any man would. But when it came to the actual act, you told her you felt it was wrong. You fought the most powerful drugs we have and told her it was wrong for her, wrong for you, wrong for Nayla, wrong for Emmis, and most of all, wrong for me." Phode takes a huge breath. He gags on the air and looks sick. "As you were having sex with her, you said you didn't want to do it and you didn't understand why you were doing it." Phode fidgets nervously. "The drugs overcame your honorable intentions. The minute you completed the act, you pushed her away and went for a swim. I took that to mean you felt the need to be immediately cleansed of what you thought was a moral transgression."

Phode hands me my shoes. "With Dariox, you were loving and kind. Perhaps you thought you owed her something. With Mavy, you were resistant, guarded, practically unwilling. I am envious of your fortitude. You tried to resist the drugs and her. You never lost your moral direction. You clung to your personal sense of right and wrong. You succumbed because she needed *you* inside of *her*. But you tried, my friend." He waves his hand down and a monitor appears. It plays back a clip of me, highly intoxicated, trying to explain to Mavy why I couldn't be with her—why it was wrong to do that to Phode.

Phode squirms as he plays back the clip. He is jealous of me having sex with her, but also jealous of the fact that if not for the drugs, I could have resisted her. "You have no idea how appreciative I am of the respect you showed me." Phode shakes his head and forces a smile. "I wish I were as strong a man as you."

22

JO-JO A GO-GO

The extraction team trains and meets around the clock in the days leading up to the mission. Kene Yorne and Mavy lead training sessions on the systems interface and communications network between command ops and the air and ground mission. Phode instructs us on how to limit the diplomatic fallout from the operation and what to do if we're captured. He is insistent on us not escalating the conflict and making sure that we limit casualties to a bare minimum. Mavy and I brief the team on contingency plans and optimized countertactical strategies to deal with FTIS improvisational plans. After days of intensive training, I feel ready. I'm ready to get Pique. I'm ready to get her back.

On the night before the operation, the extraction team has an early dinner. Phode, Kene, Trace, and Nayla join us. Trace eats more food than the rest of us combined, and Mavy expresses her repugnance. Phode reminds Mavy that Trace is their guest, and she ignores Phode. At five o'clock, Phode ends the meal and tells all of us to return to our quarters. He orders his team to get a good night's rest for the mission. We will leave one hour before sunrise and will use the cover of night for our extraction and the sunrise for our return.

I haven't spoken to Nayla in days and I feel terrible about it. After a dinner at which she will barely look in my direction, I ask her if I can walk her back to her quarters. She at first says no, but as soon as I tell her I owe her an apology, she agrees. As we walk, I place my hand on her shoulder and say, "I had no right to talk to you the way I did the other day. I'm truly sorry and I hope we can move past this."

She takes my hand off her shoulder and holds it tight. I immediately feel the static electricity from her. She glides her hand over mine and there is an unusual amount of heat. "Thank you, Max. That's all you needed to say." Nayla smiles as her hands continue moving over mine. The heat grows stronger. "Emile told me that you really tried to resist her. I guess that's all I could have wished for. The only problem is that there are still consequences for your actions. Not moral, but practical." I feel a shock of electricity from Nayla and she quickly pulls her hand away. She looks embarrassed and apologizes. I try to ignore the shock, but it stings. "Let's leave our problems for another time," she says. "Let's enjoy what remains of the day. Who knows what tomorrow will bring?"

We walk outside of Rogue headquarters and watch the sun lower itself onto the Pacifiqua. In the orange and purple light of the setting sun, Nayla looks exactly like Emmis. Like her sister, Nayla has giant blue eyes, tanned skin, and a bright uncomplicated smile. Like her sister, Nayla is beautiful. If I could look long enough into the sun, maybe my eyes could be tricked into believing Nayla is actually Emmis. But what Nayla could never understand is that I don't want *someone like Emmis*. I would sooner be with Mavy than Nayla. It's not because Nayla isn't the kind of person I might want to be with, but because she is too much like the person I was meant to be with.

By six o'clock, I am in my quarters. My mind is on Emmis and my kids and it can't be there. I miss them more at this moment than ever before and it hurts like an open wound. I quickly grab one of the books the Holy Father gave me and dive into it. I am no longer looking for answers. I'm pretty sure there are none. I just want my mind to wander so I can sleep. I open the first page of the book. It must have been written many centuries ago. It is in a voice that is very strange to me. It is beyond archaic and I have great difficulty understanding the references. It is written in an early form of English by a person who does not seem educated.

JO-JO A GO-GO

This is my story.

I moved to New York City in 1962 from a small town in Mississippi. I was sixteen. I saw *Breakfast at Tiffany's* one night, and by the next morning, my bags were packed and I was on a Greyhound headed to the big city. I knew there was no life for me in Mississippi. I could hang around and be a pincushion for all those old men's needles or I could go up to New York and reinvent myself. I decided to reinvent myself.

My name is Jo-Jo Rollins, but everyone calls me Jo-Jo a Go-Go. I'm a dancer and a mother. I'm a lot of other things, too.

When you're done reading my story some of you will think I was a hooker. That's okay. It's wrong, but it's okay. People believe what they need to believe. I used my body to get things. That's true. But I slept with men for one reason and one reason alone. I needed to protect my girls. I needed to keep my girls safe. I needed to make them strong. I needed my family to grow.

I've got three little darlings. Regina, Margot, and Lilly. They're the loves of my life. Each one of them is from a different man, but they're closer than peas in a pod.

Each of their fathers had something different we needed. God came to me in a vision one night and told me who I needed and what they needed to give me. Some of it was money and some of it was other stuff. But money was the big one I needed. So, I always took their money. But when I got a really great guy, I took their seed too. I was very selective about the kind of seeds I needed to grow my girls.

With the money I earned, I was able to leave New York City and the go-go dancing behind. In 1973, I took my three girls to Orange County, California. I bought us a house, a house built with money from the men I slept with. Timmy, Regina's papa, paid for the shag carpet. William, Margot's papa, paid for the screen door. Mike, Lilly's papa, paid for the shingles. John, whose baby got aborted, paid for the ceramic tub. You get the idea. Those men bought us a house. My girls' house.

I love those girls and I'd do anything for them. But they know there are a couple of rules they have to follow. They break any of these rules and they break me. They break my spirit.

The Rules of Our House

1. Don't stop having babies until you have a girl.

2. Only let smart men knock you up.

3. Get the seeds and then kick 'em to the curb.

4. Never sell my house.

5. Never take on a man's last name.

23

PIQUE

I wake up ready for the mission. Any thoughts of my family and any doubts I have are pushed aside. At the beginning of any mission, I cast aside all concerns. It's essential to my purpose. There is no room for uncertainty. I am not being overconfident when I say that I will rescue Pique. I am being practical.

I walk briskly toward the helipad where Asio, Dariox, Shifa, and Mavy are waiting for me. Each is dressed in a formfitting one-piece black suit. Phode and Kene stand beside them. Kene hugs his sister good-bye and whispers something in her ear.

I pull Phode aside. "Thank you for making this happen. It's been an honor to work with you. But as you know, from this point on, the command is a hundred percent mine."

"Max, we don't need to say things like this. We're friends." I pull Phode into a hug. It is very uncharacteristic of me and that's all I will say about it.

"Let's go," I shout. Mavy, Shifa, Dariox, and Asio grab hands and start bouncing up and down like it's a warmup before an international gaming match. They bounce and chant, "We are one. We are one. We are one."

We take our places in the helicraft and ready ourselves for launch. Shifa runs through a checklist before takeoff and Mavy and Asio shout back a series of "Check"s. Dariox has only one check. Shifa shouts to her, "Killer!" Dariox turns back to me and smiles. "Check!" Something surges through me when Dariox smiles at me.

I give the command for liftoff and we are sucked straight up into the sky. It is the exact same feeling as when the craft nosedived during the Trial—only now we are going up. "Thirty-eight minutes to touchdown," Mavy shouts. The engines' roar on takeoff is defeaning, and at top liftoff speed, the helicraft's parts are whining loudly. After a few minutes of ascent, we reach crusing altitude and the engines begin to quiet down. Asio swivels her chair to the control board on the side of the craft and begins inserting disks into the jamming slots. At our cruising altitude of ten thousand meters, we hit some strong turbulence. Shifa asks me if we should climb above it and I say no. We deviate from the plan only if absolutely necessary.

A few minutes before we touch down, I unstrap myself and whisper one line to each member of my team. I put my hands firmly on their shoulders and press down on them hard. I want them to feel my weight. I say each of their names slowly. *"Dariox." "Asio." "Mavy." "Shifa."* I want them to own their roles. I want them to understand that I am counting on them. I want them to feel my weight, my reliance on them. While holding their shoulders firmly down, I whisper the Rogues' battle cry in their ears, pausing in between every word. "We will take as one. We will win as one. We will kill as one."

I strap myself in for the final few minutes of flight. The ride is about to get rough. Dariox is busily double-checking each and every motion of her artilleries. Her hands are rapidly moving back and forth among five hand sensors that control the motion and replenishment of her weapons. She is quick and powerful. I'm glad she is the one who will be providing my cover.

"The *big drop* in twenty seconds," Shifa shouts as we are about to initiate the rapid descent. She counts down to one and we drop quickly in between two mountain peaks. The helicraft bobs and weaves its way through the snowy caps. The final approach is particularly dangerous, because we need to move quickly through dangerous terrain, while staying off FTIS radar.

Shifa activates the same boosters that suck up ocean water, and she uses them to bank left and right off the mountains. Snow is blowing everywhere, and the boosters are making visibility challenging, but they are ensuring we don't crash into the mountainsides. At the same time as we are careening off the mountainsides, we are avoiding radar by rapidly ascending and descending at a 2:1 ratio. This is extremely nauseating even for those of us who are battle-tested. My stomach is in my throat one second and my ankles the next.

I hear a loud gurgle from beside me. It's Asio. She's thrown up on the floor. She looks more nervous than the rest of us, and her stomach has gotten the best of her. I grab her shoulder and tell her it will be okay. She reflexively pushes my hand away.

The good news is there's not a peep from Asio's detection monitor. Shifa's movements and Asio's jamming algorithms are keeping us off the FTIS grid.

"Forty-five seconds to touchdown," Shifa shouts. I check my holsters and pack the meylon canisters, masks, and guns. I motion for Mavy to do the same. "It's all good," she shouts back. She places her hand on top of mine. "I need to bring you home, too, Max."

"Sounds like a plan."

Shifa throws the helicraft into a nosedive for the last thousand meters. We are dropping straight down over the detention center at supersonic speed. The anticraft weapons start shooting at us. Red lasers fly through the predawn sky. Shifa banks hard left to avoid them, and Asio falls out of her seat and onto my lap. Shifa then banks hard right and we crash sideways into the detention center. Asio lifts herself up and activates the disjoints. Even through our ear-protection systems, the sound is piercing. Deafening electrical currents and high-frequency pulses storm the detention center, knocking out everything in sight. Out of the windows, I can see physical assets starting to fry and human assets holding their bloodied ears while convulsing on the ground.

"Three minutes—starting now," I shout. Dariox has already started firing as Shifa lowers the helicraft's door. Asio hands me the cartogramic drill and Mavy the register and we both start running. Dariox provides cover for Mavy and me, scouting out anything that will get in our way. She creates a protective shield around us. She is lethal—maybe more lethal than she needs to be. But we are moving fast without obstacles and I can't worry about the other side's casualties.

Within thirty seconds we are at the detention center's seemingly impenetrable wall. I activate the cartogramic drill, and four massive rotating blades erupt out of the nose of the missile-like contraption. With a mind of its own, it begins feverishly drilling. It opens up a hole big enough for Mavy and me to slide down into. We jump in behind it and follow it as it burrows its way down and under the wall. It then immediately changes course and heads up on the other side. We are under the wall and in Pique's detention block in no time. We leave the drill behind and start running again. We follow the beeps of Mavy's register. The frequency of the beeps increases as we get closer. My chronometer goes off at the one-minute mark, and right on cue there is a huge explosion. Shifa and Asio activate the iotium explosives on the south and east sides of the detention center. We hear a lot of screaming. Most of the guards start running toward the injured soldiers. They are shouting about casualties and they seem disoriented.

"How much farther," I shout to Mavy. "Just keep running," she says back. We are both running at full speed. I put my mask on and take out the one we have for Pique. Mavy puts on her own mask, and for some unexplained reason, she has a spare mask in her hand.

I pass by a number of cells with people in them. And then I hear the best sound possible. *"Hey, Your Holiness!* Come back. I'm over here." We ran right past Pique's cell. The register must have been wrong. It says we have another hundred meters to go. I immediately stop and turn back toward Pique, but Mavy, mask in hand, keeps running. I shout at her to stop, but she doesn't listen.

I run back to Pique. Her hands are bound in a thick rubber casing and there are rubber plates covering her head. This must be a mechanism for containing her powers. I pull out a laser and slice through the rubber manacles. We grab hands through the cell. I pull her in close for a hug through the bars. "Are you okay?"

"Couldn't be better!" She pulls off the rubber plates and smiles.

"We don't have a lot of time, Pique, so put this on." I hand her the mask and she places it over her face. I don't know where Mavy went and I don't want to draw extra attention, but I have to let her know I'm activating the meylon. "Mavy," I shout. "Mask on. Activating canisters . . . now." A guard hears me and fires his weapon. I duck, but a projectile hits me in my left shoulder, piercing my protective vest. The explosive doesn't fully detonate, but there are some large shrapnel fragments embedded in my shoulder. The pain is intense, but I can manage it. I pull out my weapon with my good arm and shoot the soldier in between his eyes. There is no blood. A clean shot through the head. I'm sorry I had to kill this boy.

I activate the meylon canisters and they explode into the air, spreading the meylon everywhere. I instantly hear bodies hitting the ground. Guards and prisoners alike are knocked out cold. The hallways are filled with a dark cloud and it's difficult to see.

"Back away from the cell door," I tell Pique. I place an explosive inside the input box and detonate it. The door opens and Pique jumps into my arms. Pique is not one to take orders, so before I can say anything, she says, "Let's get out of this place."

"Not yet. We can't leave Mavy behind."

Mavy comes running up on cue, holding the hand of another prisoner wearing a mask. "Hello, Pique," she says.

There's no time to figure out why Mavy has taken another prisoner, so we all just run down the hallway. There is one guard standing in our way. Mavy quickly shoots his right ankle and he falls to the ground, writhing in pain. He may never walk without a limp again, but Mavy was clearly more conscientious about keeping an enemy soldier alive than I was.

We go back through the same tunnel we came from. We make a mad dash for the helicraft. Dariox again provides a perfectly choreographed cover for us. Asio and Shifa help by detonating explosives along our escape path. We reach the helicraft. I push Pique, Mavy, and the other prisoner ahead of me through the helicraft's doors. I jump in and slam the door behind me. We quickly take off into the sky.

I put my arm around Pique and she scoots into me. I catch my breath. I unstrap my safety harness. I want to put my other arm around her. I exhale and I feel her exhale.

I have Pique.

24

DANG

We climb to thirteen thousand meters and fly at the fastest speed possible. We planned our escape route to be different from our approach so FTIS couldn't anticipate it. We fly slightly out of our way—due west, with an even slightly northerly path, until we hit the Pacifiqua, and then hug the coast as we head south. FTIS radars haven't locked in on us yet, so early signs are that the escape plan is working. With the exception of this wavy-haired boy sitting to the right of me, the mission went according to plan. "Did they hurt you?" I ask Pique. We are both closely watching the boy. "No," Pique says. "I'm fine." She looks at my bleeding shoulder. *"But you don't look so good."* I tell her I'm fine, but she knows that's not true.

"There's a lot I need to tell you, Judge." She turns toward Mavy. "But let's figure out who this guy is first."

Before Mavy answers, the boy nervously says, "I'm nobody. Really. I'm just a writer for the *Omniplex Daily Standard*. I write about celebrity gossip. The inside scoop in the Actors' Guild. I write about the stars. I have no idea why FTIS wanted me."

I ignore him. We are safely at thirteen thousand meters, and for the time being, our detection monitors remain quiet. I stare coldly at Mavy. I get up and walk over to her. I stand in front of her chair. Her eyes stare at my midsection. She does not want to look up at me. I gently cup her chin and lift her face so that she will look at me. "Three questions—yes-or-no answers. Are we clear?" She nods yes.

"Is this man dangerous in any way?"

"No."

"Did Phode or anyone else on this team know of your plans to rescue him?"

"No."

"What's his name?"

"That's not a yes-or-no question." She places her hands on my face. They are warm. The gesture seems honest. So, too, do her answers. "Our God commanded me to rescue this boy."

"You mean your father asked you to compromise my mission so that you could get this boy."

"The Holy Father is the conduit of Our God."

"Please stop talking about your father that way. I'm sick of all this nonsense. The Holy Father hears what he wants to hear and does what he wants to do. He's a man—and like most men he operates according to his own interests." Mavy's face turns red with anger. I feel her hands warming up. Electricity is building on my face and it begins to tingle. Pique's hair stands on end as does mine. For the first time, I realize Mavy has the same power that Pique and Nayla have.

"Mavy," Pique says, feeling the electricity. "Don't forget, I'm sitting right here." Pique is very calm as she says it. "Now take your hands off the judge and put them back at your side." As Mavy drops her hands, Pique smiles. "The judge didn't mean to insult the Holy Father. He just doesn't appreciate being lied to. *And neither do I.*" Pique's anger isn't real. She gives me a wink when Mavy's not looking. "The judge asked you a question. What is this boy's name?"

Mavy does not like being put in her place, especially by a child. But it's clear that Mavy knows how powerful Pique is. Mavy bites hard on her lip. "His name is Dang. Dang Forque."

The name unsettles me and I quickly realize why. "Did you say *Forque*?" I ask.

The boy sits up in his chair. "Yes, my name is Dang Forque."

"Forque," I repeat.

"Yes, Forque. It's an Erabian name. I'm of Erabian descent. *Is that a crime?*

Is that why the Federacy locked me up—because I have ancestors who were Erabian? I'm a Federacy citizen just like you, Judge." Forque turns to Mavy. "Is that why you're kidnapping me?"

"We're not kidnapping you," Mavy says. "You have been summoned by the Holy Father. You are his guest. I am to escort you to Yerusalom for a meeting with His Grace."

"Forque," I ask again. "Like F-O-R-Q-U-E. That's an unusual name."

"Yup," Dang says. He still thinks I'm being racist. "I guess those of you with snowy white skin and rich Anglican roots think Forque is a strange name." He shakes his head in disgust. "What year are you guys living in?"

"Are you somehow related to Saool Forque?"

"Who?"

"Saool Forque?"

"Never heard of him."

"Cecilia Forque?"

"No. What's this all about anyway?"

"It's nothing," I say. He doesn't need to know what I know. "And by the way, Dang, I'm not as snowy white as you think. My ancestors were not Anglicans or early Ameriquans. I'm the furthest thing from a purebred. My forefathers were a lot closer to your forefathers than you think. We both can trace our roots to the Ancients of Yerusalom. Maybe different sides of the wall, but we were one people once. Neither your ancestors nor mine were Anglicans."

There is no point in questioning Dang any further. Saool Forque lived centuries ago, and it's very unlikely Dang would know of him. But it is obvious that the Holy Father believes that this celebrity-gossip writer is somehow important.

And then it hits me. I'm an idiot for not realizing this earlier. *Rollins. Jo-Jo Rollins.* One of the most common Anglican names, so when I first read about Jo-Jo Rollins it didn't occur to me that there might be a line of Rollinses that dates back so many centuries. I thought nothing of it when I read her last name. But Emmis, Nayla, and Pique are Rollinses. They must be the descendants of Jo-Jo Rollins. And Dang Forque must be a descendant of Saool and his daughter Cecilia. This must have something to do with why the Holy Father had me read those books.

"What does your father want with Dang?" I ask Mavy.

"I asked him the very same question. He told me that he will reveal that to me when the time is right. He will reveal God's intentions when the Divine Spirit commands him to do so."

"You mean he will tell you when he wants to tell you," Pique says.

"No, I mean when we are ready to understand his divine intention, we will know. Until then, we must remain patient. Our God is a mystery to most, but there are some individuals who are so deeply interconnected with the spirit of the—"

The detection monitors go off, and Asio's control board starts flashing. We're not out of danger yet. Three Federacy S-class fighter craft enter our airspace from the north, trying to intersect us. The detection monitors blare, and flashing red lights fill the helicraft. We are under attack. Pique whispers in my ear. "At least we don't have to listen to Mavy anymore."

"Secure your restraints, everyone," I shout. "We hard-dive in ten seconds." I tell Shifa to get ready. I want the fighter to catch up to us and then I want Shifa to throw the helicraft into a nosedive heading full-speed to the Pacifiqua. The S-class fighters do not have our maneuverability. They have more specialized firepower and can reach higher speeds and altitudes. But they do not do well climbing out of dives. I'm betting on an ambitious young Federacy pilot who is unwilling to accept his craft's limitation.

I count down from ten and then shout, "Dive."

One of the craft locks in on us just as we start our dive. "Hold the dive," I shout to Shifa. "On my command, break the dive and roll north toward the other two fighters." We're going to crash the first fighter into the water. After we take that one out, we'll head straight toward the other two. This will catch them off guard, because they're taught to believe we'd run. "Get ready, Dariox. You're going to take out the other two fighter crafts on my command. The craft to the east first." I'm hoping that as we fire from east to west, the debris from the first explosion will fill the airspace of the second.

Shifa is focused on her controls. Her job is to draw the fighter toward the Pacifiqua and lift up just before we crash. Dariox's hands are fixed to her firing monitors. Asio is trying to jam the fighter's detection beams. *Dang is throwing up.* He's white as ghost and almost crying. He's absolutely terrified. Any fears I may have that he's military or a threat to us quickly disappear.

I can see the fighter craft diving just above us. It's trembling wildly. I would bet anything the pilot is a young officer who thinks he's better than he is. Unfortunately for him, he's taken the bait. I don't relish the idea of killing yet another Federacy soldier.

"Get ready, Shifa." I wait three long beats. One. Two. Three. "Pull up! Pull up!" Shifa yanks back the controls and the helicraft jerks up into the sky. We narrowly avoid hitting the ocean and fly straight up from where we came. "Roll northeast," I shout. As I say those words, there's a huge explosion. The fighter craft explodes against the Pacifiqua. A ball of fire rises up into the sky, and the craft shatters in thousands of pieces across the water. "Hold your fire, Dariox." I want the enemy pilots focused on the explosion of their fellow pilot, not our firing. I want them to absorb this initial defeat. We wait until I see that the craft have leveled off at a similar altitude to ours. They think we're going to run and they're preparing for a chase. Textbook Air Corps maneuver, especially for junior pilots.

Dariox's focus is intense. I hold back for just a second, admiring her, and then shout, "Now Dariox! Fire!" Her first two shots miss. But she is moving so effortlessly, adjusting to Shifa's diversionary banks left and right. On the third shot, she clips the wing of fighter craft to the east. "I need *an explosion,* Dariox. I need debris." As I say "debris," Dariox has her next shot flying, and it goes straight through the fighter craft's fuselage. The fighter craft bursts into pieces, and flames pour out of its main cabin. Debris flies into the path of other fighter craft, and it banks left to avoid it. The fighter craft just keeps going and going. The pilot doesn't have the stomach to fight. He speeds away from us and I'm glad to let him go.

"Turn south and climb quickly," I tell Shifa. "Lock in on Rogue headquarters." I turn back to the others. "Is everyone okay?"

"Not really," Dang says. His brown skin has turned a pale shade of yellow. There is still some vomit running down his cheek, and his helplessness reminds me of how the drool used to run down Emmis's cheek. I take out a cloth and wipe Dang's face. "You're going to be okay," I tell him. "Just sit tight. We should be on the ground in less than ten minutes."

We have clear sailing for the next few minutes. But just before we are about to make our initial descent into Rogue headquarters, I hear a strange series of pings emanating from the control board. I have never heard a transmission signal like this. "What is it?" I ask Asio.

"I don't think it's much of anything," Asio says. She fidgets with the board and looks nervous. Mavy unstraps herself and walks to the control board. "Let me take a look," she says. Asio initially says no, but Mavy orders her to move aside. It seems that Asio doesn't like being bossed around by Mavy.

"I think it's some type of encrypted official transmission," Mavy says. She is squinting and looking perplexed. "I think this may be from the Federacy." Her eyes relax. "Yes. It looks like it's coming from the Omniplex. Should we take it?"

"Of course we should take it," Pique says. Pique doesn't think in any kind of logical way, but her intuitions seem to be right. Mavy ignores Pique, though, and continues to look at me. I think for a moment about whether there's any danger in taking it and decide the risk is minimal.

Shifa lowers one of the helicraft's monitors, and a bald-headed man immediately appears on the screen. Behind him are two digital flags. One says THE OFFICE OF THE PREMIER and the other says THE FEDERACY. The bald-headed man says, "Good morning, Judge Cone, Ms. Rollins, Ms. Sway, Mr. Forque, and others." The man clears his throat. "Please, all rise, the Premier of the Federacy will now enter the chambers." Dang and I are the only two people to unfasten our seat belts and rise. I'm not sure whether this is habit or I still respect some of what the Federacy stands for. "Please be seated," the Premier says.

The Premier sits behind his writing desk with the two digital flags pulsing behind him. He is a handsome man with high cheekbones, thick silver hair, and intense eyes that appear gray against the black-and-red pulsing flags. Unlike me, he is a purebred and he wears it well. The only other aristocrat in this impromptu conference, Mavy, eyes the screen with great suspicion. "Hello, Pique," the Premier says. "I trust that your kidnappers are treating you well."

"Very well, *Your Greatness.*"

The Premier cracks the smallest smile—undetectable to anyone other than me. "Max, please let me offer my sincere and heartfelt sympathies about your family. Emmis was a true Federate and your children should not have been dragged into this war. Please know that the Federacy had nothing to do with it. No one in any government position was involved. I swear by Our God."

"Lies," Mavy shouts. "Complete and utter lies."

"Mavy, control yourself," I say. "Let the Premier speak. I want to hear what

he has to say." Mavy's outburst was a sign of weakness and not very characteristic of her. I'm surprised.

"We had nothing to do with your family, Max. I would never do anything
to harm you or your loved ones. You know I never supported what happened
to Emmis. But my hands were tied. The procedure was wrong. I'm on record as saying that to you and others. I have always supported you in your
career and I have done whatever I could to make life for you and Emmis as
easy as possible. I considered you a trusted adviser."

The Premier waits for me to respond, but I say nothing. This unnerves him.

"Our relationship may not be salvageable, Max. I understand that. But you
and Pique are in danger. Mr. Forque is in danger. That is the sole reason
I am contacting you. We took Pique and Mr. Forque to protect them, not to
prosecute them. There is something that you don't understand. We were
contacted by—"

The transmission goes cold. It is replaced by static. I don't feel an electric
current in the air, but I immediately assume Mavy is to blame. I look at her
and she simply shrugs. "Get him back on," I say to Asio. She scrambles to
find the transmission frequency, but has no luck.

I look at Pique. "What do you think he was trying to tell us?"

"I have no idea," Pique says. "The only thing I know is that the Federacy
treated me pretty well. I even spoke to the Premier once. All he wanted to
know was if I needed anything."

"Me, too," Dang says. "They treated me great."

I look at Mavy. She's been waiting to talk. "Go ahead," I say to her. I suspect she was the one who ended the Premier's transmission, but I want to
give her a chance to explain.

"You don't want to hear what I have to say." Mavy looks down at the floor.
"You don't trust me and there doesn't seem to be anything I can do about that."
For the first time since I've met her, she looks weak, vulnerable. That boundless confidence of hers has been sucked away—*sucked away by me*. She
knows I don't trust her, and that hurts.

Pique and I sit silently, watching each other as we head back to Rogue headquarters. She has a lot to tell me, and I have a lot of questions to ask. But now
is not the right time, especially with Mavy sitting right next to us. So Pique and
I just look at each other. I know she is okay, and that's enough for now.

25

KENE

The helicraft lands, and Mavy grabs Dang's hand and rushes out the door with him. She doesn't want to be in this craft, *with me,* for another minute. We all follow behind her, except for Shifa and Dariox, who remain to power down the craft's weapons and equipment.

Kene runs up to the craft to greet us. He pumps his fist in the air and begins clapping aggressively. "Flawless! You guys were absolutely flawless!" Kene smiles. "Commander Phode could not be more proud. Come, he's waiting for us in his office and we're going to celebrate." I ask him where Nayla and Trace are, and he says they're waiting in Phode's office.

We follow Kene through the hallways, which are far too quiet. Kene pushes us along, while Asio shows Pique something in one of the rooms off the hallway. "Amazing work, Judge Cone," Kene says. "I can't tell you how impressed I am."

Mavy is the first one to go into Phode's chambers. Dang follows her. Within seconds, I hear a chilling scream. It's Mavy. "No," she screams. Over and over again she screams. "No."

I quickly follow behind. I push open the doors and immediately see what Mavy is screaming about. She is bent over the pool of water. The water is red. There is a body floating in it. I don't have to look at the face to know.

Mavy turns over Phode's body and cries hysterically. She screams, "Emile." Her screams are primitive grunts from deep inside of her. She kneels beside the pool, pounding her fists into the tile until they are bloodied. She drags him from the pool and kisses his lips. I walk over to Phode and check his pulse. Nothing.

Before Mavy and I can stand up, different hands have reached in and removed our weapons. Someone drags Mavy away and quickly binds her hands in rubber manacles and places a rubber restraint around her head.

Kene is staring at me.

"Probably not the celebration you were looking for," Kene says to me. He smiles and points his gun at Mavy's head. "Maybe it's not so much fun for all of you, but it's definitely fun for me." He has ten heavily armed NFF troops behind him, and they're pointing their weapons at me. They all wear the same smile Kene wears. NFF troops are trained in the art of callousness.

Pique pushes open the doors, but stands just outside of Phode's office. It seems as if she does not want to come in. She, too, is bound in rubber manacles. Asio pushes her into the room.

"What the hell is going on," I ask Asio.

"I don't think we owe you an explanation," Asio says. "But some of it's kind of obvious, *don't you think*?"

"There's no reason not to tell them," Kene says. Kene paces in between Phode's dead body and me, but his weapon never leaves Mavy. The NFF soldiers' guns are all pointed at me. "It's not very complicated," Kene says. "I'm loyal to the NFF. I always have been. So has my sister. Our job was to monitor Commander Phode and his staff and report our findings back to the NFF. As you can probably imagine, Chancellor Vrig never fully trusted Commander Phode."

Kene laughs. "Vrig doesn't really trust anyone." Kene's laugh is easy—too easy. He feels too comfortable. I assume this means the NFF is in complete control of Rogue headquarters. I feel a sickening knot in my stomach that hurts almost as much as the pain coming from my wounded shoulder. "As you know all too well, the Rogues and the NFF have always shared a common enemy in the Federacy and we share a common heritage. So my initial mission was to ensure a smooth relationship between both sides and report back any anomalies."

Kene's voice takes on an angrier tone. "But then we find out that the Rogues' esteemed leader, the noble Commander Emile Phode, is nothing more than a puppet for the Holy Father." Kene looks at Mavy with disgust. "We find out that the Holy Father's whore of a daughter is leading Commander Phode around by his cock. And to make matters worse, we find out that our esteemed commander is cozying up with one Maxomillion Cone, one of the highest-ranking officials in our common enemy, the Federacy. We then confirmed early intelligence reports stating that the Holy Father, with the Rogues' support and perhaps even the complicity of the highest judge in the Federacy, is on some crazy holy mission to collect unique individuals with highly specialized powers and pedigrees."

He temporarily points his gun at Pique and Dang and then immediately puts it back on Mavy. "The Holy Father is rounding up freaks of nature like these two. And there's so much more I can tell you. But . . . *I don't want to.* And I know that Chancellor Vrig doesn't like it when I give away too many of our secrets." He walks over to Mavy and presses the gun firmly against her head.

"Oh—and there's just one more thing I think you'd like to know, Judge. I know you have your doubts about your family. I know some small part of you still thinks they're alive." Kene laughs. "I want you to rest assured—they are very much dead." He laughs more. "I know because I'm the one who killed them."

26

ASIO

It takes every ounce of restraint not to charge Kene at that moment. But it would be a certain suicide. And if I'm dead, I can't kill him. I block out any thought of my family. I also try, without much success, to block out the pain shooting through my shoulder. I must stay focused. I need a plan.

I quickly survey the entire room. Phode liked his office bare, and that's not a good thing for my purposes. There are twelve armed hostiles in the room and certainly many more beyond. By the look of the soldiers, they are not specially trained forces or Vrig's Elite Guard. They are regular military, but they are fully equipped. Each one has a handheld weapon and a few microgrenades strapped to his belt. They are probably average in their ability to accurately fire a weapon and probably below average in hand-to-hand combat. I'm familiar with Kene's training. He is quite adept, as is Asio. It will be no easy task taking the soldiers, Kene, and Asio out. But I have no other choice. I'm not talking my way out of this. I need a diversion and some luck.

My eyes scour Phode's office, but the only things I see are the pool, the cushions, the towel container, the retracted monitors, and the display case. It's a wide-open room with few places to find cover. I struggle to block the pain—I can't lose focus. My kids pop into my head, but they can't be there. I keep looking and looking and the only thing that makes sense to me is to make a dash for the display case. If I can knock it over, it will cause a distraction, and if I get lucky, some of the large items on the shelves will hit the soldiers. Then I can run toward one of the soldiers, grab a handheld weapon, or better yet, some microgrenades.

Mavy and Pique are looking at me and they see me searching the room. I subtly nod once and Mavy nods back. She understands I'm about to take a chance and I can use her help. She starts lecturing Kene and he is immediately annoyed. It's clear how much he genuinely despises her. Mavy takes her usual condescending tone, but ratchets it up to get even deeper under Kene's skin.

"My dear sweet, Kene—I know you think you have this grand understanding of the world. You are so wise in so many ways, but to think you comprehend the inner workings of the Nation of Yerusalom or the Rogues is truly foolish. To think you understand all plans, all purposes, and all designs is false pride on your part. You are leaving out a monumental part of this political equation."

"Oh, do tell me, Mavy," Kene says. "This will be the last time you will ever lecture me. So you might as well live it up."

"You are forgetting about the eternal will. The grandeur and mystery in *his plans*. You are forgetting that Our God speaks in a language of destiny and longing for truth. His will manifests itself through aspirations and desires, through evolution and commitment, through destiny and fortitude. Our God does not make his purpose clear to the debased, the depraved, or the debauched." Kene tightens his hand around his weapon. "You are a practical man, Kene. You should know *you're not worthy* of his grand vision. It's foolhardy for you to make assumptions about—"

Kene punches Mavy in the face with his weapon. She crumbles to the floor and a river of blood pours out from a huge gash on her cheek. "That would probably hurt tomorrow if there was a tomorrow in your future." He then mimics Mavy's condescending tone. "But only Our God knows the truth of whether a tomorrow is in your future, *my dear sweet Mavy.*"

Kene looks at Pique and Asio. "Knock the little one out, too," Kene yells to his sister. Asio slowly raises her weapon above her head. She doesn't want to strike a young girl.

"Touch her and you're dead," I say to Asio.

"That's kind of an idle threat given the position you're in."

"You wouldn't want to try me."

Asio smiles at me. I never realized how wicked her smile could be. She licks her lips and says, "You showed me a pretty good time at the Bonding. You surprised me. But I doubt you have any surprises left."

I bend down and bow to Asio. Out of the corner of my eye, I catch a glimpse of Dariox peeking through the doorway. "I'm flattered you enjoyed our time together," I say. The pain in my shoulder is excruciating, but I swallow it down as I get ready to run. "But you know, Asio, I'm a much better fighter than I am a lover." She laughs, and in that instant, I take my chances. I roll to my right as quickly as possible and then hop to my feet. I crouch low to make myself as small as I can. But I'm moving like I have never moved before. Kene's gun is still pointed down toward Mavy, and he is slow to fire at me. Three soldiers fire wildly, but miss. I make it to the display case and duck behind it. I take a deep breath, and with all my might, try to push it over. It doesn't budge. I have to tip it over. On the second push, my adrenaline kicks into overdrive and I get it to topple. The ammunition, plaques, glass orbs, and hundreds of mementos topple toward the NFF soldiers, shattering glass everywhere. I run behind the falling case and reach a soldier who has a huge cut in his leg from a glass orb. I elbow the soldier in the back of his head and his face hits the floor hard. He's out cold. I pull him on top of me for cover and grab a gun and a grenade off his belt. I press the grenade's detonator, wait two clicks, and throw it toward the other NFF soldiers. The grenade explodes, instantly killing four of the soldiers and shearing off the arms and legs of another two. Smoke fills the entire room.

As bullets fly past me, I crawl through the smoke with a gun pointed toward the surviving soldiers. I reach the first one and kick him in his groin. He falls to the floor and I grab the hair on the back of his head and slam his face into the floor. My weapon falls from my hand and I can't find it. I roll quickly to another soldier and immediately take out his legs. We wrestle on the floor. He swings at me and connects with my bad shoulder. I grab his arm as he tries to pull away from me. With my free hand, I pick up a shard of one of the glass orbs and stab it directly into the neck of the soldier. He bleeds out quickly.

I jump to my feet as the last soldier charges me. As the smoke in the room starts to clear, he picks up a piece of metal from the broken case and swings it at me. I duck under it and square off with the soldier. He swings again and this time I grab his arm with one hand and the back of his head with another. I pull his head down into my knee, breaking his nose. I then punch the back of his head, and a piece of skull lodges in between my knuckles. As he falls to the floor unconscious, I grab his weapon. I point the weapon toward Kene, and just as I do, Asio fires a shot at me. She misses. She tries to fire again, but before she can, Pique leaps in the air and—with both feet—kicks Asio in the jaw. I hear a loud snap. Asio's jaw is broken. She falls to the floor, writhing in pain.

Kene sprints toward Pique and grabs her. His weapon is pointed at her head. "Place your weapon on the ground, Judge, or I'll shoot her." I have no choice but to listen. "Now kick it over to me." The instant I kick the weapon toward Kene, Dariox, who has been waiting for the right moment, comes charging through the door. Kene sees Dariox running toward him and throws Pique to the floor. He aims his weapon and fires. He hits Dariox in the stomach. She tumbles over, but has enough forward force to roll toward Kene and take out his knees. She slams into him, reaches up, and grabs his shirt. She drags him to the floor. They struggle for his weapon and it comes free. Dang, who has been hiding behind the fallen display case, runs to the gun and grabs it before I can. Kene raises his hand to strike Dariox.

"Not going to happen," Dang shouts. He points the weapon at Kene. Dang motions for Kene to move away from Dariox. Kene does what Dang says.

"You ever use one of those?" I ask Dang.

"No, but I'm pretty sure I hit this button and he dies."

"You got it," I say. I kneel down next to Dariox. I force a smile as I look into her eyes. I pull her shirt off. It is soaked in blood. I take off my own shirt and press it against Dariox's wound. But it's no use. The blood just keeps coming. There is nothing I can do to stop it. Her stomach is blown apart. I try my best to look calm.

"I don't know, Judge," she says. Tears fill her eyes. She tries to return my halfhearted smile with her own. She reaches for my hand and coughs. It's hard for her to speak. "I don't care what you say." Her smile gains some authenticity. "I think you're a better lover than you are a fighter." I laugh.

"I'm going to get you out of here, Dariox. I just want you to relax." I apply pressure on her stomach, but there's just so much blood pouring out.

Her smile fades. She cries, but in a controlled way. Pique comes over and

I take off her rubber manacles. I wonder if there is something she can do. Can those magical hands of hers help Dariox? I don't have to say anything to Pique. She understands. She just shakes her head no. She looks more like a little girl than ever.

"Just take a deep breath, Dariox. It's going to be okay."

"I'm scared to die. Really scared. But you lying to me doesn't make it any easier." She coughs and blood comes out of her mouth. She shakes. She's terrified. "Just hold me, okay," she says. "Hold me as tight as you can."

I don't know if I held her for a minute or an hour. But at some point I realize Dariox is dead in my arms. The second I realize she's gone, I stand up and walk over to Dang. I grab the gun from him. I sit Kene up, look into his eyes, and put a bullet through his head.

PART IV
THE NFF

27

ANTHER VRIG

I feel a sharp pinch in my arm and the smell of sulfur. A thick saline-based solution escapes from my eyes and pours down my cheeks. They're like tears, but the viscosity is more like engine oil. It's as if my pain has congealed. Shapes slowly start to come into focus. Before I can make out the large outline in front of me, I hear a voice. The voice speaks slowly in a deep authoritative tone with little inflection.

"We have never actually met, Judge. I am Anther Vrig, Chancellor of the NFF." My eyes slowly clear and I see that Pique, Mavy, Dang, and Nayla are strapped to medical gurneys alongside mine. They're unconscious. They're hooked up to hundreds of wires and tubes, which connect to a central unit that pumps different liquids into their bodies.

"You put up a valiant fight. Every intelligence report I've read about you is right. *You are a fighter.* But I had a hundred of my best Elite Guards waiting just outside Phode's office. They were just too much—even for you." Vrig wipes some dust off the top of the central unit that seems to be our life source. "I have some news that may unsettle you. *You've been in a medically induced coma for over six months.*" He taps the top of the unit. "I felt it necessary to keep you asleep during this time. You and your friends were too dangerous to keep awake." The central medical unit beeps, and Vrig hits a button that silences the noise. "Much has happened, and unfortunately, you may find it even more troubling than the fact you've been unconscious for so long.

Before I tell you what's happened in the world, I would like you to keep one important thing in mind—one very important thing. *I could have killed you any time I wanted to.* I could have killed Pique, Dang, Nayla, and Mavy. I killed everyone else. I killed your pilot. I think her name was Shifa. I even killed our spy, Asio. She was very unprofessional. But I have my reasons for wanting you and your friends alive. I even kept your brother-in-law alive for your sake, though I had no choice but to turn him. He's a very susceptible man. In my experience, Abstainers are the easiest to turn, because they have no strong belief system."

I pull at my restraints, but I'm too weak.

"No point in struggling, Judge. You're not going anywhere. We have many things to discuss. Let's agree that we will both keep open minds. Please *never* forget that I could have killed you at any time. I hope that will count for something with you."

"Thank you *so much* for not killing me."

Vrig has no sense of humor. He ignores me. "First off, let me apologize for the behavior of Kene. He and his sister lost their way in the Rogues' camp. The way you found out about your family was highly unprofessional. It's not the way we do things. The NFF is brutal in war. No one would ever dispute that. But there is a reason for our brutality. We want to spread fear to control the population. Telling a man that you massacred his family is poor judgment. Bragging about it is profane. I must apologize on behalf of the NFF. We are brutal, but always with a singular purpose in mind. *Control.* We kill to control people and resources. We're not sadists. We gain no pleasure from inflicting extra pain on those we vanquish. My decision to have your family executed was a calculated one and for that I do not apologize. The desecration of their bodies was after their death and designed to send a message to the Holy Father. Know that I had them summarily executed in a painless manner. They never knew what hit them."

I swallow hard, trying to fight back my tears. I close my eyes in a vain attempt to hold them in, but I can't help what flows down my cheek. It's not that I'm afraid of seeming weak. I just don't want to share my pain with the man who gave the order to kill my family. I will kill Vrig, just as I killed Kene. But it will require patience—lots of it.

"Over the last six months, we launched concerted campaigns to wipe out the little that remained of the Rogues, and more importantly, we took down the major elements inside the Federacy. We were shocked at how quickly the Federacy's military folded once we destroyed the Omniplex, burned down all nearby military installations, and dismantled your Phoenix VOID system. The Federacy was really a house of cards. *It was shocking,* even to me. I should tell you that all the people who ordered the procedure on your wife are now dead. All of those pathetic creatures were on my payroll at one time or another. The decision for the procedure, you should know, was mine. I paid a lot to have Emmis's brain altered. She was too dangerous and too great an asset to the Nation of Yerusalom. I hope you understand, it was just a function of this quirky business I'm in—*war.*" Vrig rubs his forehead and I notice he has no eyebrows. "I am called 'Chancellor,' but this is a clumsy political title. I'm really nothing more than a chief executive of a very large corporation, which happens to be called the NFF. We're a highly sophisticated conglomerate with our hands in a lot of different businesses, the most important of which is the business of war. Our corporate charter is simple: Maximize power, consolidate wealth, and maintain stability. It's all about control. It's a simple mission and one that I adhere to as if it were my religion. For that, I can never apologize."

Vrig sees me pulling at my restraints again. I want to destroy him.

"Please just relax, Judge. I know—*you want to kill me.* You're not the first person. You certainly won't be the last. I get it. You hate me because I killed your family and destroyed your country. Few things could make more sense than that. But there's nothing you can do and you just need to remember that I could have killed you at any time and still can. I can kill all of you." Vrig walks over to Mavy, who is still unconscious. He places his hand on her stomach.

I notice for the first time that Mavy's stomach is huge. He pats her bulge.

"I could have killed your child." Vrig walks away from Mavy. "Yes, Judge. It's yours. We've conducted the DNA tests. But there's so much more to tell you. Our geneticists have learned quite a bit about all of you. I think you're going to be surprised by what they found. We certainly were. *Would you like to take a guess at who else is related?*"

Vrig waits for me to answer. When he realizes I won't play his game, he answers his own question. "These two." He points to Pique and Mavy. He smiles for the first time. "They're half sisters. That's right. The Holy Father is both of their fathers." I say nothing. I just lie there in silence, feeling sick. Pique would never want my sympathy, but the very first thing I feel is sad for her. I understand now why she and the Holy Father had such a strange dynamic. I can't imagine having a worse father—including my own abusive one.

And poor Nayla. I doubt Nayla would willingly be with the Holy Father.

My eyes finally adjust to the light. I can finally make out Vrig clearly. I have seen videos of him in intelligence reports and on the news, but they do not do justice to this man's size. He is almost a head taller than Trace, who has just entered the room, and his forearms are massive clubs. His head is shaven, and in keeping with NFF military traditions, his eyebrow hairs are permanently burned away.

Vrig tells Trace to have a seat right next to Nayla. Trace obediently complies. Vrig pats Trace on the back as he walks by him. Trace doesn't react. "I've been waiting to tell the Holy Father the good news. Can you believe, after all of the children he's had, yours will be the first grandchild? You must be very proud, Judge. You and Mavy will make the Holy Father—that sheep in synthetic skin—very proud. I'm almost jealous. Maybe I should make him proud, too." Vrig slowly makes his way to Pique. He walks over to her. He smiles at me. He puts his hand on Pique's stomach. "Maybe the Holy Father will be proud of me, too."

28

TRACE

A few weeks pass without anyone other than a cleaning attendant and a food service provider coming to my secured quarters. I assume I'm in the NFF's main detention center which is centrally located in the capital and connected to the Fortress of Freedom, the seat of the NFF's government, as well as the Citadel, the chancellor's official residence. Vrig has me staying in a nice room with a bed, a colidor full of premium foods, and a spacious water closet with a privacy door. I have a monitor that plays thousands of programs, but I spend most of my time watching the NFF News Network. This state-run news station is surprisingly open about politics and the NFF government. I can't figure out why Vrig would allow this, other than he genuinely believes in a free press.

The NFF News Network reports on developing stories throughout the world, and most importantly, the new developments in the Federacy. I am surprised by what I learn. It appears that after the initial cleansing, as Vrig calls it, and a brief two-month campaign of state terror, the Federacy fell in line with the NFF's provisional government, and life, more or less, returned to normal. According to the reports, which I'm inclined to believe, the NFF had so many loyalists implanted in the Federacy government that following the war, which was remarkably brief, the transition to a puppet government loyal to the NFF was relatively seamless.

I am of course shaken by what happened in the Federacy, especially the loss of life. But the Federacy has not truly been my country for a long time—not since Emmis's procedure. With what's happened in my life over the last year, it's hard to be anything but numb, and when I'm not numb, I'm mostly just confused. I can't make sense of what's going on in the world or that my wife and kids are really gone. I can't believe that Mavy—a woman I don't really know and one I'm not sure I trust—is pregnant with my child. And I can't believe that the Holy Father is Pique's father or that Nayla may have slept with him. I'm hoping at the very least that Pique came about from artificial means.

After three weeks of limited contact with humans, I hear a knock on my door and someone entering a code to open it. Thankfully it's not the cleaning attendant or food service provider. It's Trace. He tells me that Vrig has asked to see me.

"Vrig must like you," Trace says, as he steps into my room and looks around. "You're in the VIP wing."

I immediately slap Trace across the face and tell him to wake up. I'm hoping I can snap him out of the NFF's brainwashing. "He killed my wife and kids. He killed your sister, your niece, your nephews. He doesn't like me. He's our enemy, you fucking idiot."

Trace looks down as if he's embarrassed. He shows no outward signs of brainwashing. His expressions are just as they always were. His eyes are clear. There is nothing resembling mind control. In almost every way, Trace is Trace. But Vrig did something to him. "I'm sorry, brother," Trace says. "I don't think we see eye-to-eye on this one." Trace opens my room's door to the hallway and holds it open for me. "I'm not here for you to criticize my choices and I'm definitely not here for you to slap me around. I'm here to take you to the Citadel to meet with Vrig. That's it."

I walk behind him toward the Citadel. As we walk, I reach toward Trace and forcefully tap him on the shoulder. He stops walking. "You know I could knock you out right now and escape."

"But you won't."

"And why is that?"

"First off, you wouldn't tell me you're going to knock me out if you were actually about to do it. Second, you're not leaving here without Mavy, Pique, and Nayla. You're probably not leaving here without me either. If I know you,

you'll probably even want to take that Dang kid. With the exception of me—*who's clearly brainwashed*—they're all in medically induced comas. So I don't see you ripping their tubes out and carrying their dead bodies out of here. Third, you and I are brothers. You may give me a quick slap across the face to try to wake me up, but you're not going to knock me out cold. That's not you."

"I think the brother thing is a little overstated based on who you're working for now. Vrig's got you wrapped around his finger. If someone were really my brother, and had my back, they would wake up." I yell directly into Trace's ear. "They would wake up!" I grab the hairs on the back of his neck and pull as hard as I can. "Wake up, Trace! Wake up for Nayla! Wake up for Pique!" This is a standard Federacy deprogramming technique. Pain followed by abrupt exclamations followed by references to family. But it doesn't work with Trace.

"I am more awake than I've ever been." Trace hugs me—and this "new me" that I don't really understand and don't really even like kind of feels close to him. I want him back to normal—*normal* for Trace.

"You're my brother, Max. Really, you are. I would do anything for you. I would do anything for Nayla and Pique. I would never cause any of you harm. I could live without Mavy, and I don't know this Dang kid from a hole in the wall, but just because I support the NFF now, doesn't mean I don't care about my family."

"You realize they brainwashed you, right?"

"I realize something's changed in me. But I wouldn't call it brainwashing. I've been lost for a very long time. I was broken. Something was missing. I've been searching for so long and finding nothing but dead ends. I was a partisan. Then I was a revolutionary. Then I gave it all up and became an Abstainer. Then I gave up even more and tried being a morzium addict." Trace shakes his head. "Nothing worked."

Trace is entirely Trace. He's sad, confused, and full of emotion. This goes against everything I've ever understood about military brainwashing. Trace places his hand on my shoulder. "Nothing worked, Max. I had no real reason for living. I had no meaning in my life." Trace bites the inside of his cheek. "You can call it brainwashing if it makes you happy. But I call it purpose. Vrig gave me a purpose."

"And if that purpose means killing me, or Pique, or your sister?"

"That's not going to happen."

"How about the fact that he made some sick comment about getting Pique pregnant?"

"That's Vrig playing mind games with you. He would never do something like that."

"He killed my kids."

"There's more to that story, Max. I don't know what it is, but trust me on that."

"How can you be so sure of all of this?"

"Because during the months while you were in a coma, I got to know Vrig. I learned what he really wants. My purpose is the same as his purpose."

"Which is what?"

"To pull off the Holy Father's mask and reveal the devil underneath." Trace's smile is filled with confidence. "Vrig wants to prove that the Holy Father is a scam artist and that there is no God. So do I. That is my new purpose in life—to prove there's no God. It's bullshit. There's only one thing in this world that's true. Men are men and they do what's in their own interest." Trace is beaming. He's a true believer. "We need to show the world that the Holy Father is a fake. We need to show everyone that the Nation of Yerusalom is built on lies. We need people to understand that all this *Our God talk* is nonsense. It's the only way the Holy Father can be checked. It's the only way there can be peace among men."

"Vrig doesn't care about peace. He told me himself. He just wants to acquire as much power, money, and land as he can."

"If you think that, you really don't understand Vrig. I'm sorry, Max, but you don't understand everything. You're smart—but in all the wrong ways."

Trace hugs me again. His arms are wrapped tightly around me. As he holds me, he says, "I would never let Vrig hurt anyone I love. You, my sister, Pique. Never. I have a purpose now. I know why I was put on this earth. Brainwashed or not, I've got your back, brother."

Some part of me thinks that Trace is lying about caring about me—that Vrig has him so brainwashed that Trace has become one of the greatest actors of all time. Another part of me, the foolishly optimistic part, thinks that Trace is pretending to be loyal to Vrig in order to trick him. Either way,

I believe that Trace is acting, which, given my instincts of late, is probably totally wrong.

Trace and I walk silently the rest of the way. We arrive at a large sliding titanium door which automatically opens. We pass through a security checkpoint, and with four of Vrig's Elite Guards now following us, we walk through a long corridor with small red lights in the ceiling. Trace tells me that the NFF's central command and its communication monitoring apparatus lies just beyond the corridor's walls. We take a few turns, pass through some more checkpoints, and end up in a waiting room just outside a strange wooden door with a beautifully illustrated axe on it. Above the axe is an unassuming sign that says, "The Citadel of Men." This old-fashioned door has a manual opening mechancism, something similar to a rotational handle. One of the Elite Guards talks into his mouthpiece to ask for approval to enter, and when he receives it, he turns the odd handle to open the door and we enter. I'm shocked by what I see inside. It's an enormous room—the size of the Omniplex's amphitheater. There are towering ceilings and muruals of horrific scenes playing out on the soaring walls. It has the famous *Cryzon Tales* written all over it—*literally*.

The Cryzon Tales is the only book my father ever read to me. This is probably true for millions of children, as it is the most widely read set of fables in the advanced world. Being in this room is absolutely chilling. But it's not because of the images of maimed bodies on the walls. It's because of my father. His ghost haunts me far more than these murals. Like Vrig, my father was a man best defined by his propensity for calculated violence. He would beat me every Tuesday and Thursday, with an especially fierce beating reserved for Sundays after church. I couldn't possibly say why Tuesdays and Thursdays were my *lucky days*, but clearly Sunday was somehow related to going to church. I guess Dad was really moved by our holy pastor. Thankfully my father died before I was old enough to ask him why he chose those days. Thankfully he died before I became a trained killer—because surely I would have ended his life. I felt guilty enough as a child, always wondering what I had done wrong to deserve his beatings. If I killed him, the guilt would have been permanent.

My relationship with my father wasn't all bad and certainly others had it worse. I enjoyed the times when my father read me *The Cryzon Tales*. My father was passionate about reading the stories. He would use a different voice for each character, and at important points in the story he would stand up and act out the scene like a fine stage actor. It was not in his nature to do so, and I think he did it because he really wanted me to absorb the lessons of the Cryzon. In each tale there was an everyman who had a singular human imperfection—a flaw in his character—that seemed mostly innocuous and rarely impacted the life of anyone but the everyman. The everymen were simple fools. But the Cryzon didn't suffer fools gladly.

The Cryzon accentuated their flaws until they grew into full-grown deadly sins. An overeater became a glutton. An excessively shallow simpleton became a vain egomaniac. A lazy learner became a slothful ignoramus. And the Cryzon had no mercy for these flawed everymen. Each had his human wants met—and then some. In "Gratitude Day's Stuffing," the overeater is stuffed with succulent food until his stomach bursts. He dies a slow and excruciatingly painful death. He is then prepared as a delicacy, neatly carved by the Cryzon, and served to others guilty of the same human flaw. The Cryzon throws an all-you-can-eat Gratitude Day feast for unsuspecting overeaters, the most gluttonous of whom will be next year's meal.

On the far wall of the room is a floor-to-ceiling mural of the Cryzon, in a white smock, holding salt in one hand, and a huge carving knife in the other. Beneath him is the butchered body of the glutton. I am not one who appreciates art, but there is something oddly beautiful about this mural. Maybe it's because it's an impeccably detailed replica of the image on the front cover of the collector's edition my father used to read to me, or maybe it's because the craftsmanship is in fact that good. Either way, I am taken in by it.

On each of Vrig's walls is a depiction of human suffering from *The Cryzon Tales*. These enormous murals end at a huge emerald-green dome that spans the entire room. The dome is covered with thousands of silver words that form a mesmerizing pattern. It's hard not get lost in the swirling circles of words. These same silver words repeated over and over and over again. These same silver words replicating themselves into concentric circles that cover the entire dome. These same silver words that turn and turn and turn with no apparent beginning and no apparent end. These same silver words:

To win the Game of the Gods, men only need to know one thing. Gods need men more than men need gods.

Vrig sits in a chair underneath the center of the dome. There is nothing in this massive room Vrig calls the Citadel of Men, other than the one singular, oddly placed chair. I would say it is like his throne, but the chair itself is a no-frills chair that a university student might buy at a neighborhood economy market.

"Please come in, Judge," Vrig says to me. As I approach him, he says, "So, how are you feeling?" He goes to shake my hand and I slap it away. I immediately hear the sounds of mechanized guns moving. Vrig waves up toward the emerald dome, and the sounds stop. He's not scared. He barely reacts to my slapping of his hand.

"You really want to know how I feel, Chancellor. Let's see. Last we spoke, I wanted to kill you. Today, I want to kill you. I'm pretty sure I'll want to kill you tomorrow. So, the most appropriate answer is that I'm feeling the same. I'm feeling like I want to wrap my hands around your neck and choke you until you die."

As I take a step forward, I hear the sounds of the guns moving again. I look up and I see them embedded just above the murals and below the dome. I count at least twelve different guns pointing down at me.

"Sit down, Judge," he says. There's no "please" this time. A teenage boy in a white cloak runs into the room and places a chair across from Vrig's chair. It's a nicer chair than Vrig's, but not by much. "There's no need for threats. I understand you want me dead. You have every right. I'm not going to justify my actions. You wanted your family alive and I wanted them dead. I got my way. Next time, maybe you get your way and I'm dead. This is the kingdom of men we live in."

I refuse to sit down. I decide I will walk around the room until stopped. Surprisingly, no one tries to stop me. But the guns follow me. Vrig sees what I'm doing. He points to my chair, and the teenage boy quickly removes it. "I want to share with you news from the front and make you an offer that I hope you will take." I don't respond to Vrig. I assume we are about to negotiate, and one of the most underutilized forms of negotiation is complete silence.

"We have consolidated our gains," Vrig says. He crosses his legs in a surprisingly effeminate way. I don't point this out to sound sexist or homophobic. I point it out because it's clear to me that this is a tell of some sort. "Artiqua has surrendered, Middle Afrique, the Aziatics, Latvonia—all of the states under the Federacy's influence. There are very few exceptions. I am really surprised by how easy all of this has been. Once the mighty Federacy fell, the rest of the world gave up. So there are only three players of consequence left standing. The NFF, the Nation of Yerusalom, and Kolexico."

I am circling Vrig at this point and following the concentric silver circles on his dome, slowly closing in on him. I like that the guns are following me. It means I control them.

"Kolexico is the key to defeating the Nation of Yerusalom. If we can break Kolexico of its nonconformist ways and have it join the NFF's new order of civilized nations, Yerusalom will be irreparably crippled. The NFF needs to cut off Kolexico's illegal supply of oxygenated and carbonized hydrogen to Yerusalom. Without these supplies, and with my new hydrogen-rich friends in Middle Afrique and Artiqua, Yerusalom will be vulnerable to a marketplace that I now completely control."

"Why don't you just drop a few VOIDs on Kolexico and call it a day. That's pretty much in keeping with the way the NFF operates. Or better yet, skip that step, and drop the VOIDs on Yerusalom."

"For you to say that shows just how little you actually understand me. I have not used a single VOID in this war. I do not indiscriminately kill. I kill for a purpose—always for a purpose." Vrig's face registers his disappointment. He genuinely doesn't understand why I would think this about him. To hammer home his point, he says, "And if I must remind you, the only nation to have ever used a vehicle of immense devastation is your own in your war against your own people in the Penumbra. I don't recall you making a public statement condemning your nation's butchery."

As I close in on Vrig, he calmly continues talking. "Kolexico is not ready to be conquered by an army. It's not organized in a way that can be conquered. It needs to be tamed first—tamed by the right kind of leader. I need someone who is strong, but fair-minded. I need someone who can kill, but can also show compassion. I need someone who can unify them, so that they can be controlled as one entity. I wish I were the right man for the job. But I'm not." He rubs his bald head and smiles. "But you are."

I say nothing.

"This is the reason I kept you alive. I need you. I don't want to hide that fact. *I need you.* I think you're the only candidate for the job. Your military and judicial experience is unmatched. Your reputation for fairness is well known. And maybe the most important part—you're not NFF. You're not Yerusalom and you're not really even the Federacy. You will appear neutral to them. Kolexico's cartel leaders will respect that. One of the cartel leaders, Xylo Borne, is currently on my payroll and my intention is to have you rendezvous with him and use his resources to coordinate a unification strategy. He is extremely powerful, and although I wouldn't want to micromanage your leadership style, I would strongly encourage that you use him and his cartel's economic and military power as a starting point." Vrig stares into my eyes and then his gaze rises up to the words on his dome. He stands and looks at me again. "So . . . what do you think? Will you consider my offer?"

I don't make eye contact. I say nothing.

"If you do this, I will give you anything you want. I'm not negotiating with you. I'm telling you that you can have anything."

I raise my eyes to meet Vrig's stare. There is no expression on my face. I walk out of the room and no one stops me. Trace follows me back to my quarters. I put my arm around Trace as we walk. "You're right, Trace. We are brothers."

29

THE PRETTY SCIENTIST

A week goes by without any contact with Vrig. I know Vrig wants a response about Kolexico, but he needs to show me that he's patient and in control. I play the same game. I don't want him to think I've given Kolexico a lot of thought. But I have. The truth is—I don't have a lot of options given the state of Pique and the others. If I can get everyone to safety in exchange for doing what Vrig asks, I will.

I watch a lot of news during the week. Much of it is focused on the anarchy in Kolexico and the skirmishes between the Nation of Yerusalom and NFF in what used to be the Federacy. For whatever reason, Vrig and the Holy Father have decided not to escalate the war beyond some small battles over hydrocarbon facilities and other strategic locations in the former Federacy.

I'm surprised to find that there is a biopic on the Great Men Channel on the Holy Father that paints him in a very favorable light. The NFF's freedom of information is truly an enigma to me. The Federacy would never have allowed this. There is an extraordinary sequence in the biopic in which the Holy Father first finds Spiro de Yerusalom, known then as Ellee Torquoise. Spiro, who looked more like a girl as a small child than a boy, was living in a brothel in the South Ameriquan city of Save Paul. The footage shows the young Spiro doing a simple magic trick in which a loaf of bread appears out of thin air, then disappears, and then reappears in the hand of the brothel's madam. The Holy Father then takes the bread from the madam, kisses her on the forehead, and proceeds to feed each and every prostitute by hand. He slowly breaks the bread up into small pieces and feeds the prostitutes as if they are infants eating for the first time.

The commentator notes that each of these prostitutes probably carries a terrible disease, but that the Holy Father is either immune to their diseases or that he has so much love to give that he is willing to risk getting infected. The commentator doesn't say which explanation is the more likely, but he makes it seem as though one explanation has to be right and the other wrong.

Vrig eventually summons me. I don't feel as if I have won the waiting game. Instead, I feel as if I lost slightly less than he did. Time is the ally of neither of us. When I arrive at Vrig's Citadel of Men he is sitting in his nondescript throne of a chair reading what looks to be intelligence reports. There are no pleasantries exchanged. He barely even acknowledges that I walked into the room. He seems angry. He motions toward the door, and two gray-haired men and a pretty young woman enter. Each is dressed in a white uniform with silver trim. Vrig introduces them as lead scientists. They appear to be members of the NFF's Science Corps. The Science Corps is infamous in the Federacy—or I should say what used to be the Federacy. It had its own paramilitary groups of secret agents who would abduct senior Federacy scientists and administrative bureaucrats and turn them. Many of these agents were women who had to do little more than smile and offer to buy an old bureaucrat a drink and he was turned.

None of the scientists move forward to shake my hand. They just stand in a straight line and nod when introduced. Vrig motions again and twenty troops in light gray uniforms with charcoal lines across the shoulders quickly march into the room. Each has a bronze nameplate with a number. These are members of Vrig's Elite Guard. The last intelligence report I read—which, given what I now know about the Federacy, may have been grossly wrong—stated that Vrig's Elite Guard numbered around eight thousand. These guards are loyal to Vrig alone. There is a marked distinction between these guards' loyalty to Vrig and their loyalty to the NFF's military apparatus. These guards would fall on a sword for Vrig, but fall on a sword for the NFF only if Vrig commanded it.

If my intelligence reports were right, Vrig maintains loyalty by paying these guards five times as much as the highest-paid official in the NFF, which is

Vrig himself. No one should worry about Vrig's finances, though—his salary isn't where he makes his money. Vrig is one of the wealthiest men in the world.

Although the Elite Guard maintains a rigid hierarchy in strategic decisions, there is complete social equality among the eight thousand guards. Each is known just by his serial number. Prominent family names are discarded and each has a direct personal relationship with Vrig. There are no women. Vrig tried to incorporate women into the ranks of the Elite Guard, but he found that women were incapable of the degree of detached brutality he required of his guards.

The oldest of the Guard members, an ashen-skinned man with hard wrinkles, a white crew cut, and a titanium hoop earring in his right ear, walks over to me. He smiles at me and seems almost friendly. When he smiles, all of his hard wrinkles fold together like the sides of an accordion. He asks me to sit as he gently guides me to a medical chair that was just wheeled into the room by the same teenage boy from the other week. Before I can react, the chair's manacles have automatically locked around my arms and legs and dragged me into a seated position. "Sorry about that, buddy. None of this is going to hurt." He pats me on the back and says, "I'm Major Torne Lau, but everyone calls me Atom because I used to be in charge of the Federacy's decommissioned fissionable materials program. I'm sure you wouldn't remember me, but we met once or twice. I have a lot of respect for you." I immediately do not like Atom. It's not just that he is a defector from the Federacy. Everything about him seems fake.

Without the slightest warning, the pretty female scientist walks over to me and injects a thick salmon-colored liquid into my arm. My lungs quickly feel heavy and my eyes start to twitch. But the feeling quickly fades. The scientist places a metallic patch on my right forearm and left temple, and then does the same to my left forearm and right temple. On each of the patches are tiny robotic caterpillar legs that scour the few millimeters of contact as if looking for treasure.

I'm surprised they're using such an old technology. The Federacy was far ahead in terms of measuring truthfulness. We were always skeptical of these antiquated lie-detector machines. It just goes to show: Technology doesn't win wars. Purpose does.

"This should be very quick," Vrig says to me. "I'm going to ask you a few questions and all that I ask is that you answer them. You can be honest or lie. It ultimately doesn't matter."

"I'm always honest, except when it's strategically unwise."

"Of course that's true for us all. It probably would make sense for you to lie now, but I know that, so you'll probably be honest, but I know that, too, and so you'll be dishonest . . . but I know that . . . and on and on. So, that's why we have the machine. We have modified it in ways that you probably don't know about. The Federacy was using an outdated methodology. The machines you were using were fine. But how it was being used made it ineffective. The scientists could explain it better than me, but basically our machines measure motivations more than honesty. The machine gets to the core: *What are your interests and how genuine do those interests seem?* Honesty and dishonesty are not really the measures. The measure is self-interest. We're measuring the relationships between neurochemicals like dopamine, oxytocin, and endorphins, and electrical pulses. The machine measures your responses to your interests and sees if there is an electro-biochemical alignment in your brain. The assumption underlying this machine is that you are generally a self-interested animal and we can measure biological deviations in that self-interest. Your wife would understand this better than soldiers like you and me."

I would like to kill Vrig for even mentioning my wife, but I don't think his intent is malicious. Vrig is neither a thoughtful man nor a malicious one. I believe him when he says he kills for a purpose. He has a remarkable ability to remain detached from the actions he takes or the people they impact. His motivations are not evil. But that doesn't stop me from wanting to slam his face against the wall and watch as his blood spills out onto the floor.

30

ATOM

The scientists and troops are standing behind me in a semicircle, and I cannot turn to see them. I'm facing only Vrig, who is calmly sitting in his chair with his intelligence reports in his lap. Vrig motions for the scientists to turn on the machine, and it makes a series of loud clicking sounds. I feel all the sensors heating up, and some of the caterpillar legs dig into my arms and suck up blood, while others hunt for information. Vrig sits forward in his chair and asks his first question.

"Let's start with an easy one." He clears his throat for maximum effect. "Would you like to kill me at this moment?"

"Sort of." This is an honest answer and the scientists relay that back to Vrig. I can't kill him now and hope to save the others.

"You need me, now, but you would like to kill me at some point, right?"

"Very much," I say, never losing eye contact with Vrig.

"I appreciate your honesty, Judge." Vrig sits back in his chair, crosses his legs, and looks up at the ceiling above me. I am looking directly into his eyes, but he is looking only at the words on his ceiling.

"Before I ask you the next question, I need you to know that I have no ulterior motive in asking for your help. You have a unique skill set that I need and I am willing to reward that skill set handsomely. There is no motive other than that." He uncrosses his legs, which is almost too obvious a tell, as if he knows I know something. It's really odd to me.

Vrig plays with the papers in his lap. "Now that the NFF is in control of much of the world, I believe that disorder is my nation's number-one enemy. There are two kinds of disorder I worry about. One is where men are allowed to run around like savages thinking there is no law or government above them. *That is Kolexico.* The other is where men are allowed to run around like savages believing in gods and bogeymen. *That is the Nation of Yerusalom.* I need to end both forms of disorder. I need to bring a new order based on the strength of men and the rule of law. I want stability so men can enjoy themselves within the norms of a civilized society. The only incivility will be in meting out punishment for those who *act* like savages or *believe* like savages. We will be brutal, but for a just cause." Vrig clears his throat and says, "Will you help me, Judge?"

Vrig would make a good prosecutor. He obscured his question, innocuously appending it to the end of his speech. I don't pause. Feigning indecision is neither a good negotiation ploy nor helpful in tricking the machines. Wherever possible, my answers need to be short and to the point.

"Yes," I say. I leave no room for doubt. I can't see what the scientists behind me are doing, but Vrig lets out a small smile. The first I've seen since meeting him.

"And your motivation for helping me is *what*?"

"To save the people I care about."

"So, in exchange for saving the people you care about, you will work with me to bring order to Kolexico?"

"Yes."

"*You*, Max Cone, formerly the highest judge in the Federacy, will work with *me*, Anther Vrig, Chancellor of your former enemy, the NFF?"

"I said yes." I pretend I am annoyed at being asked the same question again. I hope my fake anger will throw the machines off.

"You will use your every effort to bring order to Kolexico."

"I'm a soldier and a judge," I say. "I believe in order. That's what I've been dedicated to for all the years of my service. It's who I am. There's no place for chaos in a civilized society. That's what I stood for as a judge and that's what the Federacy stood for." I want to distract Vrig. He despises the Federacy. It works.

"I believe you stood for that, but the Federacy stood for nothing because it was weak and placed false gods above men. That's why your Omniplex was filled with hypocrites, liars, and turncoats. But we can debate that some other time." Vrig, of course, is not totally wrong.

He stands from his seat and moves behind his chair. He places his hands on the top of the chair and lifts his body so that he is standing up straight. "So, what would you do to end the chaos?"

"I don't know, but you seem to think I'll know what to do. I will leave it at that." I hear the scientists mumble something, and it seems the machines do not think I'm being forthright. The machines are right.

"It's not just me that thinks you're especially well suited to lead," Vrig says. "The Holy Father clearly shares my assessment. That's why he had his top man, Spiro de Yerusalom, take you. He doesn't use Spiro for just any task. So, like me, the Holy Father sees you as a leader with unparalleled skills of force and judgment. *That's what started this whole adventure of yours.* The Holy Father thinks he needs you. And if that's what he thinks, then it must mean that one of his precious Palmitors whispered something into his ear or yours. I can only imagine what you saw in that Palmitor." Vrig looks at my face and notices that I'm surprised. I had no idea he knew about the Palmitor. "I know the Holy Father wanted to show you something."

I pause for a second, which is not good in terms of the machines. I'm not sure what to say. A vague truth seems like my best option.

"Yes, I had a Palmitor, but it wasn't the Holy Father who gave it to me."

"Trust me, he gave you that Palmitor. Whether you or the messenger who gave it to you knows it, it was the Holy Father's will. He controls all the Palmitors. If a Palmitor goes somewhere, it's with his permission." Vrig walks to the front of his chair, and before he sits down again, he smiles at the pretty female scientist. The smile suggests something more than just a professional relationship. I would like to think I could use this to my advantage, but I don't think Vrig really cares enough about any person for it to matter.

Vrig motions for everyone to leave the room and tells the gunmen above to stand down. His Elite Guards exit quickly and the scientists follow. Before exiting, the pretty scientist turns to Vrig and asks him if he's sure she shouldn't stay to monitor the machine. Vrig's cheeks fill with color and he says that it won't be necessary. She leaves slowly and he closely watches her as she walks out of the room. Atom is the only one who remains.

When everyone has left, Vrig motions for Atom to undo my straps and take me off the machine. He quickly undoes the manacles, but before he yanks the probes off he says, "Sorry, buddy, but this is going to sting a little." The tiny caterpillar arms have burrowed into my skin and it hurts when Atom pulls them out. It feels like being stung by a dozen bees.

Vrig slowly makes his way over to me and we are both awkwardly standing a few feet from each other. "What do you want, Judge?"

"Do you mean in exchange for going to Kolexico?"

"Yes. If you can't tell, I'm not a patient man. I do not enjoy the fine art of negotiation. I need you to be content with the deal we strike. So, what do you want?"

"It's simple—you take everyone out of their comas and allow them to come with me to Kolexico. Trace, too."

Vrig thinks for a moment. "You must leave me some form of security. At least one person must remain behind so I know your intentions are true." I knew he would say this.

"Fine," I say. I feel bad about what I'm about to say next, but I have to be decisive. "Dang. You can keep Dang."

Vrig laughs at me. I didn't know he was capable of laughter. "I don't think Dang is the one you should leave behind. But if that's your choice, we have a deal." Vrig smiles. "I've just made the deal of the century. I understand the personal reasons why you might feel like you need to take Mavy. But if I were leaving behind a person, it certainly wouldn't be Dang. The Holy Father wants Dang for a reason. So should you. In all honesty, Nayla or Trace would be the wiser choice. But if Dang's your choice, we have a deal."

Atom whispers something in Vrig's ear. Vrig tells him no and continues talking.

"You have the right to save anyone you want, Judge. But I think you should be very cautious about some of the people you've surrounded yourself with. Mavy is, and always will be, loyal to her father. You can get her pregnant, maybe even marry her, but she will always be his. Phode knew this. Mavy can't be trusted. I'm sure you also know that you can never trust an Abstainer. By their very nature, people like Nayla and Trace, maybe Pique, too, have no real convictions. They have no real loyalties. I just hope you are able to exercise better judgment when you're working for me. I know with the deaths of your family, things have been hard for you. I knew that when I killed—"

The minute Vrig says the word "killed" I lunge toward him and crack him in the face with my closed fist. He falls back and I jump on top of him, pummeling his face. Atom is quick to jump on me but the old man is not strong enough to do any damage. I quickly push Atom aside and he calls for help. In an instant, I hear a series of loud clicks, and ten red beams are on my head and chest. Over the intercom a soldier says, "Back away from the Chancellor." I punch Vrig one more time in the face, and blood spurts out from under his eye. By the time I step away from him, my blood-covered fists dripping with satisfaction, I have guards pulling me down to the floor and placing manacles on me.

"Easy everyone," Vrig says. He stands up quickly. "I'm fine." There is not an ounce of anger in Vrig, at least not any that I can detect. Atom hands him a cloth and Vrig wipes the blood from under his eye. "The next time you do that, Judge, I will have you killed. No questions asked. You will be dead." Vrig wipes away the blood and places the cloth in his pocket. "Unfortunately, you will need to come to terms with the fact that I, as the leader of a great nation, ordered the execution of your family. It was not personal. Not in the least bit. I have tremendous respect for your accomplishments, as well as your wife's."

Although Vrig rarely speaks with much emotion, his voice becomes even more robotic than usual. "As you probably know, about twelve years ago, my family was killed in an explosion. It could have been the Federacy, the Rogues, a Kolexico cartel, or maybe even the Holy Father. We were never able to determine who did it. I was despondent at first, but then I realized that revenge was not something I could afford to focus on. I gave the order to kill your family. It was a strategic political decision. Your family—Emmis and your shared lineage—would have been a key asset to the Holy Father. I could not let him have this. History will prove that your family's sacrifice was warranted." I struggle to break off my manacles, but they only dig deeper into my wrists. Atom tells me to calm down.

As the guards pin me to the floor, Vrig slowly walks up to me. He hovers over me and says, "It was not an easy decision to kill them, just as my decision to keep you alive is not an easy one." Vrig gently moves the soldiers aside and pulls me up by my arms. "You are a calculated risk, one I hope you will not make me regret."

Once again Vrig orders everyone out except for Atom. Vrig points up to the gunmen and gives a series of signals with his hands. The result is a single red light fixed on my head. "You don't understand how dangerous the Holy Father is," Vrig says. "The Holy Father is an irrational man with a very dangerous view of how the world needs to change. I don't know for sure what his plan is, but he's making a concerted effort to accumulate human assets. For decades, he's been going around impregnating unique women to create a superior generation of individuals. He slept with Nayla because of her unique talents. I wouldn't be surprised if he slept with Emmis." I lunge at him, but my restraints hold me back. He is safely out of striking distance. He doesn't react. He just keeps talking. "If I were you, I would wonder if your children are truly yours." I lunge again and the result is no better. "Did your children have blue eyes like the Holy Father's?" He looks closely into my eyes to see their color and then raises his burnt eyebrows in a mocking manner.

"Did you know that the Holy Father is writing a new chapter in the Book of Our God called 'Genetisis'? No one in the history of humankind has dared to write a new chapter to the Book of Our God. The hubris of this man."

"You've got to give it him," Atom says. "The Holy Father's got balls."

"I'm troubled by the Holy Father's actions," Vrig says. "I have some disturbing intelligence about Spiro de Yerusalom, too. My greatest fear is that they want to burn it all down and start again with some kind of superior race of people they choose. That's not good for me. That's not good for you, Judge. We are men of reason."

"Well, if Pique and Dang are part of this superior race, then why don't you just kill them?"

"You, too, Judge—don't forget that the Holy Father thinks you're a special breed. So you're right to suggest that I may have to kill the lot of you. But for now, I believe you are an asset to me. I'm questioning that the more we speak. But I still believe that we, as men of reason, can work together to contain the spread of irrationalism."

"Listen, Judge," Atom says. "You and the Chancellor need to make a deal, and you need to do it soon. You need to understand that the Chancellor's got it right, and the Holy Father's got it wrong. Gods, heavens, all this lovey-dovey scripture—it's all crap. People need to know what they can do and what they can't. That's all. What goes on inside their heads or inside their bedrooms, we don't care. In the NFF, we don't give a rat's ass if some guy wants to worship a lizard god or walks around town in nothing but frilly pink underwear. It's not our business. The NFF is in place to keep order. We're not in the business of moralizing or micromanaging people's lives. People are free and we make sure they're free by enforcing the rules and ensuring stability. *It's a good little system.*" Atom's wrinkles fold into each other as he smiles, and his eyes disappear. I'm looking only at the folds of skin. "You know I'm right," Atom says, as he slowly makes his way to me and pats me on the back. "*It's a good little system.*"

31

GUARD 512

Atom, the pretty female scientist, and one of Vrig's Elite Guards, who wears a bronze nameplate with the serial number 512 on it, walk me back to my quarters. It seems like I must be handcuffed at all times now, but no one is holding my arms. Atom gently nudges me into my room and tells the guard something that I don't understand. It almost sounds like another language. Atom guides me over to the bed, and the female scientist removes my shoes. She then takes out a needle, sticks me with it, and I quickly fall asleep. I dream of Pique playing with my kids.

I wake up and I'm not sure exactly how long I've been out, but I soon realize that it's been almost a full day. My monitor is on and it is tuned to a station called the Alike Network. The logo in the bottom right corner of the screen is two men holding hands. On the screen, there is a man wearing a tuxedo, but he is naked from the waist down. The camera focuses in for an extreme close-up on his erect not-so-private part. It is decorated like a one-eyed clown. It has a curly blue wig, a tiny red clown nose, an animated mouth, and its hole serves as a Cyclopic eye. The monitor has a split screen, and on the other screen there are two people on lower platforms, their backs—or I should say backsides—facing the camera. They wear white coats, but they too are naked from the waist down. The camera focuses in on their backsides, which are connected to two wobbly springs, each with a fake eyeball on the end. Just above the wobbly eyeballs of the man on the far left is graffiti text saying *Claimant: Hyron Meagar.* On the backside of the man on the far right is a similar graffiti-style text saying *Defendant: Pinta Vien.*

The music becomes very dramatic, similar to the acoustical arrangements in a Federacy initiation proceeding. The camera closes in on the talking clown's *mouth*. "Court will come to order. I'm Judge Jimmy." The clown's mouth is animatronically rigged and it moves as if Judge Jimmy is speaking with great passion and eloquence. A bright white light shines on the character as he says, "Welcome to another night of *Clash of the Queens.* Tonight's clash stars former lovers Hyron Meager and Pinta Vien. What started as a steamy romance blossomed into an avant-garde creative partnership. From hot sweaty nights and oiled-up queen bodies to late-night discussions over staging, lighting, and dialogue. Of course none of you have ever heard of Mr. Meager or Mr. Vien. But they thought they were going to be the next great playwrights—another Dyon and Green, if you will. They dreamed of harnessing the power of their passionate romantic partnership and becoming the creative darlings of the NFF. They had no money, and to be brutally frank, no real talent to speak of. But they had grit and determination. They couldn't afford to purchase a well-written play and they didn't have the talent to write their own. But as fortune would have it, they stumbled across an obscure book and fell in love with it. Ironically, they fell more in love with the book than each other. The jealousy was intense. As each came to interpret the book in different lights, the romance, as well as the creative endeavor, began to unravel." The camera dramatically moves away from Judge Jimmy and heads toward a table with a book on it. "I would like to call your attention to Exhibit One," Judge Jimmy says. There is an overconfident SFX as the camera closes in for a tight shot on the book's cover. Judge Jimmy takes a deep breath and says, *"Electric Gods and Other Love Stories."* There is a slow fade to black as Judge Jimmy says, "And now a brief word from our—"

Guard 512 knocks on my door and announces himself. I don't have time to process the fact that this strange channel is showing an obscure book that the Holy Father wanted me to read. I don't understand how this book could be on the monitor just as I am waking up from a medically induced daylong nap. It makes no sense and although *coincidence* is the most rational explanation, it's not my first choice.

512 knocks on the door again, but before I can answer, he has entered the

code and walked into my quarters. He confidently walks into my room as if he owns it.

"You should really wait to be invited in," I say.

"Maybe next time."

The guard, who is tall and thin and beginning to lose his hair prematurely, quickly kneels down by my bed and then crawls underneath it. He comes out the other side and scoots along the wall, pressed tightly against it. He points to the corner of my room by the bed. I never noticed it before, because of the way it's embedded into the corner of two adjoining walls, but there's a tiny hidden camera. The guard is pressed up against the wall, underneath the camera, in order to avoid being detected. He then reaches up and twists a small wire behind the camera. He quickly pulls out a radio and says, "Detainee Cone's security camera is down. Permission to move detainee to a wired location." There's a long pause, and then "Granted" comes over the line. There's an even longer pause as the guard waits patiently for further instructions. I hear people talking over the line. "Transport detainee to the Watering Hole. Atom would like to meet him there."

"Let's go," the guard, who tells me to call him "512," says. "Atom wants to see you."

"Where are we going?"

"Please come with me, Judge."

"I'm not sure I want to go."

"You should," he says. He reaches for my shoulder and moves close to whisper in my ear. "Did you ever have a gut feeling that someone you just met is about to help you?"

"Not really."

"Well now would be a good time." He opens the door. "At the very least you can have a drink with Atom. Let's go."

I follow 512 out the door and into the hallway. We walk through a few corridors in the detention center and then through two security checkpoints. We enter a lobby with large NFF flags on the wall and then walk across a guarded indoor plaza with two more security checkpoints. After a few hundred meters, I see a huge neon sign ahead that says THE WATERING HOLE. As we get close I notice that there are five evenly spaced doors, each with a monitor over it. Each monitor says something different:

GAY   STRAIGHT   BISEXUAL
TRANSGENDER   NON-IDENTIFIED

The monitors have numbers next to them, which I assume are the numbers of people in those sections of the drinking establishment at the time. The numbers are constantly changing as people enter and leave. There is a window on the second floor above each door, and each window has a naked person dancing. They are looking at the people below and waving for them to come into their part of the drinking house. I wonder if the former citizens of the Federacy have abandoned all the Old Morals and dived headfirst into this NFF lifestyle. When your conquerors bring with them unrestricted access to sex, drugs, and alcohol, it probably makes the conquest a little more palatable.

As I stare at a stick-thin woman who is caressing her artificially inflated breasts, and begging me with her similarly inflated backside to come in, Atom walks up to me. He greets me with a firm handshake. Atom is an older man, but he still can project power and a sense of authority. Atom pushes me and 512 through the STRAIGHT door. He turns to 512 and says, "I can't remember what you like, but the judge and I are Federacy boys. We only go for the women."

Atom walks us to a crowded section of the bar, and has us sit right in front of the music's speakers. The speakers are blaring and I feel their sound waves pounding against my body. I can barely hear a thing other than the thumping of music.

"Maybe we can sit somewhere a little less noisy," I shout over the music. Atom and the guard shake their heads at the same time. I understand.

We are sitting at a huge glass and polypropylene bar with bright red-tinted lighting. The DJ, a topless girl with purple-spiked hair and tattoos all over her face, is only a few meters away. To our right, there is a completely naked pregnant dancer who hangs upside down from a trapeze. I order a three-year-old synthetic scotch that is infused with Moya berries. 512 orders a double blue agave over ice. Atom orders a real scotch and gives me a hard time for ordering the fake stuff. The metaphor of me being fake and him being real is lost on neither of us.

The bartender serves our drinks. I stare at my glass and I can't help but think about Emmis and the kids. During my last few years as a judge, I would go to a bar every Friday before going home. I always felt guilty about doing it, but apparently not enough to stop me. I felt I needed it, maybe even deserved it. At the bar, I would fiddle with my drink and think nonstop about my family. The irony was that I could have just bypassed the bar and gone home to be with them. The irony now is that I cannot.

I swirl the synthetic scotch across the cubes and watch as the berry's blue hues change from dark to light. For the first few sips, I allow myself to think my family is alive. I shouldn't. But I do.

Atom is eyeing the bartender while slowly sipping his scotch. I motion to her to order another and Atom gently grabs my arm to stop me. I pull it away. "One drink is enough, Judge. You're going to need to stay sharp tonight."

"I don't know why," I say to Atom. "But I just don't like you."

"It's probably because you've grown stupid. Everyone used to say that Judge Max Cone was this great judge of character. That's what I believed when I was a citizen of the Federacy. You decided who was in and who was out. We were all supposed to be so impressed with you. But now, you wouldn't know a friend if they plopped right down next to you at a bar."

"I doubt you're a friend and I don't believe a word you say."

"Maybe that's because some part of you realizes I'm here to help you. You probably don't want that. Based on what I've seen, with you attacking Vrig, I think you've got a death wish. I think you're done living. You don't bear the slightest resemblance to the commander of the Federate Forces that I remember." Atom shakes his head in disgust. "Your judgment sucks lately."

Atom takes a sip of his drink. "I need you to stop acting like an amateur and start acting like the man we all know you are. There's no way the Max Cone I remember would have attacked Vrig in his own headquarters. The judge I know would have kept his cards hidden and waited to make the right move."

"You don't know me."

"Actually I do. I've been watching you for years and let me tell you—you're acting very out of character. You're lucky to be alive. I can tell you one thing: Vrig won't let you live much longer. He may act like it was nothing, *but it wasn't nothing.* When you attacked him, you wrote your death sentence. Vrig pretends to be above it all, but he's not. He can be vengeful like anyone else and you don't slap around a man like Vrig, especially in front of his troops, and get away with it. That's why you forced my hand, Judge. That's why I'm here talking to you today, instead of a few months from now, like I originally planned." Atom's face shows his frustration. "Damn it, Judge. That was so stupid of you to attack him. I've got a lot of blood and sweat invested in you." He downs his drink in one gulp and then slams the glass back onto the bar. "You've put us in a really terrible position. You're acting like a complete moron!"

"I could end your life right now," I say to him. "With one blow, I could kill you."

"That's great, Judge. Congratulations. Kill me. *The smart decisions keep coming and coming.*" Atom shakes his head. "Your brain has become so useless that now you just jump to violence at the drop of a hat. I can't believe you're the person I'm supposed to protect."

"Protect me. *You're going to protect me.* I should end your life right now, you miserable traitor."

"*Traitor?* You're calling me a traitor? Do you not understand what's going on here? You've lost your mind." I cannot see Atom's eyes. His face is contorted into a series of angry wrinkles.

"I'm warning you."

"*Can't think your way through a problem anymore*—well, why not just beat the hell out of it. Like I said, your judgment sucks lately."

"Who do you think you're—"

512 jumps in between Atom and me. "This is not going to be about whose prick is bigger. We've all got a lot at stake. So let's get to it, Atom. And most respectfully, Judge, please keep quiet while he talks. We don't have a lot of time." Both Atom and I shoot angry looks at 512. But we take his advice.

"Fine, I'm just going to come right out with," Atom says. "I work for Emmis." He chokes up a little and says, "*Worked* for Emmis." He lowers his head. "At first, we worked together on the Palmitor. I provided all the fissionable materials and the working knowledge of how to use them for what she needed. I was her collaborator and confidant. She was like a daughter to me."

Atom has trouble going on. He says, "Fuck it," and reaches into the bar and grabs a bottle of scotch and pours a drink for both of us. He takes a big gulp. "Emmis knew that the Federacy was on to her and wouldn't allow her research to continue. She understood that her work, and maybe even her life, would be coming to an end. So, right before they performed that fucking procedure, she made me promise her something. She made me promise that I would help you. She made me promise that I would protect you. She saw something in you—more than you just being her husband. The Palmitor showed her something incredible. It showed you becoming the leader of a pan-national military force that defeats the NFF and its allies and forges a lasting peace with the Nation of Yerusalom. But she couldn't tell you that. If you thought this was going to happen, it would affect your behavior, which probably would make it less likely to happen. She also saw you getting captured one day, although the Palmitor was unclear about who your captor would be. She worried it might be the NFF. So I ended up with Vrig because Emmis thought that would be the best way to protect you and help you achieve what the Palmitor saw for you. Emmis had contacts inside the NFF's Science Corps and she arranged for me to be abducted by their agents. Emmis wanted me on the inside of the NFF so I would be here to help you one day." Atom smiles and his eyes disappear. "Well, here I am."

"This is just too convenient. I'm finding this hard to believe."

"It doesn't get any easier to believe from here. Palmitors are peculiar little machines, but Emmis believed in them and so I believe in them. Emmis thought that in the right hands—and by 'right hands' she meant *your hands*— the Palmitors would save the world. She said that the day would come when you would restart the world with them. That's exactly what she said: you would restart the world. She said when the time came you would know exactly what to do."

"I have no idea what she was talking about."

"Can you think of anyone who might?"

Pique immediately jumps into my head, but I quickly say no. Just as Atom is about to ask me another question, 512 gets a call on his radio. "Come in, 512." 512 pulls out the radio. The voice on the other end says, "Vrig wants to see the detainee and Atom at nineteen hundred hours in the Citadel of Men."

"Copy that," 512 says. "We'll be there." 512 turns to Atom and says, "You think they know?"

"I don't know. But I'm not waiting to find out. We have to get the judge and the others out of here." Atom turns to me. "How about you have a little faith in me? And if not me—have a little faith in Emmis."

It's hard to have faith in Emmis. She lied to me about so many things. I don't know where her lies end or where the truth begins. But Atom said one thing that made sense. Vrig won't let me live much longer. So, for that reason alone, I tell Atom I'm in.

32

JENELINE

Atom and 512 tell me we have to go right now. I don't trust Atom, but I would rather gamble on him than play my cards out with Vrig. I attacked Vrig. I attacked him in *his Citadel* in front of *his men*. Atom is right. It was stupid and it likely sealed my death. But it felt really good at the time and few things feel that good these days.

We walk quickly to the exit of the bar and head through a series of back alleyways. As we pick up our pace, I start firing questions at Atom and 512. "How many people do we have?"

"There's you, me, 512, that pretty scientist Vrig has been chasing, and another guy."

"Can someone get Pique and the others out of their comas?"

"512 should know what to do. He's been watching surveillance tapes of the medical teams monitoring your friends. He could've used a few more weeks, but thanks to you, he'll have to be ready. You'll have to keep in mind though that they'll be weak and may not be able to walk. But getting them out of the coma shouldn't be too hard. Once you and 512 get them out, you'll have to find some ground transportation and head to the NFF's Airbase Nine, which is just outside the capital. It's a small mixed-used base which is primarily used for the delivery of military and civilian supplies. There's not a strong military presence. It's basically an airstrip and a few transports. I will have an airship waiting and ready to go. 512 has all the details."

We turn another corner and enter a dark tunnel. We are splashing through dirty water on the tunnel's floor. The tunnel descends into the ground, and at the bottom is a door. 512 enters a code and the door opens. The hallway beyond the door is even darker than the tunnel. Atom enters first, followed by 512. I cautiously take a few steps in. But then I hear footsteps charging toward me. They're moving quickly. Atom and 512 don't react at all. The shadow runs right past them and bolts toward me. I brace myself for a fight. It's too dark to make out the person's face, but it's a man, a large man. I crouch down as he picks up speed. His arms are wide open and he's sprinting toward me. I go in low and tackle him to the ground. I get on top of him, but he throws his arms around me. He moves his head close to my forehead. I think he is about to head-butt me, but instead he plants a kiss right in the middle of my forehead. "Surprise," he shouts. He quickly kisses me again and again. "You know, you didn't have to tackle me, Max. It hurt."

"What the hell are you doing, Trace."

"I told you—*I got your back.* I had you fooled, *didn't I*? No one ever has faith in the morzium addict. Big mistake, brother. I had you fooled, and more importantly, I had Vrig eating out of my hand." We both stand, and Trace smacks me on my backside. His white teeth shine through the dark. "You really suck, Max."

"I know I do." I hug him. "I will never doubt you again."

"Yeah, you will. But then I'll just remind you how I managed to keep you and everyone alive for six months and figured out that Atom was working against Vrig. We don't have enough time for me to tell you everything I did. But just trust me on this, I was pretty damn awesome."

"He was," 512 says. "For a guy with no formal military training, Trace was impressive. He orchestrated this whole thing."

Trace, Atom, and 512 switch off telling me different parts of their escape plan. Atom tells me that the scientist—whose name I learn is Jeneline—is on her way to Vrig's residence now and she is going to distract him. I was only partially right about Vrig's relationship with her. Vrig has been trying to sleep with Jeneline for months, but Jeneline, a trained former Federacy spy that Atom recruited, has played the cat-and-mouse game perfectly. Vrig is obsessed with her and she is in the process of making him believe that tonight is the night. It's one of the oldest tricks in the espionage playbook, but it still works.

Atom is going to detonate some small explosives laced with fissionable materials. The radiation will be no more harmful to an individual than a medical resonance test, but the bombs will be detonated near the most sensitive of the military's radiation monitors. The monitors will go off and that will cause an immediate shutdown of every major military facility in the NFF capital. Elite Guards and regular military units will be locked down in their radiation bunkers, and by the time they all find their gear and get it on, we'll be long gone. While Atom sets off the explosives, 512, Trace, and I will take out any Elite Guards or regular military guarding Pique and the others and rescue them.

Atom and 512 go over a map of the inside of the medical facility where Pique and the others are kept. There are only two main ways in and out—the front entranceway and the back emergency exit. So there isn't much to think about. We all synchronize our chronometers. "Jeneline will have Vrig drunk and in bed by eighteen hundred hours," Atom says. "The fissionable explosion occurs at eighteen fifteen. By eighteen seventeen, all the radiation monitors should be activated, and the military personnel guarding Pique and the others should be running toward radiation shelters and scrambling to find gear. They are not well trained for this kind of event, so it should be chaos. Hopefully we don't need to fire a lot of shots and bring attention to ourselves. If you can get in and out without firing a shot—that would be best."

Atom comes over to me and asks me if he can have a word in private. He sits down and rubs a few days of stubble. He wants to tell me something, but the words won't come out. He pulls at the hoop in his ear and takes a deep breath. Eventually he gets up the courage to talk. His voice is soft. "Viole," he says, before stopping. "One day Emmis brought your daughter to work. Maybe she was two at the time. Those gorgeous chubby cheeks and that funny way she laughed. She's what I imagined Emmis must have been like as a child. Viole had those huge eyes that just wanted to devour everything she saw. She was picking up books on the shelves and pretending to read them. She even licked her finger as she turned the pages. She was this little fireball of energy and curiosity and hope." He moves his hand across the top of his crew cut and then slides it down to wipe a tear from his eye. "Someday, I'm going to ram a VOID so far up Vrig's ass he won't know what hit him. You have my word, Judge. I will kill Vrig for what he did to Emmis and that little girl of yours. I need you to know I had no idea that he was capable of that kind of brutality. If I knew, I would have broken my promise to Emmis and killed him right then and there."

Atom is crying full-on at this point and whispering Emmis's name. He hugs me so hard I think he might break a rib. I know that it's not me he's hugging. It's Emmis.

33

MAVY

At 1755, Trace, 512, and I start moving quickly toward the medical facility. We can't run, but we also can't walk. 512 was able to secure regular military uniforms for Trace and me to wear, as well as NFF-issued guns and ammunition. No one stops us at any of the low-level security checkpoints. But when we reach the street leading to the medical facility, there are two Elite Guards sitting on the base of an NFF monument, smoking crushed wildflowers. They don't seem to know 512, but 512 nods at them and tries to keep walking. One of the guards stands and puts his hand on my chest to stop me. He turns to 512 and says, "Why you hanging out with these two stiffs?"

"They're all right," 512 says.

The guard looks at my face very closely. He's an overconfident sort and talks down to me, as I'm sure he does to all other regular military. "Do I know you? *Weren't you the janitor at my secondary school?* No, that's not it. *You were the captain of the girls' running team.*" He laughs while examining me. "Seriously, you look very familiar. Do I know you?"

"I don't think so," I say. I try using my best NFF accent, but it's not very good. Both guards are now looking at me closely. I glance at my chronometer. It's 1802. We can't spend a lot of time messing around with these guys. I smile and try to politely walk away.

"What's the rush, soldier," the guard asks me. He places his hand on my chest again, even more firmly this time. The invasion of my personal space makes me want to break his hand, but obviously I need to check my temper. "You seem like you're in a hurry to get somewhere."

"Sorry about that," I say. There is no inflection in my voice. "Your wife called and said her husband's a limp dick who hasn't been able to fuck her in ages. She needs me right away." I smile and shrug my shoulders. "I don't want to keep her waiting." This time my accent is dead-on and the joke works.

Both guards laugh and the one who put his hand on my chest is now patting me on the back. As we slowly walk away from them, the guard shouts out, "Say hi to my wife. Hope you two have a good time. Remember, she likes to be on top." When they're out of sight, we pick up the pace and head toward the medical facility.

The entrance is unremarkable. There's an illuminated rectangular sign above the doors that says NFF MILITARY HOSPITAL and an NFF flag which is fraying at the bottom. We walk up ten or so black-painted concrete steps to a set of sliding glass doors with cracks at the bottom. Before we go in, 512 turns to Trace and me and says, "Remember, let's try to avoid gunfire. We don't want to bring any extra attention to ourselves." I like 512. He leads without trying. It's a sign of a good soldier.

We enter through the glass doors. In the center of the entranceway is a kiosk with six military guards. Four of them are standing with guns resting on their shoulders, and the other two are sitting behind control panels that monitor the security systems in the facility. "You'll have to sign in and mark the time," one of the sitting guards says. I look down at my chronometer. It says 1808. I quickly enter the time on the sign-in monitor. At the rate we're going, we won't make it to their floor by the time the explosions go off. I look at 512 and point at my chronometer.

"Who are you going to see?" the guard at the desk asks. 512 moves in close, leaning over the desk and making sure the guards can smell the blue agave on his breath. "We're celebrating tonight. Chancellor Vrig is making my friends here part of the Elite Guard. I just wanted to show these guys what it means to be a guard." He moves in even closer and whispers, "I'm the guy that caught the detainees on floor four. Vrig gave me a bonus of a year's salary for that. I just want to give these guys a little taste of what it would be like and I want to show them who I captured."

"The Chancellor's willing to hire from the regular military now?" the guard asks.

"Quiet," 512 says. "This isn't public information. You've got to get a recommendation from a guard, but the Chancellor is definitely hiring." 512 smiles. "How about you let us go up to floor four and when I come back we can talk a little and I'll see if you're worthy of my recommendation."

Three laminated badges quickly shoot out of a small machine and we're off to the fourth floor. We ride up in an outdated elevator that is poorly lit. There are three more military guards sitting at the floor's kiosk. We exit the elevator and are waved on by them. Apparently, the guards from downstairs already radioed ahead and told the floor guards to let us go through.

We walk down a long hallway, and out of nowhere it happens. There's an enormous explosion that knocks us off our feet. My head hits the floor hard. The entire building rocks. Glass shatters. Parts of the roof fall in. Shock wave after shock wave crashes over us. Each time I try to stand, another explosion knocks me back down. When it finally stops, all that can be heard are hysterical screams and blaring sirens. I don't know what Atom did, but these were not the kinds of small detonations we talked about. These were not small at all.

I finally try to stand. I'm disoriented and my ears are ringing. There's a cut on the side of my head from where I hit the floor. I look down at my chronometer. It is covered in blood. I wipe away the blood. The chronometer says 1811.

Atom detonated these bombs four minutes ahead of schedule. Something must have gone wrong. People are running through the halls screaming. "Four minutes early," I shout to 512 over the screams. "Not good." Trace looks at me. He looks nervous. He's not a soldier. He doesn't understand that things always go wrong and that you judge a mission by how much is going right. Trace shakes his head and says, "I've got a bad feeling, brother."

"We don't have time to worry about it," I say. "We've got to get inside the room." We run in the opposite direction of most of the people who are headed toward the exits. We push open the heavy hospital doors and enter the ward where Pique and the others are being held. Just as we get to their hallway, alarms start ringing inside the hospital. All of the speakers in the hallway blast a disturbing warning sound that sounds like cats screaming. Then a voice comes over the speakers:

> *This is a message from the NFF Department of Emergency Ser-*
> *vices. This is an actual emergency. Repeat . . . this is an actual*
> *emergency. There have been multiple detonations of fissionable*
> *materials near the capital. The sources and locations are currently*
> *unknown. Dangerous levels of radiation have been detected.*
> *Other than essential emergency personnel, all personnel are to*
> *evacuate their posts and immediately head to radiation shelters.*
> *All personnel are to locate radiation gear and properly equip*
> *themselves. Find your radiation shelters and remain there until*
> *further notice.*

The warning sounds and messages keep repeating themselves over and over again, blending with the screams and the secondary explosions of generators, transports, and ammunition depots.

We quickly find Pique and the others' room. There is one lone guard outside the door. He is terrified. "Where are the others?" 512 asks him.

"They left. They told me to stay behind and guard the prisoners."

"You're excused, soldier," 512 says with authority. "Get to the shelter immediately." The guard, who looks about seventeen, runs as fast as he can toward the exit. I push my way through another set of doors. It's an awful sight. I see Pique, Mavy, and Nayla. Their skin is discolored and they are lifeless. I look for Dang, but he doesn't seem to be there. I run to Pique and hug her. I won't let her out of my sight again.

I go over to Mavy and place my hand on her belly. I think I feel a kick, but it's probably just my mind playing a trick. Trace is holding Nayla's hand and fighting back the urge to cry. Nayla looks worse than Pique and Mavy. I look around the room one more time for Dang, but don't see him. Vrig must have had him moved to a more secure location. Maybe Vrig was being honest. Maybe Dang is this special prize the Holy Father seeks.

512 has already begun reprogramming the medical devices that are keeping everyone in comas. The machines' high-pitched pings slow down and they begin to hum in a lower key. "You can start removing the intravenous

catheters," 512 shouts. I remove the catheters from Pique before turning to Mavy. As I am removing the last catheter, the doors swing open. "What's going on in here," an Elite Guard calls in.

"It's me—512," 512 shouts to the other Elite Guard. "Vrig ordered me to secure the detainees."

"That's bullshit," the guard shouts back. "Command Central just ordered me to do it. Drop your weapon now."

Just as the guard reaches for his radio, I pull out my gun and shoot him in between the eyes. He's dead.

"You didn't need to do that," 512 yells. "I had it under control."

"You're a good soldier, but I don't have time for moralizing."

"I knew that guy."

"I don't care if he was your best friend. I need to get these people out of here. He was one button away from calling in reinforcements. So deal with it. I will kill as many people as I need to get out of here." 512's not happy about what I'm saying. But it's not my job to keep him happy. I just need him to follow me.

I tell Trace to pull the dead guard in and hide him somewhere. Nayla is the first to wake up. I feel bad that Trace is not at her side. I run over to her and grab her hand. She can't speak. I gently place my hand on her cheek and smile. "It's going to be okay."

Trace runs over to her and hugs her. She is very confused and jumpy. "Stay still, Nayla," I say in a calm voice. When her eyes catch mine, she smiles. I feel a little sick, because that kind of smile is unmistakable. It's love.

Pique is next to get up and then Mavy. Pique is able to talk immediately. Her voice is a little raspy and weak, but she manages to get out what she wants. "*Hello, Your Holiness.*" And then she winks as if everything is just perfect.

"Thank God you're okay. But take it slow. You've been asleep for a long time." I kiss the top of her head and head toward Mavy on the other side of the room. Mavy is barely waking up and I have to shake her a little. She's disoriented. When she finally comes to, the first thing she does is look down at her protruding stomach. She's shocked at what she sees. She has trouble processing it. Her chest heaves up and down as she struggles for breath. She's frightened. She looks down at her stomach again and then up at me. She scans the room and sees Pique and Nayla sitting up in their gurneys. She looks at Trace and then back at me. I take both of her hands and hold them tight.

"You're safe, Mavy," I say. "Just slow your breathing. You need to calm down." She begins exhaling through her nose and her breathing steadies. "We're going to get you out of this place."

She looks around the room anxiously again and then turns her sights back to the bulge in her stomach. She places her hands over her mound and says, "I'm . . . I'm . . . I'm pregnant?"

I nod yes.

"But Emile's dead. How can I be . . ." Her voice trails off. She slowly raises her eyes from her stomach to meet mine. She tightens her grip around my hands and raises her eyebrows. She looks at me, then her stomach—me, then her stomach. She doesn't say it, but I know she's asking if I'm the father.

I nod yes.

"Good." She rubs her stomach and smiles. "That's really good."

34

NAYLA

Nayla looks sick and it's not just because she's been in a coma for more than half a year. The sight of Mavy's stomach seems to be a fate worse than death. She doesn't say anything, but every time I look at her she looks away in disgust. Pique, on other hand, lets me know that it's okay—that she and I are okay. It's almost as if she knows I need her acceptance and she gives it to me unconditionally. It's all in a matter of a few quick nods. But I know that's what she means.

"Can you stand?" I ask Pique.

She looks down at her legs. "They still seem to be there, so I guess so." She stands up and her legs immediately give out. I catch her as she falls. She laughs and says, "Colossal failure." 512 tries to help Mavy up, but her legs are also like rubber bands. Nayla is also weak at first, but with Trace's arms wrapped around her she is able to drag her legs a little.

The second Pique's legs get back their strength she moves toward her mom. She falls into Nayla's arms and they both cry. I forget that they haven't seen each other yet. I almost lost sight of the fact that Pique is Nayla's little girl. I give them a moment before telling everyone we need to go.

I have to find a way to transport Pique, Mavy, and Nayla out of the facility. They're not strong enough to walk, much less run if things get hectic. I send Trace to find a large medical linens cart. It's not the most dignified mode of transportation, but it's the best I can think of. When Trace brings it back, he smiles at Mavy, and using his best Yerusi aristocrat accent, says, "Your coach awaits you, madam."

"There is no way that I'm getting in a cart full of soiled linens." It's nice to see that Mavy hasn't lost herself. Pique laughs and says, "You're going to be a mom soon. Diapers. Poop. Spit-up. Come on now. You have to stop being so uptight. Life's about to get seriously gross for you." I think I almost see a smile from Mavy. Nayla, on the other hand, is miserable. She doesn't like Pique cavorting with the enemy. I wonder if Pique knows that Mavy is her half sister. Of course Nayla does, and Mavy must, too. I have to think Pique knows, so it's strange she never mentioned it.

512 lifts Mavy up. "Sorry, ma'am. I have the utmost respect for you and your highborn Yerusalom ways, but I'm soldier on a mission and that trumps holy folks, princesses, politicians, and all the rest of you." Mavy struggles a bit as 512 pushes her head under what looks like a pretty disgusting bedcover. But I don't feel electricity in the air, so she can't be too mad.

Pique lifts herself up and dives into the cart, while Nayla slowly lowers herself in, finding a spot as far away from Mavy as possible. "Let's go," I say. "You three are going to have to pretend to be unconscious. If anyone asks, we say you were knocked unconscious by the blast and that we're getting you to a radiation shelter." I turn to Trace and 512 and pull them in close to me. "Kill anyone you have to. This is a tight escape with only one, maybe two, exits. That means we fire first and worry about the dead later."

"That's not the code of conduct I follow," 512 says.

"I'll be sure to remember that when I give your eulogy."

I push open the doors to the hallway and we move quickly toward the elevator. Trace is pushing the cart. 512 is in the rear and I'm out in front. We get to the elevators, and there is a young woman lying facedown on the floor, blocking the elevator doors. It's a young nursing student, probably about the same age as Dariox. I feel her neck for a pulse. She's dead. There are no wounds. She's very young, but it looks like she may have died of a heart attack from the explosions. I drag her body to the side and press the elevator button. I'm not sure it will work. The elevators may have sustained damage during the explosions, or they have been manually shut down because of the emergency. But it's worth trying, because getting everyone down four flights of stairs will be a nightmare.

There are no lights indicating that the elevator is coming, but after a while, I hear the elevator's cables moving. When the elevator reaches the floor below, I hear the sound of radio chatter. These amateurs have forgotten to turn down their radios. It must be the military security guards from downstairs. I point to the elevator doors and motion for everyone to be quiet. Trace moves the cart away from the elevators, while 512 and I each stand to one side of the doors. I use my hands to show 512 the plan, and he gets it. 512 always seems to get it. He doesn't want to do what I've asked, but he knows it's our best chance to escape.

As the doors crack open, we each grab hold of a door. We let the doors open only a few centimeters—just enough to fit the barrels of our guns. While keeping the doors from opening, we stick our guns through the crack and start firing. We fire until we can't hear anything coming from inside. Not even the radios.

We let the doors open. Six dead. It's the security guards from downstairs.

"I guess they won't be joining the Elite Guard," I say to 512.

"I don't understand you, Judge. I never would have taken you for being such a callous killer."

I stop for a second. 512 is right. I don't understand what's come over me. "I'm sorry." I don't know if I'm apologizing to 512 or the six dead soldiers, but I really am sorry. This is not the kind of soldier I want to be.

We don't bother to pull the dead bodies out. We just push them to the side and pull the cart in. I feel badly about what I'm doing to these soldiers, but given the limited room, I have no choice but to quickly throw them on top of each other. As I do, I push more blood and guts out of them and the mess oozes out onto the elevator's floor. Our feet become covered in a sludge of death. A few of the soldiers have defecated and urinated from the ordeal. That elevator is a cesspool of decay and waste. I don't know what waits for me on first floor, but I know I want out of this elevator.

Before the elevator opens to the ground floor, I ask if everyone's okay. They each respond quickly, but I hear fear in their voices, especially Trace's. He feels the weight of his responsibility. He's scared because Pique and Nayla are depending on him. "It's going to be okay," I say. I want Trace feeling confident. I want him to understand that we're going to accomplish each step one at a time. This is standard psych ops for new soldiers. "We're in good shape, Trace. First we're going to move quickly to the front entrance. Then, we're going to find a ground transport. And then we're going to take the back roads to the airfield and leave with Atom. It's all under control."

The elevator eventually opens and we're back at the entranceway. It's quiet. There are about ten dead bodies on the floor and there is blood everywhere. All of the windows are shattered and most of the ceiling's tiles have fallen. It looks like most of the people were killed by flying glass or fallen ceiling. These kinds of deaths had to be caused by a massive shock wave.

I look out through the shattered windows onto the street. I don't see any people walking around. They must have all quickly evacuated and headed toward the radiation shelters. It is eerily quiet inside and outside the facility. The only thing I hear is some static coming from the control station at the kiosk.

As we approach the kiosk, I can begin to make out the dispatches coming through the security systems. The military dispatcher sounds despondent.

> This is a Level One Alert. Repeat. This is a Level One Alert. Repeat: Level One Alert. We are under attack from the Nation of Yerusalom and Federacy sympathizers. The damage sustained is catastrophic. Initial reports indicate that our own Mercury VOID system has been used against us. Reports are coming in that some of our major cities have been totally annihilated. All corridors and military bases between M71 and V22 have been destroyed. The six main suburbs around the capital are devastated. Communications are badly damaged and information is discontinuous. As much as ten percent of the population may have been killed. There is reliable information that Detainee Judge Maxomillion Cone and Major Torne Lau, also known as Atom Lau, may have orchestrated the attack. All personnel should be on the lookout for Judge Cone and Major Torne. Do not kill. Repeat: Capture, but do not kill.

"What the fuck," Trace shouts. He angrily walks over to 512 and pushes him in his chest. "Did you know about this?"

"Of course not," 512 says. "My mom and dad may be dead right now." He pushes Trace hard and Trace stumbles backward. "Don't you dare accuse me of knowing about this."

Trace's suspicions turn to me. "Max, do you know anything about this?"

I take a long time to answer, which doesn't help ease Trace's suspicion, or 512's for that matter. I can't process what's going on. There's too much imperfect information to decipher, and I need to focus on getting out of here. I just give Trace an indignant nod and say, "We've got to get out of this place and not through the entranceway." I hear sirens in the distance, and although the streets look empty, the Elite Guard is probably hiding in wait just outside the doors. Even if we got through, we certainly can't escape in one of the nearby ambulatory transports. They know we're coming from a medical facility and they will be looking for that kind of transport. The only other way out is a back emergency exit. But it's covered in rubble and impenetrable.

I order everyone to head back to the elevators. We're going to the only viable escape I can think of—the roof. We go back into the same putrid-smelling elevator as before. I hit the button for the roof. As the doors close, the smell overwhelms Trace. He tries to fight it, but he can't. By the time we reach floor fourteen, he has thrown up. I pat his back and wipe his mouth with my sleeve.

The sheets rumble and Mavy sticks her head out. "Where are we going?"

"We can't go through the entranceway. Our next best option is the roof."

"And then what?" Nayla asks.

"And then we improvise."

35

PIQUE

For strategic reasons, the NFF's capital was crammed into the east side of the Delawine River. It's a poorly planned city, with buildings built one on top of the other. The city's layout is a running joke in the NFF, but it's a very good thing for our purposes at the moment. We get up to the roof and I take note of a nearby building with a rooftop right across from the medical facility's rear. That roof is relatively close to ours and about one floor below. There's a loading dock below it with some delivery transports. Hopefully we can get across and use one of the transports to get away.

"Everyone out of the cart," I say. Pique seems to be back to a hundred percent, but the others are still a little weak. I need them to get stronger in a hurry. I tell everyone the plan. We're going to tie the hospital linens together and create a rope line to the other roof. Everyone except Pique tells me they think it would be better to go back down the elevator and fight our way out through the front door. 512 and Trace are particularly adamant. They insist we go out the front. They're entitled to their opinions, but they're wrong.

"I hear you," I say to all of them. "And maybe if we were deciding where to go to dinner tonight, I would listen to what everyone wants. But this is about saving our lives. Our only chance of getting out of here is by getting to that other roof. The front entranceway is suicide. So, you can think what you want, but we're doing it my way." I'm mostly looking at Trace when I say this, because I know he'll fall in line most quickly. He relents first and then the others do, too. They immediately get to work on what I need.

Trace starts tying bedcovers, blankets, and sheets together. We tear apart the cart, and that adds another few meters of material. There's also a fire hose made of a strong polyfiber material that will work, too. I explain to Trace that the knots need to be tied as tight as possible.

Without me saying anything, Pique says, "I'll go across first." She knows she's the best one for the job. The first person has to swing over to the other side, and it will be dangerous. The day she tied me up with a rope in my chambers was a pretty good audition for what I need now. I don't like risking her life, but given her small size and extraordinary strength, she's the best hope.

"You're not doing it," Nayla says. "I'm going first."

"I got this, Mom." Nayla and I exchange some harsh words. I don't like overriding a mother. I feel badly telling her what I need her child to do. It's not my place, but it's what I need and it will be done. As I tie my improvised rope to a metal fence, Pique says to Nayla, "Don't worry, Mom. *Just ask His Holiness over there what I can do with a rope.*"

Pique jumps over the fence and takes hold of the end of the line. I adjust the knot around her waist and pull it tight. I tell her to hold the rope firmly and explain to her how she needs to kick off our building to swing to the other. I double-check the knot on her and the one on the metal fence. Trace, 512, and I each take turns pulling all the knots to make sure they're secure. We then walk over to the metal fence and get ready to lower Pique down. "Please be careful, Pique." She looks so little against the ground below. I become filled with doubt. My plan is not as strong as I'd like. But based on the mounting military activity I hear from below, I'm certain that the Elite Guard is waiting for us outside the front door of the medical facility. We need to get to the other building and exit through it.

Trace, 512, and I get into a line and take hold of the rope. I'm closest to the fence. We hold the rope and gently let a little go at a time. We lower Pique down the side of our building. I hop over the fence and lie down with my heels wedged in between the roof and the fence's bottom crossbar. My arms and shoulders are leaning over the street below. I hold the rope as tight as I can and tell Pique to start kicking. Pique pushes off the steel frame on the side of our building.

"Don't kick off the windows," I say.

"Thanks for the tip," she says back. "I'm not an idiot, you know."

I stretch my body as far as I can over the building's edge to give her the best possible chance. I'm facedown, looking onto the street below. A few military carriers pass below us, but they don't slow down. I don't think they are looking for us this high up, and given that they have just turned onto our street, they probably can't see us from their vantage point. Pique swings back and forth over the street below. She is like an acrobat—kicking her legs in the air and moving our rope back and forth. As she does, we let a little more rope out. I try to use my arms to swing her as far as I can.

She pushes against a balcony that juts out from our building's floor below, and this gives her a huge boost. She soars more than halfway across the street and then climbs up toward the fence on the other building's roof, but falls just short.

"Kick harder."

"Why don't you swing harder," she yells back.

She flies back quickly toward our building and I shout out for her watch the window. She twists her body at the last second to avoid shattering the glass and kicks her legs off the balcony's guardrail. As she pushes off, she breaks the rail. She soars over the street below toward the building on the other side. As she closes in on a fence on the other roof, she decides to take her hands off the rope. The only thing securing her is the knot I tied around her waist. She puts her hands in front of her and tightens her body into the shape of an arrow. She moves too fast for me to tell her no. It's definitely unsafe, but she has turned herself into a speeding arrow, cutting through the air's resistance. Flying over the street below, held only by the rope around her waist, she soars toward the other building. The closer she gets to the other side, the heavier the rope gets. It digs into my hands, burning a line into my palms. I struggle to keep a firm grip on the rope. Finally, she reaches out her hand and grabs hold of the fence on the other side. "Got it," she shouts.

I let out a deep breath and let go of the rope. While Pique ties the rope to the bottom post of the fence, I get everyone else ready to go across. Mavy and Nayla are still too weak to go it alone, so we're going to have to take them on our backs. I decide to take Mavy first. I move fast because I don't want Pique alone on the other side for long.

512 lifts Mavy up and helps her over the fence. Mavy, who is almost as tall as I am, climbs on my back and wraps her legs around my waist. She puts her hands around my chest and locks them together. She then nuzzles her head in between my shoulder and chin, with her lips gently pressed against my neck.

I let Pique know we're about to start. She pulls whatever little slack there is out of the knot on her side and says, "All good." I grab the rope and lower Mavy and me down over the side of the ledge. Then, slowly, I place one hand over the other and begin our trip. Mavy and I develop a sort of rhythm as we slowly make our way across the rope that hangs over the street below. As I move hand-over-hand, she tightens her legs around my waist and lifts her body. I feel her stomach and the life within it pressed into my back.

About three-quarters of the way through, I hear a siren coming from below, and against my better judgment, I look down. I'm not the least bit scared of heights, but I'm responsible for three lives on that rope. Taking your eyes off an improvised rope that is precariously dangling seventy-five meters above concrete is not wise. When I look down, I see two military carriers pass us by. They probably don't see us, but I feel naked up here, just like when I was dangling over those falls with Asio. If those carriers were to stop and look up, there would be nothing I could do to protect us.

My arms are becoming weak, but I'm sure they won't fail me. My only concerns are the strength of the rope, which seems to be holding up okay, and the increasing wind gusts. As we approach the other building, Mavy speaks for the first time. "God must really love you, Max." I don't have the energy to respond. But in my head I tell Mavy to be quiet. I don't want to hear what her god thinks of me. I just want her to hold on so I can get her safely to the other side. Her god has nothing to do with that.

The muscles in my arms and shoulders are on fire, but I manage to get Mavy to the other side. I put one foot on the ledge of the other building, and turn my body so Mavy can grab on to the fence. I then hoist her over it, and Pique grabs hold of her on the other side. I grab the fence and lift myself over.

Pique and I tighten whatever knots are in our reach, and 512 does the same from the other side. Trace and Nayla get ready to go next. 512 helps Nayla over the fence. She's not much bigger than Pique, so Trace shouldn't have too much trouble carrying the extra load. Trace grabs the rope with both hands. Nayla climbs on his back and grabs a firm hold of his shirt. Trace lowers himself and Nayla over the side of the building. Holding the rope above his head, he begins making his way away from the ledge. Trace is moving much quicker than I did, which is not a good sign. His pace reflects his fear. He's using up his energy too quickly and being careless. "You need to slow down, Trace," I shout. "Breathe. Pace yourself."

He doesn't respond.

Trace manages to get to the midway point quickly, but he's already out of steam. The wind is picking up, and one of the gusts catches Trace off guard. His left hand slips from the rope. He frantically reaches back up, but he can't grab the rope. He's exhausted. Nayla says something to him as he reaches up for the second time. He misses again. Trace is barely holding on with one hand. Nayla knows he can no longer carry her. She reaches up and grabs the rope for herself. The instant her weight comes off him he's able to reach his hand back up and grab the rope.

Trace twists his body and tries to reach back for Nayla, but she moves away. "You need to keep going," she shouts. "It will be easier for me to move without you rocking the line. Just go." Trace starts moving again. This time he is moving fast. Nayla holds tight, waiting for Trace to finish. When Trace gets to us, he is completely spent. I grab him and lift him over the fence. His face has failure written all over it.

Nayla starts to move. Her movements are measured and her progress slow. The wind gusts are picking up at the worst time possible. They begin to move the rope back and forth. Nayla's face is bright red. She's struggling. Pique jumps over the fence and grabs hold of the rope. She starts to head out on the rope, but Nayla says no. "Stay where you are, Pique. You can't help me." Nayla's right. If Pique heads out on the rope, Nayla will lose her balance. Nayla is able to make some progress, but Pique can no longer take it. Pique is just about to go after her when a gust of wind overtakes Nayla. Her right hand loses the rope. As she dangles, Pique tightens her grip, as if that could somehow help. Nayla reaches back up for the rope, but she misses. She has nothing left. I look at Nayla. Her eyes are vacant. There's not much fight left in her. She barely holds on with one hand. Her face turns a shade of angry purple. Her breathing quickens as fear overtakes her. She knows there's no way out but down.

"Promise me you'll take care of Pique, Max. She'll need you."

"Hold on, Nayla," I shout. "You fight." I'm begging Nayla to hold on. Pique and Trace are pleading with her, too.

"I tried to protect you, Max." The rope sways back and forth as she struggles to hold on. "Mavy. The Holy Father. Even Emmis." Her hand begins to slip. "I didn't want to tell you." Her hand comes away from the rope. "Emmis isn't—"

She falls. She yells something. But "Emmis" is the only thing I hear.

Then the ground silences her.

36

512

Nayla's body hits the ground hard and makes a grotesque thud. She bounces off the concrete street and flips hard onto her side. Her head breaks away from her body. Pique screams as loud as I've ever heard anyone scream. The buildings echo her agony.

I run as fast as I can to Pique. She starts to scream again and I put my hand over her mouth. I hate doing it, but I can't let her scream. I wrap her up in my arms. I don't want her looking at her mother's body for another second. Pique wails. She's inconsolable. I rock her back and forth. She's a baby again. An infant. Weak. Vulnerable. Innocent. Pique is shaking. I tighten my hold around her.

After a few minutes, Mavy makes her way to Pique and me. She places her hand on my shoulder. I quickly remove it. I think about all the times Nayla tried to warn me about Mavy. I turn around to tell Mavy to leave us alone, but then I see that Mavy's crying. She catches her breath and says, "I'm so sorry, Max." She places one hand on her stomach and rubs her eyes with the other. "I don't understand this," she says. "It's just not right." She bends down on her knee and moves close to Pique. "Our God has a way of . . ." Mavy's voice trails off into silence. There's nothing to say. She lowers her head toward Pique and whispers, "I'm sorry." She presses her lips on Pique's head for a second and kisses her. She then gently touches my face before moving aside.

I carry Pique over to Trace. She feels as lifeless as her mother. Trace is sitting with his head buried in between his knees. His cries are muffled, but his back heaves in huge uncontrollable waves. I reach my hand out to Trace and pull him up off the concrete floor. I bring him into a hug and tell him that Nayla would want us to get out of here. She would want us to keep fighting. Trace and Pique don't want to go on. They each say it's their fault. If it's anyone's fault, it's mine. But there will be plenty of time to assign blame later. For now, there's no time to mourn, and even less time for guilt.

I look over at the roof we just came from and I notice that 512 is untying the rope. Before I have a chance to say anything, he has untied the knots and the rope has fallen to the side of the building I'm on. It dangles below and flaps in the wind.

"What are you doing," I shout across to the other building.

"Pull the rope up," he yells back. "The next carrier that comes by will stop at Nayla's body. They'll look up and see the rope. We can't have that."

512 is of course right. I can lift the rope myself, but I call for Pique and Trace's help. I want them active. I don't want their minds on Nayla. The three of us pull the rope up and push it out of sight. The fact that Nayla's body is sitting in the middle of the road probably won't give away the fact that we've crossed over to the other building. But a huge dangling rope connecting the buildings certainly will.

"I will go back down the elevator," 512 yells. "Hopefully the military and Elite Guards don't know about me yet. I'll say I was looking for you guys."

"Meet us at the loading dock in the back of our building," I say.

"If I'm not there in exactly ten minutes, leave without me."

"We're waiting for you. Just get there."

512 heads to the door on his roof and we do the same. Our door is locked, but there's a small window nearby. I break through the window with the heel of my foot and climb through. A piece of glass gets lodged in my forearm and I pull it out with my teeth. I open the door and Mavy walks through. Trace and Pique have made their way back to the ledge and are staring at Nayla's body. They're frozen by the sight. I grab each of them by the shirt and pull them back toward the door.

Before heading down the stairs, Mavy reaches for Trace. She grabs for one of his hands and places it inside both of hers. She tells him how sorry she is for his loss. He could say a lot of ugly things, given their past, but he graciously accepts.

I press the elevator call button and nothing happens. The elevators must be turned off or damaged. We have to take the stairs. It's about eighteen flights down, but we have no choice. We have to hurry, because the streets will soon be teeming with troops.

Mavy starts out strong, running from step to step, but before long she's winded. By the time we hit the tenth floor, she has fallen behind. I run back to get her and hold her hand the rest of the way, making sure she keeps up. We don't pass anyone—alive or dead. But in between the first and second floors we come up to our first encounter. It's a young boy, probably not more than five, and he's dead. He is lying facedown and there's a small stream of blood coming from his mouth. Most of the damage must be internal. It looks like the blast knocked him off his feet, and he most likely hit his head. He was probably too young to have been alone. I think about the person, probably a mother or father, who had to leave his poor dead body behind.

When we get to the ground floor, I tell everyone to be quiet. I point to the back of the lobby. This should lead us to the loading docks and delivery transports. As we start moving I notice there are a handful of dead people scattered throughout the lobby. As in the medical facility's entranceway, ceiling tiles and glass are strewn everywhere. I pass a few damaged corporate flags dangling near the rear elevator banks. The logos on the flags are torn, but I recognize one of them. It's a large NFF communications company that advertised on the news shows I watched on the NFF network. In the commercial, a beautiful woman, barely dressed, walks along the beach. As the gentle waves wash over her feet, she smiles. As the wind blows through her hair, she laughs. Then, as she reaches a dock filled with friends, she turns to face the camera. Her voice is a mix of sultry and smart. "Choice Communications. The *choice* is yours."

Pique and Nayla are lagging behind and I tell everyone to pick up the pace. We reach the back of the lobby, go through a door, and climb down half a flight of stairs. I open a heavy metal door to the loading dock, and a gust of wind blows in. I turn to the left and there are about nine land transports sitting parked in the lot. They are of different sizes, but each transport is painted white with the blue and green logo of Choice Communications. We split up and begin checking to see if the starter keys are in the transports. No luck on the first four, so we fan out to the remaining five. The next one I search doesn't have the starter keys and neither does Trace's or Pique's. Then I hear, "Got one." It's Mavy. We all run to her transport. It's a large transport but it only has seating for two, in the front. It has a rear compartment filled with bulky communications equipment, but there's room enough for the others to sit on the floor.

I try to enter on the driver's side, but Mavy is already in the seat. I tell her to move over, but she says no. It's not worth the fight. As Mavy starts the transport I realize that we have a big problem. We're supposed to rendez-vous with Atom at an airfield that is in a major suburb just outside the capital. According to the military dispatch we heard in the lobby, the suburbs have been decimated. Could Atom have been *that stupid*? Then it occurs to me—could he have been *that smart*. Ruthlessly smart. Maybe he was clear-ing a path for our escape, and civilian casualties were not his problem. I pray this isn't true.

Mavy starts to back out. "Where are you going," I say to her. I'm angry because she's trying to leave 512 behind. "He risked his life for you, Mavy."

"Would you please calm down, Max. They say that crisis can bring out a man's true character. Yours seems to be *distrust*." She adjusts the gears and spins the directional wheel counterclockwise. She turns her head to me. "I'm just turning us around so we can get out of here quicker."

The second she turns the transport around, we hear gunfire. Less than a minute later, there's a loud knock on the passenger-side window. It's 512. I fling open the door. He jumps in. His leg is bleeding badly.

"We've got to get out of here," 512 says. He smiles. "Turns out they know about me."

37

THREE ELITE GUARDS

Mavy presses the accelerator and we take off down the street. I tell her to stop and let 512 drive. But she keeps going. "512 knows the streets of the capital," I say. "He should drive."

"Look at his leg," Mavy says. "He can't drive."

"Fine. Then I'm driving."

"I'm driving, Max. You're just going to have to deal with a woman driving you around. If I can fly a state-of-the-art helicraft, I think I can drive this old delivery transport."

"Well, you're going the wrong way," 512 says. "You have no idea what you're doing."

"Thank you for your input," Mavy says to 512. "But I know exactly where I'm going. I'm going around the corner. I'm not leaving here without Nayla. She's going to have a proper burial."

"There's no time for that," I say. "They'll be coming at us from every direction. And Nayla was an Abstainer. She doesn't care about *proper burials*."

"I care," Trace says from the back.

"Me, too," Pique says. Her voice is that of a little girl's. The debate is over. As dumb as it is, we're going to get Nayla's body.

"Fine," I say. "But I'm the only one getting out. The rest of you stay in the transport and if you hear gunfire, you drive away."

"*Sure thing*," Pique says. "We'll just leave you behind to die." She shakes her head at me.

Nayla's body is on the west side of the building and Mavy gets us there in no time. I tell her to pull off to the side of the road and back into an alleyway in between this building and the next. I don't want Pique or Trace to see what I'm doing.

I look in the back of the transport and find a large plastic cover protecting the communications equipment. I rip it off and hop out of the passenger door. I run down the alleyway, turn onto the street, and quickly make my way to Nayla. I take a deep breath and try to think about anything other than the fact that I'm collecting her dead body. I don't want Pique or Trace seeing the body, especially in its decapitated form. I quickly pick up Nayla's head. I sit down and prop Nayla's body up in between my legs. We are both seated, and her back is against my chest. While holding her body in place with my legs, I place my hands on both sides of her head. With as much force as I can muster, I drive her head onto her spine. It works. I hold Nayla's cheeks and rotate her head on her spine so that it's properly aligned. It's a gruesome task, but Trace and Pique need this. I place Nayla's body on the plastic and roll her up in it. I then put her over my shoulder and start back to the transport.

As I reach the sidewalk, someone shouts, "Don't move." I turn around and see a military carrier. Three Elite Guards jump out of their carrier with their weapons drawn. I take off running. They quickly debate whether to fire. I guess they're still supposed to bring me in alive. By the time they've decided to fire warning shots, I'm heading down the alleyway with Nayla's body. Mavy sees me running. She presses the accelerator and takes off toward me. The transport's tires screech, and the smell of burning rubber fills the alleyway. Mavy slows down so I can jump in. As 512 pulls Nayla's body off my shoulder, the military carrier races in, blocking our exit. Mavy throws the transport into reverse, and we head back down the alleyway with the military carrier following us. 512 pulls out his weapon and opens the glass hatch on the side of the transport. He fires three quick rounds—each a perfect shot to the carrier's three front tires. He then fires a fourth into the engine block. The carrier spins out of control and crashes into the wall of the building.

Mavy continues in reverse. "Stop," Trace shouts from the back. She's about to hit a metal barricade in the back of the alleyway. This alleyway has only one way out. Mavy slams on the brakes, and we barely avoid crashing into the barricade. We'll have to go out the way we came in.

The military carrier is disabled and pressed up against the building's wall. We should be able to pass through, but this time, I can guarantee that the soldiers will be shooting to kill. I can't risk the others, so I tell Mavy to sit tight. Without the Elite Guards noticing, I hop out of the back of the transport and assess the surroundings. I see a small steel-plated door to the first floor of the building just behind the transport, and a window just above the military carrier. I motion for 512 to come to the back of the transport and I tell him to have Mavy blow the transport's horn for three seconds while I move to the door and count another thirty seconds so I can get in place. Then, I tell 512 exactly what I need him and Trace to do.

While Mavy blows the horn, I crawl a few meters to the steel-plated door, open it a crack, and slip through. The Elite Guards don't see me. The building is dark. The emergency lighting system is flickering a little, but not working properly. Alarms are ringing and there's a computerized voice that keeps repeating, "Evacuate to shelters. Evacuate to shelters. Evacuate to shelters." I quickly find the stairs and jump three or four steps at time. Three-quarters of the way up, I come down hard on my left ankle and twist it. The pain is sharp, but the worst of it lasts only a few seconds. I look down at my chronometer and fifteen seconds have gone by. I try to sprint down a narrow hallway, but my ankle slows me down. I come to a window and realize it's not the right one. I continue running down the hallway and I get to the right window. I see the military carrier just below. One of the guards is talking on the radio, and the other two are tending to minor wounds.

Right on cue, at thirty seconds, Trace pushes 512 from behind. 512 has his hands in the air and he is walking slowly to the carrier. Trace has a gun pointed to his head. 512 is shouting, "Shoot this motherfucker. Shoot this motherfucker." Trace acts agitated and unhinged. "Shut up or I'll put a bullet in you." I told Trace to act as unbalanced as he could and his performance is masterful. The Elite Guards react quickly. They pull open the left-side door to their carrier and draw their weapons. They shield themselves with the door as they fix their guns on Trace. I want their eyes focused straight ahead. I quietly open the window, take out my gun, and point it at the soldiers. I have wide-open shots at all three.

I feel bad for what I'm about to do. I'm about to kill these men—innocent as far as I know—in a manner unbefitting of a soldier. I'm going to execute them. One shot to the head for each. I'm only a few meters away from them and they don't stand a chance. They might as well be unarmed children. I'm sorry.

I fire rapidly. Three shots. Three dead soldiers.

The only kindness I show them is that they die before they realize what hit them. I make sure the shots are quick and clean.

I jump down through the window onto the roof of their military carrier. I wave Mavy forward. Trace and 512 hop into our transport, while I rummage through their carrier grabbing a radio, a first-aid kit, and enough weapons to arm everyone.

When I return to our transport, I see Pique covered in blood. It's on her hands. It's on her shirt. It's everywhere. My heart races and I'm short of breath. It's only for a brief moment, but the heaviest kind of oppression falls over me—despair like when I saw my family covered in blood. It ends quickly, though. Pique gives me a fake smile through her watery eyes.

The blood's not hers. It's Nayla's.

38

ATOM

512 directs Mavy through the capital's streets. There are a number of utility trucks and emergency transports on the roads, so ours doesn't stand out too much. The radio I took from the Elite Guards is a nonstop source of military chatter. The NFF military dispatcher says that roadblocks are being set up throughout the capital and that the military is forming perimeter encampments around the city. It seems to me that they're preparing for an incoming ground attack, which makes no sense. Based on what I'm hearing on the radio, the NFF's command structure has broken down. Communications are in tatters and even the snippets of strategy that are getting through are contradictory at best.

We've been driving a few minutes and I have yet to see any signs of a roadblock or even troop movements. As a precaution, we avoid all major roads into and out of the capital. But contrary to what the NFF military dispatcher has suggested, there are no checkpoints and no military presence whatsoever. I wonder if Atom knew this would happen. I wonder if he planned to destroy huge sections of the NFF and its military infrastructure. I wonder if this was always his plan and he didn't tell me because he knew I would never go along with it.

Our destination is about ten minutes away, which gives me some time to work on the different wounds—physical and emotional—in the transport. I start with 512's leg. The bullet went straight through and did not hit any major arteries. I clean the wound with the first-aid kit I took from the guards and bandage him up.

I won't be able to find the same kind of quick remedy for what ails Pique and Trace. The only thing I can offer them is my strength. I have no words to comfort them and I can't make time pass any faster. Strength is all I have. I reassure them that I will always be there for them. I tell them they are my family. But it doesn't help. It's too soon for false comforts.

The three of us sit on the floor in the back of the transport just looking at the plastic tarp that covers Nayla. I wipe away the bloodstains on the outer cover, and Pique tells me to stop. "It doesn't matter." We don't say much after that. Every time we hit a bump in the road, a few words seem to pop out. "It's so hard." "It hurts so much." "I miss her." "This sucks." 512 interrupts our misery. "We'll be there in five minutes." I hand out weapons to everyone, not knowing what waits for us at the airfield. Pique makes a face. "I don't want this." She pushes the gun away from her. I understand. It was wrong of me to even offer.

I move to the front of the transport and stick my head in between Mavy's and 512's seats. "We have to be prepared for anything," I say to them. "Mavy, assuming the airship is waiting for us, I don't want you pulling alongside it. You need to keep a safe distance. I have no idea if we can trust Atom."

"We can trust him," 512 says. "Something has gone wrong, but I have no reason to doubt him. I know Atom. He's one of the good ones."

"He's a traitor to someone," I say.

"We're all traitors to someone," Mavy says.

"Well I don't trust him."

"I understand," 512 says. "It's only been a short time I've known you, Judge. But I think I know the kind of man you are. You're honest and you care about your people. You kill too easily, but you're a good man. I want you to know— if for some reason Atom is up to something, and I'm forced to choose a side— *I choose you.*"

"I appreciate—"

Just as I try to thank 512, an FDP, a find-and-destroy projectile, pierces the back window of our transport, shattering the glass. I run back to see if everyone is okay. I tell Pique and Trace to move to the front and stay low. There are two fortified military carriers chasing us at high speed. They know it's us. The military dispatchers have yet to broadcast our location, but they soon will. I just hope we get to the airfield first.

"Slow down, Mavy," I say. She doesn't. "I said *slow down*."

"What," Mavy yells. "Are you out of your mind?"

"Just do it."

Mavy slows down the transport, and the two carriers, one in the right lane and the other in the left, speed up. They close in on us. This is precisely what I want. I tell Trace, Pique, and 512 to come to the back and help me. We release the restraints holding the communications equipment. It takes all of our strength to move these huge pieces of equipment toward the back door. When we have all the equipment lined up in the back, we swing the doors open and push the equipment out. The equipment slams into the road and breaks into large hunks of flying metal shrapnel. The carriers swerve to avoid the debris, but one of the carriers can't get out of the way in time. A large section of a transmission pod crashes into the carrier's front windshield and left front tire. The carrier skids off the roadway, hits a ditch, and flips into the air. In seconds there are flames coming out of the transport and electric shocks are flying out of the pod and carrier. An Elite Guard in flames runs from the carrier. His steps are quick at first. Then lumbering. Then slow-motion. After a few steps, his legs stop churning and he falls to the ground. His charred body shakes for a second. Then nothing. The others never even make it out of the carrier.

The second carrier manages to avoid the equipment. Mavy starts speeding away, but the carrier gains on us. It fires another FDP and it catches one of our tires. We swerve into the road's shoulder, but Mavy keeps control. The damaged tire slows us down and causes the transport to hobble over every bump in the road. 512 and I pull out our weapons. It will be almost impossible to disable this carrier, because it is battle-fortified with carbonized plating and steel armor. But we have to try something. We fire a few useless shots and then I feel a powerful pull coming from behind me. Pique grabs 512 and me by the backs of our shirts and throws us away from the back doors. The force of her toss is so strong that we both slam into the front seats of the transport. "Enough of this," Pique says. The hair on my head stands up and I feel heat coming from Pique. She calmly walks to the back of the transport and opens the door. She's crying. She raises her hands and turns her palms to face the carrier. A hot and violent cloud of electricity fills the transport. Pique fires and scorches every last bit of earth in her path. It's over in an instant. This is nothing like what I saw from Nayla or even Spiro. The carrier is in flames. The trees lining the road are in flames. The pavement is melted.

Pique shakes violently. Her eyes roll to the back of her head and she passes out. She falls back on Nayla's dead body and rolls to the side of the trans-port. I run to her and grab her head before it hits the ground. I hold her in my lap as she convulses. Her heart is speeding and she is covered in sweat. Her hands are burning hot.

Pique remains out cold for the next few minutes. Mavy speeds away and turns onto the final road to the airfield. Pique's shaking slows and her body temperature gradually returns to normal. As we approach the entranceway to the airfield, Pique gasps for air and slowly wakes.

She's groggy, but hasn't lost her edge. *"Pretty cool, right?"* Her eyes quickly fill with tears. *"I can kill people."*

"You saved people, Pique. People you care about."

"Whatever." She gives me a look of disgust. "It's wrong and you know it."

"It's not wrong. It's only wrong—"

Pique cuts me off. She puts her hand over my mouth. "Stop. Please stop. You're the only person capable of understanding the truth. So just stop." Tears pour down her face. I don't say another word.

Mavy drives up to a security post with four soldiers who appear to have been burned alive by a surging heat storm from a nearby VOID. Each and every hangar we pass is burned to the ground. I don't see how our airship could have survived this blast. The entire airfield is decimated. Airships. Hangars. Security posts. All destroyed by fire.

"This isn't looking good," Trace says.

"You're quite the perceptive one," Mavy says back.

"Perceptive enough to know that your god has really fucked us this time."

"Blasphemy's not going to help matters."

"Neither is—"

"Will both of you please shut up," 512 says. He is looking through a set of field glasses and is trying to focus on something in distance. Mavy gets close enough for 512 to make it out.

"It's there. Our airship."

"How can that be? Trace asks.

"We're about to find out," Mavy says.

I remind Mavy not to get too close. She stops the transport about two hundred meters from the airship. I tell Trace and Pique to stay put. I want only soldiers approaching the airship. Mavy, 512, and I go on foot with weapons drawn, single-file, crouched low, spaced ten or so meters apart. We get to the airship without any interference and then split up. We go once around the airship and nothing seems unusual. Nothing other than the fact that this unharmed airship is sitting in a sea of scorched ships and buildings. The entry ramp is down and the door to the ship half open. This could mean it's an ambush or Atom just wants us to get going quickly. I go up first and Mavy and 512 follow. Our guns fan out in different directions. I quickly make a left turn down the aisle leading to the cockpit door. It's dead quiet on the ship. The door is wide open and I make out the back of Atom's head peeking out above the pilot's seat. There's another person—with a white bag over his head—sitting in the copilot's seat. "Atom, it's us."

Atom doesn't turn around.

I race to him and put my hand on his shoulder, but nothing. I step forward and swivel his chair toward me. I place my hand on his neck. He has a pulse, but it's weak. I look down and he has a gunshot wound to his gut. He's bleeding out. I shake him to wake him up.

He abruptly comes to and he's extremely disoriented. He tries to speak, but can't form the words. Then, a word comes out. "Thank." He can barely form the next words. Another word. "God." Slowly, he says it, "Thank God. You made it." He then goes unconscious again. 512 tends to Atom and applies pressure on his wound. From the amount of blood I see, there's no way Atom is going to pull through. His skin is colorless. His lips are purple. His breaths are labored. These are surefire signs that his march toward death has begun.

I turn from Atom and face the person in the other chair. The person's hands are manacled behind his back and secured to the arm of the chair. He is covered with a white hood. I remove the white hood and the cloth gag underneath it. *It's Dang.*

I rip the gag off. "What the hell happened?" I ask.

He nods toward Atom. "This guy saved me."

"From the look of things, it certainly doesn't seem like he was trying to save you," Mavy says. She uses the end of her gun to break through Dang's manacles.

"The manacles and hood were for show. He was protecting me. He knew he was dying and he knew I had no idea how to fly this airship out of here. So, if you guys didn't make it, and I got caught by Vrig's troops, he wanted to make it seem like I was kidnapped. He's a smart guy. Brave, too." Mavy breaks the manacles and Dang rubs his wrists. "He rescued me. He and this woman scientist saved me. Well, it was mostly him, because this scientist was killed on the spot." Dang lowers his head. "It was awful. Even though she pleaded with them to let her live, they shot her in the back of the head. And they almost got this guy, too. But he somehow managed to fight his way through it."

Dang runs his hands through his hair. "I don't even know where I was, but all of a sudden bullets were flying everywhere, and this guy I never met is guarding me and killing everyone in sight. We're running through side streets and back alleyways and he tells me to duck into a school. We manage to find one of those school transports and we're driving like a million kilometers an hour and we get to some small airstrip right in the capital. We hop in this airship, fly for like ten minutes, and land here. He mumbles his name, Adam or something, and then he tells me I should put this gag on and pretend I've been kidnapped. And then he tells me he's been sent here by the Holy Father and Spiro de Yerusalom to save me."

"The Holy Father?" 512 asks.

"Yes, the Holy Father. That old bastard saved me again."

"Watch yourself, Dang," Mavy says.

"He rescued little ole me again." Dang rolls his eyes at Mavy. "I must be really important." Dang walks over to Atom. He is clearly concerned about the man who saved him. "I don't understand any of this. I remember getting captured by the NFF and the next thing I remember is that scientist being executed. What the hell is going on?"

"We'll explain later," Mavy says to Dang. "I'm just glad you're okay."

Atom stirs in his seat. He mumbles bits and pieces of words, but I can't understand what he's trying to say. He mutters something under his breath. He becomes more active and tries to raise his arms. Maybe he's reaching for

Dang to come closer. At least, that's what Dang thinks. Dang lowers his head to hear what Atom has to say. Dang is nervous. He's not sure he wants to hear. Atom slowly pushes the words out of his mouth.

"*Go . . . to . . . Yerusalom.*"

Atom wheezes and coughs. "*Yerusalom.*" The force of the word causes a small trickle of blood to roll from Atom's mouth. Atom reaches for a breath, but doesn't find one. "Go." More blood streams out of his mouth. Dang looks like an anxious child being told he has to do the thing he fears most. "Why? Why should I go there?"

"Yerusalom needs you." Something from deep inside of Atom wants to come out. It shoots out of his mouth. Blood and bile and mucus from deep within pour out of Atom. Dang tries to wipe away the mess, but the more he wipes, the more comes out. Atom grabs his arm. "The world needs you."

Dang does his best to hide his anger, as well as its close cousin fear, but it's not good enough. "*How do you know what the world needs?*"

Atom's eyes snap open. They look at me and only me. "I know because Emmis told me." Atom's eyelids rapidly open and close. He looks possessed. "Emmis knows the truth."

"What truth?" I ask.

"Ask her."

"How can I ask? She's dead."

Atom smiles. His body convulses. With one eye open and one closed, he says his last words. "*To win the Game of the Gods, men only need to know one thing. Gods need men more than men need gods.*"

PART V
KOLEXICO

39

MAVY

What did Atom mean when he said to ask Emmis. She's dead. I know she's dead. I saw it with my own eyes. Kene killed her. Vrig gave the order. I held her dead body. I held all of their dead bodies. I can't do this again. I won't let anybody, especially a liar like Atom, mess with my head. *She's dead. I'm alive. I have people to protect.*

I pull Atom's dead body out of the pilot's chair. He's not coming with us. Even dead, Atom is a liability. He killed thousands—maybe even millions—of innocent people and I can't be associated with that. I carry his dead body down the ramp and leave it by the side of the airstrip. I don't feel great about this, but I have no choice. The second I lay the body down, I see Pique and Trace speeding toward us in the transport. They're moving fast and I soon see why. In the distance there are five heavily armed military carriers racing in our direction. Trace and Pique get to the airship and jump out. "We've got to get out of here," Trace says to me. I push them up the ramp and Mavy already has the engines buzzing. We slam the door behind us and jump into our seats. We feel badly but we have no choice but to leave Nayla's body behind.

"Secure your restraints, everyone," Mavy shouts. "This probably won't be the smoothest liftoff." The carriers are moving fast and firing at us. But we're still out of range. One of the carriers quickly swerves onto our airstrip and closes in on us. 512 scrambles to see if the airship has any weaponry. He searches the airship's databanks. No anticraft weapons, no jammers, no disjoint technology, no ammunition of any kind. This is a purely civilian air-ship and an old one at that. 512 knows the search is futile. "Nothing." He then looks at Pique. "We may need you again."

"No," I say. "Not again." I'm annoyed that 512 asked her, but I don't think he understands. If my instincts are right, every time she uses her powers, she dies a little more.

I run to the back of the airship and look out the rear window. I don't like what I see. The carrier is in range and its FDP launcher is actively moving around, trying to lock in on us. The launcher rears back and fires a loud shot. I hear the FDP racing toward us—its intense whistle getting louder and an-grier as it approaches. There's a loud crack like thunder. The FDP grazes one of the ship's wings and takes off a piece of the outermost lift flap. The piece flies off and clips the right back landing wheel and snaps it off. The tail of the airship hits the ground and screeches. Sparks fly everywhere. "Mavy, it's now or never," I shout. Although we probably don't have enough speed to get off the ground, we can't stay where we are. One more FDP and we're dead. "Get us up. Now."

Mavy throws on the thrusters and activates the flaps' hydraulics. The nose of the ship and the front wheels lift off the ground, but the tail of the ship is still dragging behind. Mavy has the nose pointed up at a steep angle, but we can't get the tail off the ground. Metal sparks are flying from the tail, and the smell of burnt air is filling the cabin. "I wish I believed in God right now," Dang says.

"How did you ever become a Federate?" I ask him.

"I lied. Really well."

This is the first time I see Pique smile since Nayla died. Dang is panick-ing, so he just keeps nervously talking. "I had to become a Federate," Dang says. "Everyone knows the Federacy has the best restaurants." Pique, who never seems worried no matter what our situation is, smiles again.

The carrier fires another FDP, and this one takes out the already dam-aged axle that's dragging on the runway. Maybe that FDP saves us—because just as the damaged piece of axle goes flying, we get the extra lift we need and the tail comes up and we're in the air. Mavy pulls in the front wheel and adjusts the lift flaps and we go soaring into the sky, out of the range of the carriers. We're safe for now, but we need to get out of NFF airspace as soon as possible. Hopefully they're not able to scramble any fighters.

"Head northeast," I say.

"We need to head southeast, Max." I know what Mavy means, but it's not happening.

I look at the cartogramic monitor on the wall of the airship. "Lock in to sixty-four point one seven degrees north, fifty-one point seven four degrees west."

Mavy turns to look at the monitor. "The only destination I'm locking in to are thirty-one point seven eight degrees north, thirty-five point two two degrees east."

I remain calm. "Mavy, I understand where you're coming from. But I need to keep everyone safe." Mavy is annoyed. "I'm the only one who knows how to fly this ship. We're going where I say we're going."

"It doesn't work that way."

"Can someone tell me what the hell the two of them are even arguing about? Trace asks. Pique gives her uncle a look that says, *Us Rollins women understand that our men sometimes need a little extra help.* Pique speaks slowly, as if Trace were a child. "*Mavy wants to go to Yerusalom. The judge wants to go to Kolexico.*"

Trace sticks his tongue out at Pique and she laughs. "Then it's settled," Trace says. "We go to Kolexico."

"And why is that," Mavy says.

"Because I like the judge better than you." Trace tries to contain his smile and then takes a more serious tone. "The judge is right. We can buy the kinds of friends we need in Kolexico. Vrig has already paved the way by buying off Xylo Borne, the Easter Cartel's leader. The thing to keep in mind about most Kolexicans is that they like their money. They *really really* like their money." My brother-in-law is smarter than the Rollins girls or I give him credit for. I sometimes forget he was a leader in his own right—before the morzium did him in. Trace quickly becomes diplomatic with Mavy and tries his hardest not to aggravate her any further. He unlocks his restraint and takes a few steps toward her. "If we're going to find out the truth of what's going on— I'm sorry, Mavy, but Yerusalom just isn't the place to do it. We can buy the truth in Kolexico. In Yerusalom, the truth isn't for sale and it probably isn't even the truth."

Mavy doesn't respond. I can't tell what's going through her head, but it seems that some of the fight has been taken out of her. She seems almost glum. Pique gently nudges her uncle back to his seat and kneels on the floor alongside Mavy. "Men," Pique says. "They always know what's right for us."

Mavy's laugh is halfhearted.

"I don't know where we should go. But maybe Trace has a point. Yerusalom's not like most places and *our father* is not like other men." This is the first time I've heard Pique acknowledge that she and Mavy have the same father. She must have known all along. I don't think she's ever lied to me, but this certainly seems like the kind of omission that qualifies as a lie. I wish she had told me, but I'm not upset. Whereas Emmis lied to me because it served her interests, Pique lied to me because it served mine. I'm as sure of this as I am anything.

"I know you love our father," Pique says, "but I also know you're like me— you have your doubts." Mavy doesn't respond. Her hands tighten around the navigation controls, but otherwise she is completely still.

"Can I ask you a question," Pique says. Mavy continues to look forward but nods yes.

"Why do you trust our father so much? I mean, I know he's our father, but so what? We don't have to trust our fathers—*do we*? Not if they haven't earned it. You don't just go and trust some random stranger. I wouldn't walk down the street and say, *Hey there stranger, can you take care of my baby and after that take all my money and place it in the bank depository for me.* You trust people because they prove they can be trusted, right? Can you honestly tell me that our father has earned your trust?"

We are traveling at an altitude of nine thousand meters and we're out of NFF territory. We are at least a kilometer above any cloud formations and we see nothing but blue sky in front of us. We have a simple civilian radar system, but I trust what it's telling me—that there are no fighter craft nearby. Mavy flies the airship due east. She is not willing to abandon her position or adopt ours. She won't commit to flying north to Kolexico or south to Yerusalom. She stares forward at the clear sky with her hands tightly gripping the controls even though the ship's computers are doing the flying. After a few minutes, she slowly lets go of the wheel and turns her seat to face Pique and pauses.

"Faith," Mavy finally says. She turns her seat back toward the sky ahead of us and hits a switch that turns off the autopilot. "Faith in something that's better than this." We hit a few bumps as Mavy takes control away from the ship. "I trust him because I believe that there has to be something better in this world than killing, lying, and cheating. If our father—the Holy Father—is not what he says he is, then what's the point of any of this. He's the closest thing I've seen to Our God and if he's as flawed as all of you think, then so is Our God. And if that's the case, I don't want to go on." Mavy looks like she wants to cry, but she won't let herself.

Pique places both of her hands on Mavy's belly. "I don't know about God, Mavy. I'm still just a kid. But if you ask me what really matters in this world, I think a lot of it comes down to this one thing: *We need to be better people than our parents, and our children need to be better than us.*" Pique looks down at Mavy's stomach. "I think you're a much better person than our father, and I think you're going to try your hardest to help this little baby be a better person than you." Mavy puts her hands over Pique's and holds it there. She allows a tear. One hard-earned tear.

"I appreciate that," Mavy says. "You're no child. You're a very special young woman and a better person than I'll ever be. But, what I think you don't yet understand is that either there's one righteous path that the Holy Father is leading us down or there isn't. If you prove to me that the Holy Father isn't the shepherd I believe him to be, then I don't know what to make of this reality we're living in. I need to trust him. *You hear me. I need to trust him.* I don't know how to explain it to you any other way."

Pique nods her head as if she understands. She doesn't, but the most important thing for her is that Mavy feels like she does. For Pique, it's not about Truth with a capital "T." It never has been. It's about the little truths people share every day: honesty, caring for loved ones, showing compassion to strangers, being better than our instincts. Her idea of what's important couldn't be further from Mavy's. Pique lifts herself up. "I'm a good fighter and I don't lie. I don't understand a lot more than that. I'm not sure I want to. But I know one thing. Someday, I hope you and I can be close. Like sisters. Okay. You and I can be sisters."

"We already are, Pique."

"Well, then I hope I can say something you might not like. I'm not trying to be disrespectful, but I see our father as a man who's got a lot of problems. I don't see a lot of *holy* in him."

After Pique says this, the only thing that can be heard is the hum of the airship's engines. We continue flying east without anyone saying a word. Slowly, Mavy starts to slouch in her seat. Her head begins to lower. It eventually drops all the way down so that her chin is resting on the navigation controls. Her long and perfect stature becomes a hunched-over arch, awkwardly nestled into the pilot's seat. She's folded herself into a ball. She's as small as she can be. Eventually she reaches down and locks into a destination in the airship's databank. Her voice is weak. "Locking in to sixty-four degrees eleven minutes north, fifty-one degrees forty-three minutes west."

"Thank you, Mavy," I say.

She straightens up in her seat and gives me an angry look. "Don't thank me. I didn't do it for you."

40

CARTELS OF KOLEXICO

We fly for a few hours and then begin our descent into Kolexico. As we descend toward a runway outside of Kolexico's largest city—actually it's the only city—I can't help but laugh. 512 asks me what's so funny. I explain to him how ironic it is that this second-rate land of misfits and outlaws survived the Federacy, the Rogues, and all the other territories that the NFF destroyed. Now, if the NFF is in as bad a shape as I think, it's just Kolexico, a place built around a false sense of freedom, and the Nation of Yerusalom, a place built around a false sense of salvation. *Maybe the Abstainers had it right all along.*

We're going to land on a civilian airstrip in the Assembly of Cüko, the administrative center of Kolexico. My plan is to meet with Xylo Borne. I'm not worried that Borne has some strong allegiance to Vrig. He doesn't. As Trace said, it's always about the money for these cartel leaders, and Vrig's money is not worth much anymore. Vrig's finances are tied to NFF currency and his country's military infrastructure. The minute Atom unleashed those VOIDs, the economy caught fire. Even without me closely monitoring what's happening, I know inflation will run rampant and the NFF's economy will spiral out of control. Vrig's money will soon be worthless.

By Kolexican law, the Assembly of Cüko, as well as the airstrip within it, is a combat-free zone. Kolexico is a place that permits a certain amount of chaos, but it's a managed form which has served its inhabitants well for centuries. The Charter of Kolexico, or as it's more commonly known, the Ten

Rules, was established by three former soldiers from what used to be known as the state of Danemerk. This state was the smallest of the thirty states in the Great Anglican Nation. It never had more than a million inhabitants and it currently has about half that amount. As the story of the Kolexico founding goes, these three soldiers-turned-fathers-of-a-nation were prosecuted for an odious act—bestiality. Whether the founding story of Kolexico is true is questionable. But it's still important in understanding why Kolexicans are such fierce libertarians.

The victim of the alleged bestiality was a bottle-nosed dolphin. Each of the three soldiers took turns "making love" to this "intelligent female" creature who demonstrated her "consent" each time by presumably enjoying the acts. It's a very important part of the story that it was *making love*, that the dolphin was *female and intelligent*, and lastly, that the dolphin *consented*. According to the founding story, these soldiers had their reasons. It was not just that they had a wicked sense of the absurd, which they obviously did. It is clear from the story that they did not relish the idea of having sex with a dolphin. They found the whole thing grotesque and degrading. But it was the most dramatic way they could think of to protest a new and onerous Anglican law on permissible sexual practices. The old Anglicans were obsessed with sex. It's what the famous psychodiagnostician Dr. Ryson Thom wrote about in his book *The Prurience of Being a Prude*.

Following a deadly outbreak of PIV, a terrible sexually transmitted disease that had no cure at the time, and yet another war with the Kingdom of the Blessed Erabian States over the meaning of four simple Erabiat words in a peace agreement, the Anglican parliament passed the Responsible Endeavors for Sexual Practices Ensuring Custom and Tradition Act. The RESPECT Act prohibited a wide range of sexual conduct, including acts that were then widely practiced by homosexuals, bisexuals, and transgendered. The act went to great lengths to prohibit specific types of conduct. For example, the act stated that "a man's penis shall not come in contact with the rectum or anus of another man under any circumstance." It also prohibited "the practice commonly known as *scissoring*, a practice in which one woman causes her vagina to be pressed up against another woman's vagina for the purpose of causing sexual gratification in one or both women." Perhaps the cruelest part of the act was that it required any individual in the process of changing genders to register with the Ministry of Health and sign something called the Registry of the Changed.

The laws were draconian on their face, but in practice, they often had ridiculous unintended consequences. The soldiers wanted to exploit this. *Cue the dolphin.*

The RESPECT Act allowed heterosexual couples to file an affidavit with the Ministry of Health that certain acts they engaged in—oral sex, for example—were like "making love." If they filed the affidavit, then they were considered outside the scope of the law for that particular act. Homosexuals, on the other hand, were not afforded this "privilege." To protect couples, many lawyers advocated that their newlywed clients file broad-reaching affidavits with the Ministry of Health to protect themselves against any potential prosecution. Even though the vast majority of married couples were not going to engage in most of these acts, they signed the affidavits anyway. It was at first embarrassing to the population, because it was a mostly religious population. But eventually every heterosexual couple was signing a document that made it seem like they were porn stars.

To highlight the absurdity of the RESPECT Act, the founding story tells us that the three soldiers digitally recorded themselves engaging in bestiality. First, they recorded themselves signing affidavits about how having sex with the dolphin's various orifices was like "making love." They then recorded the dolphin "signing" the affidavit—supposedly the dolphin held the pen in her mouth and moved it across the paper. Then they placed the dolphin in a rotating harness and proceeded to digitally record themselves, one by one, mounting the dolphin and "making love" to different orifices, including the blowhole. The soldiers then sent the digital recording to a number of different outlets, and large portions of the Great Anglican Nation viewed this spectacle. Most were outraged at the bestiality. However, a small but soon-to-be-growing segment of the population embraced the absurdist message. The recording turned the soldiers into folk heroes.

Many Kolexicans treat this founding story like one of the great stories of the Book of Our God. The story has been handed down from generation to generation, and although writing about it is generally frowned upon, Kolexicans take great pride in the soldiers and their sacrificial dolphin. There are even groups of avid "Dolphiners," who, like adventurers trying to find the lost treasure of some sunken ship, spend their lives hunting for the missing recordings, which most Kolexicans believe were destroyed by the Great Anglican Nation. The recording is a holy grail—a fascination for many. The story of the soldiers and the dolphin gives one just a little taste of what lurks beneath the surface in Kolexico.

It's a very, very strange place.

After releasing the recording, the three soldiers immediately fled Danemerk. They were prosecuted in absentia for their actions, even though they technically did not violate the RESPECT Act. Bestiality was not expressly prohibited, and therefore, strictly speaking, shoud have been permissible between consenting heterosexual parties that signed affidavits. The soldiers never had any intention of going to trial for their alleged crime. They planned their escape well in advance of the release of the recordings and started a colony on Emerald Island, a remote island outpost far from the population centers in the state of Danemerk. The ten thousand or so Danemerkians who inhabited this massive but mostly unpopulated island were by no means loyal subjects of the Great Anglican Nation. They were "tribes," for lack of a better word, of loosely affiliated individuals who disliked the idea of a centralized government. These tribes were the precursors to the cartels of Kolexico.

Emerald Island, now Kolexico, was a sprawling island abundant in hydrogen forms, but with little or no infrastructure. There was only one main road on the island, and it was poorly maintained. Without any loyal boots on the ground, the Anglican Nation had a hard time tracking down the soldiers. The will to capture the soldiers quickly faded. The soldiers were free to build a new community, and foremost on their minds was the unfairness of the RESPECT Act.

That is how Kolexico was supposedly started. Whether the whole story is true or not, who knows. But there was a RESPECT Act and there were three soldiers who opposed it and started Kolexico. Most importantly, Kolexicans believe in the story—or at least the moral of the story. Freedom is the core value underpinning Kolexican society. "The less government the better," reads the Kolexican charter's flag. Kolexicans even refuse to call themselves a nation, though they are. They consider themselves members of a charter, a charter to ten simple rules.

Just as it is frowned upon to write about the story of the dolphin, it is customary not to write down the Ten Rules. Writing in general is frowned upon. A strong anti-intellectual current runs through Kolexico. But by the sixth grade, every child knows the Ten Rules by heart. I, too, have them memorized, as a result of my first-year Anthropology of Law class. My instructor insisted on us roleplaying as members of the society we were learning about. I have never forgotten the rules.

Rule 1:

There shall be no laws regulating the type of sexual practices engaged in between consenting adults.

Rule 2:

There shall be no laws establishing a religion or regulating a religion, and no laws interfering with an individual's moral beliefs or restricting an individual's speech.

Rule 3:

Any group of one thousand or more individuals can form a cartel and elect a single leader to represent the cartel in the Kolexico governing body. Cartel leaders will be responsible for all intra-cartel matters, except they shall not pass any laws in violation of these Ten Rules or restricting the unfettered right of individuals to switch cartels.

Rule 4:

Each cartel shall have an equal vote in the governing body, which shall be called the Assembly of Cüko.

Rule 5:

The Assembly of Cüko, and the one-kilometer area surrounding it, shall forever be a combat-free zone and weapons shall be strictly prohibited. Any individual or cartel that uses violence in this combat-free zone shall be summarily executed by a firing squad of the leaders of the five largest cartels at that time. Each leader shall fire a lethal bullet.

Rule 6:

A cartel leader may call for a vote on any matter not specifically prohibited in these Ten Rules. A leader shall call for no more than five votes in a calendar year. The results of the vote shall be binding for no more than one year, and subsequent votes on the matter are prohibited for that one-year time period, except if a unanimous vote by all cartel leaders calls for a new vote.

Rule 7:

If there is a dispute between two or more cartels, the disputants shall simultaneously produce a list of all cartel leaders, ranked from highest choice to lowest, and the leader that is mutually highest on both lists shall have sole authority to resolve the dispute based on economic equilibrium principles and minimal harm to the five least wealthy cartels.

Rule 8:

Each cartel shall contribute ten percent of its Gross Cartel Product as defined by the International Atlas of Economic Designations to the administration of the Assembly of a Cüko and the one-kilometer combat-free zone.

Rule 9:

There shall be one Administrator for the Assembly of Cüko. The Administrator shall be elected by two-thirds majority of all cartel leaders and serve a one-year term and shall never serve again. The vote shall take place on the last day of each calendar year. If a two-thirds majority cannot be reached, the leaders of the five least wealthy cartels shall select an Administrator by simple majority.

Rule 10:

It is the intention of the framers of these Ten Rules that Kolexico be a land that promotes freedom, individual liberty, and limited government.

41

ORION

The right side of our rear landing gear is destroyed, so we let the Kolexico air transport controller know this. If this were the Federacy, the controller would initiate a crisis landing procedure that includes fire-retardant foam on the airstrip, emergency transports, and an immediate landing clearance. But the controller does none of the above. No foam. No emergency transports. No assistance whatsoever. "Best of luck" is all the controller says. He probably then goes and gets a cup of tea, because it's about five minutes before he comes back and assigns us a landing strip at the far end of the Assembly of Cüko airfield.

Mavy's descent is slow and controlled. Some strong winds from the north occasionally cause some imbalance, but Mavy does a good job of keeping the airship steady. At about five thousand meters, we can make out a few lights on the ground in Kolexico. I have lost track of time, but my chronometer seems to think it's close to midnight. I'm glad to put this miserable day behind me.

I move close to Pique and reach for her hand. She quickly reaches back and grabs a firm hold. Trace unfastens his seat belt and sits before both of us. He grabs our hands, too. We're all unsure about what awaits us. Kolexico is not known for its hospitality, especially toward people like us, and so we're more than a little apprehensive. Dang sees the three of us huddled together. I'm not sure I believe in prayer any longer, and I know that Pique and Trace

certainly don't, but it is sort of what we're doing. I can't say who we're praying to or even what we're praying for, but when three people in our states of
mind sit in a circle holding hands, prayer is the only way I can think to describe it. Dang slowly makes his way toward us. He's cautious. "Hey, would
it be too weird if I joined in?"

"It would be totally weird," Pique says. "But get in here."

The four of us are holding hands. It's beyond out of character for me. But
I don't care. They need me. Or maybe it's just that I need them.

"You guys better get your restraints on," Mavy says. "I'm beginning the
final descent and I don't know how I'm going to set the rear of this bird down.
But I will bring her down and it will be rough."

I make sure everyone is strapped in and then make my way to Mavy. I put
a flotation device on her and snap each strap together. Mavy tries to stop me,
but she needs to keep her hands on the controls. She quickly tries to slap my
hand away. "Stop it already. We're not going over water."

"It's protection for you and the baby." I place my hand on Mavy's shoulder. "I know you can take care of yourself. But I'm here for you." She reaches
back, and briefly places her hand over mine before returning it to the controls. I strap myself in and tell everyone to cover their heads and brace for
impact.

At one thousand meters, Mavy says she can see the airstrip. Besides a few
strong gusts of wind, conditions are the best they can be for an emergency
landing. It's a clear night. The airspace is empty. We are the only people landing on this remote airstrip.

"Five hundred meters to touchdown," 512 shouts from the copilot's chair.
The front landing gear comes down and our lift flaps turn to landing position. The airship is shuddering, and the thrusters, which are trying to slow
us down, are deafening.

"Would you all think I'm a complete loser if I threw up again?" Dang
shouts.

"Yes," Pique responds.

"Well, I may just . . . have to . . . oh . . ." Dang throws up. He's not made
for soldiering. It's hard to believe this boy shares a gene pool with Saool
Forque.

"*Impact* in fifteen seconds," 512 shouts.

"You mean *landing*," Trace shouts back.

"Feel free to choose your own words," 512 says. "But it's going to be anything but smooth." Mavy descends another few hundred meters and positions the ship so the airstrip is directly in front of us. Just as she prepares to touch the ship down, she banks hard to the left. The nose of the ship, which is pointed high in the air, crosses over the airstrip. The right wing arches up in the air and the ship rolls to its left. Mavy wants the operational rear left wheel to touch down first. She throws all the thrusters in reverse, and the engines fight the forward pull. The rear left wheel touches the ground and we bounce back in the air. She slowly lowers the nose at the same time as she brings the right wing down. The rear left wheel hits the strip again, but this time it sticks. The front wheel comes down hard and takes a small skip before hitting the ground and sticking. The airship then violently falls back to its right. It's as if we just tried to sit on a three-legged chair. The tail hits the ground fast and scrapes along the airstrip. Sparks fly as the back of the airship drags along the concrete strip. Mavy swerves the airship onto a nearby patch of grass and we slide across it, burning up the grass behind us. The back of the airship catches fire, and black smoke starts to fill the cabin. I unfasten my restraints just as the airship is slowing down.

"Everyone out," I shout. The smoke makes it hard to see and breathe. "Get to the front exit." The smoke is thickening and the exit lights have malfunctioned. It's hard to see where to go. Pique and Trace push open a door on the side of the airship and drop an emergency ladder down. "Go," I shout. Pique and Trace quickly head down the ladder. 512 and Mavy are busy trying to turn off the engines and slow the spread of the fire. But there's no use and I tell them they have to get out through the side now.

Dang and I are the only ones left. It's hard to make out what's going on through the smoke, but he's shaking badly. As I get closer to him, I realize it's not shaking, but dry-heaving. He is struggling to undo his restraints and having no success. He's confused. The smell of his vomit mixing with the smell of burning plastic and rubber can't help matters. He's a mess. I can't see the releases on his restraints, but I feel around for them. I mostly feel a warm sludge, which I try to convince myself is anything but Dang's fresh vomit. I eventually find the restraints, and pull him out of them. I don't know whether he's up for running or not, and I don't wait to find out. I throw him over my shoulder and run to the exit. I have one hand on him and the other on the emergency ladder as I quickly go down it. I keep running until I find Pique and the others on the other side of the airstrip. When I look back, our airship is completely engulfed in flames.

I collapse on the ground next to Mavy. She lies alongside me. The air is frigid, but we don't mind. Her back is on the ground and her belly is pointing up toward the stars. Shoulder-to-shoulder, we both look up at the night sky.

Right above us is Orion. He's bursting with life.

42

XYLO BORNE

An older woman approaches us on the airstrip. She's dressed in plain clothes and wears a very unofficial-looking badge that says her name, Echa Magor, and her title, assistant administrator of the Assembly of Cüko. Her hair is white and the moonlight shines on a prickly set of faint gray whiskers around her chin. "Are you okay," she states matter-of-factly. The way she asks makes it clear that she couldn't care less.

"We're quite well and you," Pique says with an over-the-top interest. The woman doesn't find it funny.

"Do you have any weapons?" the woman asks.

Pique will not let another one of us answer. She holds up her fists and says, "Just these." She waves her fists in the air like a clown challenging another clown to a fight.

"That's cute, little girl," the woman says. There is zero inflection in her voice. She's all business. "Any real weapons?"

"Do you consider words weapons?" Dang asks. "You can ask any celebrity I've ever written about. My words are weapons."

The woman sees me as the only sensible one in the group, probably because of my age. I don't think she recognizes who I am, but I barely recognize myself these days, so why should she?

"Does your group have any weapons?" she asks me.

"We have many and we know this is a demilitarized zone. We will hand them all over." I tell everyone to hand over their weapons and they do.

"Do you grant me permission to use an armament detector on you?"

"Of course."

She takes a small device out of her pocket and asks us to spread our legs and put our hands in the air. She runs the detector across each of our bodies. There's not a peep. She takes out a radio and says, "They're clean. Bringing a party of six to the Airstrip Receiving Center. Judge Cone is safe. Please wake the Administrator."

"So you do know who I am," I say.

"Of course I know who you are. This is Kolexico, not Mars. We can read the news." I see the right side of her lips rise. It almost looks like a smile. "Welcome," she says. But she can't possibly mean it.

I want to ask her more questions, but just as I try she walks away from me. She places our weapons in a container in the back of her transport and jumps in. "Meet me over there," she says, pointing to a large structure at the northern edge of the airstrip. She doesn't offer to drive us, even though there's plenty of room in her transport.

Mavy doesn't seem to care at all. The minute the woman leaves, Mavy returns to lying on her back. She's in no rush. She's lost in thought, staring at the night sky. I look at her for a few moments. Her big green eyes are fixed on the sky. She's hypnotized by the stars. She's breathing slowly. The baby's temporary home gradually rises and falls with each breath. Mavy may be the most beautiful woman I have ever seen. I eventually reach down to her. She grabs my outstretched hand and I pull her up. As soon as she gets up, she reaches around me with her other hand and pulls me into a tight embrace. Our baby is firmly pressed between us. Her lips come close to my ears. "How crazy would it be if you and I ended up together?" She moves back so I can see her face and she mine. Then what she says surprises me. She turns away from me and says, "Emile would be so hurt." She lets go of my hand. The two of us walk behind the others.

"You ever wonder what that might be like?" she asks me.

"You mean what it would be like for us to be together?"

"No. I mean what it must be like for someone like Emile. Did you ever

think about what it would be like for a man who died too young to watch—
from up above—as the woman he loves, falls in love with another man?"

"Nope. I've been kind of busy lately trying to escape from people who are
trying to kill us."

She ignores my response. "Think about it. You're a young man, early thir-
ties, with a perfect wife and two beautiful children. Life couldn't get much
better. Your wife is sweet and gorgeous and you're madly in love with her.
Then one day, out of nowhere, God decides to take you. Maybe you get struck
by a transport. Your wife is devastated, and perhaps because of this, or maybe
despite it, within a month or two, she meets another man. He's taller than
you. Richer than you. Smarter than you. He's better-looking than you. She
sleeps with him after only a few weeks. You have to watch how nervous
she is getting ready for a date with him. You watch how excited she is for it.
You watch how she laughs at his jokes at dinner. You watch as her hand 'accidentally' touches his. You watch him order for her. You watch as she invites
him back to the bedroom you used to sleep in. You watch him taking off
her clothes. You watch how eager she is to take off his clothes. You watch
how excited she is to please him and how excited she is to be pleased.

"You watch as he kisses her neck and gently strokes her hair. You watch as
he kisses her breasts. You watch him go inside of her. You watch her moan
with a kind of pleasure you have never seen. Day after day, week after week,
you watch her tell him how amazing he makes her feel.

"And then the fateful day arrives, when all that passion turns to love. He—
not you—is her true love. She tells him this and you're right there watching.
You watch as she says *I've never felt this way before* and *I love you more than
anything.* The pain. I can't even begin to imagine that kind of pain. You have
to watch her tell another man how much she loves him. With all her heart,
she loves this other man."

Mavy exhales a deep breath, as if she's exhaling the hurt of every pained
lover. She feels more than I do. I have no idea what Mavy wants me to say to
her. But I know she wants me to say something. All I can come up with is
"I wouldn't want that to be me."

She looks up toward the sky. "It's just that love is so cosmically screwed
up. I wish Our God had a better answer for this kind of pain."

We walk along the scorched grass, tracing back over our airship's path.

Pique runs back and walks alongside me. I put my arm around her. She's so little—especially compared to the woman on my other side. It's hard to believe Pique and Mavy have the same fathers. They're so different.

We get to the Receiving Center. It's a large box of a building with a white stone exterior and metal grates over the windows. We walk inside and find that the interior is even less inviting than the exterior. The single room is basically empty, except for a few old desks and chairs. There are no Kolexico flags or digital posters defining regulations or any ornaments to speak of. The bare walls are painted a drab gray. The floors are creamy white slabs of concrete and silicon. There is one bench and it's made of a strange white rubberized material that looks rigid and unwelcoming. The assistant administrator, who is the only person in the room, is seated at a rickety metal desk that is beginning to oxidize.

As we walk through the door and approach her, she doesn't look up. In about as unfriendly a voice as I've ever heard, she says, "Have a seat over there." She points to the bench, but still doesn't look up. She is busy entering some information into an old-fashioned microprocessor.

Everyone but Trace sits down on the bench. He's a bit antsy, but it also seems like he wants the assistant administrator to understand that he doesn't like the idea of being told to sit and wait. He doesn't like how rude she's been. The assistant administrator doesn't seem to care.

I sit quietly for a minute or two and then say, "We would like to see—"

"Leader Borne," the assistant administrator says. "We know."

"May I ask how you know?"

"The Administrator will be here shortly. He will answer all of your questions."

"You know that we just came from the NFF. It's been devastated—"

"By over twenty-five VOIDs," she says. She still doesn't look up at us. "I know. We all know. If the Administrator so chooses, he will discuss these issues with you."

"Do you know how many people died?" She doesn't answer. She lifts her head up for a split second, makes a face at us, and then goes right back to her work. "Do you even care how many people died?"

"Forgive me, Judge," she says without interrupting her work. "I'm very busy. I don't mean to be rude, but when I said the Administrator will answer your questions—*that* is what I meant." Pique elbows me, and in a singsongy way says, "Someone's getting in trouble." I elbow her back.

Trace walks around picking up things off desks and moving around chairs. He is trying his hardest to get the assistant administrator to tell him to stop. But she doesn't. It's a childish antic, but fun to watch. Either she's an excellent actor or she genuinely doesn't care. Eventually he walks over to her and says, "So, *whatcha* working on?" She doesn't take the bait. She ignores him. He tries one more thing—picking up a writing instrument from her desk and annoyingly throwing it up and down over her head. She doesn't flinch. He has no choice but to give up. He squeezes himself on the bench in between Dang and Pique, slouches down, and closes his eyes.

After ten minutes, the door swings open and the Administrator flies in. He is underwhelming in stature, not being more than a few centimeters taller than Pique. He's very thin and walks faster than any man I have ever seen. He seems like the kind of person who is always in motion—always moving with a purpose. He doesn't go to shake any of our hands. Kolexicans do not shake hands as a general principle. He passes us on the bench and says, "Welcome." He does not make eye contact. He quickly walks to the assistant administrator, hands her an envelope, and then grabs a nearby chair. He pulls the chair toward our bench and sits down.

"Where to begin? Where to begin?" He talks the same way he moves. Fast. "Let's start with the NFF. A terrible tragedy. Millions are dead, but we don't have more information than that. Could be as much as ten million. Terrible. Terrible. As you know, Kolexico is neutral as to all foreign matters. We have no official position on who did what to whom. You are welcome here in Kolexico, as would be Chancellor Vrig, the Holy Father, or any of their staff." He barely pauses before moving to the next topic. "Now, it seems like you would like to meet with Xylo." He stammers for a second. "I mean, Leader Borne. Sorry. It's hard to get used to calling him 'Leader' even after all this time." He forces himself to slow down. "Xylo . . . Leader Borne is my twin brother. We're identical twins. I'm older by six minutes, but how could that possibly be relevant to you. So, you want to meet Xy—" He cuts himself off and takes a quick breath. "Leader Borne is amenable to meeting you. I've arranged transport. It's about a six-hour drive from here." He stands up. "Now,

I have an emergency meeting in the Assembly that I must attend, so do you have any questions of me before I leave?"

"Can you tell me where the bathroom is," Dang blurts out. I give Dang an angry look and he shrugs. "I really have to go." The Administrator has no problem answering the question and points Dang to the back of the room. I give the same angry look to Trace and Pique as a precaution.

"I have a few questions."

"And I have a few minutes. Go ahead."

"How can you demonstrate to me that we will be safe?"

"I can't."

"You can't make any assurances."

"I can give you back your weapons once you leave the Assembly of Cüko zone."

"Okay. Who will be driving the transport?"

"The assistant administrator."

"Will anyone else be coming?"

"No."

"Does anyone else know about our arrival?"

"I have no idea."

"Can you assure me that—"

"Let me stop you, Judge. In Kolexico, we are not overly concerned with the business of others. We want to live our lives, and some, like Xylo, want to get rich. You're complicating this."

"I'm not sure I'm complicating anything. In case you haven't noticed, the world is falling apart."

"Yes, but the truths of daily life remain. You want something from Xylo—maybe information or safe passage to Yerusalom or some mercenaries. I honestly don't know what you want and I don't care. Xylo wants his money. If someone can offer him more money than you, you may have reason to worry. But if you're prepared to give him more money than that other person, you should have nothing to fear."

"Maybe you would turn me in for money."

"I'm not interested in money. I'm the Administrator. I take that duty very seriously, as have all before me." He stands up. "And since I can only assume you have no further meaningful questions, I shall leave now." I've obviously insulted him. He quickly scurries away just as Dang returns from the bathroom. Dang reaches his hand out to say thank you, but the Administrator breezes right by him.

Trace looks at the assistant administrator and says, "I guess we're stuck with you."

"You could do worse," she says. It's hard to tell if she means this as a joke. She then points to the bathroom and says, "It's about a six-hour drive. So if anyone else has to use the bathroom, you better go now."

"I don't have to go," Mavy says. She grabs her stomach. "But this little guy does." Trace holds the door for Mavy as she walks in. Pique follows her. When they come out, Trace, 512, and I go in. I've always found it strange to be at a urinal and talk. But of course Trace doesn't want to a let second silently go by. As we head to the urinals, Trace starts talking. Thankfully 512 is in between us, so he feels more obligated to field Trace's questions. I don't want to talk.

"What do you make of all this?" Trace asks him.

"I think the Administrator seems honest," 512 says. "I don't see any reason to be overly concerned."

"Maybe it's nothing, but why are they bothering to drive us all the way out there. Six hours away. Why can't this leader guy just meet us here? They're putting us in a car and driving us away from the combat-free zone, the airstrip, and the only bit of civilization that exists in Kolexico. It just bothers me."

"You have a point," 512 says. "But I don't think these people are political. They never have been. And I don't think we need to worry about Borne, or even Vrig, who'll have his hands full maintaining order at home. So what are we really worried about?"

"I don't know. I'm just worried. But I guess we'll have our weapons. It'll have to be enough."

I walk toward the washbasin and turn on the water. I don't want to get involved in Trace and 512's conversation. There is much to worry about, but I can't be overly concerned about going six hours away from the Assembly of Cüko. It seems relatively benign, especially in light of what we've been through. Without a doubt, there are many more risks that lie ahead. The Holy

Father and Chancellor Vrig are dangerous men who will not rest until they've achieved what they want. But, for the time being, I think we're safe.

Trace and 512 leave the bathroom and I linger behind. I look at myself in the mirror above the washbasin. New lines have formed on my face. Angry patches of gray have sprouted in my beard. I splash water on my face. I run my hands under the warm water and scrub them with cleanser. I get my hands clean—very clean. Yet I keep washing. Over and over, I wash my hands while staring at an unfamiliar face that seems to age before my eyes. I wash and wash. I'm trying to wash them clean of something. I just don't know what it is.

43

ECHA MAGOR

We squeeze into the assistant administrator's transport. It has three rows. Mavy sits in the front passenger seat. Dang, Pique, and I sit in the middle row. 512 and Trace, who are fast becoming friends, sit in the back row.

The assistant administrator is the last one to enter the transport. She tells us there has been a small change of plans. Maybe I should find the last-minute change troubling, but I don't. The assistant administrator tells us that we're going to stay the night at a lodge that's a two-hour drive from the Assembly of Cüko. She doesn't want to drive all six hours tonight. It's late, and the assistant administrator thinks it's too much for her. Mavy seems suspicious, but I have no reason to doubt her.

We drive for a short while and she pulls over to the side of the road. She goes to the back of the transport and removes our weapons from a secured container. She returns to the car and hands the weapons to me. She pulls back onto the road and it soon turns from two lanes each way to one lane. There are small reflectors every hundred meters or so on the side of the road, but our route is otherwise dark. I have never seen so many stars.

Trace is sitting two rows behind the assistant administrator. He leans forward in his seat and pulls his restraint along with him. "So, your name's Echa," Trace says. "What kind of name is that?" She doesn't say anything. "Oh, that's *so rude of me*. I should have asked permission to address you first—Madame Assistant Administrator, is it okay if I call you Echa?"

She takes a long time to respond, but then says, "No."

"No, it wouldn't be okay?"

"I find your double negatives irritating, but *yes*."

"You mean yes, I can't call you Echa."

"Yes," she says, now very irritated. "I would rather you not call me Echa."

"May I ask why?"

"No."

"So I can't call you Echa and I can't ask you why."

"Oh, that's enough," Echa says. "The name Echa was given to me by my slaveholders."

There's a long awkward pause followed by an even more awkward "Oops" and "Sorry." Trace has no idea what to say next, so he doesn't say a thing. The silence is beyond uncomfortable. Mavy feels the need to fill the void. As we continue driving down what seems to be an ever-narrowing road, Mavy and the assistant administrator get into a lengthy discussion about slavery. Although slavery has been illegal for many generations, there were small pockets throughout the world that continued to permit it. One such place was the Island of Ire, a reactionary enclave just seventy-five kilometers off the coast of Kolexico. It was an independent principality of about five thousand citizens, most of whom practiced an ancient form of religion called Evantism that they used to justify slavery. As recently as fifty years ago, there were still some on the island who had slaves.

The assistant administrator tells us that she was captured as a very young girl and enslaved. She tries to hide her pain, but it breaks through. She tells us that at age twelve she was sterilized. For Mavy, this crime seems to be the most egregious of all. "I can't imagine someone enslaving me," Mavy says. "But taking away my right—my God-given right to bear children—that's un-forgivable." Mavy gently places her hand on the assistant administrator's shoulder. "Anyone who takes away a woman's right to bear children should be put to death. Our God may take pity on their soul, but I sure as hell don't."

The remainder of the ride is mostly silent. Some are nodding off and others are lost in their own thought. Pique rests her head on my shoulder. She hasn't said anything in hours. I know she's mourning Nayla, but that's not the only pain on her mind. She finally breaks her silence and blurts out what's bothering her. "How many people were killed?"

"I don't know."

"Millions, right? Maybe tens of millions?"

"It could be that bad."

"I don't even know what to say to that. I'm struggling to understand what happened to my mom. *I really miss her.*" Pique wills herself not to cry, but she's so choked up she can't speak. Eventually she catches herself long enough to say, "But my mom dying is kind of nothing compared to this. All this death is so . . . so . . . *sick.*"

"It really is." I exhale, but there is no air to escape. "I wish I knew what to say to you, Pique. I wish I could explain things to you in a way that would make things easier for you. But you know I can't."

She swallows hard. "Could we have done something to stop it?"

"You couldn't have done a thing. Absolutely nothing. *But maybe I could have.* I don't know. I really don't know." Pique goes back to resting her head on my shoulder. It's hard to describe how I'm feeling. I know one thing—*I want to feel more.* I've never really understood those monks who whip themselves to feel like the Son Savior did when he was tortured on his altar. But I sort of understand now why the monks wanted to feel something. That's what I want now. I want to share the pain of those who suffered. But I can't. I just can't. I can barely process what happened on an intellectual level. Connecting on an emotional level is impossible. I'm detached—utterly and brazenly detached. *My world* continues to spin just as it did before. *My world* effortlessly turns unimpeded by anything that has happened. But it shouldn't. For just one day, it should stop. At the very least, it should slow down to take note. For just one day, Pique and I should be standing on a world that has a hard time turning.

44

DANG

Up ahead I see the first building lights I've seen since leaving the Assembly of Cüko. There is a long building with a flat roof surrounded by a few small residences, a hydrocarbon refueling station, and a grocery depot. The building sits perched atop of snowy bluff overlooking the Sea of Wül. The assistant administrator pulls the transport up to the entryway. We get out, stretch our legs, and breathe in the cold air. I walk toward a railing at the edge of a cliff and stare at the views below. Huge waves are crashing against the rocks. The whitecaps glow in the moon's light. It's a sight that insists on being noticed.

The assistant administrator goes to the back of the transport and pulls out two containers. One is marked MALE and the other FEMALE. She calls us over and hands one to Trace and one to Mavy. "Clean clothes," she says. "You need them." We walk through a small lobby. There are a few pictures of animals on the wall, but not much else. There is a middle-aged woman at the front desk. She recognizes the assistant administrator.

"Welcome, Echa," the woman says.

"It's good to see you, Rinda."

Trace runs up to Rinda, as if defending his woman's honor. "She would rather you not call her 'Echa.' That's her slave name."

Rinda laughs. "Not that one again, Echa. You told them the slave story. You can do better than that."

Echa puts her arm around Trace. "This guy just wouldn't stop. He's been so annoying from the moment I met him." Echa smiles. "I just had to."

"I don't think that's funny," Mavy says. "You're making light of slavery and sterilizing women. You should be ashamed of yourself."

"You're right," Echa says. "I'm sorry." She's not sorry in the least and I don't think she understands how offensive her joke is to someone like Mavy. "I just need to have a little fun sometimes," Echa says. "I'm sure you've noticed, I'm an older woman. There's not much pleasure I can take in life anymore." Mavy refuses to accept her apology.

Rinda walks out from behind the front desk. "Echa's good people. One of Kolexico's finest." She points at Trace, while looking at Mavy. "I'm sure your friend here must have been a real pain in the behind."

"Well, that's true," Mavy says. "He's a bit of a buffoon, but—"

"I'm right here, Mavy," Trace says, cutting her off.

"Can we just get our rooms," I say. I have no patience for joking or small talk. "It's late and I'm tired. We all need our rest." I look at Rinda. "How many rooms do you have available?"

"I have four rooms left. They're all on the third floor. Echa gets one room and the rest of you can split up the other three however you like." Mavy takes the three keys and walks toward the elevator. She pulls me aside. "You want to bunk with me?" she says.

"We can't. You need to keep an eye on Pique. She needs you now. I'll share a room with Dang, and Trace and 512 can share."

"Your loss."

Pique needs a big sister right now and I want Mavy to spend time with her. And even if that wasn't the case, I couldn't be with Mavy. I might want to, but it would be for all the wrong reasons. I need to feel unhappy tonight. I need to feel connected to others' suffering. I need to find my own version of the monks' whip.

Dang and I carry the clothes we got from Echa into our room. I let Dang shower before me. He's still wearing puke-soaked clothes, and he needs a shower more than I do. As he turns on the shower, I head toward the room's balcony. A gust of wind blows through the balcony's door as I open it. I step outside. The crashing waves are loud and unrelenting. The frigid air that comes off the sea cuts through me. I like it. I look out onto the whitecaps skipping through the Sea of Wül. Orion is the closest I've ever seen to the horizon. It's almost as if the crashing whitecaps are nipping at his ankles. Like me, the cold doesn't seem to bother him.

Dang and I start to switch places. But he's just in a towel and sopping wet. I'm too young to be Dang's father, but that doesn't stop me from telling him to put some clothes on before he goes out into the cold. Dang's too old to be my son, but that doesn't stop him from acting like an exasperated teenager. "I'm fine," he says. I've never had a teenager, especially not a twenty-five-year-old one, but I'm pretty sure that his *I'm fine* means *Leave me the hell alone.*

It's late and we've both been through a lot. We eventually crawl into our beds and shut the lights. I quickly fade. I don't fight the overwhelming urge to sleep. As I start to drift off, I hear Dang restlessly moving in his bed. He is being purposefully loud.

"You up?" he asks.

"No."

"You sound up."

"I'm not."

"You're talking, so you must be up."

"Fine. I'm up."

"I need to tell you something?"

"Okay."

"I'm pretty sure I know why I'm here. If I'm honest with myself, I may have even known all along."

I sit up and turn the lights on. The lights flicker before turning bright. My eyes are heavy, but I force them open. Dang is sitting on the side of his bed, his feet dangling above the floor, shoulders hunched over. His body is rocking back and forth, while his head shakes from side to side. He's nervous. But Dang always seems nervous.

"Just come out with it. It's okay."

"I don't know why I didn't say anything earlier. Maybe I didn't want to admit it to myself. Maybe I didn't want you or Pique or Mavy to know. Maybe I just wanted to feel normal, like someone was making a big mistake. I don't want this responsibility. I just want to be able to sit back and—"

"Just spit it out already, Dang. What is it?"

He takes a deep breath and spits it out. "Numbers—I'm really good with numbers."

I laugh. "I don't think the fact that you got an A in calculus is the reason you're here."

"It's not like that. I have a unique ability to manipulate mathematical fields."

"I don't even know what that means, but that's not the reason you're here."

"You don't understand. I can see things that other people can't see. I see things other people don't even realize exist."

"Okay," I say. I'm highly skeptical, but now I'm really up and I want to get back to sleep as quickly as I can. "How about you give me an example?"

"Dimensions. I was born with the ability to visualize four dimensions— sometimes I can even visualize five or six if I concentrate really hard." Dang stands from the bed. "The Holy Father probably wants me because I can see mathematical abstractions." He pauses. "I can see things like time."

"I don't think a person can see time, Dang."

"Of course you don't." Dang is the angry teen again. "You can't fathom the idea that time is a tangible thing. It's beyond you."

"Okay. So explain it to me so my little brain can understand."

"It's not easy to put into words. It really requires a profound understanding of high-order math and a suspension of a lot of what you think you know to be true. At this point in my life, I really can't even come close to explaining it. Maybe when I was younger I could, but I was forced to give it all up. I can try and give you an analogy though. Pretend you were to receive a transmission from a really faraway place and you had two receivers—a one-of-a-kind powerful receiver and a garden-variety weak one. The powerful one would receive the transmission first and would be able to perceive a high degree of detail. Pretend that multiple realities over multiple space-time continuums are all part of that transmission and that the receiver is the person who is deciphering it. You may receive a singular transmission based on one simplified dimension that folds into one easily comprehensible reality. A more powerful receiver, like me, may be able to see multiple dimensions and process the disharmonies of the competing realities."

"I have no idea what you're talking about."

"Oh, I know you don't." Dang smiles. "I'm not sure I really comprehend it all either, but I know I'm different. I know I have a gift. I know that my brain is able to understand things that others can't."

"So that's why you decided to join that rarefied profession—entertainment writer. You wanted to use that massive brain of yours to write trashy articles about reality-programming stars."

"That's *exactly* why I became an entertainment writer. My parents made me choose a profession that would require absolutely no intellectual rigor."

"You're losing me, Dang."

"Do you know what the Book of Our God's Paradox of Boundless Polygons is?"

"Sort of." I remembered Aquarius telling me that Emmis was one of only a handful of people to have decoded it.

"I solved it. I solved it when I was eleven. When my parents found out, they took me to a family friend—a Mr. Glass or something like that."

"Veriton Glass? The judge?"

"I don't know if he was a judge. He was a family friend. I was eleven for God's sake." Dang stands up and begins pacing in the small space between our beds. "He was someone my parents really trusted. I don't know, maybe because he was a judge. He told them to never tell anyone about what I'd done. He told them I should never look at another math or science or religious text again. They forbade me and I listened. They took me out of school, hired private tutors, and hand-selected a profession for me—entertainment writer. That's how they kept me safe. But the Holy Father must have known what I could do."

"Your explanation seems highly implausible. I think it's just because you're a descendant of Saool Forque and the Holy Father is collecting gene pools or something like that."

"You're not hearing me." We've become father and son again.

"I think you're way off, Dang."

"You're being a real jerk." Dang walks to the balcony. He opens the door and says, "Sixteen million, five hundred eighty-three thousand, four hundred and fifty-two."

"What?"

"Sixteen million, five hundred eighty-three thousand, four hundred and fifty-two. That's the number of people who were killed by the VOIDs. When you turn on the news tomorrow, you will see that is the number of people who died in the NFF. Well, they won't get the number exactly right, but they'll be close."

"How can you possibly know that?"

"Because I'm fucking smart. I told you already. I'm some kind of math genius who somehow figures shit out. And that's why the Holy Father wants me. He probably wants to put my brain in a bottle or some crap like that." Dang walks out onto the balcony. "I just want to write about actors cheating on their spouses." He starts to close the door behind him, but before it's fully closed, he shouts out to me. "By the way, Judge—fuck you. Fuck you."

45

THE HOLY FATHER

When I wake up in the morning, Dang is fast asleep and snoring loudly. I want to wake him and tell him I'm sorry. He's a good kid. He deserved better from me last night. But I let him rest. Sleep will do him a lot more good than my apology.

I go down to the lobby and the leading Kolexico news station is on the monitor. Breaking news is flashing all over the monitor. A reporter is standing in the rain outside one of Vrig's vacation homes. The reporter's voice is solemn. "I am standing outside Lalinport Estate, Chancellor Vrig's official vacation home. Sometime within the hour, the Chancellor will be holding a news conference from here. I have been told by sources close to the Chancellor that he will substantiate an earlier report that the death toll has surpassed sixteen million."

I don't understand how Dang could have predicted that number last night. He said I couldn't possibly fathom what he can see. He's right. *I can't count that many dead.*

I head toward the tea stand, even though I'm sick to my stomach from the news. There's no way I can eat or drink tea. But I need to do something. Rinda is standing behind the front desk watching the newscast. She calls out to me. I raise my eyes to meet hers and instantly regret it. "So, this is what the world has come to," she says. She looks me up and down. "You had something to do with this, didn't you?"

I slowly shake my head. It feels particularly heavy this morning. "I don't think so."

"What the hell is that supposed to mean?"

"It means that I hope I had nothing to do with it."

"You look guilty to me. It's just one girl's opinion, but you look guilty."

I know I didn't push the button that launched those VOIDs. That was Atom. And I know I didn't order Atom to do it. That had to be the Holy Father. But that doesn't stop me from asking myself whether it was my fault. Could I have stopped this? Is this what the Palmitor was trying to show me? Did Veriton want me to understand that this could happen? Maybe Rinda is right. Maybe Dariox was right. Maybe the Palmitor was right. *Maybe I am to blame.*

I quickly walk away from Rinda, as well as the questions I'm asking myself. I reach the tea counter. There's a small pot of fresh-brewed Crimson. I pour myself the cup I really don't want. My hands shake as I pour, and some spills on me, instantly burning my left arm. It scalds me, but it doesn't bother me at all. This is a kind of pain I can understand. Like a good little monk, I appreciate the ease with which I can process it.

I want to check in on Pique and Mavy, so I go back toward the elevators. "Wait a minute," Rinda shouts out to me. "I have a delivery container for you. It came Global Direct this morning. Looks like it's from Yerusalom. Maybe it's payment for blowing up the NFF." I ignore the woman's glib comment and grab the container.

I take the elevator to the third floor and walk to Mavy and Pique's door. I give the door a single knock. Mavy answers. "Good morning, Max."

"I just wanted to check on you guys. Everyone okay?"

"Pique's still asleep," she whispers. "We both tossed and turned all night. Pique had a tough night. She was restless and mumbling all sorts of horrible things. I kept waking up and going over to hold her, but she was in this strange state between sleeping and delirium. I think we both can use some more sleep." Mavy kisses me on the cheek and closes the door. I don't even consider telling her how bad things are in the NFF or that I have a delivery container, probably from her father. She should sleep. They should all sleep . . . for just a little longer.

I walk back to my room with the delivery container. I'm not sure if it's because my left arm is burning or that I don't want what's in this container, but it feels unwieldy. I open the door to the room and see that Dang is still sleeping. I don't want to wake him, so I head out to the balcony and sit on a small chair. The first thing I do is closely examine the outside of the container. In my early years of being a judge, there was a citizen candidate by the name of Veandor Moon who sent me a container filled with explosives after I denied him citizenship. My security detail intercepted the explosives. But since that day, I'm always careful about examining containers before I open them.

On the surface, there doesn't seem to be anything dangerous about this container. But it's a little suspicious that most of the shipping details have been redacted. The only word that can be made out is "Yerusalom." I slowly open the container. It doesn't surprise me to see what's inside. It's a book from the Holy Father. On the cover of the book is a small silver-laced piece of antique notepaper. It has textured etchings and rounded corners, and it's silky to the touch. It's the single most pretentious piece of paper I have ever seen. The written message is more sensible. "Perhaps you have stopped searching for answers."

I pull off the note and reveal the title of the book. *Who Wrote the Book of Our God?* This is one of the books the Holy Father wanted me to read, but it never made it out of Rogue headquarters. Either the Holy Father has more than one copy or somehow he managed to get my copy back. I open the cover and see that there is an envelope inside with the Holy Father's seal. I place the book on the floor and pull a letter out of the envelope.

> *On this Day of Remembrance, 211 A.E.O.O. Praise All that*
> *is Divine.*

Dearest Judge:

I was so relieved to learn that you, Mavy, Pique, and Dang are safe. I furthermore cannot express to you the depth of joy I felt upon learning that you and Mavy are expecting a child. The Glory of Man lies in the generations to come.

This overwhelming joy stands in such stark contrast to the profound anguish I feel over the tragedy we all experienced yesterday. I have never felt more like a helpless child than yesterday. I have officially declared this day "A Day of Remembrance" for all those who were martyred. May my sons and daughters rest in eternal peace.

Like so many great men before me, including the Son Savior, I was betrayed by a wayward disciple. This insubordination resulted in unimaginable death and suffering. I have prayed to feel the kind of pain I need to feel. Men like us cannot easily grieve. Our God has yet to answer my prayers. But I will continue to seek his assurance that my sons and daughters are being cared for.

I hope you believe me, Judge. I had nothing to do with this abhorrent act. We have all been betrayed. We are all pained. We are all bewildered. But we must find the path to truth. We must find the divine path that has been laid before us.

I hope you will join me in praying for the Holy Truth to reveal itself. We can begin this prayer from afar, but we must pray together, for the End of Days is coming. It will soon be upon us and we must be in place. You, Pique, Mavy, Dang, and Spiro need to be with me in Yerusalom.

I know you do not believe. I know you do not have faith. But the end is coming and you and your loved ones will soon be reunited.

May the glory of the divine open its heart to you. May it heal your wounds. May it cast aside your enemies. May it rain truth upon your soul. May it bring you and the others I love back to Yerusalom.

With an Open Heart and Boundless Love,
Father

I crumple up this ridiculous letter and throw it into the sea below. The waves quickly swallow it up. I don't need Pique or Mavy seeing the letter. Their father is a very dangerous man. I reach down and grab the book off the floor. I open it. In meticulous penmanship, the Holy Father has written on the inside of the book's cover.

Time is no longer a generous friend. As the end approaches, time becomes miserly and fakes its finiteness. Time and its allies have become my enemies, and like it or not, yours too. I have taken the liberty of underlining some passages. I would like you to read them. You will find them at pages 23, 131, 277, 307, 431, and 557.

This glorious book was written by one of the greatest men to ever grace this earth, my Grandfather, the Cardinal of Petyrsburg. The book was never published for public consumption. It could never be. Only a handful of copies exist and only a handful of people have read it: my father, Spiro, Emmis, and one other person who might surprise you. Now you will share in what we know. I hope it does not pain you as much as it pained me when I first read its truth.

A large part of me doesn't want to open the book. Even the book's cover feels inhospitable. It's an abrasive material—perhaps a crude wood composite. I tell myself that I will read the first passage only. I reluctantly open the book to page 23. The following passage is marked:

The truth lies in the intersection between human and divine. There is an arithmetic elasticity to the space between human and divine. It is neither completely predetermined nor infinitely full of choice. It is both yielding and unyielding across multiple dimensions. Inertial forces contract and expand this space in a never-ending push and pull between human and divine, finite and infinite. Past behaviors pull. Genetic mutations tug. Godlike dynamisms prod. Aberrant synapses lag. Miscommunicated threads atrophy.

It all comes down to this one truth: the manipulation of the infinite is our enemy's primary means for maintaining a monopoly over the divine.

I close the book. I have no desire to read more. I don't know where the Holy Father is trying to take me, but I know wherever it is, *I don't want to go.*

When I open the balcony door, I see that Dang has woken up. I sit at the foot of my bed as he sits up in his. "I'm sorry about what I said last night."

"No problem. We're okay, Judge."

"You were right about the number of people killed."

Dang answers slowly. "I know." He walks into the bathroom and closes the door. He's in there a long time. I don't know what he's doing. Eventually, I just shout out over the running water. "Meet me in the lobby in ten minutes."

Dang doesn't respond, so I repeat myself. When he doesn't respond again, I chalk it up to him being a moody teen again and so I move on.

As I'm heading back to the lobby, I run into Pique. She beats me to the line. "Are you okay?"

"Me? *I'm perfect.*"

We take the elevator down to the lobby. The door of the elevator opens and we see Echa, Trace, and 512 watching the news. Rinda is switching between entering data into the front desk's micro-processor and watching the news. She turns away from the micro-processor for a second—to give me a dirty look as I walk by. On the monitor, there's a flashing caption that says BREAKING NEWS: MILLIONS DEAD IN THE NFF. This is followed by a far-away shot of Vrig at a podium, surrounded by so many Elite Guards I can't even count. The camera slowly moves toward Vrig as a melancholy version of the NFF national anthem plays. The camera moves in close to Vrig. He looks despondent. As he starts to speak, he doesn't even try to hide his misery. There is no optimism in his voice—just sadness, and eventually, anger.

"The NFF has suffered over sixteen and a half million confirmed deaths," he says. "We expect that number to double over the next few months. I have temporarily disbanded all elected legislative bodies at this time and suspended all rights. These are dire times, and under the Emergency Powers Convention, I have assumed all governmental authority." Vrig stands up tall behind the podium. The NFF's state-run news cameras close in for a well-rehearsed close-up. He grabs the podium firmly and looks deep into the camera. "I want to make one thing very clear. I know who did this monstrous act. And I will take my revenge in the very near future. My revenge will most certainly not be measure for measure. I will annihilate my enemy. For the sake of every human being on the planet, I must annihilate this monster."

The camera pulls away as patriotic music plays and Vrig walks off the podium. The camera focuses on the NFF flag and then goes up to the sky. There is an abrupt cut, and a new camera, much shakier than the one before, is tight in on a young reporter from the field. The reporter looks nervous. She is surrounded by a crowd a few blocks from Chancellor Vrig's vacation home. Only a few seconds go by before something goes terribly wrong. The reporter quickly says "We're live from Chancellor Vrig's—" and then just stops dead in her tracks. She starts breathing heavily and the look of worry on her face turns to terror. She starts running. The camera moves fast. It shakes and skips as the cameraman tries to keep up with her. They're both running and screaming. The mob chasing her is yelling and chanting, but I can't make out what they're saying. The camera then falls to the ground and the screams of the reporter and cameraman become louder, more shrill. We can't see what's happening, but from the sound of the screams, and what I know to be the sound of broken limbs, they are being ripped apart by the mob.

The camera lens cracks and then our screen goes black. The black lasts for about ten seconds and then, unexpectedly, we are in a quiet newsroom. The news anchor can barely speak. "We have lost contact with our field reporter and cameraman." The anchor tries not to choke up, but he can't help it. "Apparently, they've been attacked by . . ." His voice trails off. The anchor sits there silently before someone off-camera shouts, "Go to break."

Trace and Echa are shaking their heads at what they witnessed on the monitor. Like the good soldier he is, 512 is stoic. There's very little that affects him.

Mavy comes down and she looks out of sorts. One of the buttons on her shirt is undone and her hair is pulled into two uneven parts. She slowly moves toward the monitor, squeezes in between 512 and Trace, and watches with everyone else. Echa takes a quick break from the news and walks over to me. "I think we need to get going. Leader Borne is not the kind of man who likes to be kept waiting." Rinda loudly chimes in, "Even if it is the great Maxomillion Cone."

I once again ignore this unbearable woman, but Pique stares her down. I tell Echa that Dang will be down soon and then we can go. Echa nods and quickly goes back to watching the monitor. Everyone is transfixed by the news, which is moving at the speed of light. Spontaneous riots are breaking out all over the NFF. There are reports that the NFF has lost control over its entire Mercury VOID system. The military leadership is fracturing. The Head Chaplain of the NFF's religious minority is broadcasting on its network that the End of Days is coming. Elite Guard generals are maintaining that everything is under control, but even the most naive viewer knows this to be untrue. There is death in the streets and the NFF is in chaos. And I can't stop thinking that it's my fault.

46

DANG

Twenty minutes go by, and because we're all so wrapped up in the ever-changing landscape of news from the NFF, we forget that Dang still hasn't come down. When there is a brief break in the coverage, I realize that Dang is more than just a little late. I find the hotel's communication set and ring up to the room. Dang doesn't answer. I quickly move past the point of being just a little worried. I don't wait for the elevator. I take the stairs up to Dang's room. As I make my way up, my worry increases. Dang's been thrown into this situation. Pique and Mavy grew up with a father who is known to every human being on the planet. Nayla and Trace were leaders in the Abstainer movement. 512 is a soldier like me. But Dang is not like us. He and his parents tried to avoid this world at all costs. They tried to suppress all the things that could have made him a part of it. They tried to hide his enormous talents, while the rest of us tried to exploit whatever talents we had. I don't know that Dang is cut out for this world. I don't know that he's strong enough.

As my concerns grow, I pick up the pace on the stairs. By the time I hit the third floor, I am running full-speed to the door. My fears have gotten the best of me. I knock a few times and there's no answer. I take out my key and try to open the door. But Dang has turned the internal lock on. I become uneasy. *Why would he lock himself in?* I try to kick the door open. The first kick does nothing. I put more force into the second kick and the door swings open. Freezing-cold air pours through the door. The chill runs through my body and by now my fears are full-blown. I look into the room and see that the balcony door is wide open. "Dang," I shout. The beds are torn apart and there are sheets everywhere. An image of Dang hanging from a noose made of sheets flashes through my mind. Is he hanging from the balcony? We've had enough death to last many lifetimes. Please, I need Dang to be okay.

I run into the room and frantically look out to the balcony. But I don't see him. I check the bathroom. Nothing. I search the closets, underneath the beds, behind the couch. I don't want to go out to the balcony. I don't want to see his dead body on the rocks below or hanging from a sheet tied to the rails. I jump over some blankets and step out onto the balcony. I notice in the far corner that there's a mound of blankets huddled together. I look over the balcony railing. Nothing. I look back at the blankets again. Then I see it. Feet. Dang's feet. *And they're moving.* Thank God they're moving.

I kick the bundle of blankets about as hard as I can.

"What the—" Dang shouts.

"You scared the hell out of me."

Dang sticks his head out from under all the blankets. He looks at me for a long time without saying anything. Then he gives me the saddest smile imaginable.

"You think you were scared," Dang says. Dang sits up against one of the balcony walls. He shakes his head. "The world's coming to an end."

"Really? Okay, well, I better shave. I want to look good on the last day." I don't hide my frustration. Dang is being overly dramatic.

He reaches down into the blanket, looking for something. He quickly finds it and pulls it out. He lifts up *Who Wrote the Book of Our God?* "The smartest man who has ever walked the earth, the Cardinal of Petyrsburg, thinks it's about to end."

"Oh, please."

"I know I'm wasting my breath with you. I know you won't believe me. But I've been reading it for a while now, and it's a call to war. It's a call to end the world as we know it. The book is actually a complex mathematical code. I'm not going to be able to crack it in twenty minutes of reading. But I think I understand a few things so far and I'm starting to get the hang of the math."

"I skimmed the book. I didn't see any math."

Dang tries not to laugh. He knows it's condescending, but he doesn't mean it to be. He's far too frightened to be condescending.

"Like I said, I believe there is more to this than meets the eye. Even the page numbers the Holy Father chose for you to read are mathematically significant. You may have noticed that some chapters have just one word for the entire chapter and others may be twenty pages of highly dense ontological ideas." Dang stops himself. "You don't know what 'ontological' means, right?" I shrug. "Well, it's a theory of existence or reality, and in quantum numerical theory, it's the relationship between numbers and existence. But you don't need to understand any of this. Just follow me with this. Chapters one, four, six, eight, nine, ten, twelve, fifteen, and sixteen are each just one word. And if you string the words together it says, 'We Shall Strike When Two Holy Fathers Procreate Righteous Births.' These patterns exist throughout the book. They are all about events that need to trigger human actions."

Dang thumbs through the book. He moves quickly through the pages with an intensity I have seen only once before in him—the time he pointed a gun a Kene Yorne. Like that time, Dang feels that he is the only thing that stands between death and the rest of us.

"Here's another example. Look at the pages the Holy Father annotated. He wanted you to read the first page of chapters two, three, five, seven, eleven, and thirteen. All prime numbers. Then look at the pages he chose for you to read—twenty-three, one thirty-one, two seventy-seven, three hundred and seven, four thirty-one, and five fifty-seven. All primes. The statistical chances of these pages being chosen in a random fashion based on their content as opposed to being chosen because they are prime is approximately point zero zero two six seven percent. So it's definitely not random."

"So?"

"Well, here's where it gets into conjecture. Clearly, the Cardinal is trying to present an argument about how and when to attack the enemy and the Holy Father is highlighting the significance of prime numbers to the Cardinal's theory. I can't be sure who the enemy is or what the numbers mean. It's very cryptic and I'm a math whiz, not some literary or ecclesiastical scholar. My idea of good writing is coming up with a catchy phrase to describe how some soap-opera star got caught with his pants down. But it's obvious that the Cardinal is calling for a war. It seems like the enemy is time, but that doesn't make a lot of sense and I can't say for sure what the hell is going on. I can see the math patterns, but I'm guessing about the rest."

"I only read one passage and honestly I thought it was nonsense."

"It might be. But I'm sure of at least one thing. The Cardinal didn't think it was nonsense and the Holy Father certainly doesn't think so. I also have a theory about why this book was sent to you. I hate to crush your ego, Judge. But I don't think you're the intended audience. I think I am."

"So why didn't he just send it to you."

"I don't know. You're a judge. You tell me."

I don't answer Dang. I don't even agree with the premise. "Let me ask you something, Dang. So you've strung together some chapter titles and found some prime-number patterns. Why is it even important?"

"Like I said before, I don't really know. But if you want, I can take a wild guess."

"Go for it."

"Well, a prime number is a number that can only be divided by itself or one. The most interesting part about the Holy Father's annotations at the back of the book is that they're focused—almost obsessively—on the fact that prime numbers are in infinite supply. Although prime numbers become less common as numbers grow larger, they still exist, into infinity. The Cardinal and the Holy Father are fixated on the fact that prime numbers—numbers that cannot be divided by other numbers—go on in an infinite manner. Intuitively, you might think that as numbers get larger, there would be a point at which those larger numbers would have so many smaller numbers within them that they would be capable of being divided by them. But the answer, somewhat paradoxically, is that the inability to divide will always exist. And I think this has something to do with the enemy the Cardinal is talking about. This enemy is infinite and indivisible, but as it grows larger, the likelihood of coming in contact with an indivisible part of the enemy grows less likely. These prime numbers are like tumors that become exponentially rare as the universe of numbers expands." Dang swallows hard. "But they never go away."

Dang slides back into his ball of linens. I really don't know what he's talking about, but whatever it is, he's genuinely frightened by it. At the same time, he's consumed by his desire to find answers and so he keeps searching. He compulsively flips through the book while scribbling equations in the margins. I have no choice but to rip the book out of his hands.

"What are you doing," he yells.

"I'm probably saving you from a nervous breakdown. And besides that, it's time for us to go."

"I have a lot more to do. Just leave me here with the book. I'll be fine."

"I can't do that."

"Why not? Go and meet with this Borne guy—*I'm sure he'll have loads of information to tell you*—and I'll be right here figuring out what's really going on."

"No, you're coming with me. I need to protect you—not because you're some math whiz or you have some exceptional genetic makeup or because the Holy Father thinks you're some grand prize. I have to protect you because—" It's hard for me to finish the thought.

"Because you care," Dang says.

"Yes. That."

"Can I at least have the book back?"

"Under one condition—you tell no one about it. Not Pique. Not Mavy. No one. You can figure out whatever the hell you want. But you keep this book hidden at all times. I don't want them knowing about it."

"You've got a deal, Judge," Dang says. He reaches his hand up toward mine. I go to shake it, but then I realize he isn't reaching for my hand. He's reaching for the book.

47

LEADER BORNE

I force everyone away from the newscasts. The latest report is about Province 12 breaking away from the NFF. The governor of Province 12 is about to hold a news conference and he's going to announce his province's secession from the NFF, as well as an alliance with the Nation of Yerusalom. Multiple news sources are also reporting widespread military defections in the NFF's southern provinces, including Elite Guard units stationed there to keep the peace. If the Elite Guard is defecting, things must be extremely bad for Vrig. I worry that he will get desperate.

512 and Echa are the easiest to pull away from the newscasts. Both act more like dispassionate scientists watching an experiment than concerned citizens of the world. But Mavy and Trace are glued to the screen. They hang on every word, as if somehow conditions in the world will miraculously improve. I think they understand that every minute we sit watching these monitors is another minute that we can't help to improve things. But they're still slow to get up.

I call for Pique and she moves quickly toward me as if she has something in mind—a purpose for the day. The way she runs reminds me of the way Viole used to run up to me when I came home from work. I imagine that Viole would be a lot like Pique if she had been given the chance to grow up.

I head toward the transport, a few meters ahead of Pique. 512 opens the door for me and we all pile in. Rinda runs out from behind the counter and hands Echa a receipt for the stay. "You know you won't get reimbursed by the Administrator without this," she says to Echa. The woman then knocks on my window. I grudgingly tap the descend button and my glass drops down. "You didn't even have the courtesy to say good-bye," she says to me. "You must really feel guilty about what you did."

"Oh shut up," Pique yells. "This man has more decency in his pinkie than you and every other mean-spirited Kolexican have in your entire bodies. So get back behind your counter before I come out there and teach you a lesson." I notice Echa's hair begin to frizz from the static electricity. Pique hits the ascend button and tells Echa to drive. Echa quickly hits the accelerator and we head down the driveway. Echa knows that Pique was yelling at her, too.

We sit in silence for a while. Pique's anger has surprised everyone. Well, everyone except for Dang. He missed it entirely. He is lost in his own thoughts. I assume complex mathematical formulas are racing through his head. I asked him not to show the book to anyone, but that's not stopping him from thinking about it obsessively. He has a crazed look, which doesn't go unnoticed by Pique. Few things do.

We drive for a few hours and Echa says very little. Mavy and Pique are still tired and they sleep for most of the ride. Trace and 512 listen on a receiver to what's going on in the NFF and the Nation of Yerusalom. The Holy Father has issued a statement condemning the attack on the NFF, and like his letter said, he has called for a Day of Remembrance. All of the Yerusalom news networks are broadcasting the Holy Father's sermon from the San Bernardino Basilica. I can't hear much of what the Holy Father is saying, but every once in a while I hear Trace say something like "that lying bastard" or "I hate that phony." The Holy Father's sermon lasts for at least two hours, and when it's over, I feel compelled to ask Trace what he said.

"He offered his condolences to the people of the NFF. He told them that although they may not be looking for divine compassion, he will continue to shower them with his love. It was the usual religious nonsense where the Holy Father pretends that he's God himself." Trace then imitates the Holy Father and I'm just glad that Mavy's sleeping. "You don't know what's good for you, my children. But guess who does? Me. That's right—I and I alone am the divine spirit that knows what's good for you."

GAME OF THE GODS • 265

Trace continues to tell me what the Holy Father said. But at a certain point I just tune him out. What lies outside my window interests me more. Hours pass and I watch as the ice-covered fields turn to grass. The mountains slowly flatten. Young wildflowers bud in between the bleakest of spaces. I even manage to see a herd a reindeer grazing—perfectly oblivious to it all.

We eventually pass a bit of civilization—a hydrocarbon refueling station with some parked transports that are being repaired. Echa slows as she passes the station. She then says, "Leader Borne's headquarters is up ahead." Echa turns the transport down a long pebbled road that has planted pines on each side. The road is a few hundred meters long. I wake Pique and Mavy and tell everyone to be prepared for any and all possibilities. We have no idea what to expect. 512 and I check our weapons, and Trace copies us. The transport comes to a stop outside of a large metal structure with a single gabled roof. The roof is held up by four steel posts and there are no walls to the structure. We step out of the transport and are immediately hit by an overwhelming smell of rancid fish. I turn to my right and notice a sign that says EASTER CARTEL HEADQUARTERS. There is another sign, almost as large, that says FREE COD FRIDAYS. There are outdoor grills, park tables, industrial heating lamps, and seating for hundreds of people. Echa sees me looking at the rows and rows of tables and benches. She smiles. "This is the political life of a cartel leader. It's not as glamorous as you're probably used to—being a judge in the Federacy and all. Out here, it's a lot of free-cod outings."

The dirt pathway to the main structure is about thirty-five meters. There are no guards along the path or near the front door of the structure. There are no visible signs of any security whatsoever. My first reaction is that it's a trap. Maybe someone is going to ambush us. But there are no tracks on the dirt path and it hasn't rained in a while, so that seems unlikely. The whole place seems abandoned.

Echa is walking along the path as if she's going to her friend's house. So if there is an ambush, she's not in on it. As a precaution, I send Mavy and Pique back to the transport while I check out the headquarters. They're not happy about this. Maybe I should send Echa, too, but I may need her. I tell Trace and 512 to go to the side entrance of the structure. I warn Trace that he should use his weapon only if directly fired upon.

Echa climbs the steps to the entranceway and I cautiously hang back a

little. There is a tinted glass door and Echa pushes it open. I'm a few steps
behind her when I hear a loud thud, followed by Echa screaming. Echa, who
is writhing in pain, is on the ground. She's tripped. I look down and realize
what she's tripped over. It's a dead body. It looks like a member of a security
detail. He reeks of rotten flesh. The whole room reeks. The heat in the headquarters has been left on high and it's causing this body, and probably others,
too, to decay much quicker than normal. I quickly flip over his body. There
is a single bullet hole to his head. I lift Echa up and hurry back through door.
I shout for Trace and 512 to stay put and I carry her back to the transport as
fast as I can.

I run back to the side of the building and explain to Trace and 512 what I
saw. "There's at least one dead body in there, but based on the smell, I think
there may be more. I'm going to go through a window on the other side of the
building in case someone's in there expecting me to come back through
the front door. Trace, you go through this side door, and remember, do not
fire unless fired upon. 512, you go up through the raised porch in the back.
Everyone stay low and keep quiet. We're going in on the count of twenty-
five and we'll meet at the center of the building. Starting . . . now."

I run to the other side of the house. I quietly break the lock on the window
and let the remaining six seconds count off. Then, I jump through the window and hit the ground rolling. I stop in a kneeling position and my gun follows my eyes as it scans the room. There's no movement and no sound,
except for when Trace barrels in. He immediately trips over something and
shouts, "Oh, gross!" I abandon any attempt at caution and sprint to him. He's
found another dead body—another member of the security detail. 512
checks out the rest of the area to make sure it's safe and then makes his way
to us. He whispers, "I think it's clear down here, Judge. There's four dead
bodies in total. Three security, one older female dead at her desk chair. She's
probably an admin. All executed with a single bullet to the back of the head."
He points to a metal ramp going up to a loft. "The ramp leads to what looks
like another office. I'll go check it out."

"No. You stay. I'm going up. It's a small space and if there's anyone up there,
it can't be more than a few. I can manage that. Only come up if you hear me
discharge my weapon."

I head up the ramp quietly. At the top of the ramp is a landing and a closed door. I kick it open and jump past the door's opening. I get a quick look in as I move by. There's someone sitting in an office chair with his or her back to the door. I didn't see anyone else in the room. I peek my head into the room—definitely no one else. I see one small closet on the right side of the room. It's the only place there might be another person. I call out to the person in the chair. "Turn around slowly." No response. I move quickly to the chair and I realize the person's not moving. I immediately reach for the closet door, step to the side of it, and yank the door open. A bunch of files fall off a shelf and make a loud noise. Trace calls up to me to see if I'm okay and I yell back that everything's fine. As I turn around the chair, I realize everything's not fine. The person is dead. And there's a note pinned to his chest—*a note addressed to me.*

The person sitting in the chair is an exact replica of the Administrator, only his hair is cut close and dyed in black and white stripes. It's Borne. He's wearing the traditional clothes of an Easter, which is similar to a hunting outfit, with greens, grays, and blacks in a camouflage pattern. There is a single bullet to his head—executed at close range just like the others. And then there is this strange note. It is pinned to his jacket and written in handwriting that is hard to decipher. I have never seen such poor handwriting. It looks like the handwriting of a child. I pull the note off Borne's chest.

Hello Max,

You were right to come here. Leader Borne knew a lot. I'm sorry to say he knew too much. He was more cunning than I hoped. Like poor Atom, he played every side. So he and the others had to be killed. They did nothing wrong other than knowing things too early. That's often the problem with this world. People know things before it's time.

I wish they didn't have to be killed. But they died in the service of a greater cause. I think when we talk, you will agree. I will find you in the next day or two so we can properly meet. Please do not leave Kolexico. You can't. You and Pique will be safe here. I will make sure of it. In the meantime, if I can make a suggestion. Get some rest. You look exhausted. You will need your strength for what lies ahead.

48

ECHA

We return to the transport and Echa immediately asks me if Borne is dead.
She knows the answer, but I tell her anyway.

"That's not good," Echa says. She's panicked. "Not good at all."

I try to comfort Echa. The rest of us have seen so much death recently
that we're hardened. But Echa is not used to this. "Yes, it's a tragedy. I'm very
sorry."

Echa looks at me as if I have three heads. "I don't care about Borne. I only
care about the fact that the other cartel leaders are going to need to blame
someone. Borne didn't have any enemies in Kolexico." Echa's nerves are getting the best of her. She puts her head in her hands. "What are we going to
do? They're going to blame us. I know it. You had an appointment to see him.
You had a motive to kill him. Your fingerprints are all over that house." Echa
grabs my hands. "Look, there's blood all over your hands. First you're a part
of something awful in the NFF and now it looks like you killed Borne."

Pique takes a step forward. She aggressively removes Echa's hands from
mine. It is strange to see such a young girl being so combative with someone
who's her grandmother's age. Pique gives Echa a menacing look and says,
"We had nothing to do with what happened in the NFF. And we had nothing
to do with killing those people in there. So, that's exactly what you'll tell the
Administrator and the other cartel leaders." Pique doesn't wait for a response.
She turns and walks a few steps away.

Echa calls out to her, but Pique keeps her distance. "Of course I'll tell the Administrator the truth. But it won't matter. Even if he believes me, there's a good chance you'll get blamed. We haven't had a cartel leader killed in thirty years. The leaders maintain stability in Kolexico. They're untouchable. Trust me—the Administrator is going to have to string someone up for this and he'll do it quickly. And let's not forget, it's his brother who's been killed."

"Echa's right," I say. "We'll be blamed. They'll assume the worst of us because of what happened in the NFF and because we're outsiders. We're the easiest target. We have no choice but to get out of here quickly and stay out of sight. Then, we'll have to plan an escape that doesn't involve us going back to the main airstrip."

Pique gives me a strange look and walks toward me quickly. I don't think I said anything odd, but she has a determined look on her face as if I just said something that bothered her. She marches up to me and reaches into my shirt pocket before I can stop her. She pulls out the note that was pinned to Borne. She knows that my decision to leave quickly is not just based on the dead people in that building. She then walks away.

"That's not for you, Pique. It's addressed to me."

Her pace picks up. I'm not going to chase her. Even if I wanted to catch her, I couldn't. She reads the note once and then again. She walks back to all of us, but instead of returning the note to me, she slams it against Dang's chest. "Here. You can use it as a bookmark for that book you're reading. You know—the one you took from the judge." She looks at me. I can't make out her expression at first, but then I realize what it is—*disappointment*. "How many other things are you guys hiding from us?"

"We're not hiding anything," I say. "I'm just trying to protect you."

"I'll take my chance with the truth. You don't get to decide what I hear and what I don't. The note, the book—*what else are you hiding*? You should know by now that I don't like secrets. They're the same as lies. I don't lie and you can't either." She turns to Dang and punches him in the shoulder. She punches him hard and he shouts in pain. "You, too, Dang. I might under-stand the Judge keeping secrets from me. But not you."

Pique walks off angry. Mavy gives me a dirty look before going after Pique. I feel bad. But I don't think I'm wrong. Pique's barely a teenager. She's just lost her mom. She has enough to deal with.

I walk over to Echa. I stick my right hand out to her. Like most people, she reflexively grabs it and starts shaking, even though she has no idea what she's tacitly agreeing to. "This is the end of the line for us, Echa." She's confused and she lets go of my hand. "I'm sorry to do this, but I'm going to need to take your phone and transport keys." Echa is very old and she badly twisted her ankle when she tripped over the dead body. So I don't feel good about what I'm doing. But I don't trust her—not in the least. She would sell us out in a heartbeat. We need time to get away. "I will leave one set of starter keys at the end of the road—by the intersection with the highway. Then you should make a right turn onto the highway and walk another kilometer or so and your transport will be on the right. Your phone will be locked in the transport's back container. Feel free to tell the authorities whatever you like. But, as a man who spent a decade and half as a judge, I would recommend you tell the truth. That's your best hope for saving yourself."

I take Echa's other set of starter keys and her phone and tell everyone to get in the transport. Mavy doesn't like the idea of leaving Echa behind, but I convince her it's the only option. As we leave, Trace hits the descend button on his window and yells out, "Sorry about all this. Be safe, Echa."

Echa raises her middle finger.

Mavy insists on driving. No matter the mode of transportation, Mavy is now *officially* the driver. We quickly reach the turn onto the highway and I hop out of the transport. I grab a tall stick with branches, plant it in the ground, and hang the keys on it. I'm trying to be nice by getting the branch so that Echa won't have to bend down too far. I don't want her to bend, but apparently I'm fine with an elderly woman having to walk more than a kilometer on a twisted ankle.

I put her starter keys on the branch and we speed away. We drive exactly one kilometer and I tell everyone to get out of the car. I lock her phone and the other set of keys in the back container and we go on foot the rest of the way. We are heading back to the hydrocarbon refueling station, because it has a parking lot full of transports. We will need to take one of the transports without anyone knowing. For the same reasons we can't escape in Echa's car, we need to take a transport that the authorities can't trace.

It's about a fifteen-minute walk to the station. The highway has very little traffic, but we can't be seen. We are six people who look very different from everyday Kolexicans. So we head into the brush and make our way along the road, out of sight of the delivery transports that occasionally speed by.

When we get to a clearing a few thousand meters from the station, I send 512 up ahead to look around. I tell him to scout out the number of people working in the station and to look for a large transport we can borrow. Technically we're stealing the transport, because I have no intention of returning it, but it feels more like borrowing.

512 sprints there, gets the information we need, and comes back quickly. He's one of the best soldiers I have ever worked with. His report is to the point. "One worker, five large transports in working order, starter keys on the wall of main office, manifests by the rear entry to office."

I call for Dang to come over. I can't find Trace, so I start explaining to 512 and Dang that we need to come up with a plan to get the keys without the worker noticing. Eventually, I see Trace in the distance. He's been talking to Pique and Mavy but he makes his way toward us. I have to reexplain everything to Trace, and of course he asks a lot of questions. Most of his questions are of the stupid or redundant variety. I have to remind him multiple times that we stick out in Kolexico and that we don't want the station worker to be able to identify us or be able to report the transport missing right away. While I'm talking to the guys, I notice that Pique and Mavy have moved closer to the road and farther from us.

I continue explaining my plan, with Trace demanding multiple explanations over and over again. I tell Trace and the others that we will look for the rear entry into the office and sneak up on the worker without him knowing. 512 and I will subdue him, blindfold him, and tie him up without him ever seeing us. I emphasize the importance of not harming the worker. I have enough blood on my hands. At the same time as we are subduing the worker, Dang and Trace will place large refuse containers on the highway to divert traffic—potential witnesses—away from the station.

Everyone except for Trace seems to get the plan. He continues to bombard me with one dumb question after another. While he is asking one of his more long-winded ones, I notice that Pique and Mavy are no longer near the road. They're nowhere to be found.

"Did you see where Mavy and Pique went?" I ask Trace.

Trace shrugs his shoulders, but he is smiling.

"Where are they, Trace?"

He waits a little while and then finally points to the station. "They went that way."

"Is there some reason you didn't stop them."

"Oh, absolutely." Trace's smile grows. "I have a great reason."

"Do you want to share this reason?"

"Sure, Max. They asked me to distract you."

"*Distract me?* Why would they want to do that?"

"Well, let's see," Trace says. He rubs his chin as if he's a professor. "First of all, you called this all-boys meeting and never even thought to invite Mavy and Pique. Mavy probably has more military experience than me, Dang, and even 512 combined. You've been treating Pique and Mavy like these delicate flowers. It's pretty damn sexist, don't you think? Either one of them could probably kick my ass—definitely Dang's." Dang nods in agreement. "If they ever did get into trouble, they have their hands to bail them out. And worst of all, Max, you've been keeping secrets from them. *Me, too, by the way— thank you very much!* So when they said to me that they were going to handle this little mission, and at the same time teach you a lesson, I said absolutely, how can I help? And then they said, well how about if we try to—"

"Oh shut up already, Trace. Mavy's pregnant if you haven't noticed and Pique is young girl. Sexist or not, they shouldn't be playing soldier."

"There you go again, Max. *Playing soldier?* Mavy is a soldier. She doesn't just play one. And Pique could best you any day of the week. She's proven that. They're real fighters. Just like you and 512."

"I don't have time for this." I take off running down the highway. I'm out from the brush in plain sight. I stick out like a sore thumb in this place. I look nothing like a Kolexican and I'm sprinting down the highway with a shirt covered in blood. Any delivery transport driving by can see me. But I need to get to Mavy and Pique.

As my heart pounds and sweat fills my eyes, I close in on the station. Out of nowhere, a speeding delivery transport heading in the other direction crosses over the road and pulls up alongside me. I'm not sure what I'll do to the driver. The window descends. I'm ready to jump in and take out this innocent driver.

"Get in," a voice says through the window. The door flies open and a hand extends out to me. It's Pique. She grabs my hand and yanks me into the land transport as if I weigh nothing more than small child. I'm mad, but I don't let them know it. I immediately start asking Pique questions about their heist.

"Was there anyone in the hydrocarbon—"

"There was just the one worker."

"Was he able to identify—"

"He didn't see us."

"How were you able to—"

"We waited for him to go in the stockroom. We locked the door behind him. Then we took the keys."

I look at Mavy. Her hands are firmly fixed to the wheel. She is powerful, in control, self-assured. She looks over at Pique. They're proud of what they accomplished. But more importantly, they're proud of each other. They should be. I ask more questions and I quickly realize that their execution was flawless.

"One last question," I say.

"No more questions, Max." Mavy's had enough.

"Just one more, please."

"Fine."

I hop on the other side of Pique and squeeze in between the two of them. I put my arms around them. "Can you guys forgive me?"

They don't answer. But I can tell by their half smiles—the answer is a definite maybe.

49

512

We pick up the guys in the delivery transport and head in the opposite direction from the Assembly of Cüko. I want to put as much distance between us and the administrative authorities as possible. As an added measure, we take only back roads and constantly change our direction so that our route can't be easily traced. Mavy and Pique lifted a communications receiver with a digital cartogram from the hydrocarbon station's office. 512 navigates us using it. He is insistent that we head as far south as possible.

We drive deep into the night and we're all exhausted. 512 leads us to a series of small dirt roads, far removed from any paved state roads. When we finally hit a dirt path that isn't wide enough for the delivery transport, 512 asks Mavy to stop. He steps out of the transport with the communications receiver and surveys the area. He's gone for about five minutes. When he comes back he says that one of the maps shows a small abandoned hydropower facility about halfway up the mountain ahead. "There's water, wildlife, and shelter in the station. We should be fine up there until we can figure out an escape plan." We can't go any farther on the road, so we decide that we will hike up the mountain in the morning. We're safely hidden on this desolate dirt road, so we will sleep in the delivery transport, wake up, and go.

Everyone is tired. It doesn't take long for most of us to fall asleep. Trace is snoring within minutes, and Pique and Mavy are not far behind. 512 is more apprehensive. He takes a few tours around our transport and makes sure we're safe. He's done an excellent job of keeping us off the radar, but he doesn't feel like his job is done yet. Eventually, he comes back to the transport and dozes off. But his sleep seems like a restless one. It's just Dang and me left. We're both wide awake. My body is exhausted, but my mind is not.

I quietly open the transport door, making sure that I don't wake anyone. I walk to the back of the transport and hop up on the ledge of the back container. My knees are almost touching my chest, and my back is up against the transport's rear window. My head is looking up at the clear night. Kolexico has the most unbelievable views of the stars. There's so little light pollution. On most nights, the Omniplex lights went to battle with the stars—and almost always won.

My mind starts to relax and I feel like it might be possible to sleep. The stars have this numbing effect on me. I think about the baby inside of Mavy and for a brief moment, I'm something other than miserable. I start to drift off to sleep, but then I hear footsteps, followed by a hushed voice. "Judge." The voice gets louder. "Judge. It's me." Once again, Dang does not want me to sleep.

Dang has *Who Wrote the Book of Our God?* folded underneath his arm. He hops up next to me and we are shoulder-to-shoulder on the back container of the transport. He launches into his theories about what the book means. I try to get him to slow down, but he can't stop himself. He's obsessed. Dang points up to Orion. "The stars that make up Orion's belt are hundreds of thousands of times brighter than our sun. And each of those stars is, on average, about a thousand light-years away. A thousand light-years. A thousand times ten trillion kilometers." He laughs. "And those immense amounts of energy and trillions and trillions of kilometers are nothing in the grand scheme of things. They're not even the microbes on the fleas on the dog. For me to quantify how mathematically unimportant they are would take an eternity. And yet there is our good friend Orion—shining bright. It's like you can reach up and touch him." Dang takes the book and places it underneath his head as he sits back. "But can you even begin to imagine what we can't see?"

"I'm not even going to try." What I really mean to say is that I have no desire to try.

"I've been thinking more about what the Holy Father wants."

"*Oh, really?*"

"That's funny, Judge. But this is serious. Based on the math, I was beginning to think that the Holy Father and Cardinal somehow thought that their enemy was *time* itself. But I don't think that's right anymore, at least not entirely. It's something equally as intangible and infinite as time, but it's not quite that. I think time is the weapon or the messenger or the soldier or the servant or something like that. There's this strange chapter in the Cardinal's book. It's not one the Holy Father pointed out to you and that has me concerned, too. It's about irrational people, but I think it's a metaphor for irrational numbers. The Cardinal talks about the behaviors of irrational people, kind of like the people in *The Cryzon Tales*. But I'm pretty sure the Cardinal is really talking about numbers—irrational numbers. As you probably remember from secondary school, the most famous of these irrational numbers is pi. It's the constant that's used for measuring a circle. It's a really simple idea—and of all things, *it's a constant.* Yet it leads to a number that is anything but simple. It never ends and it appears to hold no rational basis for its pattern. It's a never-ending recital of numbers that has its own infinite universe. It goes on forever in a random manner, never allowing for a rational understanding of it. So, this chapter started me thinking. Is the Cardinal saying that his enemy is irrationality? Or is he saying that by embracing irrationality we can transcend all that keeps us apart? I think he wonders whether it's rational to think we can find a pattern of meaning in a string of infinite numbers or in the universe itself. I think he's saying it's a form of hubris—a sort of irrationality—to assume a rational universe based on a singular divine presence?"

"Can we go back to talking about how Orion has a really big and shiny belt?"

"Can I ask you something, Judge?"

"Sure, as long as it's not a math problem and you don't use the word 'irrational' again?"

"What do you think the Holy Father wants?"

"That's easy. It's what every political being wants—power."

"That kind of begs the questions, doesn't it? I mean *what is power?*"

"You said one question, Dang. But I'm going to cut you some slack because you're a good kid. I think it depends. If you're one of those stars in Orion's belt, I would think power is how bright you shine. Being a star, it seems to me, is all about shining bright. Being a human, it's all about how many humans, especially powerful humans, you control. The bully controls the weak kid. The mom and dad control the bully. The dad and mom control each other. The boss controls the mom and dad. The boss's boss controls the boss. The local town leader controls the boss's boss. The governor controls the local town leader—on and on and on. You get the idea."

Dang hops down from the transport and leaves the book behind. I think he's done with it. As he's walking back, he says, "Yeah, I get it. But the real question is who controls the powers we consider divine?"

I answer him, but he's already back in the land transport. It wouldn't have mattered if he heard my answer.

I manage to fall asleep on the back container. It's a heavy sleep—the kind that sucks you in and won't let you go. My dreams pin me down and demand to be heard. I dream all night. I mostly dream of war. In particular, I dream of Saool Forque's soldiers, lying dead at the crumbled walls of Yerusalom. They're holding hands in Forque's Infinite T. The dream starts innocently enough. It's almost pleasing. But as the rain starts to come down, and my eyesight, which is somehow also Forque's eyesight, begins to blur, the faces on the soldiers begin to change. Soon the soldiers become people I know and love. Lying dead on the ground are Kase, Jax, Viole, Emmis, Aquarius, Nayla, Trace, Dang, Veriton, 512, Mavy, Pique, and one other person. It's hard to make out at first, but then I see who the other person is. It's the baby—a little girl. She and Pique are holding hands. They're dead. But they're holding hands.

I'm suddenly woken up from my dream. There's loud banging coming from inside the transport. It's Trace. He has to go to the bathroom, and for some reason, everyone needs to know it. I hop down from the back of the transport. My back aches. I walk around to stretch my legs. I find 512 sitting on a tree stump, looking at the communications receiver. Before I have a chance to say anything, he says we should get moving. "There's no real rush," I say. But he insists. "We need to establish a source of fresh water," he says. Before he walks away, I let him know that I think he's doing a great job. I let him know that he is exactly the kind of soldier I admire. He almost looks sad when I tell him.

"I just wish I had more time to serve you, Judge."

"You will." I pat him on the back and 512 hugs me. I'm surprised, but I'm glad he feels that way about me. I walk back to the land transport and tell the others to get ready.

We start heading up the mountain. I stay close to Pique and Mavy. At one point, Trace gives me a look like *you'll never learn.* Dang is nervous as usual and I notice something about him for the first time. Even though he is only twenty-five, his hair is turning gray. Almost before my eyes, it's turning gray. He doesn't look right.

As the climb up the mountain steepens, I reach for Mavy's hand. Her palms are sweaty and they seal to mine. I help her over some of the steep inclines and she doesn't seem to mind my sexist chivalry. I look at Trace and raise my eyebrows—*take that.*

When I ask Mavy if she's okay, she reminds me that there's another living person inside of her. "We're okay, Max."

We hike through a rocky terrain of pines and shrubs. It's not long before we hear a rushing river in the distance. Up ahead, we see a clearing and a small sliver of the river. 512 looks at his communications device, hits a few buttons, and tells us that if we follow the river another five kilometers, we should hit a hydropower facility. 512 is strangely out of breath and I wonder if the cold air and altitude are making it difficult for him.

We walk along the winding banks of the river and steep inclines for hours without anyone saying much, but the time passes quickly. "There," 512 eventually shouts. He looks down at the communications device, while pointing at slabs of concrete and metal in the distance. Within a short time we are standing on the path that leads to the hydropower facility. There is an old stone and concrete building with no windows about a hundred meters ahead. "That should work," 512 says. There's not a hint of enthusiasm in his voice.

"Let's go check out the building," I say to 512. Trace gives me the *you'll never learn* look again and I ask Mavy and Pique if they want to join us. They say they're going to stay with Dang, who looks ill. I'm relieved they're not coming. I don't invite Trace.

512 and I head toward the gray concrete building. As we walk along a path overgrown with weeds, I watch as concrete walls grow out of the river and steel cylinders churn in the river's currents. It's jarring. We are surrounded by nature, mostly pristine but for these huge slabs of concrete and metal jut-ting out of the water. The water is beginning to win the battle again. It is slowly chipping away at the concrete slabs and turning the steel cylinders to rust.

512 is walking slowly and it takes a while to get to the concrete building. But we finally do. There is a faint smell of smoke just outside of it. Like the concrete slabs, the building is also losing its battle with nature. There are cracks in the walls, and like a decaying tooth, it has brown fissures forming by the foundation, which are causing it to crumble. The doorknobs and hinges are rusted over, but still look like they function.

I stare at the door for an unusually long period of time. It feels out of place. 512 takes a deep breath and then gives me a gentle nudge. I pull out my weapon and slowly open the door. The door creaks and the hinges hiss. It's dark inside and I can't see much. The smell of fire is strong, but it's not wood. It smells more like burning rubber. I take a step in and yell, "Anyone in here!" There's no response. I take a few more steps in and notice a boxlike machine in the distance. There's very little light but I can see what looks like a metal-lic surface. 512 steps in behind me. He puts his hand on my shoulder and moves his mouth close to my ear. "The end is here, Judge." I turn around and 512 is no longer behind me.

A small light goes on. It's just enough for me to see a few meters ahead. I hear 512 breathing heavily, but I can't see where he is. My heart picks up its pace. In the distance, I can make out the metallic shape, taller than wide—maybe the size of an office chair. This machine is gently humming. I see it has wheels. There are wires and receiver panels all over its surface. I hear a sharp click and the machine begins to turn around. As it does, I notice there is an orb or some type of ball-like object sitting on top of the machine. I look again. It's not an orb. It's a head. It's the head of something. No, it's the head of *someone*. It's the head of a person.

The machine rolls closer. The head has long hair. I think it's a woman sit-ting inside this machine. She looks at 512 and nods once. 512 acknowledges her command and says, "Thank you for everything, Judge. It's been an honor to serve you." He raises his gun to his head and pulls the trigger. His brains splatter on the wall behind me. His body collapses to the floor.

I raise my gun and point it at the machine coming toward me. Then I see her face. My gun drops to the floor. My eyes must be playing tricks. I close my eyes and open them again. It's no trick.

It's Emmis.

PART VI
YERUSALOM

50

EMMIS

I slowly take a step forward. It may be the hardest step I have ever taken.

The woman sitting encased in this machinery is most definitely Emmis. But she just had 512 kill himself. The Emmis I knew would never do that. The person I cared for all those years would never do that. She has more wires coming out of her than a power grid. She is almost lifeless. There is no expression on her face. There is no happiness to see me. There is no remorse for ordering 512 to kill himself.

I take another difficult step. She rolls toward me easily.

The top of her shoulders stick out of the L-shaped metal box she sits in. I bend over and grab hold of them. I awkwardly hug her because it feels like the right thing to do. But I don't feel like I've just been reunited with the woman I loved. Her cold stare won't allow for that.

I kiss her on the top of her head and there is still no response.

"Are you okay, Emmis?"

"I'm fine." Her eyes meet mine. "It's good to see you again, Max."

"*The kids?*" Tears are forming in my eyes, and my heart is pounding. "Are they okay?"

"Yes, Max. They're fine. We're all fine."

"Thank God. Thank God they're okay." I hug her again. I cry. I'm not even sure I believe her, but I want to believe her so badly. I break down and cry—uncontrollable tears of joy followed by fear for their safety and then complete and utter confusion.

Emmis watches my tears with dispassion. She's like an alien encountering a human for the first time. It's a very uncomfortable feeling and it helps me to quickly compose myself.

"What happened?" I ask. "How are you alive? The kids—tell me everything."

"I'll answer all your questions later. I promise you the kids are fine. But right now I need to explain some things to you. There isn't a lot of time. We can't stay here. You're going to need to let me talk." She rolls over to the gun I dropped. She blinks and it causes a metal arm to appear from her machinery's casing. The arm lowers itself to the floor, retrieves my gun, and hands it to me. "This is why you were chosen. You're a soldier. You're the best and most trustworthy soldier I've ever known. Every revolution needs a great fighter." She rolls toward 512. She blinks and an electric current shoots out from a small chamber in the center of her metallic casing. It's the spot where I imagine her heart is—*where her heart used to be*. The current cauterizes the wound on 512's head. She blinks quickly. "Arrangements will be made for 512. He was a good soldier, too. But he knew too much. Same as Atom and Borne. Their knowledge was outliving its usefulness. Dang is coming dangerously close as well." Emmis opens her eyes and relaxes them. It seems as though it's exhausting for Emmis to control the machinery.

"I need you to understand something, Max. Certain events are going to happen. The Palmitors have been coalescing around a relatively fixed set of events. There is a small probability these events won't happen, but in all likelihood, we are near—maybe hours, maybe days, maybe weeks—the end of the world as we know it. I've spent my entire life predicting what would happen and trying to avoid it. But it seems inevitable. The Palmitors have told you and me the same thing—the world is going to end, Max, and you're going to be the one who ends it."

There's not the slightest hint of compassion. *Guess what, person I used to love, the world's about to end and you're the reason why. Have a nice day.* I don't believe anything she's saying, but that doesn't stop me from being annoyed at how cavalier she is.

I raise my gun up to my temple. "How about I kill myself right now? I can't end the world if I'm dead, right?"

"I wish it were that simple, Max. You were always simple. *I mean that in the nicest of ways.*"

"I have to tell you—it doesn't seem like you're paying me a compliment."

"Well, I am. You always knew what's right without all the moral ambiguities. You're smart, maybe even a genius, but your morality is simple. I guess that's part of the reason I fell in love with you." Even as she says "fell in love with you," there's no emotion. Her face is a deep void.

"You won't kill yourself, Max. You will need to take care of our children. They will survive this destruction. So will Pique, so will Mavy, and so will your new baby. I, on the other hand, will not be as fortunate. Neither will Dang or Trace. The three of us will die. The Palmitors seem very clear on this point."

"Sorry, but I don't believe any of this. I mean you say you and your brother are about to die and you don't even seem to care."

"We all die, Max. Trace is a statistical aberration as it is. He should have died years ago. The morzium alone gives him a life expectancy well below the norm. So, I cannot get too upset about the fact that he's already outlived what any reasonable statistical model would have predicted."

"You're so callous. What did they do to you?"

"*They freed me.* The procedures freed me."

"How can you say that? Can you even feel compassion or love or happiness anymore?" I don't wait for an answer. I just blurt something out that I immediately regret. "*Is there any part of you that is still even capable of loving me?*"

"Of course I knew you would ask this. I understand how you must feel. But I'm sorry to say that I don't feel love anymore. I don't love you, at least not in the way you want me to. I am beyond that kind of love and I'm grateful to be relieved of that heavy burden. Love was my greatest restraint. I hope you can understand that."

"No, I'm too simple for that."

"I can still appreciate you, even your sarcasm. I just can't love you."

"That's fine, Emmis. But can you love our children? Please tell me you still love them."

"I care for them very much. I understand the importance of my role as a parent. I understand that I share in the collective responsibility of protecting and nurturing future generations. But most parents who say they love their children are just trying to fill some selfish need. I'm committed to our children, but I'm not so self-centered as to label it 'love.'"

"I cannot believe what they did to you." I can no longer hold my anger in. Without thinking, I pull my hand back and punch the wall. Pain shoots through my body and I scream from it. In an instant, all of the nervous energy that was pushing me forward drains out of me. I rest my back against the wall and slowly let my body slide down until my backside hits the floor. I stare at my bloody knuckles.

Within seconds, the door swings open. It's Pique first, followed by Mavy. Trace and Dang are far behind. "I heard you scream," Pique says. "Are you okay?" I don't answer. She then sees 512.

"What happened," Pique says. There is fear in her voice. Pique sees Emmis, and her head jerks back in shock. She can't believe what she's seeing.

"Hello, Pique," Emmis says.

"Emmis? Is that you?" Pique cautiously walks toward her. "You look so . . ."

"*Different.* I can say the same of you. The last time I saw a picture of you, you were a little girl in pigtails."

Trace and Dang run in and I jump up to meet them at the door. I'm scared Emmis might harm Dang. I tell him to wait outside until I can figure out what's going on. I grab Trace just inside the doorway and quickly explain what's happened. He's in disbelief. I tell him that it's Emmis, but that he shouldn't expect her to be like he remembers. Trace doesn't listen. *How could he?* He pushes me aside, runs over to her, and hugs her. Her response is no better than it was to me. "It's nice to see you, Trace." Trace is so happy that he doesn't dwell on the icy reception. He also has upsetting news that he's compelled to tell her.

"I have some bad news," Trace says to her. Emmis's arms are in immovable metal sleeves, which are attached to two thin horizontal platforms that are similar to the arms of a chair. Her fingertips stick out of the ends of the sleeves, but their movement seems limited. Trace reaches for them, but his touch doesn't register with Emmis, even though I think she feels it. "You've been through so much, but I have to tell you something. It's about Nayla and Mom." Trace swallows hard. "They're both dead."

"I know." Emmis looks at Trace, and a flicker of pain shows on her face. It's a remnant from some previous existence. "I'm sorry for your loss, Trace." Trace takes a step back. The chill has finally hit him. Just as he is about to say something to Emmis like "what's with you," the door swings opens. It's Dang. I should have realized he wouldn't listen. I'm worried Emmis might kill him. I step in between Dang and Emmis. She immediately knows what I'm doing. She was always smarter than me.

"There's no need for that, Max. There's not enough time for him to be a real threat."

Emmis makes her way to Mavy, rolling to her slowly, but with purpose. Mavy seems in awe. Her eyes are fixed on Emmis's every move. I have never seen Mavy this way. Emmis moves close to Mavy, and her head is eye-level with Mavy's bulging stomach. "We have never met, Mavy, but I have heard many great things about you."

"It's an honor," Mavy says.

"Congratulations on your baby." Emmis then turns to me. "To you, too, Max." She turns back to Mavy and says, "Would you like to know the sex of the child?"

"No," Mavy quickly says. "There are so few surprises in life."

"I wish that were true," Emmis says. She's serious. She genuinely believes she knows every event that is about to unfold.

Emmis rolls to the door and asks everyone to follow her. She exits the concrete building and starts moving along the path. Most of us follow Emmis, but Pique grabs Dang by the arm and they both hang back. The wheels on Emmis's machinery are thick as a motorsport's and she easily tackles the rocky terrain. We follow her, single-file, up the mountain and away from the power station. Pique and Dang lag behind. We soon reach a large plateau that sits high above the river. Emmis looks around as if she's expecting someone. "This is as good a spot as any," she says. She moves to the highest ground— like some great Ancient prophet about to reveal God's truth—and asks everyone to sit down around her. Pique and Dang catch up, but choose to sit away from Emmis.

"I am going to share everything I know," Emmis says. "Max, is it okay if I speak freely in front of everyone? Some of this is personal and it may be painful for you. Because of what we'll be doing with the Palmitors, I think it is necessary for everyone to have as much information as possible."

"We shouldn't be here," Pique says. "I hope you don't take this the wrong way, Emmis. But I don't need to hear what you're going to say, especially if you're going to say something that would hurt the judge."

"Your loyalty to Max is more than I would have expected. We sent you to him because we knew you would protect him. But the Palmitors never predicted this kind of fierce loyalty."

"What do you mean, *you* sent *me*. I went on my own. I wanted to get away. Maybe I even wanted be like my *aunt Emmis*—who I thought joined the Federacy to help change the world. I thought she was leaving behind the Abstainers because they wanted to sit quietly while the world fell apart. I thought I was like you. But something tells me we're nothing alike. *Not anymore.*"

"As special as you are, Pique, there are things you cannot understand. But I'm here to try to explain them to you. It's important that you listen, because I'm sorry to say, but the world is coming to an end."

"The world's not coming to an end." Pique is angry. "Maybe your world or my father's world is coming to end, but my world's not. You can tell everyone whatever you want. But I know what I know."

"You know what you've been spoon-fed to believe."

"I'm sorry for everything that's happened to you, Emmis. But you're acting like a real jerk to the judge. And I won't sit by while you take him down. He still loves you. He loves his kids. Remember that or you'll have to deal with me. I think you and your fancy Palmitors know what I'm capable of."

"Pique, you don't need to protect me," I say. I smile at Pique to let her know how thankful I am for her support. "I'm a big boy and Emmis can say whatever she wants." I tell Emmis to go ahead.

"Everyone who is here should be here," Emmis says. She blinks. This time it seems more like a tick than a conscious effort to control her apparatus. "Except for one of you." She looks over at Trace. "I'm sorry, Trace, but the words I'm about to say are not for you. The things we need to discuss are not for your ears. I'm not sure why the Palmitors have told me this, but there's a strong chance that it's your past morzium addiction and the biochemical vestiges left on your brain. The rest of us will be using the Palmitors in order to anticipate the strategic moves of our enemy. Unfortunately you cannot be a part of that. I'm very sorry." She blinks rapidly and her head jerks to the left, then the right. It looks like a demon has taken over her body. "It's time for you to go home."

Pique really doesn't like what she's hearing now. She's furious. "If it weren't for Trace saving us, we'd all still be in comas or worse. He's not going anywhere."

"You can't just come in here and tell him to leave," Dang says.

"I've had my differences with this man," Mavy says. "But he's a good soul. He has lived a life filled with sin. But Our God has begun to shine his light on this man. Trace is becoming a righteous soul." Mavy looks at Trace, then Emmis. "If Trace goes, I go."

"Me, too," Pique says.

"And me," Dang says.

I nod in agreement.

Trace walks over to Mavy and places his hand on her shoulder. "Thank you, Mavy. You're not half bad either. But you know what. If Emmis thinks I shouldn't be here, then I probably shouldn't be here."

"It's what's best," Emmis says. "I see good things for you at home. I see a peaceful end. Go home, Trace. Go back to where we were born." Trace looks at her for a long time. When anyone tries to tell him he must stay, he politely asks them to be quiet so he can think. His eyes become watery, but he won't let himself cry. "I'm going" is all he says.

I don't understand Trace's logic for saying he will leave. It may just be that old patterns are hard to break. He's the little brother and his older sister has told him to go home. Pique and Dang put up the biggest protest, but Trace's mind is made up. He's going somewhere where he believes he's meant to be.

Trace makes his rounds hugging everyone good-bye. First Dang, then Mavy, then me. I hold on to the hug longer than Trace does, which surprises him. He saves Pique for last. He kisses her on the cheek and lifts her off the ground with a big hug.

"I don't think you should go," she says to him one last time.

"You're the one person who's always had some faith in me. All I can say is—keep it up. I know what I'm doing."

Trace turns and waves good-bye. As he heads down the path, Pique shouts, "Wait." Pique runs after him. She whispers something in his ear and kisses him. Trace turns back to look at me. He actually looks happy. There are few things I feel certain about these days. But I feel sure of this one thing. This is the last time we'll see Trace.

51

PIQUE

Emmis watches Trace disappear into the thick of the forest. I want to run after him, but I don't think there's anything I can do to stop him. Emmis slowly turns her machinery away from the forest and moves close to me. She looks only at me, but talks loudly enough for the others to hear. "It will be personal, Max."

"It's fine. Get to it, Emmis."

"I want you to know that I have only lied to you about one thing—my life's purpose. That may sound like an enormous thing to lie about, but it doesn't diminish what we had. I lied to protect you and the children. I hope you understand that when I was capable of love, I did love you. When I was capable of sharing my life with someone else, I did share it with you. And when I needed love, I was able to receive it from you. Our relationship was an honest one, built on love and respect. Although I am no longer capable of that kind of love, you can always find solace in what we had."

Emmis blinks and a flexible metal canister, no wider than a writing instrument, comes out of one of the thin arm-like platforms. It shoots a liquid into her mouth. It's not water. The liquid is green and there is a slight smell of ammonia.

"I'm not going to debate how deep or significant your deception was," I say. "It doesn't matter right now. Let's just get to what happened. Why are you here and how am I going to get my kids back? I need to know they're safe."

"Max, I promise you the kids are absolutely fine. They're in a safe place. They were never harmed to begin with. It was all an orchestrated subterfuge to protect them. Please be patient. I will address all of that shortly. But I need to start at the beginning. Then, hopefully everything will become clear to you and the others." Emmis looks around to make sure everyone is paying attention. "When I was young, I was discovered by one of the Holy Father's emissaries. I was given the Book of Our God's Paradox of Boundless Polygons. I solved the paradox in a matter of weeks. Now we've all been led to believe that this long-lost testament was discovered in the San Bernardino Basilica by one of the Cardinal of Petyrsburg's servants. The reality is that the Cardinal himself, a mathematical savant like his grandson the Holy Father, wrote it. It's actually nothing more than an exclusive entrance exam for those of us with a capacity to understand a particular strain of high-order mathematics—a strain related to the physics of divinity. When the Holy Father was a young man, the Cardinal made clear to him that his life's mission was to find and nurture those of us capable of passing his test. It turns out that it's a very short list—me, Spiro, Mavy's mother, Dang, and a handful of others. The Holy Father spent decades studying us. He was, and still is, consumed by every aspect of our genealogy. Family, the genetic idea of it, is a critical component of the Holy Father's vision for humanity." Emmis scans the others' faces to see if they're paying attention. Mavy and Dang are riveted. Pique, on the other hand, has a stick and is meticulously etching a drawing of the hydropower facility in the dirt.

Emmis coughs to get Pique's attention. "The Holy Father also found what he initially thought was a genetic by-product of the ability to comprehend high-order mathematics—the ability to manipulate electromagnetic fields. I used to have this power, and of course, Nayla, Pique, Spiro, and Mavy have it. It only exists in females, as it seems that the Y chromosome has a corrupting effect. This power appears to be connected to the ability of our minds to manipulate numbers in extraordinary ways. It turns out that this manipulation of electromagnetic fields is not an inconsequential by-product of a dexterous brain. In actuality, it is the brain's electrical currents and unique gravitational behaviors on a molecular level that allows us to comprehend complex mathematical abstractions."

I'm trying to understand everything Emmis is saying. But a lot of it is not registering. Certain things feel stickier than others, especially the smaller details. The thing about the Y chromosome feels particularly sticky, mostly because Spiro has the power, but he's a man. At least I thought he was a man. It never occurred to me that he wasn't genetically a man. Then I remember the biopic about the Holy Father that featured Spiro. In it, Spiro had long hair and looked like a little girl. And although there was no reference to gender, the child's original name was Ellee, usually, but not always, a girl's name.

Emmis blinks and I hear a series of mechanical clicks followed by the hum of hydraulics. Two large monitors rise up on forty-five-degree angles from underneath each of the arm-like platforms. Red lasers appear from the top of the monitors and begin to gyrate. They home in on Emmis's eyes. She rhythmically closes and opens each eye three times. The red lasers pulse to those same rhythms. I assume she is calibrating the lasers. She looks down at the monitors, and by blinking and moving her eyes, she's able to quickly move to the screen she wants. She looks disturbed by what she's seen. She looks toward the forest in the distance. "There's not a lot of time."

She takes one last look at the monitors and starts talking more quickly. "The Holy Father and I want peace and prosperity on earth. In order to achieve this, humankind needs to advance. Our genetic anomalies are the beginning of that advancement. We need to use this progress to improve the human condition. All of us have extraordinary intellectual gifts." She stops herself and turns to me. "I didn't mean you, Max. Your genetics are more common. You are obviously very intelligent and have shown extraordinary heroism and an ability to problem-solve. But you do not have the kind of genetic intellect we're looking for."

"Thanks."

"It's not an insult. You have many important talents that none of us have. We're all uniquely positioned. The Holy Father is incapable of doing what Pique can do with an electromagnetic field, and she is incapable of doing the kind of high-order mathematics that he can do. You have your own special talents that we all admire."

"You probably could have done better—you know, genetically speaking—with some other sperm donor."

"Not at all, Max." For the first time, I hear a hint of compassion. "You were exactly what I needed. You must understand that this has never been just about me. The Holy Father recognized your importance right from the start. He saw our marriage long before I did. It's no coincidence we were bonded. It was his doing." Her compassion quickly dries up. "Since the Y chromosome can only corrupt the intellectual perfection of humankind, the Holy Father likes to marry off his intellectually superior women with men who show great leadership, judgment, and the ability to problem-solve. That's why you and I were bonded. That's why Mavy and Emile were going to be bonded. And that's why you're an excellent partner for Mavy. The Holy Father, Spiro, and I are very excited about the genetic potential for the baby that grows inside of Mavy." Emmis almost smiles.

"By now you must realize why the Holy Father gave you the books about Pique and Dang's ancestors. Jo-Jo Rollins, the matriarch of my genetic lineage, stressed the importance of maintaining a pristine line of female genealogy that self-selected its men. Saool Forque, the patriarch of Dang's lineage, asked Ray Tyne to seek out the brightest and best woman he knew for his genealogy to continue through a superior female partner. That is how we end up with people like Pique and Dang." Pique erases part of the roofline of her dirt sketch and decreases its angle on the next try. "Perhaps you can see where the Holy Father and I are trying to go with this. We believe that Dang and Pique would create the kind of genetic product that would advance humanity by leaps and bounds."

Pique looks up for the first time. She's been listening all along. She and Dang exchange awkward looks, but both are too embarrassed to say anything.

Emmis is oblivious to their discomfort and she just continues talking. "I need you to know, Max, that the Holy Father has chosen you. He cares about you very much." She blinks and the metal cylinder that seems to nourish her reappears. The ammonia-smelling liquid is shot into Emmis's mouth again. "You should know how much the Holy Father cares about our whole family. Years ago, when Chancellor Vrig and his Federacy coconspirators decided to perform the procedure on me, the Holy Father used all his resources to ensure that it could be reversed. He outmaneuvered Vrig without

Vrig ever knowing. Years later, he again protected us from Vrig. He staged everything so that Kene Yorne and his assassins would think they killed us, instead of DAKs made to look like us. If he didn't take us from the Federacy, we would most certainly be dead." She points to her machinery. "Then—in what may be the greatest miracle of all—the Holy Father brought me back to life. It took his scientists years and years to create, but he made sure they did. As the End of Days approached, he invested immeasurable resources into the completion of this incredible vessel. You must know, Max—the Holy Father sees himself as the caretaker of you, me, and our children. They're his family. *They're his children.*"

A horrible thought claws its way into my head. Vrig said it to me and I brushed it aside. I hate myself for thinking it, but is Emmis trying to say to me that my kids are really the Holy Father's kids. Is that why he has such a vested interest in saving them. *Did Emmis sleep with the Holy Father?* He slept with Nayla. He slept with Mavy's mother. He slept with countless exceptional women in order to reproduce his own genetic gifts. The thought of him being with Emmis sickens me. It can't be true. It just can't. I have to know.

"Did you and the Holy Father . . ." I say, before stopping myself. I take a deep breath. "I mean was there ever anything between—"

"Max," Emmis snaps. She is aggravated. "No. It wasn't necessary to the cause and I had no interest in it. As you might suspect, he tried. He tried very hard. But when I was capable of these kinds of emotions, I loved you and only you. He was persistent, but I'm not like Mavy's mother or Nayla." She turns to Mavy and Pique. "Sorry, I meant no disrespect by that."

"*I'm sure not,*" Pique says angrily. "But I wouldn't go there if I were you. Although my mom loved me, being with my father was the biggest mistake of her life."

"You're right, Pique. We should leave the past in the past. It's not important. The future is all that matters." Emmis rolls closer to Pique and politely asks her to stop sketching in the dirt. "I hope you know that the future holds great things for you, Pique. You are perhaps the most special of all of us. You are the only person who shares two great gene lines—the Holy Father's and mine. You are filled with so much promise, but then there's . . ." Emmis stops herself and makes a quick correction. "Then there's . . . *your age.* You're still so young." This is not what Emmis was going to say. I think about whether I should find out what Emmis was about to say, but I don't want Pique hearing anything painful about herself, even if it's untrue.

Emmis activates her monitors again and the lasers immediately lock in on her eye movements. She scrolls through a few screens and finds what she's looking for. She faces the others and says, "Can you please excuse Max and me for a moment."

"Gladly," Pique says, taking Mavy and Dang by the arms and pulling them away.

Emmis focuses on her monitors. She blinks and they rotate to face me. Two flaps open in the arm-like platforms underneath Emmis's hands. Two small square devices come out and move along a thin rotating belt. The devices quickly lock into the palms of Emmis's hands. "These are unlike any other Palmitors. They are specifically designed for me and are intertwined with my own electromagnetic biochemistry. They're hardwired into me. The connection is unique, intimate." Her voice picks up. She's almost excited. Her face reddens, almost like she's blushing. As the Palmitors touch her hand, I see a flicker of the woman I fell in love with and realize that her only passion is resting in her palms.

Emmis concentrates hard and her hands slowly close around the Palmitors. It's painful for her to move her hands. "I want to show you something. I'm doing this because I want you to trust me. I need you to believe in what I can do." The Palmitors begin to howl and the metal sleeves that house her arms begin to vibrate. The monitors shake from the motion. "My insights into the future have become complex, convoluted to the untrained mind. I wanted to show you something very simple. It's a model of future behavior that I think you can process." She blinks and two graphs, one on each screen, turn from white to blue. "Each screen shows a possible future related to the birth of your child. The graph lines on the top of the screen represent different probabilistic distributions. I know Mavy didn't want to know, but I'm pretty sure you do. The monitor on the right shows Mavy having a girl and the different genetic probabilities associated with it. The monitor on the right shows Mavy having a boy and the genetic probabilities associated with that. Overall, it very much looks like it will be a healthy girl who carries much of the Holy Father's genetic material." The monitors go black. "I can't show you more than that now, but I wanted to give you a glimpse of what I can do. I need you to trust me, Max. It's very important that you trust me."

"I can't do that." I look deep into her cold eyes. "I can't trust you." Emmis's monitors beep. Her eyes squint. She looks up quickly from her monitors and looks around.

"You're not going to have much choice, Max." There's an increased urgency to her voice. Emmis looks up to the sky. "You actually have no choice."

"There's always a choice." I hear some sounds in the distance. They're getting louder.

"No, I mean now. You really have to trust me. Now."

I soon realize what she means. The sound gets louder. I don't see it yet, but I hear the blades slicing through the air. It's a helicraft. I pull out my gun and point it in the direction of the oncoming helicraft. Emmis shakes her head. "The helicraft is here to save you. I called for it a few minutes ago. It's the cartels you have to worry about. They'll be here any minute and they've been instructed to kill."

I run toward the others, and Emmis follows me. "There's nothing to be nervous about, Max. The helicraft is here to take us back to Yerusalom. That's where we're supposed to be. The Palmitors are certain of it." Emmis and I get to Pique and the others just as the helicraft reaches a clearing a few hundred meters away. It hovers above the clearing. "No one needs to worry," Emmis says. "We're going back to Yerusalom where we'll be safe."

"How can you say Yerusalom will be safe," I say. "Yerusalom is the first place Vrig will attack."

"We've taken care of everything," Emmis says. "Trust me. There's no reason for me to lie. We need you. Please, all of you need to trust me."

"I don't trust you one bit," Pique says. "And I won't be going anywhere with you." Mavy and Dang don't understand Pique's anger. Dang is scared and wants be anywhere but here and Mavy is excited about returning to Yerusalom.

The forest begins to rumble. The churning and crushing of earth and brush overtakes the sounds of the helicraft's blades. The trees begin to move. The helicraft is at our backs and the forest is moving in front of us. We're caught in the middle.

I hear metal turning. It comes from behind us. The helicraft's artillery guns are moving. I hear two quick blasts. I turn and two projectiles are heading right at us. I grab Pique and Mavy and pull them to the ground. Dang sees us and follows suit. Emmis calmly watches as the projectiles fly right over her head. There is a flash of light and two huge explosions. I sit up and see two armored carriers on fire. They had just come out of the forest.

Emmis looks down at her monitors. "In less than two minutes, there will be twenty more of those. The cartels know you're here. They've sent every carrier in the area. We need to go."

Emmis blinks a few times. I assume she is sending a message to the heli-craft, because the door of the helicraft immediately folds down and a ramp appears. "We need to go right now," Emmis says.

"I'm not going anywhere," Pique says.

"We don't have a choice," Mavy says. "We can't fight all of those carriers. We have to get on the helicraft."

"She's right," Dang says. Dang is his usual *calm self.* "Please, Pique, let's go. Please."

"I'm not going, but you should get on board."

"Either we all go or none of us goes," Mavy says.

"You two need to get on board," I say to Mavy and Dang. "Emmis, please take them." I pull Mavy in close so no one else can hear. "I will get Pique on board. But having you and Dang here will only make it harder. I promise I will get her to go." Mavy reluctantly agrees and she, Dang, and Emmis head to the helicraft.

"I'm not going," Pique says stubbornly.

"I don't see a better option right now. I don't want to go to Yerusalom either. But we can't stay here. We can't fight twenty armored carriers, even with your magical hands. It would kill you. We can't stay, Pique. We have to go with Emmis."

"That's a terrible idea. This isn't Emmis. It's her body inside that machine, but it's not her. I'm sorry, Judge, but I just don't trust Emmis's ghost."

"I don't either. But those burning carriers, the ones that were ready to fire on us, are real. And I believe Emmis when she says a lot more of them are coming." On cue, the forest rumbles, much louder than before. "Please, Pique. Just do it for me."

"I can't."

"Please, Pique. I will do anything you ask." The sound of the trees being crushed grows louder.

"*Anything?*"

"Yes. Anything. But ask me quickly."

"Okay. The next time I ask you to do something, no matter what it is, you just do it."

Three gigantic pines topple over and I hear the carriers' wheels grinding up brush. "Okay. I will."

"No, promise me. The next time I ask you to do something, no matter what it is, you just do it. No questions asked."

"I promise."

"Swear on your children's lives."

"I swear on my children's lives. The next time you ask me to do something, I will do it. No questions asked."

"Deal."

Pique takes my hand and we start running—running to Yerusalom.

52

DAKS

Pique and I run as fast as we can toward the helicraft. Just before we hit the ramp, an armored carrier fires a shot. The projectile speeds toward us. The buzz is deafening. I feel the heat of the projectile on the back of my neck. Just as it's about to take me out, a burst of supersonic energy blasts out from the helicraft. It knocks Pique and me off our feet. I look up from the ground and watch as the projectile explodes into a million pieces. I help Pique to her feet and we both run onto the ramp and into the helicraft. The door closes just as another armored carrier appears and fires a shot. The helicraft discharges another sonic burst and disorients the projectile, causing a massive explosion. A DAK runs to the transport's access area and quickly ushers us into our seats alongside Dang and Mavy. I look up and see two DAKs in the cockpit.

"Ignition sequence initiated," one says to the other. Their voices are mechanical, but soothing. "Full thrust," the other responds. The helicraft blasts off into the sky with a mind-blowing force. This helicraft makes the Rogues' craft seem like an old-fashioned copter. A surface-to-air projectile starts toward the helicraft, but the speed of this otherworldly helicraft is too much. I glance out my window and the armored carriers have already become specks. In no time, we are at the end of the Earth's atmosphere.

It looks peaceful below, but I realize anything can look good at a distance.

The DAK that ushered us in approaches us. It places down a movable tray with a lace cloth, a silver-plated cup, and a honey biscuit. It then pours

Damascian tea into our cups. Ecclesiastical music, which was playing softly in the background, is now playing more loudly. After serving the tea, the DAK asks if we want anything else. None of us wanted anything in the first place.

The two DAKs in the cockpit announce that we have reached our cruising altitude. They press a series of buttons on the control panel in front of them and stand upright. They walk to the DAK serving us and form a straight line. They bring their feet together and snap to attention facing us. They lock hands, and in perfect unison, announce, "Spiro de Yerusalom."

A panel in the ceiling slowly lowers and a blue light pours into the cabin. A stairwell descends from the ceiling. Spiro slowly walks down the steps, reaches the floor, spins his body, and then heads toward me. "So nice to see you again, Judge." He extends his hand to me. I don't take it.

"So we're not even pretending to be civil," Spiro says to me. I don't respond. "Very well, Judge. Then the pleasure is all mine." Spiro takes a few steps back and lines up with the DAKs. He locks hands with one of them, and in unison, they announce, "The Holy Father." I hear the footsteps. Slowly, deliberately, step over step over step, the Holy Father makes his way down. A circle in the floor slides open and a red velvet chair rises up on a metal plate. The headrest of the chair has the Nation of Yerusalom seal on it—a white-gloved hand reaching up to the sky. The chair locks into place facing us.

The Holy Father moves to Pique and Mavy first. He gradually kneels between their seats. He takes a deep breath. "My loves." He grabs each of their hands and kisses them. Pique is quick to pull away. Mavy is not. He then moves to Dang and me. He places a hand on each of our heads. He mouths a blessing, but no words come out. He smiles and says, "It's so good to have you here." He walks back to the red velvet chair and sits. Spiro takes his place on one side and Emmis's machinery comes to a stop on the other. The two DAKs that were in the cockpit return to it, while the other polishes the silver in the craft's galley.

"We will soon be home, my children. All that I have put you through—it causes me such pain. But this was . . . *as it was supposed to be.* This was . . . *as it had to be.* Emmis, Spiro, and I have seen all of this. The end is upon us. The new beginning will soon arrive. Here we are. Seven divinely inspired men and women flying at the edge of space in a human masterpiece. Flying

302 • JAY SCHIFFMAN

in a monument to human ascension. Flying in a soaring tabernacle of devotion. Flying in an unyielding testament to the very glory of man."

The Holy Father motions to the DAK in the galley. The DAK approaches and the Holy Father instructs him on what needs to be done. The DAK walks to a brightly colored touchscreen with pulsing lights. He enters a code and then touches a red button in the lower left portion of the screen. My seat immediately vibrates and I try to jump out of it. But it's too late. Rubber manacles, like invincible mythic snakes, coil around my legs. The same happen to my hands and head. I look at the others. They're also wrapped in thick rubber. Normally, my first instinct would be to fight. Anger would course through my veins. This would immediately be followed by some kind of formulation of a strategy, some attempt to come up with a plan. But in this case, the only thing I muster is regret—overwhelming regret. I let everyone down. I should have listened to Pique. Her instincts are better than mine. I should have known this was a trap.

Pique struggles hard to get out. She's not going down without a fight. But it's no use. The rubber has neutralized her powers. Mavy and Dang do not fight at all. For Mavy, I think it's blind trust. I think she believes that her father and Emmis would never hurt us. For Dang, it's the opposite. Fear rules Dang and he regrets that he ran from one dangerous situation into an even more dangerous one. But he's resigned to his fate.

"Please don't struggle, Pique," the Holy Father says. "This is simply a protective measure. I have to keep you all safe. One of you might try something foolish that will endanger us all." The Holy Father looks at each of the DAKs. They chant "The end is here" over and over again. Their eerie tone clashes with the ecclesiastical music. This discordant symphony sends a harsh chill through me. Spiro's smile doesn't help matters.

Pique quickly fills with rage. She's like a wild animal. At one point she tries to bite through the manacles, but they're far too thick. "Let me go," she screams. She's frantic. I think she understands more about what's going to happen next than the rest of us. She thrashes, but the restraints refuse to yield. "I will kill all of you if you don't let me go. You, too, Father. Let me out now, or as god is my witness, I will kill you."

Spiro's smile has grown more sinister.

"Knock that smile off your face or I will do it for you, Spiro," Pique says. She's not herself. What she knows has unhinged her.

The Holy Father allows the slightest grin to escape. It's pride. Pique is his favorite. She always has been. "You are the most human of us all, Pique." His eyes become wide. "And also the most divine. Perhaps that is why I love you so much."

"I despise you—everything about you."

"I know, my child. We always hate what we fear."

I see a brilliant flash of light outside my window. It's like the sun has exploded. A strong vibration hits the helicraft. I look over at Pique. She's no longer struggling. A tear rolls down her face and it's quickly followed by more. She closes her eyes, which forces out even more tears. Her chest heaves. There is another brilliant flash and another. With each, Pique shudders. The DAKs' chants continue and Emmis yells at them to stop. There is still a sliver of humanity left in her.

I watch as the VOIDs explode over and over again, and before I can even ask Emmis about the safety of the children, she says, "The kids are nowhere near those explosions, Max. They're in a detonation shelter thousands of kilometers away. I've made sure they're safe."

"She means they're mostly safe," Spiro says.

"What the hell does that mean?" I pull at my restraints with all my might and they don't budge. Emmis gives Spiro an angry look. "Don't listen to him, Max. I promise you they're safe."

Spiro walks behind my chair and places his hands on my shoulder. I want to throw my head back and slam his face, but my head is immobilized by the restraints. "The judge values honesty more than any other trait, Emmis. You should know that having been married to him for so many years. Why don't we just tell him the truth?"

"You're beginning to try my patience," Emmis says.

"Some say patience is a virtue. I think it's overrated. I prefer an equally unoriginal saying—'throw caution to the wind.'" Spiro comes around to the side of my chair and then leaps in front of me. "Your children are our insurance, Judge."

I spit in Spiro's face. It's nothing I have ever done, but it's the only means

I have for striking at him and I don't regret it. "Oh that's lovely, Judge," Spiro says. He takes my spit and rubs it in between his thumb and index finger. "Quite the gentleman."

"If any harm comes to them, you know I'll kill you," I say. I turn to Emmis. "You better not have had anything to do with this."

"That's enough," the Holy Father says. "Spiro will be dead soon enough. As will Emmis. And I will be in another state altogether. But your children will be alive. We've all seen this end."

Spiro bows before Emmis. "I'm sorry for inserting myself between you and your husband. It's not my place . . . *to tell him the truth.* You've obviously done such a wonderful job over the years of being forthright with him—your Abstainer background, your work on the Palmitor, your alliance with the Holy Father . . . I could go on and on."

"I'm warning you, Spiro," Emmis says.

"Your warning is duly noted." Spiro faces me. "But the judge should know the truth. I feel compelled to tell him what I've done. He has every right to know that I've inserted small explosive devices at the base of his children's skulls. He should know that I control the detonator for these devices. He should also know that his little girl—Viole, I believe—squealed the loudest. A father should know these things. It was so hard to get that device in between those tiny little vertebrae. She has been having such a hard time turning her head lately. *You may want to have that looked into.*"

I try to pull the manacles apart. I feel a superhuman strength come over my body, as if I can rip these manacles to shreds. But I can't. It's just the adrenaline talking. I want to kill him so badly.

"Emmis, how could you allow this," I say.

"I'm sorry, Max. I know what I saw and the children will be safe. No matter what Spiro is saying, I can guarantee their safety."

"You can't guarantee anything. I don't care what you saw. You can't guarantee they'll be safe." I shake my head. "It's not okay. What you've done is unforgivable."

I know I have to make a move soon. As I start looking around the craft for an escape strategy, a monitor comes down from the ceiling. It has the Nation of Yerusalom seal on it. The Holy Father stares at the seal. "A short while ago I contacted Chancellor Vrig. I let him know that we are in the process of launching a series of VOIDs against major population centers that have been deemed *genetic or tactical impediments to human ascension.* I explained to him what I shall now explain to you." The Holy Father swivels in his chair toward us. He folds his hands in prayer as he speaks. "The days of nations fighting one another will soon be behind us. A new humanity will spread across the world like buds sprouting in spring. But for there to be a true re-birth, we must discard the old. From the ashes will rise a new humanity."

Another brilliant light flashes outside of our windows and then another. These vibrations are smaller than the earlier ones, but the light is just as strong. A DAK looks up at the explosion for a moment and then returns to folding a silk napkin.

"Only a few more VOIDs and the first wave of destruction will be over," the Holy Father says. "It took many millennia to build humanity in Our God's image and yet only a few minutes to destroy it."

Pique clutches her seat. She whispers, *"How could you let this happen? You can't possibly exist."* I don't know that Pique ever believed in Our God, but if she did, she certainly doesn't now.

The Holy Father hears Pique. "You're wrong, my love. You should never doubt the existence of Our God. It is a dangerous endeavor. I tried to ex-plain this to Chancellor Vrig, but he would not listen. I have a great respect for the Chancellor—more than he realizes. I even gave him an annotated copy of *Who Wrote the Book of Our God?* because I truly appreciate Vrig's belief in the greatness of human beings. Vrig and I share a profound respect for the potential of humans. But he never believed in Our God. I explained to him that I have had many a conversation with Our God over my lifetime. *This God* very much exists. I tried and tried to prove this to the Chancellor, but he refused to believe. He insisted that it was nothing more than a pretense. With such human arrogance, he would say that I was merely playing what he called 'the Game of the VOIDs.' He was so sure of himself. He thought that people like me upheld this game so that we could maintain power over ordi-nary men." The Holy Father laughs. "The irony of this. Our God has all the power—not me. Our God is the one playing the game. How absurd it is to claim that I used Our God to maintain my power. The opposite is true. *Our God used me to maintain his.*"

Another flash of light hits our window. Dang turns to face Pique. His voice breaks in a million pieces. He now knows what Pique knows. He whispers to Pique. There is defeat in his voice. "I get it now. I should've known a long time ago. I'm so sorry, Pique."

"I knew you two would be the first," the Holy Father says. "That's why the two of you are meant to be together. I know how painful it can be at the beginning. It was just as painful for me. My grandfather, the Cardinal, killed himself because he couldn't deal with the pain. Of course the history books fail to tell the truth about his death. But, in fact, he took his own life rather than fight for what he knew was right. He was incapable of doing what I have done. I loved my grandfather, but regretfully, I must say he lacked courage. I have always understood what must be done. We must defeat our enemy by taking away his monopoly over space and time. These are his only true weapons—his only means for controlling us. They always have been. If we master them, the hegemony dissipates and humanity ascends."

I need to make my move. I have to find a way to take control of this craft, and if it's at all possible, stop the launch sequences from continuing. I yell as loud as I can and make sure my voice conveys a kind of desperate insanity. I scream, "What are you talking about? What are you talking about? What? What?" I need them to think I'm losing my mind. I need them distracted. I can't sit here any longer with VOIDs exploding around me. I need to act.

"Please control yourself," the Holy Father says. "There's no reason for you to raise your voice."

"You're destroying the world," I shout. "And you're still talking nonsense about time and space and some enemy."

Pique is motionless. Her eyes are bright red from crying—bright red from bearing all that death. She understands how senseless it all is. She understands the truth about who the Holy Father sees as his enemy.

"Who is this enemy you're talking about?" I ask. I don't shout this time. I see how distraught Pique is, and although I think the Holy Father is delusional, part of me genuinely wants to know. "Who is this enemy?" I take a commanding tone. "Tell me already—who is he?"

The Holy Father stands from his chair and walks toward me. He places his hand over mine. He leans over to whisper in my ear. "My enemy," he says before pausing. He straightens up and folds his hands behind his back.

"My enemy . . . is *God*."

53

SPIRO

Spiro motions to one of the DAKs and it quickly returns to the panel and presses a few buttons on the screen. The rubber manacle around my head starts to vibrate and then unfolds like a rubberized butterfly springing from a cocoon. Two flaps meet to cover my mouth. There are two small breathing holes over my nostrils, but otherwise it's airtight. Words cannot escape. I look over at Mavy, Dang, and Pique and they are also gagged.

"We will be contacting Chancellor Vrig soon," Spiro says. "And we can't have any of you running your mouths. You might *accidentally* try to give him information about our whereabouts."

"I am truly sorry for any discomfort this may cause," the Holy Father says. "Especially for you, my dear sweet Mavy. I know this can't be comfortable in your state."

The Holy Father asks Emmis to show him something about Pique on one of her monitors. I assume he is most worried about her interfering with his grand plans. He reaches down to Emmis's monitor and scrolls through the different screens. At one point, he touches the screen and shakes his head, clearly disappointed. Emmis then whispers something to the Holy Father and he responds, "You must."

Emmis blinks and her monitor retracts. She rolls toward Pique. She occasionally looks at me, but talks directly to Pique. "I know this must be very hard to accept, Pique. I know you've always had your doubts about the existence of Our God. Anyone with your genetic makeup would. And even if you did believe, I know you would see the version of God that you know as a force for good. It took me decades to accept the fact that Our God or any god for that matter is neither good nor bad. Our God is nothing more than an infinitely successful appropriator of power. There's no judgment in that statement." Emmis turns to me. "This is a major point of contention between the Holy Father and me. I see Our God as a neutral force, like a form of artificial intelligence that is designed to acquire more information. By its very nature, Our God is an aggregator of power, no differently than a lion is a hunter. Again, there is no moral judgment in the lion killing and taking what he must. Same with a god taking what it must. Our God is programmed, for lack of a better word, to exploit power."

"'Exploit' is the operative word," Spiro says.

"Let's not get into semantics," the Holy Father says. "We have our differences with Emmis, but our goals are the same."

"They very much are, Father," Emmis says. She does not hide her deep admiration for the Holy Father. "Because of your particular genetic constitution, Pique, it will be very difficult for you to accept that Our God's monopoly over time and space is detrimental to the advancement of humankind. It took me quite some time to realize philosophically what I understood mathematically at a very young age. The laws of space and time have been intentionally distorted so that humans cannot properly master them. This is the essence of the Cardinal's discovery. Some of the difficulty you are having is that you and Our God are in some ways kindred spirits. Each of you is a naturally gifted aggregator of power—electricity, gravitational forces, intelligence, judgment. You both live to increase your powers."

Emmis couldn't be more wrong about Pique. She doesn't live to increase her powers. She would give away her powers tomorrow if she could. She wants nothing more than to live a normal life. She's particularly exceptional because she doesn't want to be.

"Of course Our God's powers are exponentially more developed than yours. But for a human, you are beyond compare. You don't even try to cultivate your capabilities and yet you are the most advanced of us. If you worked on your powers, as we would like, you would be capable of many divine feats. The interesting thing about this kind of extreme power is that it makes you unpredictable. The Palmitor is far more imprecise when it comes to a life force like you or Our God. There's a marked erraticism to you both. It's an interesting paradox—the more power you aggregate, the less predictable you are. Some might say you and Our God think with *your hearts*. Of course there is no such thing as a metaphysical heart. But like Our God, you often favor nonrational modes of decision making." Emmis closes her eyes. "This is a big problem for us."

"I suggested we just kill you and harvest your genetic material," Spiro says. "Or at least lock you up in a rubber prison and run experiments on you." He points to the Holy Father. "But *Daddy* said that's not an option."

Pique sees me looking at her, and I think she winks at me. She pulls at the manacles as if she wants to break free and attack Spiro. The Holy Father tells Pique to relax and then angrily points to a fold-down seat on the wall of the craft and motions for Spiro to take a seat and be quiet. Pique quiets down, and when I'm the only one looking at her, winks at me again. She's up to something.

"I would be lying to you, Pique, if I said we didn't need you," Emmis continues. "You are the closest thing we have to a divine force. With you, we have a very powerful processor for our Palmitor. But it's a double-edged sword. We can harness your enormous powers, but as I said before, we also add a level of unpredictability."

Out of nowhere, Spiro jumps from his seat. He's extremely agitated. "How did you do that," he yells at Pique. He moves to the panel, taps the screen, and her gag folds back into its cocoon.

"Do what?" she asks.

"You know what you did."

"No. I don't. I know that I hate you and want to kill you. But I don't know what you're talking about."

"It was you. You got inside of my head and spoke. You said, *I am Our God, the One True God, and I will destroy all those who defy me.*"

"I heard no such thing," the Holy Father says.

"In *my head*, Father!" Spiro shouts. "She got inside *my head*. She spoke to me. I don't understand."

"Maybe it really was Our God—if you believe in that kind of thing," Pique says. "But it wasn't me. I mean—I'm not Our God, *right*? I've got some electrical power in my hands, but it's nothing that a little rubber can't control. I can't imagine that qualifies for being Our God." Pique is playing with Spiro.

"You can communicate telepathically," Spiro says.

"Not through this high-density rubber," Emmis says. "Her manacles are near-perfect insulators."

Spiro shakes his head angrily and presses a button on the screen. Pique is again gagged. The manacle unfolds over her mouth and silences her. "Sorry, my love," the Holy Father says. Spiro starts to talk and the Holy Father cuts him off. "I think you've said enough." The Holy Father and Spiro remind me of an old married couple. They bicker, but there is an unbreakable bond that only they can understand.

The Holy Father slowly lifts himself out of his seat and takes a few steps toward us. "You may find this hard to believe, Pique. But I have in fact talked to Our God. It's not often and it's not easy for me to do. Frankly, it's quite painful—similar to the pain you probably feel after you've expended a great deal of electrical energy. The only difference for me is I have neither your physical manifestations of electromagnetism nor your innate abilities. Mine are completely within the realm of my cerebral cortex."

The Holy Father begins to walk around the helicraft. His hands are interlocked behind his back. "For most of my life, I have felt very close to Our God. I saw Our God as a great influence in my life. But as I grew older, and I acquired certain key proficiencies—divine powers if you will—the closeness I felt began to fade. I began to read my grandfather's teachings in a different light. I can't say for sure but I believe Our God felt threatened by my powers. The thing you must keep in mind is that Our God does not like to share. It's not in his nature. It's not a coincidence that monotheism became the only basis for religion in both the Old and New Orders."

A DAK brings the Holy Father a syringe on a silver tray. The DAK stretches its arms out and the Holy Father takes the syringe from the tray. The Holy Father inserts it into his neck and presses a small hydraulic button on the end. The Holy Father grimaces for a second and then places the empty syringe back on the tray. The DAK moves away and the Holy Father walks toward one of the windows near where Spiro is sitting. He doesn't turn back to look at us. He just stares out the circular window. *"What does it even mean to be divine? What are the types of qualities and powers that gods actually possess?* The truth is that a god, in actuality, is little more than a master scientist—an expert in biology, chemistry, physics, genetics, and all the great sciences. Most importantly, a god controls space and time—the main ingredients of all science." As the Holy Father walks by Spiro, he lovingly places his hand on his shoulder.

"I believe we are put on this earth to improve ourselves. Human life is the struggle to reach the divine. Every religion throughout history has heroic humans whose defining characteristic is their brush with divinity. Prophets split apart oceans. Priests turn water to wine. Holy soldiers slay superhuman giants. Humanity's mission is to create a race of humans that can masterfully manipulate space and time. Imagine, for example, if Pique's progeny could not only manipulate electromagnetic fields, but could move celestial bodies or travel at the speed of light. They would be divine. They would be just as powerful as Our God. They would break his monopoly. I am creating this very future for humankind." The Holy Father turns to face us. "When we form the future with our own hands, we master our destiny and free ourselves from the shackles of Our God."

While the Holy Father continues his sermon, I see Mavy nod at Pique. It's subtle, but I see it. Mavy immediately starts breathing heavily. The manacles rise and fall as she takes larger and larger breaths of air. I'm not sure what Pique and Mavy are up to, but I know it's something.

"Let's be fair, Father," Emmis says. "Our God is doing what is in Our God's nature. You are right to suggest that he has complicated the laws of physics and mathematics so that we cannot easily see the truth. But Our God has no motive. Our God is not shackling us. Our God is expanding into the infinite as any god must. That's all."

Spiro throws his hands in the air. "*Greed. Desire. Selfishness.* Our God is infinitely expanding in those directions as well, *is he not?*"

Spiro again jumps from his seat. He nervously looks around the helicraft. He's tense. "Stop it," he shouts. "Stop saying that." Spiro's head twitches and sweat begins to form on his brow.

"Are you okay, my child?" the Holy Father asks. "Is it the voice again?"

Mavy's breathing becomes deep and labored. The Holy Father looks at her for a moment but turns back to Spiro. "Maybe you are in fact hearing Our

God," the Holy Father says. Spiro nervously shakes his head back and forth. He doesn't want to believe it's possible, but he's a lot more susceptible to belief than I am. He may hate Our God, but he believes in his existence. The only thing I believe in is Mavy and Pique's plan. Somehow Pique got inside Spiro's head and she's driving him mad.

As Spiro becomes more and more unhinged, Mavy pretends to hyperventilate. Her breaths become desperate and her face reddens. Emmis instructs the DAK to return to the panel and release Mavy's gag. Through labored breaths, Mavy says, "Father, I don't feel right." She heaves and gasps while fighting to say the words. "Please help me. Please, Father, help me."

Her voice becomes weak. "The baby," she cries. Mavy forces herself to stop breathing completely and it looks like she's about to pass out. Emmis tells the DAK to release Mavy's restraints. Mavy falls out of her seat and collapses on the floor. The Holy Father moves as quickly as he can to her. He bends down and takes her hand. As soon as he feels for her pulse, she springs to her feet and grabs his arm. She pulls it tight behind his back and places her right hand on his temple. He grimaces in pain.

"This is wrong, my love," the Holy Father says. "You have misunderstood my intentions."

She ignores him. With the Holy Father as her hostage, she backs away from Emmis and Spiro. "Release everyone or I electrocute him."

"You're not going to kill your own father," Spiro says.

Mavy immediately sends a small electrical charge into the side of the Holy Father's temple, and he screams. The room fills with static energy. My own body sizzles with energy. Mavy's enraged. Everything she's ever believed in is gone.

"I don't know this man," she says. "The father I knew wouldn't bind his daughters to a chair. The father I knew wouldn't say these unspeakable things about Our God. The father I knew was filled with love and compassion. This man is not my father."

"Please calm down, Mavy," Emmis says. "We can work this out." She turns to the DAK and says, "Release them. All of them. Now."

"We will do no such thing," Spiro says. He rushes toward the panel to stop the DAK.

"It's okay, my child," the Holy Father says to Spiro. "Emmis is right. We can work this out. Please let the DAK release them." The DAK heads to the panel, and Spiro intercepts it. Electricity warms the room. Spiro puts his hand on the DAK's chest and sends an electric current through its body. Smoke pours from the DAK's mouth as it convulses. The DAK falls to the floor. The other DAKs, in the cockpit, hit the autopilot and run toward the panel. But Spiro quickly disposes of them.

Emmis begins blinking rapidly. Her monitors rise out of her machinery, and her eyes move with a focused speed across different screens. I think she's trying to override the control panel. Spiro quickly steps over the dead DAKs and heads toward me. I'm covered in protective rubber, but there are a few spots where he can hurt me. "Let the Holy Father go or the judge is dead," Spiro shouts to Mavy.

Spiro then stops in his tracks. He grabs his head and covers his ears. He shakes his head violently. "Stop it already. Stop it. Please . . . stop." He tries to shake off the voices, but they continue to haunt him. He raises his right hand and aims it at me. I try to drop my head to increase the amount of rubber facing him. He fires an electric blast. It hits me, but only a small current gets through to a part of my shoulder not covered in rubber. It speeds through my body—from my shoulder, down my side, and out through my feet. My body shakes wildly and I smell my hair burning. Then, all of sudden, my arms and legs come free. I don't know if Emmis hacked into the panel or Spiro's short-circuited my manacles, but I'm able to get free. I quickly dive behind my chair just as Spiro fires another shot.

Spiro runs toward me. He needs to get close, because I'm tucked behind the rubberized chair. I decide to sacrifice my left arm as a target. As he gets close to me, I raise my left arm far above the left side of the chair. Spiro reacts to my decoy and fires another blast. I absorb the blow, and pain surges through my left hand and arm. I then leap out over the right-side chair and kick Spiro in his chest. He falls backward and his head slams into the floor. I jump on top of him and punch his face. My second punch breaks his nose. Blood splatters everywhere. I pummel every part of him. *He must die.* I raise my hand back for what I hope is the final blow. I bring it down with all the force I have. But someone grabs my fist. I turn around. It's Pique.

I would not normally tolerate someone stopping me. Not when I'm in a fight. Not when I've made a conscious decision to kill a bad person. But it's Pique.

"We're better than this," she says. She stares directly into my eyes. She wants me to stop. She needs me to spare him. "Please, Judge." She could easily pull me away herself, but she wants me to do it on my own. I take a deep breath and gather myself. I eventually step away from Spiro. I do what Pique asked. "You see," Pique says. "We really are better than this."

"You may be," Emmis says. "But I'm not." Emmis blinks twice and a flexible mechanical arm appears from her machinery. It's like the tail of a scorpion.

"Don't," Pique shouts. "He's the only one who knows where the kids are." Pique doesn't necessarily believe this. She knows Spiro will never tell us where he's hidden them. But she wants to save Spiro's life. She cares, even about him. She wants us to be decent. She wants us to show mercy.

But Emmis is no longer decent or capable of mercy. For the first time since she returned, I see her acting on a genuine human emotion. *Anger.* All reason is gone. She's nothing more than an enraged animal. She feels a primal urge from deep within—an urge that the procedures couldn't remove. Her mechanical arm springs out toward Spiro. Pique jumps toward it. But it's too late. Emmis plunges her mechanical arm into Spiro's chest and claws out his heart. His body seizes on the floor. He coughs up blood and is dead in an instant.

"Emmis," the Holy Father shouts. "No!" The Holy Father is in a state of disbelief. *"How could you?"* Pique tries to revive Spiro, but it's hopeless. The Holy Father slouches down and Mavy immediately lets go of his arm. The Holy Father covers his face and turns away. It is not dignified for a Holy Father to cry. He slowly stands and straightens out his robe.

"This is not how it was supposed to be," he says to Emmis. The Holy Father becomes more indignant. "This is not what I saw."

"It may not be what you saw, Father. But it's what had to be done. He was not essential."

"He was essential to me," the Holy Father snaps. "That is all you need to understand." He turns his back again. His voice is weak. "He was essential to me."

The Holy Father becomes small. He slumps over and rhythmically bobs his head up and down. He speaks in a soft voice. "Spiro was my redemption. *My redemption.*" The Holy Father rubs his eyes and takes a deep breath. "The prostitutes found Spiro as a little orphan girl. From the beginning, they trained this little girl in their profession. Of all the names to choose, they chose Ellee, the most righteous of the Old Order prophets. How could they do this to a poor innocent girl? By the time she was just nine, she had a client list that would make even the most corrupt souls sick to their stomachs. She had impurity rammed down every orifice of her young body." The Holy Father begins to weep. "I had to rescue her. I wasn't sure how to save her and so I prayed. I prayed and I prayed and I prayed. *Did Our God answer my prayers?* Of course not. That coldhearted bastard remained silent. Complete silence. So I took it upon myself to decide. It's what we humans always do when our gods remain silent. I decided she could no longer live as Ellee. She needed to be reborn. So I turned her into a him and named my new son Spiro, the most divine of the Old Order prophets. It was not a perfect transformation. Nothing ever is. My Spiro was scarred and had many imperfections. He was damaged and always would be. But he was reborn. My son was reborn."

54

PIQUE

Dang and I remove the DAKs and Spiro's dead body. We place the DAKs in the galley and lock the door. We treat Spiro's body with more dignity. We wrap him in a blanket and place him in the storage compartment in the rear of the helicraft. I quickly return to the cockpit, where Mavy is already in the pilot's seat trying to figure out the controls.

"Can you fly this thing?" I ask.

"You know I can." She pokes me and says, "The real issue is—*can I land it?*"

I debate whether I should secure the Holy Father and Emmis, and decide against it. My reasons are not the same for each, and suffice it to say, Emmis is the one I'm truly concerned about. The first order of business is to get Vrig on that monitor. I want to make sure there's no more needless death and suffering. Vrig may be readying to launch hundreds of VOIDs and I need to quickly put an end to this madness.

I look outside the window and I can see the lights of Yerusalom in the far distance. We have enough fuel to circle for a while and I need a plan. "Mavy, take us down to five thousand meters and circle." I turn to Emmis. "I need to know if there any more VOIDs in the launch queue?"

"No," she says. I look at the Holy Father and he agrees.

"Can you help me get Vrig on the monitor?" I need to convince Vrig to hold off on retaliating. Emmis stares into space, ignoring my question. I ask her again and this time she forces out an answer. But it's not an answer to my question. "You're right. I shouldn't have killed Spiro." She then returns to staring into space. I recognize this stare. It's that same one from when she was in her wheeled chair, staring vacantly out the window, watching the owl that lives in our backspace.

Dang realizes that Emmis isn't going to be much help. He jumps up and starts examining the control panel, scrolling through every screen and making a mental note of screen numbers and configurations. It doesn't take him long to figure out how things work. He moves to a screen with a digital dial, and within a minute, he has a message sent through the communications system. No more than thirty seconds pass before the monitor comes on. There's no seal. No ceremonial music. No velvet chairs. There's no introduction. It's just Vrig's face. He's sitting on his airship's chair. He looks worn. His face is unshaven and there are knapsack-size bags under his eyes. He probably hasn't slept in days. Behind him is a cabin window. Like us, he is far above the exploding VOIDs.

Vrig is not a man for pleasantries on a good day. So on this horrific day, he angrily jumps in. "This is what you wanted? This is the kind of world you want to lord over? You sick egomaniac. If you wanted my surrender, you should have just asked for it."

The Holy Father looks to me. "May I address him?" Vrig answers before I can. "You don't have to say a word. But you better hope that *that God* of yours takes some pity on your soul, because you're a monster. You're an absolute monster."

"You're being hysterical, Chancellor," the Holy Father says. "If anyone is being an egomaniac it is you. You place far too much emphasis on the life of any individual or group of individuals. Humanity is larger than the sum of the humans that comprise it. Humanity will only survive if the unhealthiest forms perish and the hardiest are permitted to flourish. This is what we must aspire to."

"You've killed countless millions of people. Parents. Babies. Saints. The infirm. The handicapped. You've killed people who this god of yours must love. What kind of perverse aspiration is that? What kind of humanity do you want? I can assure you it's nothing I want to be a part of."

Vrig looks at me. He's despondent. His voice is hushed. "You and I have failed, Judge. We should have foreseen this kind of insanity. We should've known that men like this—men with their heads in the clouds—cannot ensure the safety of our race. We were reckless to think otherwise."

Vrig is right. We should have known. Men like us are to blame, because we know better than most that humans are quick to violence and slow to mercy. The Holy Father is one of the most human creatures I have ever met. We should have known how easily violence would come to him and how challenging it would be for him to show mercy. The Palmitor was right all along. *I am to blame.* I should have seen this coming.

"I hope you will take my advice," Vrig says.

"That depends," I say.

"I recommend that you torture this monster until blood pours out of his eyeballs. You need to cut small pieces off him until you get the information you need. You need to know what he's planning next. This is just the beginning."

"There's no need to torture me," the Holy Father says. "My work is mostly done. It's for the rest of you to rebuild a better humanity—one that aspires to divinity, rather than cowering before lesser gods. Humility is for the weak. Find the greatest among you and raise them up as gods. Raise them up to the heavens. That is our destiny."

"Stop it already," Pique yells. "You've lost your mind. I would laugh at you if you weren't so dangerous." Pique turns to face Vrig on the monitor. "You, too. Both of you are so full of yourselves. I'm pretty smart and I have no clue if God exists. It actually doesn't really matter right now. I want him to exist just like I want the fighting to stop, and my mom to be alive, and Trace to be there when we land. But I won't pretend to know one way or the other." Pique stares at her father for a long time. He knows his judgment is coming. "I can't imagine if there was a god that he would leave the world in the hands of you or the Chancellor." The Holy Father looks down, but Pique doesn't stop. "There was a time when you were a good person. I know that. But you've lost your way. The only thing that matters now is that you're a killer and I can't allow you to—"

"I'm sorry, everyone," Vrig says, cutting Pique off. "I can't take any chances. It doesn't seem like you'll be willing to get the information we need. I hope you understand." The monitor goes off and ten seconds later a projectile slams into the side of our helicraft, knocking us into a tailspin. I'm thrown against the farthermost wall of the helicraft. Pique flies through the air and I'm able to grab her leg before she slams into a metal bar that sticks out from the wall. I can't see Mavy or Dang, but I hear Dang yell, "Someone needs to get to the panel. There's an emergency parachute. Screen five or fourteen. Maybe nineteen."

The gravitational force of the spinning craft pins me down to the front part of the helicraft, just outside the cockpit. I think I see Mavy strapped in the pilot's seat, but when I call for her, she says nothing. I know our best hope is to get to that control panel. But the only time I feel like I can move is when the tail flips over the nose, which is hard to time. I miss the next time we flip over, but I take note of the sound the craft makes just before it flips. After a few seconds, I hear the faint beginning of that sound again. I know there aren't too many more chances before we hit the ground. So I take a deep breath and let go of the wall. I fall through the air. Objects are flying at me. I'm pelted by silverware, jars of foods, metal shards, and slabs of fiberglass. I think I see Spiro's body fly by. I barely get my hands in front of me before crashing into the opposite wall. I hit the wall inches from a piece of metal that would have gutted me like a fish.

I pull myself along the wall. I cross by a window and see the hills of Yerusalom quickly approaching. We can't be more than a few thousand meters above land. There's not much time. I move as quickly as I can, hand over hand, grabbing anything I can to get close to the panel. We flip again and I grab on to a loose cable. When we flip back, I am again pelted by items falling from the craft's compartments. It's like a violent sandstorm, only instead of sand it's sharp metal pieces and flying fiberglass. I hear Dang screaming in the background as he absorbs the blows of these objects. Pique shouts out something trying to comfort him. Still, there are no sounds from Mavy or anyone else.

I'm able to pull myself along the wall and get my hands on the control panel. I grab on to a bent piece of metal, which rips though my left hand. Blood pours down my arm. With my right hand I start scrolling through the screens. Five—no luck. Fourteen—no luck. Nineteen—nothing. "Dang, it's not those numbers," I yell. "Quick, pick another one."

"I don't know."

"Pick one."

"Fifteen?"

I quickly get to that screen and there it is—the emergency landing button. I hit it and the chute immediately flies out. The chute unfolds and instantly fills with air. We get sucked back into the sky faster than the speed we were falling. Everything slows down and the helicraft's nose points directly to the ground. "Everyone okay? I shout. Pique answers first, then Dang. Dang begins to explain his minor injuries and I cut him off. "You'll be fine."

I make my way to the cockpit. It's relatively easy to get there, because the pull of the craft is nose-down. Mavy's unconscious, but breathing regularly. Her head must have hit the steering controls. I gently shake her and she jumps to. Besides a huge bump on her head, and what will be a certain headache, she's fine. I look back for Emmis and the Holy Father. I call out to them, but I hear nothing. I look out the cockpit window and see we're only a few hundred meters above what looks like a flat patch of land between two hills. I tell everyone to brace themselves. Mavy tries to use the manual override to lift the helicraft's nose, but she can do just so much. I watch as we fall toward the ground and count down the seconds to impact so everyone's ready. Mavy slows us down just enough, and the helicraft's nose hits the ground hard, but the craft stays in one piece. We skid across the dirt before sliding up against the side of a hill.

I release Mavy's restraints with my good hand. She gets up slowly. Pique and Dang run up to the cockpit. I tell everyone to get out quickly. Pique and Dang each put an arm under Mavy and help her to the exit. I run back to find Emmis and the Holy Father. I search the whole craft and eventually find Emmis in the last place I would ever think to look. She is wedged into the helicraft's latrine behind two chairs that separated from the floor. The chairs, toilet, and Emmis's machinery are all intermingled together. Mangled metal tubes from the machinery are wrapped around the chairs. Pipes from the latrine are sticking into Emmis circuitry. Emmis's wiring is knotted together with the chairs' rubber manacles. I can barely tell where Emmis begins and everything else ends. There's water shooting everywhere. Sparks are flying. And the smell of ammonia and burnt metal fills the cabin. I'm able to move one of the chairs to see Emmis's head. She's awake, but not moving. Not that she physically could, but she doesn't want to get free.

"Get out, Max. There's nothing you can do for me."

"I'm getting you out of here." I start pulling the chairs off her, trying to separate them from Emmis's machinery. But the chairs are too heavy and there's too much mangled metal. Her machinery is now part of this helicraft. There's no way I'm getting it out. Even if I did, it can't possibly still work.

I don't know how long Emmis will live without her machinery, but I'm going to get her out. I rip through her machinery, breaking motion belts, pulling out rubber hoses, crushing aluminum pipes, and shattering fiberglass casings. I tear through a cable connecting her spine to the machinery's processing center. Like an animal chewing through its newborn's umbilical cord, I gnaw through a thick blue line that recycles blood. I yank out a tube that connects her lungs to a pump. I break a small generator that sits at the base of her spine.

I don't want her to die. Not in this craft. Not in this way.

I pull and rip and tear everything that stands between us until there is nothing left but Emmis and me. Her body is naked like the last time I bathed her. I lift her up in my arms and begin running.

I run down the exit ramp with Emmis. I run as if I'm saving her life, but I know that I'm not. Life is already done with her. Dang quickly takes off his jacket and covers Emmis's naked body. Her head rests in my lap. I hold her. I'm holding the woman I fell in love with all those years ago. I'm holding the mother of my three children. That's all that matters to me now.

I look around. We are in the hills of Yerusalom. The Holy Father's Golden Library and Holy Temple are in the far distance. So is a smoldering San Bernardino Basilica. There were no VOIDs in Yerusalom. Yet it burns.

Emmis's breaths are uneasy, confused. She doesn't want to live. But she's not sure death is the better option. She blinks—like an amputee who still feels a leg—and then stares up at the sun.

"I always imagined death differently," she says. "I assumed I would be on my deathbed and I would reflect on all of the terrible things I did. I would know I wasn't a good person. But I was hoping I could say—I did all these terrible things for a good reason. I did them for a just cause." She looks at me. "But, I can't say that. So all I can do . . . *is die.*"

"You don't need to talk."

"The machinery. The metal. The wires. The tubes. That wasn't me. *Right, Max?* It wasn't me. There was a time when I really wanted to—"

"It's okay. It doesn't matter."

Emmis smiles at me. "It does matter. It's the only thing that matters. We're supposed to do what's right, especially for the people who love us." She reaches up and places her hand on my face. "I did love you once." She gasps for breath. She stares at the sun. "I failed." Her eyes flutter, and without any ceremony, she dies. There is nothing peaceful about the look on her face. There is nothing peaceful about the body she left behind.

Pique moves close to Emmis and kisses her on the forehead. "You did fail," Pique says. She wipes away her own tears and then mine. "Emmis failed. And when we think about her life, that's what we'll need to remember most."

PART VII
THE BEGINNERS

55

ELLEE

We bury Emmis right where she died. I think it's fitting. For people like Emmis, Yerusalom should be something that always remains in sight, but is kept at a distance. She got too close and lost herself. At least that's what I'll tell our kids when I find them.

I go back into the helicraft to look for the Holy Father. I search everywhere. The only thing I can find is one perfectly intact Palmitor lying on top of a torn piece of red velvet from the Holy Father's mangled chair. I can't find him, though. There's a small gash in the helicraft where the projectile hit. It's big enough for a person to fall through, but the chances that actually happened seem very small. Mavy, Dang, and I have different theories about what might have happened to the Holy Father. Mavy's theory skews toward the metaphysical, whereas Dang's is firmly grounded in the laws of aerodynamics. But Pique is the only one who has an answer that makes any sense. She doesn't know.

I walk back to Pique, Mavy, and Dang with the Palmitor in my hand. I hate everything about this thing. I hate what it did to Emmis and I hate what it said to me. But I have made so many deals with devils recently that I'm willing to use it just one more time if it will help me find my kids. Before I can wrap my hands around the Palmitor and glimpse into a future with or without my children, Pique rips it away from me. She is about to smash it on the ground.

"Wait," I shout. "We can use it to help us find—"

I don't have to finish. Pique just shakes her head. No one is better at finishing my thoughts than her.

"I know what you want to use it for," Pique says. "And we can't."

"Just this one time. Then, we'll destroy it."

"No. Even if it works, I don't want to know and you shouldn't either. If it tells us something bad, we're still not giving up. We're not believing in it. If it tells us something good, I'm not listening to that either. We don't need *this thing* to tell us who we are or what we should do. The future doesn't control us. It can't tell us what's right or what's wrong."

"Maybe the Palmitor will tell us exactly where they are?"

Mavy senses my desperation. She puts her arm around me. "It doesn't work that way, Max. You know that."

I take the Palmitor back from Pique. She could stop me, but she doesn't. "You made me a promise," Pique says. "You swore on the lives of your children that you would do anything I ask. I only came with you on that helicraft because of your promise. *No questions asked*—you would do whatever I asked you. Well, I'm asking you now. I'm begging you to destroy it."

I'm pretty sure Pique had the Palmitor in mind when she made her deal with me. She knew I would be tempted, just like Emmis, just like her father. She knew that for a *good reason* I might want to use it. But for Pique, there is no good reason. There's no good reason for gazing into the future.

I look at Mavy and Dang. Both are nodding in agreement with Pique. I look at the fresh mound of dirt and the parched wildflowers that lie on top of Emmis's grave. "Please, Judge," Pique says. "You've spent your whole life making decisions for others. You've spent your whole life telling soldiers what to do and deciding whether people become citizens. You've been leading us and making every decision about how to protect us. We're thankful for that. But how about you let me make this decision for you? *How about you have a little faith in me?*"

I think about my children and what it would be like to play with them again. I tighten my grip around the Palmitor for the last time. I place it on the ground and stomp on it. It doesn't put up a fight. It breaks apart easily.

Mavy reaches for my hand. "You did the right thing, Max." She holds my hand and starts walking. She's pulling me in the direction of Yerusalom. Pique and Dang follow. Mavy tells me we need to head to the Holy Father's residence. We need to search through Spiro's quarters to see if we can find anything about the children. I don't ask any questions. I just follow. I fight the urge to look back at the spot where we buried Emmis.

As we walk through the hills of Yerusalom, the sun begins to lose its shine. Thick smoke creeps across the sky, reminding me that the rest of the world is still on fire. We move quickly through the hills and pass only a handful of people, who are fleeing in the opposite direction. I stop one of them in their transport and she tells me that NFF troops and Elite Guard units have just swept through Yerusalom. Most of the city and the Yerusi troops defending it are destroyed. They hanged a few hundred citizens to send a message and then quickly left. They told everyone else to leave, too. Supposedly, there are refugee camps in northern Damascia, and that is where everyone is heading.

As we approach Yerusalom, we see the poor souls hung like meat on racks. Every other light post has one. Most are very old men, which says something, however small, about Vrig's humanity. The speakers are blaring with an eerie computerized voice that repeats every twenty seconds. "Citizens of the Nation of Yerusalom—you must evacuate immediately. A VOID will hit the center of the city at nine P.M. standard Yerusalom time. Repeat—a VOID will hit the center of the city at nine P.M. standard Yerusalom time. You must evacuate immediately." Vrig wants the city, and more importantly what it stands for, destroyed. But he doesn't want to needlessly kill innocent people. Vrig is not a compassionate man, but I believe what he told me—he kills only for a purpose.

Most citizens have heeded the warning to evacuate, and so the streets are empty. I tell everyone that we need to learn what we can about my children and get out quickly. We follow Mavy through the desolate streets to the Holy Father's residence. Mavy's mother allowed her to spend summers here, so she knows the area well.

We get to the entrance of the Holy Father's residence and there are hundreds of bloodied soldiers lying facedown. There is no sign of life as we make our way through the residence. Dismembered DAKs are scattered throughout the hallways, as are hundreds of National Yerusi soldiers who lost their fight with the NFF. We quickly make our way to the Golden Library. Most of the library has been looted. Thousands of books, the priceless artwork, the ornate furniture—it has all been taken. Mavy quickly ushers me into Spiro's quarters. The only thing that Vrig's troops left behind was a framed picture of Spiro as a little girl. In the picture, Spiro is surrounded by the prostitutes that raised her. She's probably around nine. It may be a photographic illusion, but her feet are floating a few centimeters above the ground. She's smiling, but there's a definite sadness in her eyes.

We turn Spiro's quarters upside down looking for any clue that can help us find my kids. For hours, we search the Holy Father's entire residence. Dang watches the clock closely. Every ten minutes he nervously announces the time. By the time he announces that it's eight thirty, his voice is filled with desperation. For the last few hours I haven't even thought about the VOID that's coming. But with only thirty minutes left, I need to start. We don't have a lot of time and we're looking for a needle in a haystack.

"It's no use," I say. "We're not going to find anything."

"Five more minutes," Pique says. "We'll find something. I know it."

"Absolutely not. We have twenty minutes, thirty most, to get out of here. There's no more time."

We're going to escape using the Holy Father's emergency escape craft. Mavy was one of the few people permitted access to the craft and she did her initial pilot training on it. She has assured me that it's fully functional. But I have some doubt. "We still have to get to the craft and make sure everything's operational. We need to go . . . *now*."

"Stop worrying, Max," Mavy says. "It'll be fine."

I insist on leaving and we all follow Mavy through a series of winding hallways toward the emergency escape craft. We climb eight, maybe nine flights of stairs and arrive at a door with a small placard that says EEC, presumably an acronym for what we're about to use. Mavy opens the code box below the placard and enters an alphanumeric code. The door swings open and there is another hallway ahead of us with arrow signs on the wall. But instead of following the arrows that point to the emergency escape exit, Mavy tells us to go in the opposite direction. Mavy explains that this misdirection ruse was designed to protect against a hostile party that breaks through. We turn down two hallways and reach a metal grate on the floor. Mavy lifts the grate. Beneath it is a circular metal plate—just enough for one person to fit through—and a metal handle that spins. Mavy turns the handle three times to the right, two times to the left, and then lifts it up. "Fifteen minutes," Dang says. He's shaking at this point and his thick mop of hair, which appears to be getting more gray every moment, is dripping with sweat.

Mavy lifts up the metal plate and a mildew smell creeps out. She lowers herself down into the dank space and we follow one by one. I go through last and see that there is a single light, which shines weakly on an old helicraft. It's not what I was hoping for, and worse, I don't see how we're getting it out of here. It's sitting in what looks like a room in a museum for old aircraft.

"How are we supposed to fly this piece of junk out of here?" I ask.

"I trained on this piece of junk, Max. Before it became our emergency escape craft, it was used in actual combat. It's battle-tested."

"Maybe that's true. But so is the fact that I'm looking at four walls, a floor, and a ceiling. That's not very good for a takeoff."

"Really, Max. Come on now." Mavy points at the far-right wall. There's a sliver of light coming from underneath it.

"I don't mean to be negative here," Dang says. "Especially not at a time like this. But that thing you're pointing at—*it's called a wall*. They're not very easy to fly through."

"It's not like other walls, Dang. A little faith please." Mavy heads to the door of the helicraft. She presses a red button, and the helicraft's ramp slowly makes its way down, creaking the entire time. We head up the ramp and find seats. The interior of the helicraft smells like the inside of a sweaty shoe. The seats are ripped. The carpet is stained. The windows are cracked.

"Ten minutes," Dang shouts. "Please, Mavy."

"Calm down, Dang," Pique says. "It's Mavy. She's got this."

"Sorry, but, there's only ten—strike that—nine minutes left."

"How many times has she saved you?"

"A lot," Dang says. "About the same amount of times as I've thrown—" Dang fights back the urge to throw up.

Mavy turns on the control and initializes the engines. Everything seems to be working, but then all of a sudden a warning alarm comes on. The sound is jarring. "Not good," Mavy says.

"What do you mean *not good*," Dang says.

"I mean, *not good*." Mavy runs to the back of the helicraft looking for something. She then runs over to me. "There's some problems. There's no coolant, the engine's feedback cable is fraying, and we will eventually need new transistor bundles. We can fly for a few minutes, but that's about it. With takeoff and landing, and trying to get far enough away from the VOID's initial blast, we're going to need more than a few minutes of flying time. For now though, the coolant is the main problem."

"What about water," I say. "Will that work?"

"Maybe that gets you thirty minutes at most. It's not a long-term fix."

"It will get us out of the VOID's range if you can max out on the boosters," I say. "It will have to do." I grab Pique and Dang and we run off the helicraft. "Find anything that holds water." We all run as fast as we can. Pique is way out in front of me and Dang lags far behind. By the time I catch up to her, she's just outside the library, holding recycling containers. We fill up the containers in a baptismal sink that was used by the Holy Father for his ritual morning washing. We seal the containers and head back to the craft. I start running and soon pass Spiro's quarters. That photo of Spiro with the prostitutes catches my eye again. I'm not sure why, but I have to take it. I put it in my back pocket and sprint toward the helicraft.

Mavy meets us by the ramp. She tells us to leave two containers and bring the others on board. She opens a panel in the tail of the helicraft and pours the water from the two containers in. She runs back.

"Five minutes," Dang yells. "Five minutes."

Mavy powers up the engines. "Damn it. The wall. Someone needs to open the wall."

I unfasten my restraint, but Pique is already running down the ramp of the helicraft. Mavy shouts out an instruction telling Pique which levers to turn. Pique pulls the wall open and there's nothing but blue sky in front of us. We're about ten stories up and we're going to launch the helicraft right out of the side of the building. I can't see how this will work.

Pique runs back, but before she can strap herself in, Mavy pushes the thrusters forward. The exit is not much wider than the helicraft, and our runaway is not much longer than a residential rampway. Mavy needs to get up enough speed to generate lift, but she has to worry about maintaining a perfectly straight line to the exit. The margin of error is thin. We barrel toward the exit, but Mavy is holding back some thrust to keep us straight and steady. We hit the air and the nose takes a frightening dip down. As the rest of the craft goes through the wall, I feel the nose gently lift up and the back of the craft slip down. Our first few moments have us heading tail-down toward the ground. I quickly glance at Dang. His eyes are closed and he's clutching his seat's arms. As the tail of the helicraft is about to slam into the pavement below, Mavy throws the thrusters into full gear and they push off the ground. We immediately shoot up into the sky. We rapidly climb above the clouds and eventually see the approaching VOID and its fiery tail. Our paths cross.

"Where to?" Mavy asks me.

Pique doesn't give me a chance to answer. "To my house." Pique knows what she wants—she wants to find Trace. I don't disagree. Vrig has no reason to target the Abstainers. There is nothing strategic about the barren land they inhabit. We should be safe there and I also want to see if Trace went home.

We can't get over the Atlantique using water as our coolant and we need to find a new feedback cable and transistor bundles. We have to locate an airfield and supply station, but we can fly only in thirty-minute stretches using water as our coolant. The problem, we come to realize, is that Vrig has destroyed most of the airfields in a thousand-kilometer radius of Yerusalom, and the Holy Father has destroyed much of the rest. Even when we find an airfield, it usually doesn't have the kinds of supplies we need.

What we initially think will take a day or two ends up taking us twelve weeks. During that time, Mavy's stomach grows large. So does Dang's. He spends those weeks eating his way through his pain. He beats himself up for not figuring out the Holy Father's plan sooner.

Between three different airfield supply stations, we eventually are able to stock up on the helicraft supplies we need so that we can head to Abstainer territory. The flight over the Atlantique is uneventful. We touch down in a field of weeds just in front of Pique's house. We're all glad to leave this helicraft behind. I walk toward the house, and everyone follows. Pique is happy—as happy as one can be under the circumstances—to be home. I walk up to the front porch and notice muddy footprints. They look fresh. I open the rickety metal door. The footprints do not seem to extend into the house, but I still need to go room by room making sure it's safe inside before I let the others go in. Mavy and Pique take a seat on the porch, while Dang goes for a walk. Dang finds a stone path through an overgrown garden that leads to the woods and he decides to follow it.

As I walk into the house, I hear Pique tell Mavy that she and I should take the spare bedroom. Pique tells Mavy that she was born in that room and that it would be the perfect place for Mavy to give birth. Mavy doesn't ask me what I think about sharing a room. She just decides she and I are going to be together. I don't put up a fight. But I'm not there yet and I doubt I ever will be.

The first room I check is that spare bedroom. I place my one possession—the picture of Spiro and the prostitutes—on a dresser by the window. As I try to squeeze it in next to a picture of Emmis as a little girl, I put it too close and it falls to the floor. The frame shatters and the picture of Spiro falls out. I lift up the picture and see that there's a note on the back of it. It's dated a few months ago. The note says:

Dear Ellee:

We found this picture and thought you would like it. It is painful for us to look at it, as it reminds us of how we mistreated you when we were willful sinners. We thank you for giving us a chance to redeem ourselves. We thank you for sending us the three children. We are old women now. We are still with sin. But we are so sorry for everything we did to you. We promise, on Our God himself, that we will protect these children.

With Fondness,
The Nuns of Save Paul

I sit down on the bed. I close my eyes. The relief I feel overwhelms me. I begin to shake. I cry. My kids are actually safe. They're in Save Paul. I know it. Maybe Spiro—as troubled as he was—wanted to keep them safe. Maybe he wasn't *just cruel*. I go to find Mavy and Pique to tell them, but just as I do, I hear yelling from the backyard. "Come quick," Dang yells. "Hurry." I run out the door. My heart races as I run along the path. I get there in seconds and Mavy and Pique are already there. They're standing around four identical tombstones. The only difference is the first names on them.

Aquarius Rollins.   Emmis Rollins.
Nayla Rollins.   Trace Rollins.

Pique kneels down beside the gravestones. She runs her fingers over the engraving—first Aquarius, then Emmis, and then Nayla. She refuses to touch Trace.

"How can this be?" Mavy asks. "Who would even know that Emmis or Nayla is dead? Who could have done this?"

"Trace," Pique answers quickly. "It has to be Trace."

"Why would he make a grave for himself?"

"To make someone think he's dead," I say. I honestly don't know if Trace is in that grave or not, but I want to believe he's alive. And more importantly, I want everyone else to believe it. "Maybe he wants Vrig or someone else to think he's dead. It's been a couple of months since we've seen him. Who knows what he's been up to."

Everyone seems satisfied—perhaps too satisfied—with my answer. As we walk back to the house, I hand Pique the note from the Nuns of Save Paul. She jumps into my arms. "You see. I told you we'd find them." We make plans to leave for Save Paul the next morning. That night, we all have dinner together. Dang is a surprisingly good cook and he is able to take a bunch of sustainables from the cabinet and whip them into a really delicious stew. As we all eat together, I think about my childhood dinners. My father made me say Our God's Dinner Prayer every night. I always mumbled through it. I hated that he made me say it. On most nights, he would slap me across the face with the back of his hand. Even though I knew the hit was coming, I still mumbled. I wanted to show him he couldn't break me.

I don't think I have prayed at a dinner table since my childhood. But sitting at this table where Trace, Nayla, and Aquarius once consoled me, I feel the need to say something. I don't know that I would call it a prayer. It's more like a simple wish cast out into an unwitting, and perhaps even uncaring, universe. There's no intended recipient and no expectation of a divine entity being on the other end. My wish is simple. I hope that Aquarius, Trace, and Nayla are happy. I would include Emmis in the list, but I think it would be futile.

The next morning we wake up and fly to Save Paul in the old escape helicraft. The flight is smooth, but I'm on edge the whole time. I can't wait to land and find my kids. When we finally touch down, I am no less on edge. We quickly walk to the former brothel, now a monastery for the Nuns of Save Paul. As I walk through the paved entranceway, I naively think I will open the monastery's doors and my children will come running into my arms. But that foolish hope is quickly extinguished. My children do not run up to me. The only people I find are some old battered-down nuns. My children aren't there. I'm not sure how much more of this kind of heartbreak I can take.

I interrogate the nuns for hours and I believe they're telling me the truth. Jax, Kase, and Viole were there, but not for long. According to the nuns, a large bearded man who said he worked for Spiro picked them up after only a few weeks. He moved them to another location, but the nuns have no idea where. I try to get the nuns to tell me more about the man, but they are very old and all they can agree on is that he had a beard and he was large.

We spend a few days searching Save Paul and the surrounding area. I bribe anyone I can—local officials, kids on the streets, patrons of newly formed brothels, anyone. But it's clear my children aren't there, and we can't afford to look much longer, because Mavy's not feeling well. Her contractions have sneaked up on her and she's in a lot of pain. The baby's coming.

The flight back home isn't easy. Mavy clutches her stomach most of the flight. By the time we start our initial descent, the baby is banging hard on the door. It's ready to come out. We land and I quickly get Mavy up to the room. As she gets comfortable in the bed, I look around for extra sheets and blankets. I walk by the picture of Spiro and the prostitutes. I lay it facedown. I don't want them to be a part of this. I grab some linens and leave them at the side of the bed. Mavy's labor kicks into high gear after about an hour. I grab hold of one of her hands, and Pique holds the other. Her pain begins to sharpen and it's hard for her to sit still. She thrashes around the bed like a fish out of water. Childbirth seems like it's both the most natural and least natural thing.

Pique tries to settle Mavy down by rubbing cold cloths on her forehead and stroking her hair. When Mavy is finally ready to push, each of us grabs a leg and pushes it up to her chest. Mavy pushes for twenty minutes, grunting and shouting obscenities about the pain. When the baby finally peeks its head into the world, it is Pique who gently reaches in and grabs the baby's shoulders. She tells Mavy to push again and Pique guides the baby out. I don't know how Pique knows what she's doing, but she does.

Just after sunset, in the room where Pique was born, Mavy gives birth to a little girl. Mavy takes the baby in her arms and I sit beside them in the bed. I kiss them both. Mavy looks at Pique and says, "I want you to name her."

Pique thinks for a while. She looks at all the pictures on the dresser. There's Aquarius, Emmis, Nayla, and Trace. She then lifts up the picture of Spiro so that it's no longer facing down. She picks it up and studies the little girl in it. She thinks for a few seconds. "Let's name her Ellee." Pique gently places the picture back. "That's it—Ellee."

Mavy's exhausted. I take the baby from her, so that she can get some sleep. Dang and Pique follow me as I take little Ellee outside to meet her new family. We sit by the gravestones. I introduce Ellee to everyone. Pique asks me if she can hold her. She takes Ellee and sits down. I look over at both of them. Pique is resting against a tree near Aquarius's grave, while holding Ellee in her arms. Pique extends her pinky and Ellee wraps her tiny fingers around it. "You know what tomorrow is," she says to Ellee.

"She can't talk," I say.

"I kind of figured that out."

"Well, do you know what tomorrow is?"

"Thursday," I say.

"Yes, *Your Holiness.* Tomorrow is Thursday. But I was sort of looking for a different answer." Pique is already in love with this baby. I'm not sure she'll ever give her back. "I was thinking that tomorrow will be the first full day of her life. And maybe tomorrow will be the day that we find her brothers and sister." She looks up from Ellee and smiles at me. "I'm going to find them, you know."

Ellee is still holding on to Pique's finger. I reach out a finger, and Ellee latches on to it with her other hand. Pique kisses the top of her head, and for the first time, Ellee opens her eyes. If Ellee could see far enough, the first thing she would see is the night sky. She would see Orion. She would see Orion's bright stars—winking at her from light-years away. Then, as she brought her gaze back down to earth, she would see Pique and me. She would see us holding her hands. And she would know—Pique and I are never letting go.